[redacted]

[redacted]

THE RETURN OF ZITA THE SPACEGIRL

Ben Hatke

First Second
New York

First Second

New York

Text and illustrations copyright © 2014 by Ben Hatke

Published by First Second
First Second is an imprint of Roaring Brook Press,
a division of Holtzbrinck Publishing Holdings Limited Partnership
175 Fifth Avenue, New York, New York 10010

Cover and interior design by Colleen AF Venable

Cataloging-in-Publication Data is on file at the Library of Congress

Paperback ISBN: 978-1-59643-876-7
Hardcover ISBN: 978-1-62672-058-9

First Second books may be purchased for business or promotional use. For
information on bulk purchases please contact Macmillan Corporate and
Premium Sales Departement at (800) 221-7945 x5442 or by email at
specialmarkets@macmillan.com.

First Edition 2014

Printed in China by Macmillan Production (Asia) Ltd., Kowloon Bay, Hong Kong
(supplier code PS)
Paperback: 10 9 8 7 6 5 4 3 2 1
Hardcover: 10 9 8 7 6 5 4 3 2 1

for Anna

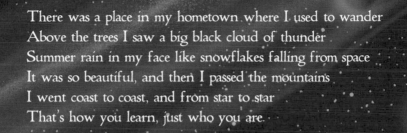

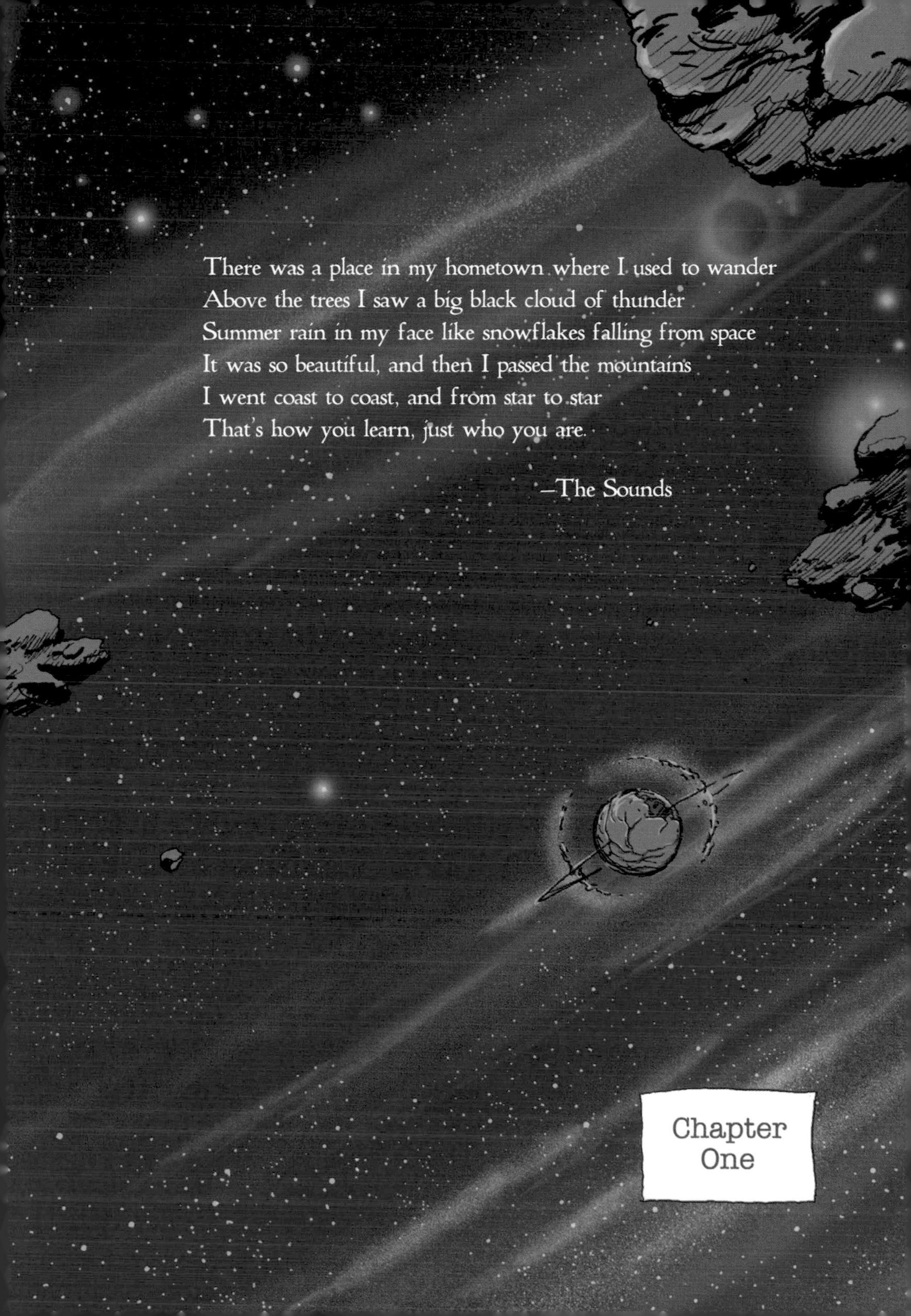

There was a place in my hometown where I used to wander
Above the trees I saw a big black cloud of thunder
Summer rain in my face like snowflakes falling from space
It was so beautiful, and then I passed the mountains
I went coast to coast, and from star to star
That's how you learn, just who you are.

—The Sounds

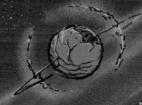

Chapter
One

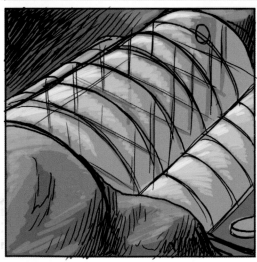

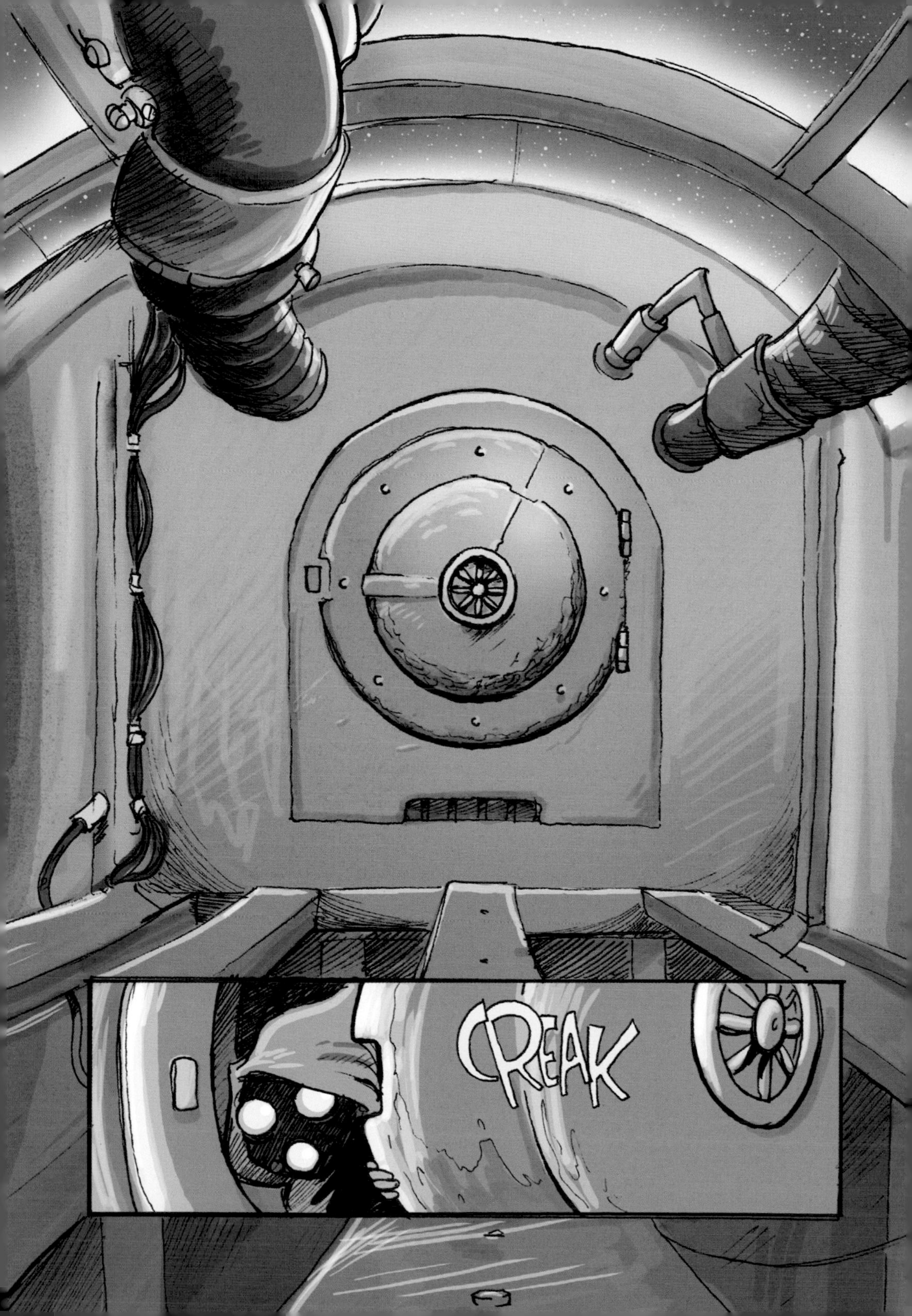
CREAK

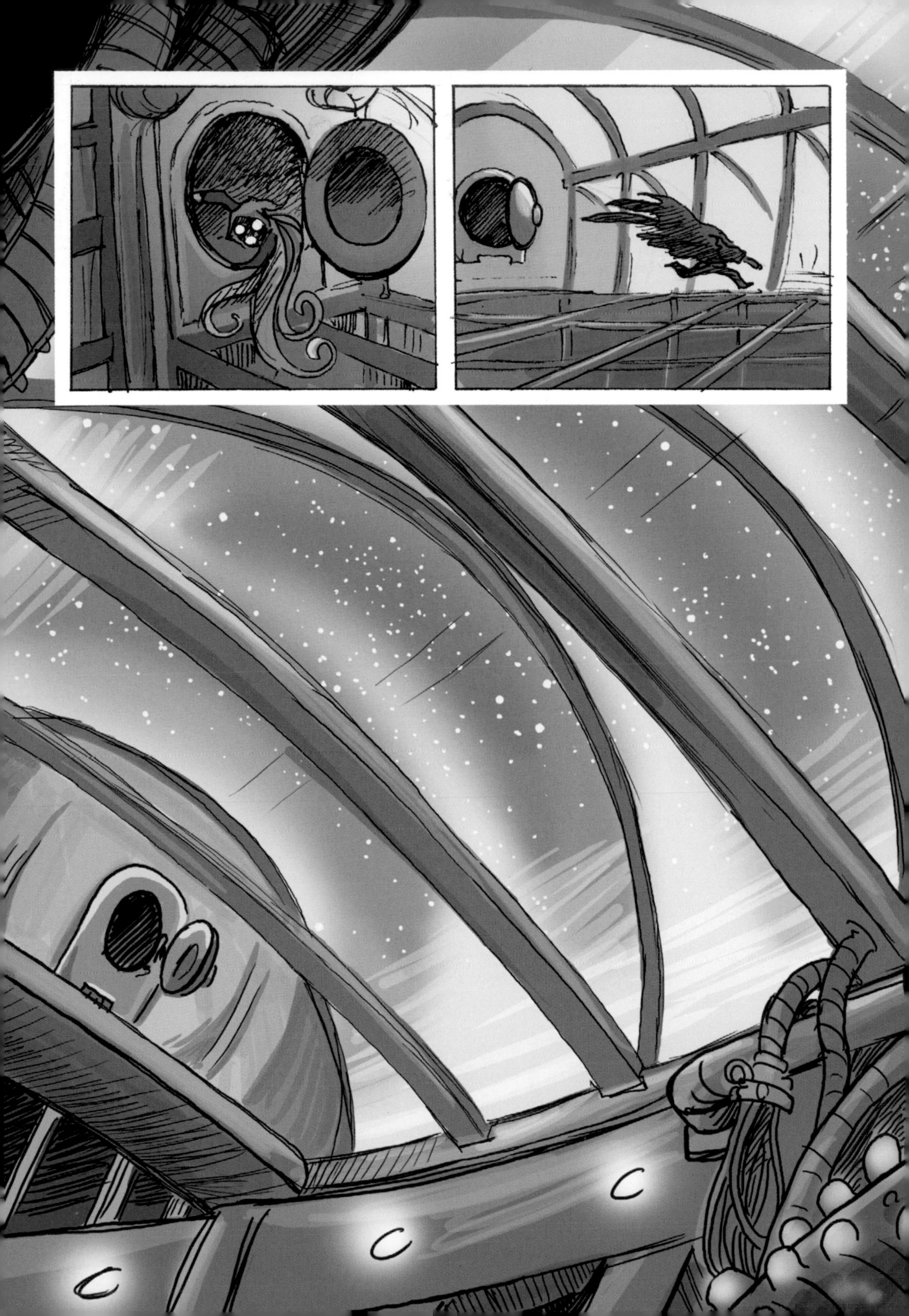

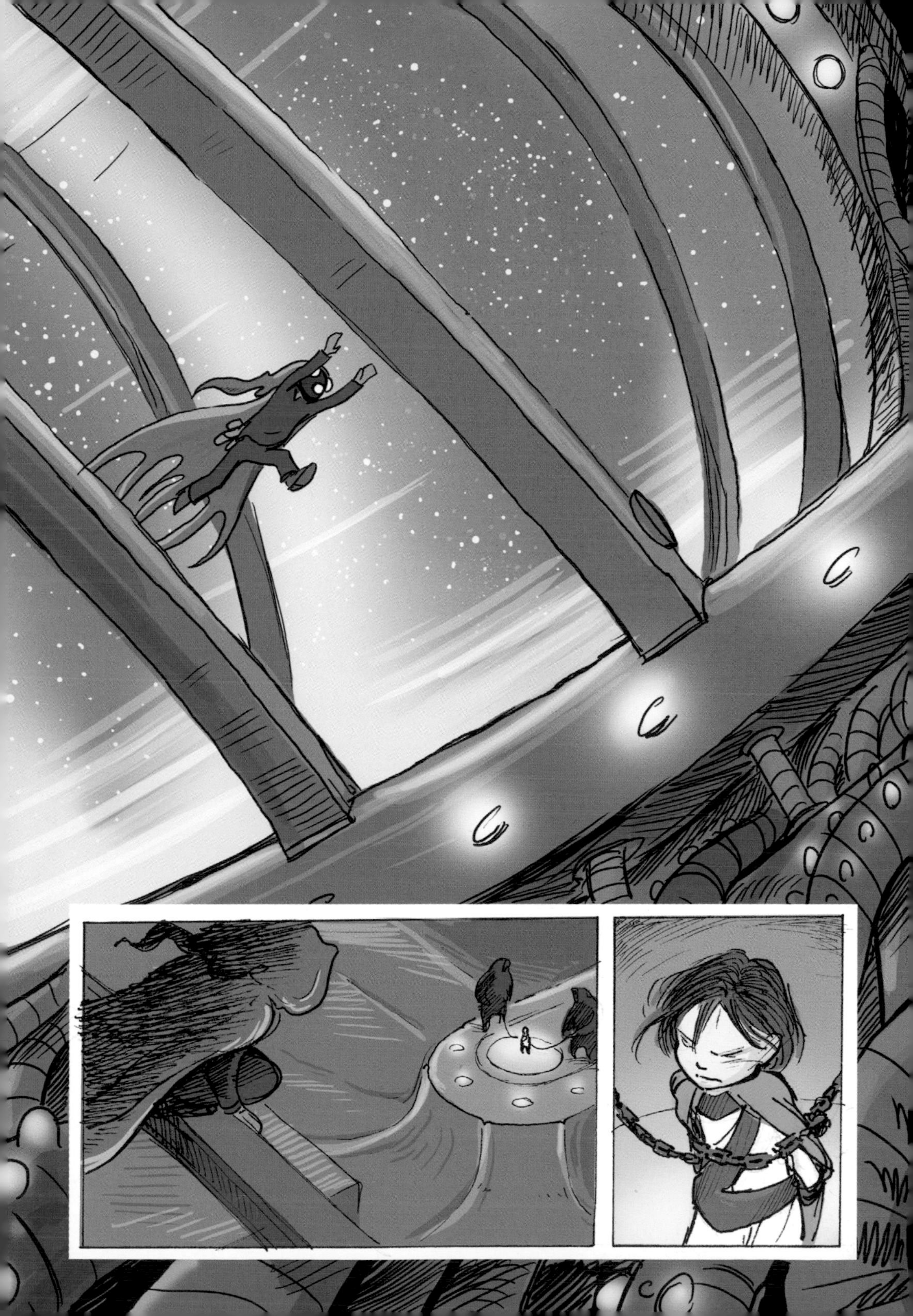

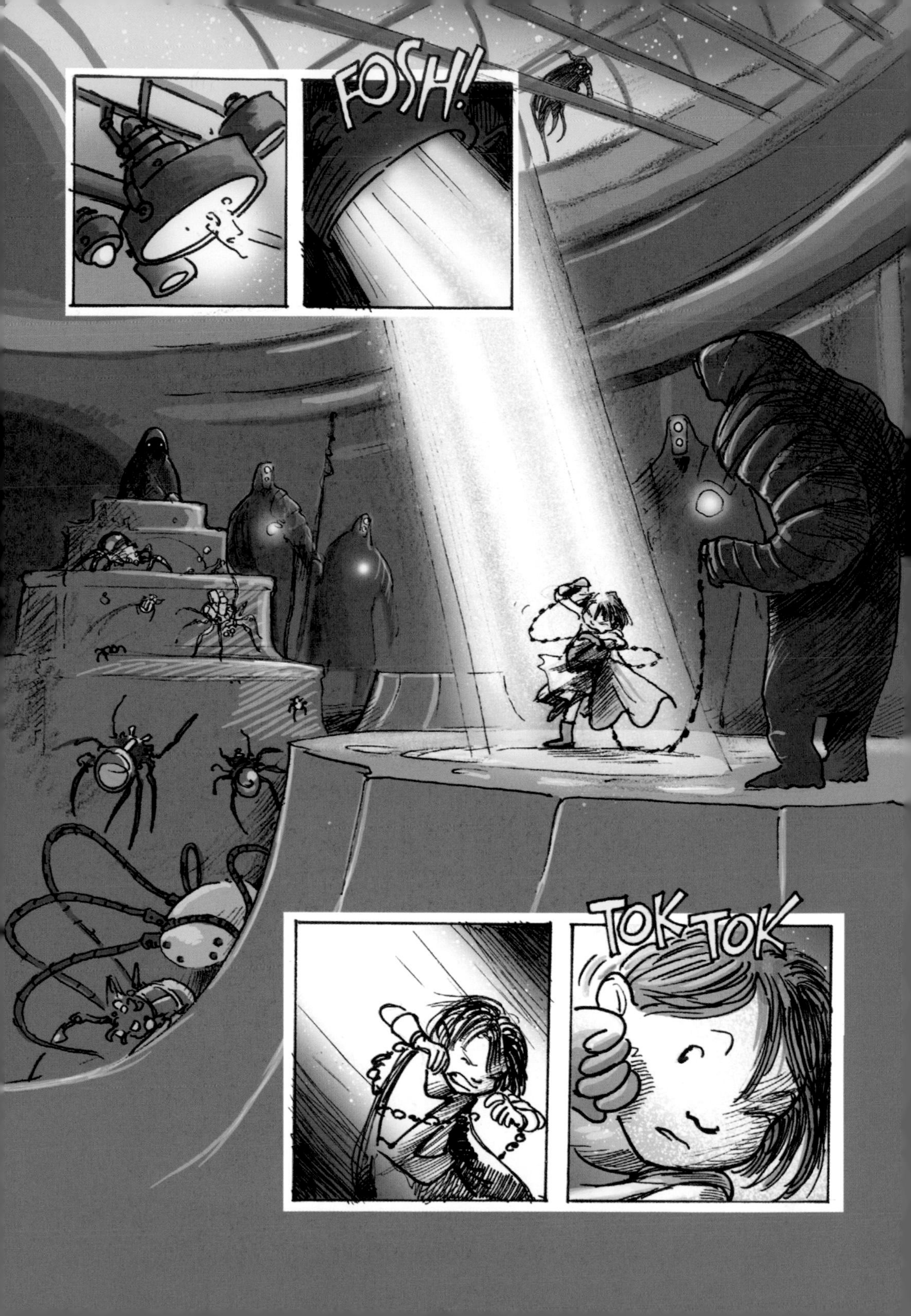
FOSH!
TOK TOK

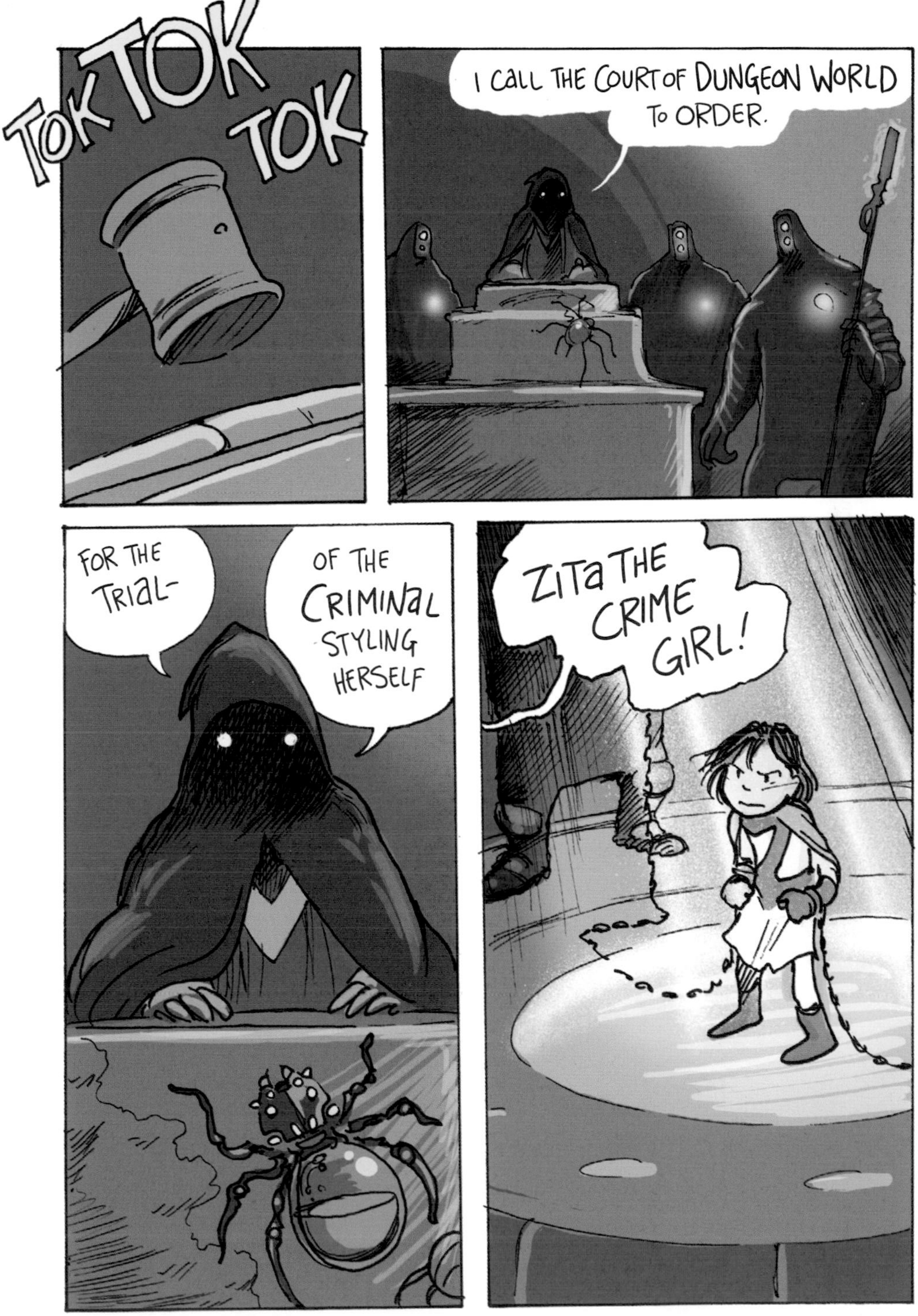
TOK TOK TOK
I CALL THE COURT OF DUNGEON WORLD TO ORDER.
FOR THE TRIAL-
OF THE CRIMINAL STYLING HERSELF
ZITA THE CRIME GIRL!

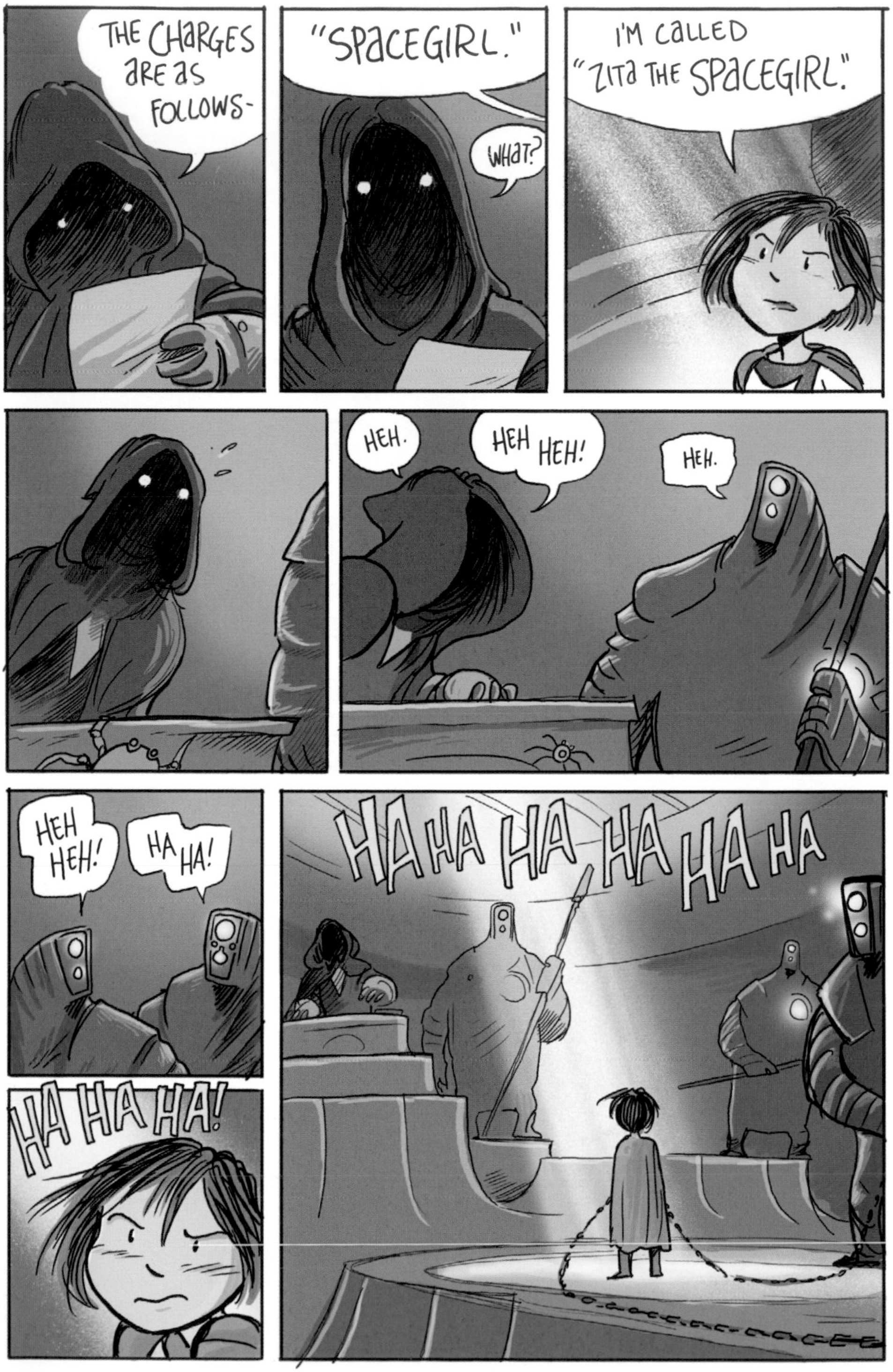
THE CHARGES ARE AS FOLLOWS-
"SPACEGIRL."
WHAT?
I'M CALLED "ZITA THE SPACEGIRL."
HEH.
HEH HEH!
HEH.
HEH HEH!
HA HA!
HA HA HA HA!
HA HA HA HA HA HA HA

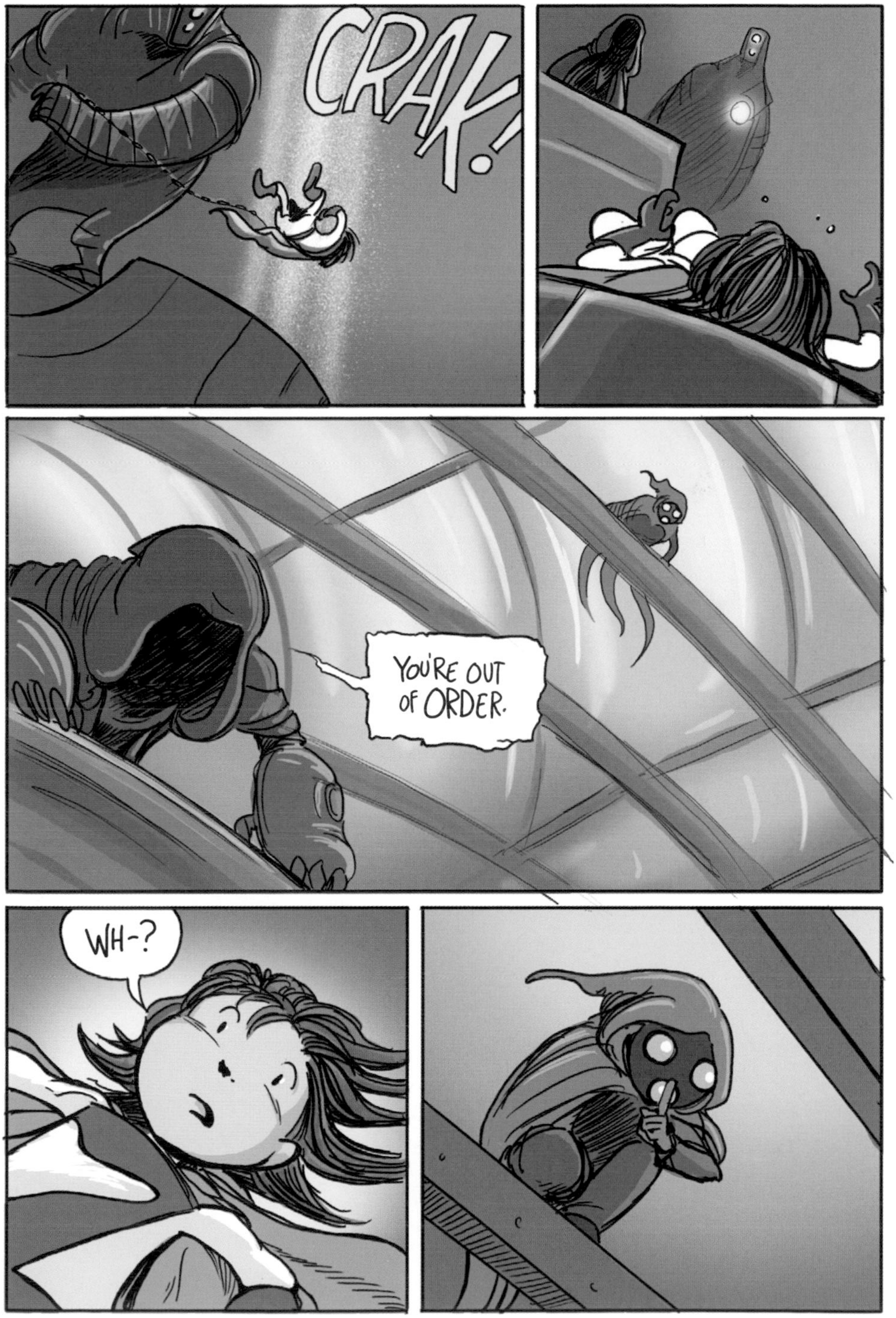
CRAK!
YOU'RE OUT OF ORDER.
WH-?

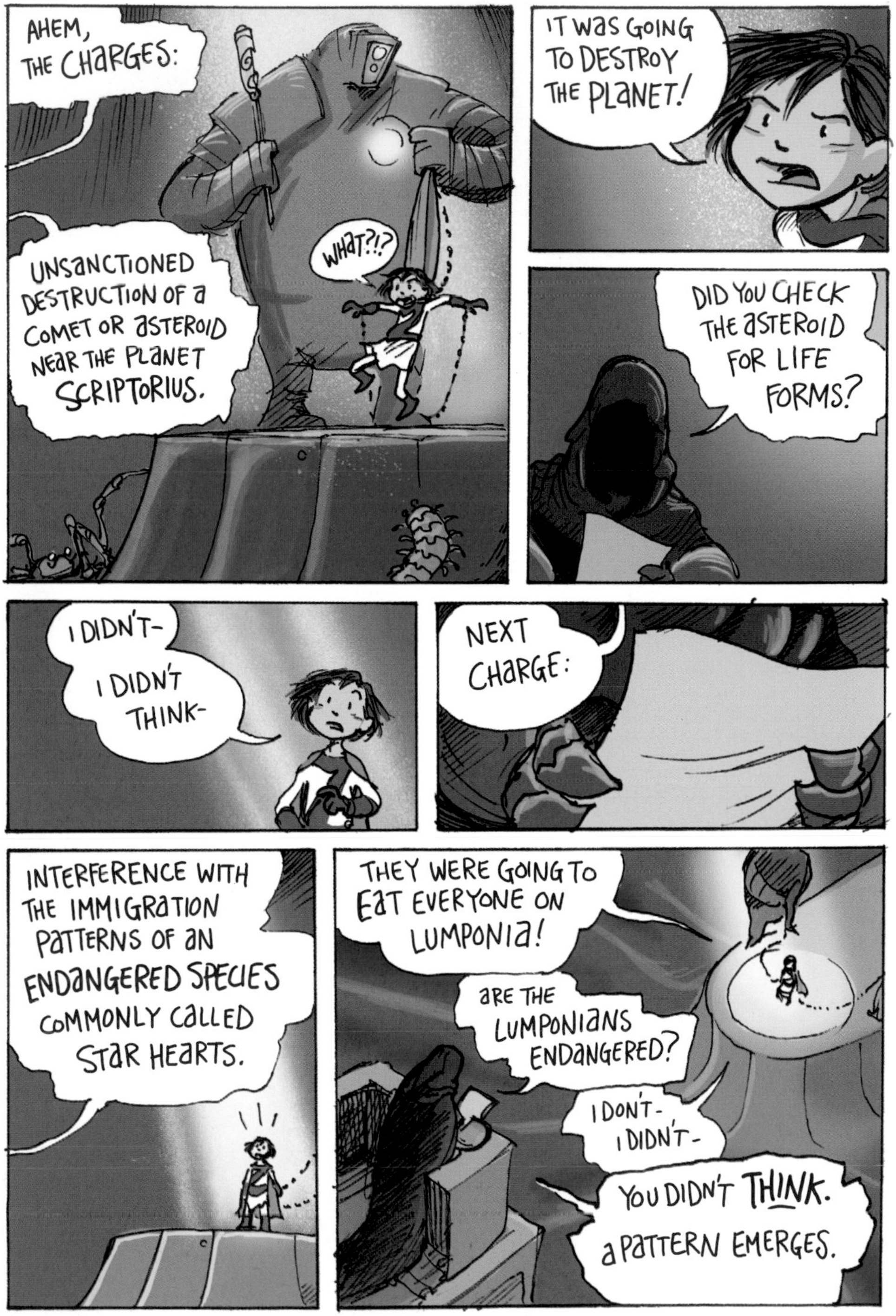
AHEM, THE CHARGES:
UNSANCTIONED DESTRUCTION OF A COMET OR ASTEROID NEAR THE PLANET SCRIPTORIUS.
WHAT?!?
IT WAS GOING TO DESTROY THE PLANET!
DID YOU CHECK THE ASTEROID FOR LIFE FORMS?
I DIDN'T-
I DIDN'T THINK-
NEXT CHARGE:
INTERFERENCE WITH THE IMMIGRATION PATTERNS OF AN ENDANGERED SPECIES COMMONLY CALLED STAR HEARTS.
THEY WERE GOING TO EAT EVERYONE ON LUMPONIA!
ARE THE LUMPONIANS ENDANGERED?
I DON'T-
I DIDN'T-
YOU DIDN'T THINK.
A PATTERN EMERGES.

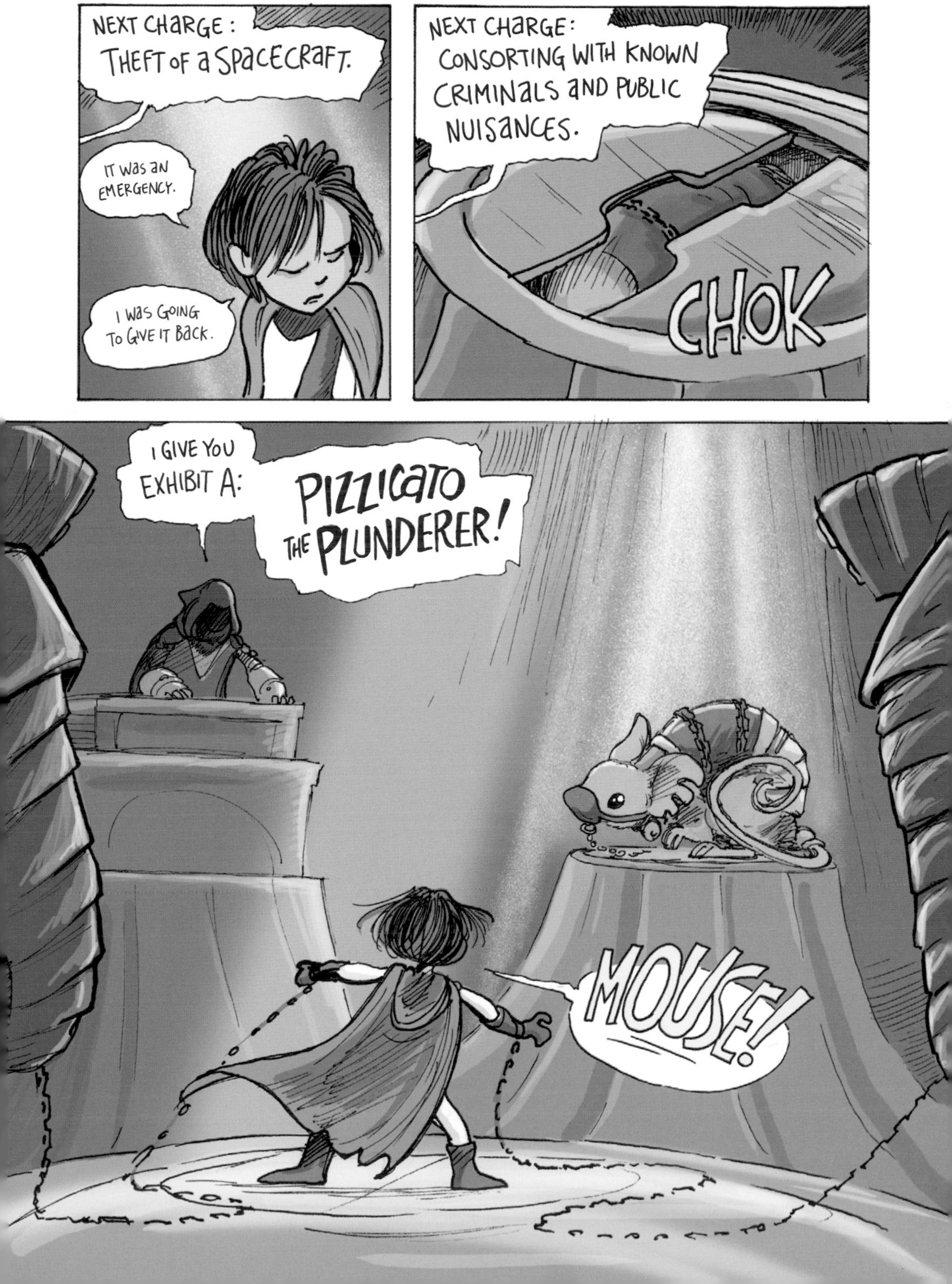

NEXT CHARGE: THEFT OF A SPACECRAFT.
IT WAS AN EMERGENCY.
I WAS GOING TO GIVE IT BACK.
NEXT CHARGE: CONSORTING WITH KNOWN CRIMINALS AND PUBLIC NUISANCES.
CHOK
I GIVE YOU EXHIBIT A:
PIZZICATO THE PLUNDERER!
MOUSE!

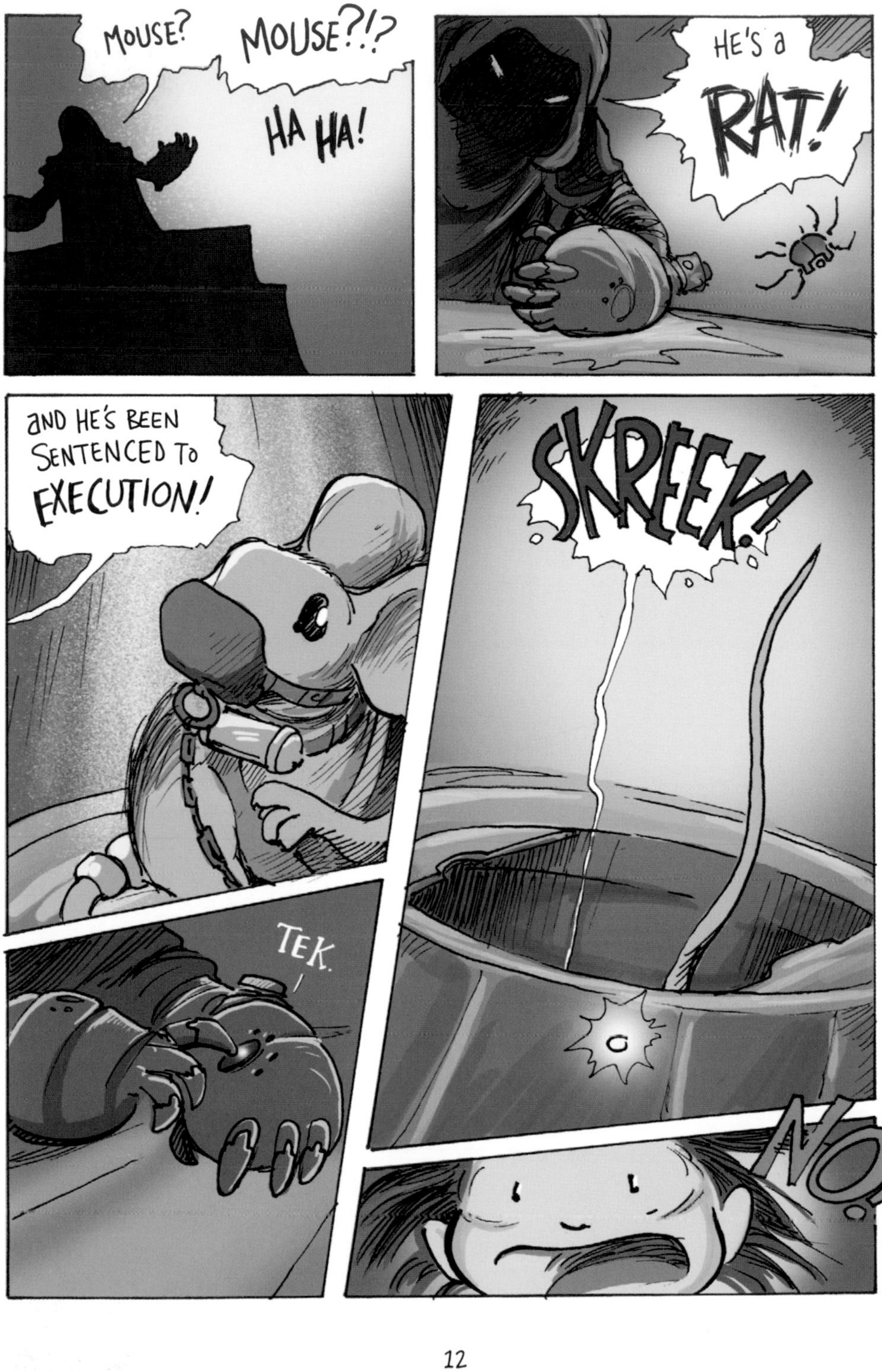
MOUSE?
MOUSE?!?
HA HA!
HE'S a RAT!
aND HE'S BEEN SENTENCED TO EXECUTION!
SKREEK!
TEK.
NO!

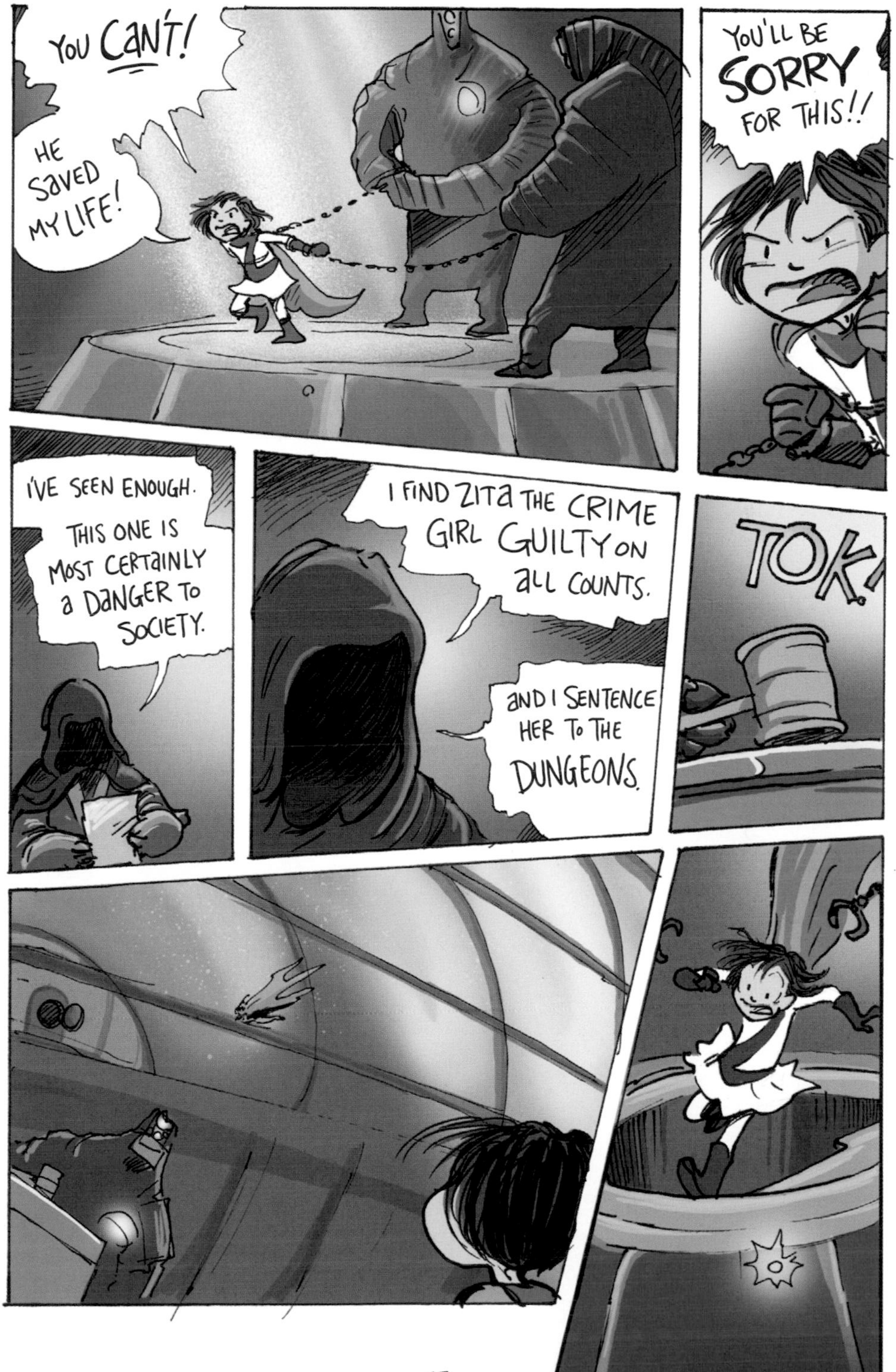

YOU CAN'T!
HE SAVED MY LIFE!
YOU'LL BE SORRY FOR THIS!!
I'VE SEEN ENOUGH.
THIS ONE IS MOST CERTAINLY A DANGER TO SOCIETY.
I FIND ZITA THE CRIME GIRL GUILTY ON ALL COUNTS.
AND I SENTENCE HER TO THE DUNGEONS.
TOK!

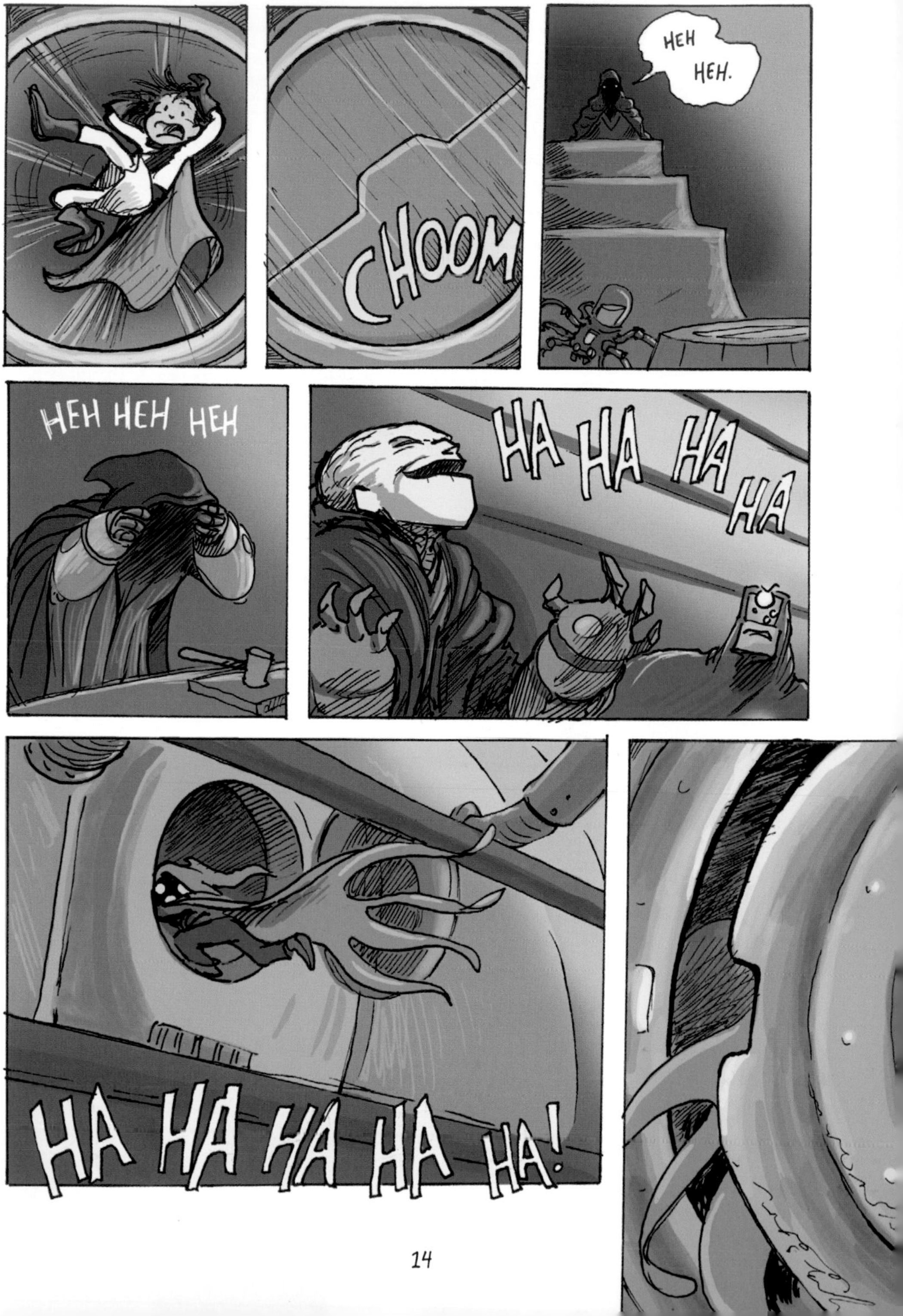
CHOOM
HEH HEH.
HEH HEH HEH
HA HA HA HA
HA HA HA HA HA!

Chapter Two

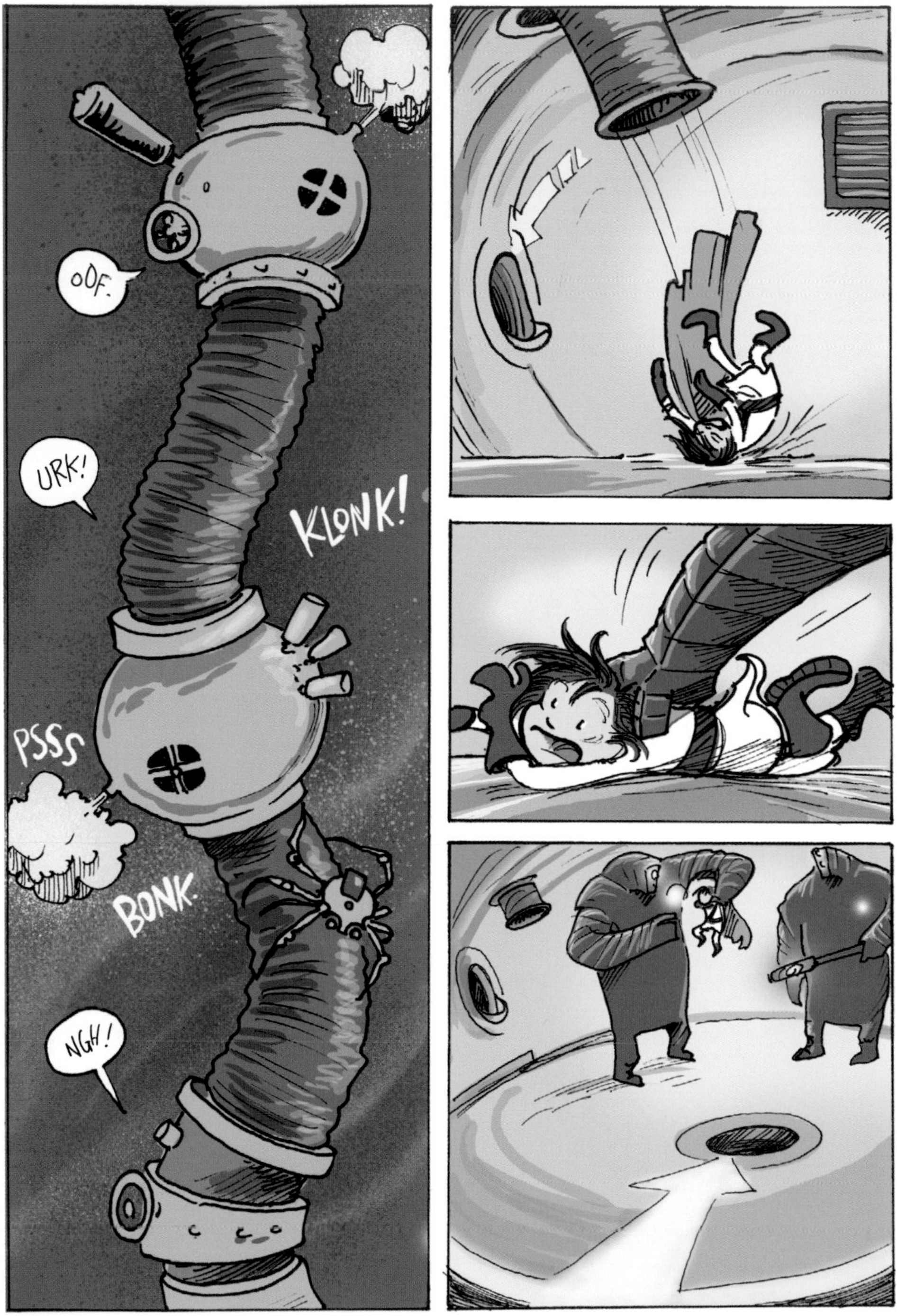
OOF.
URK!
KLONK!
PSSS
BONK.
NGH!

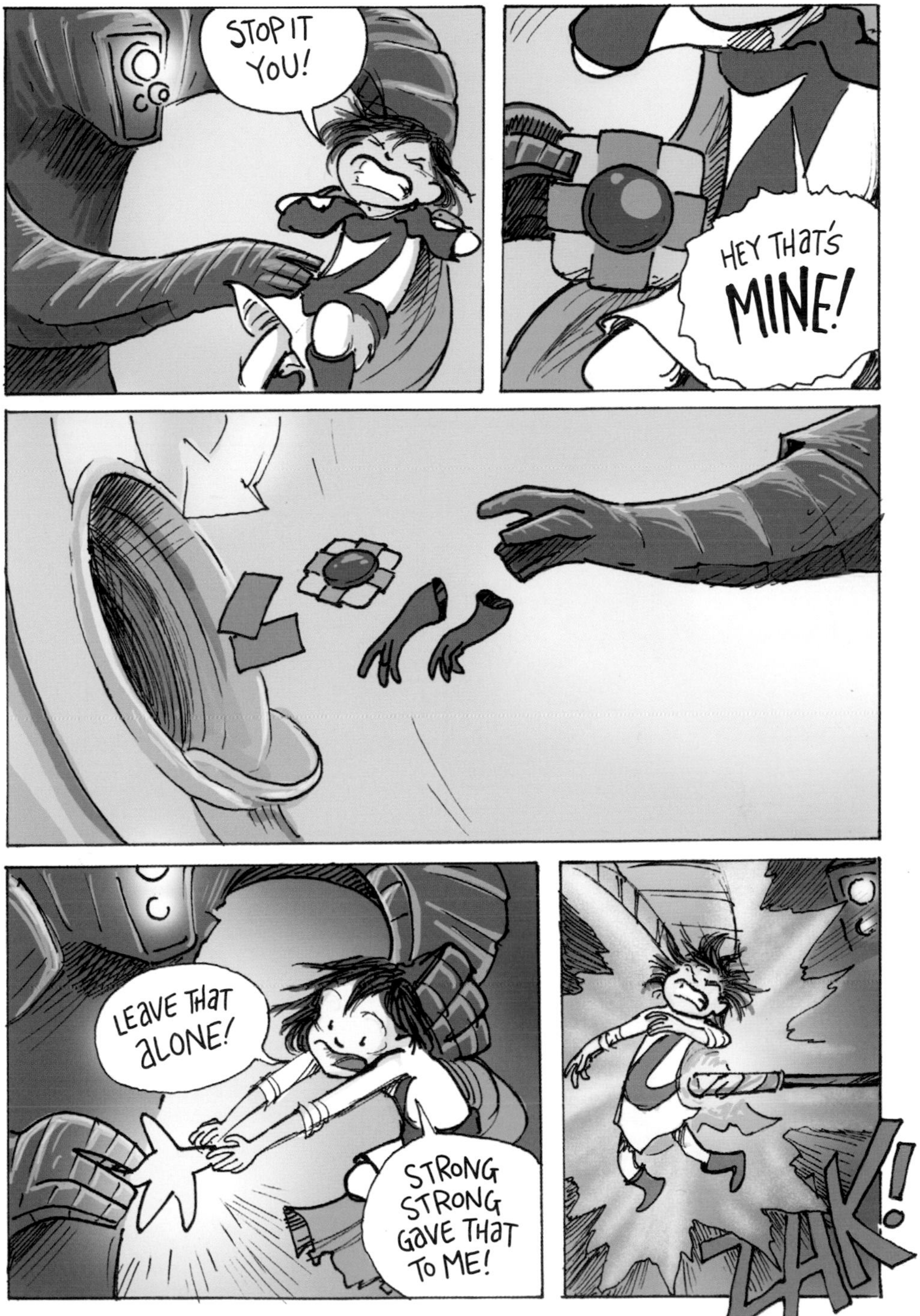
STOP IT YOU!
HEY THAT'S MINE!
LEAVE THAT ALONE!
STRONG STRONG GAVE THAT TO ME!
ZAK!

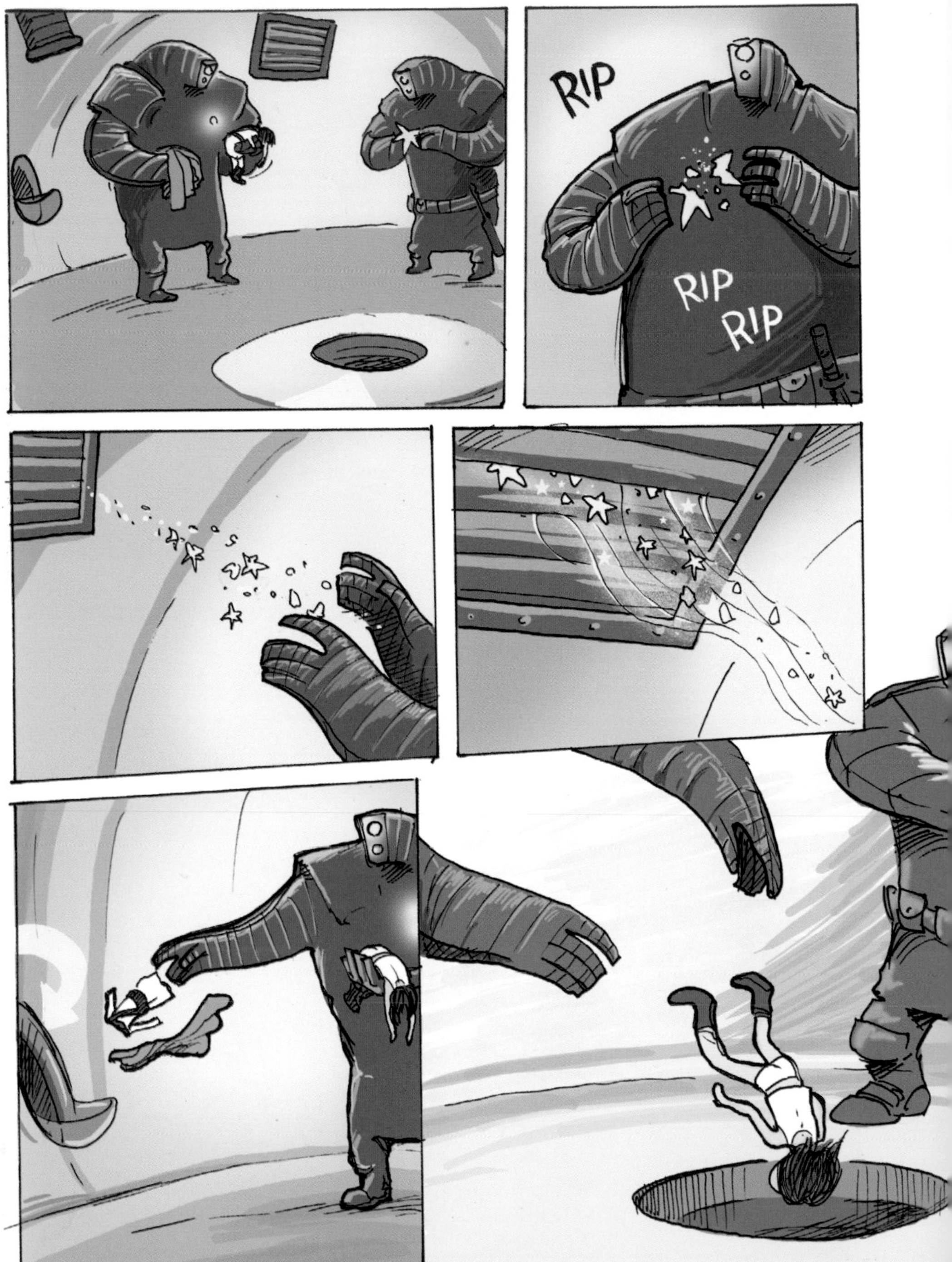
RIP
RIP
RIP

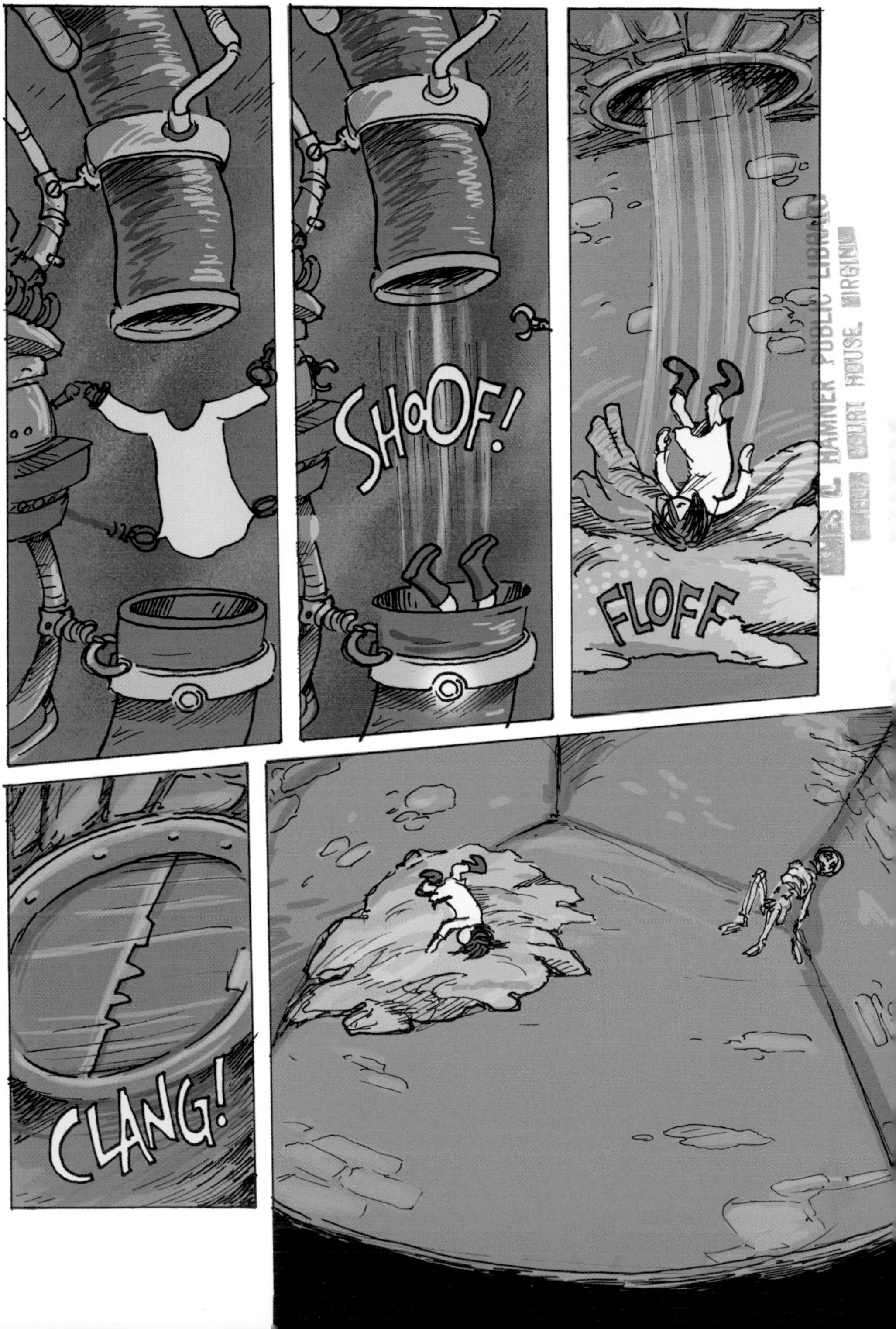
SHOOF!
FLOFF
CLANG!

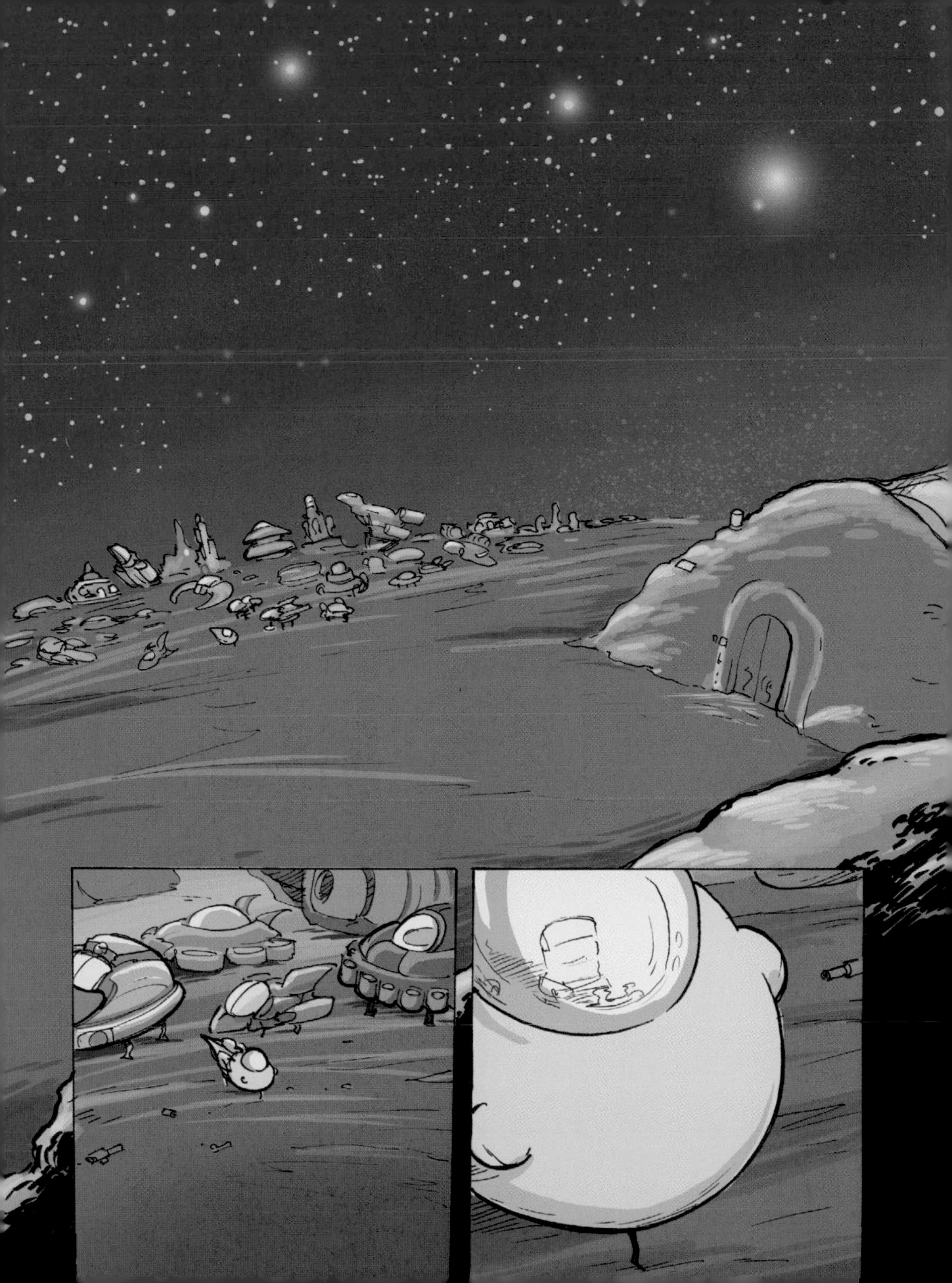

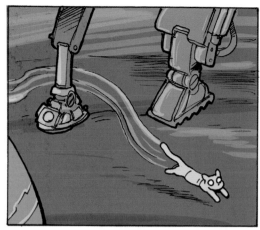

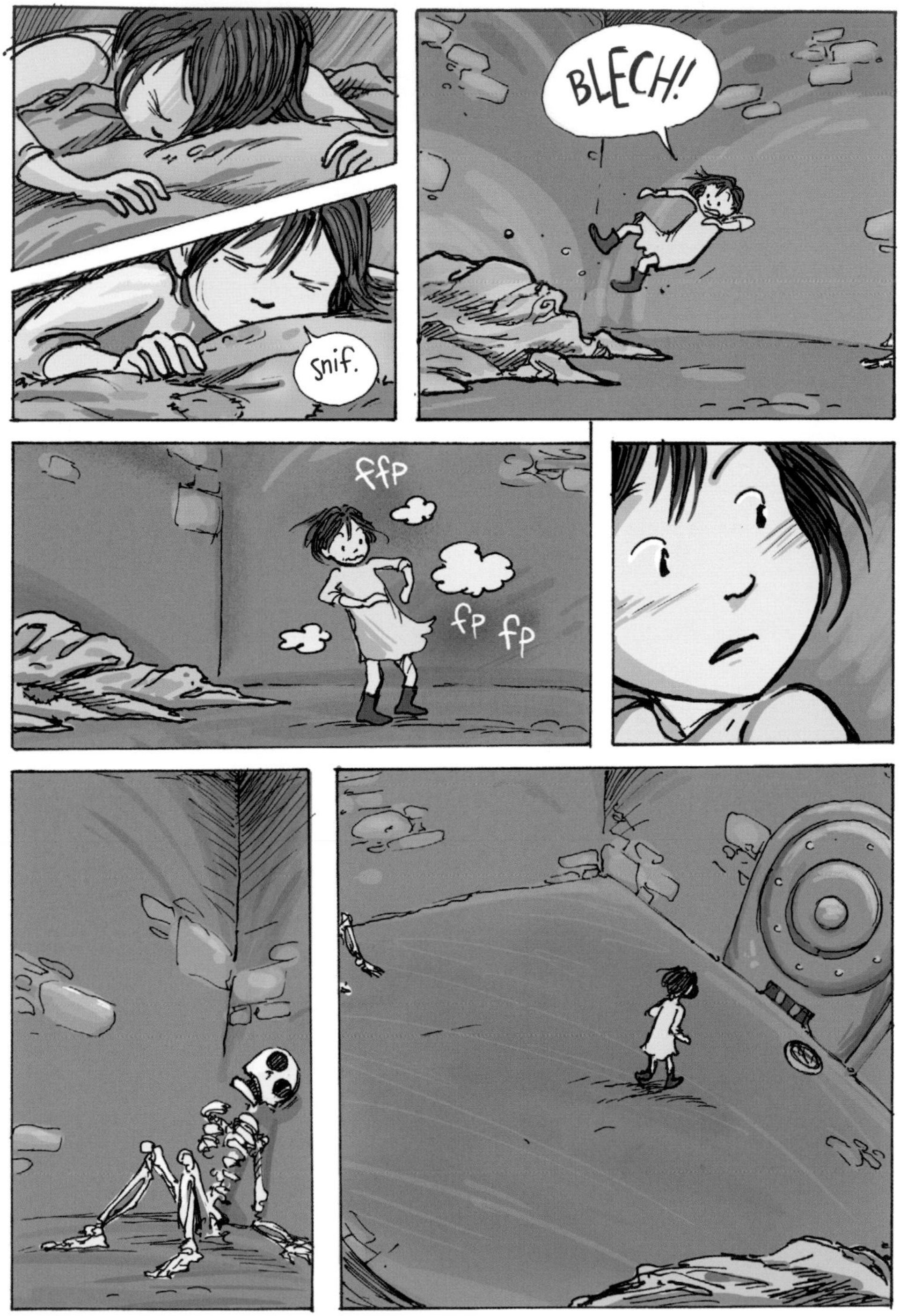
snif.
BLECH!
ffp
fp fp

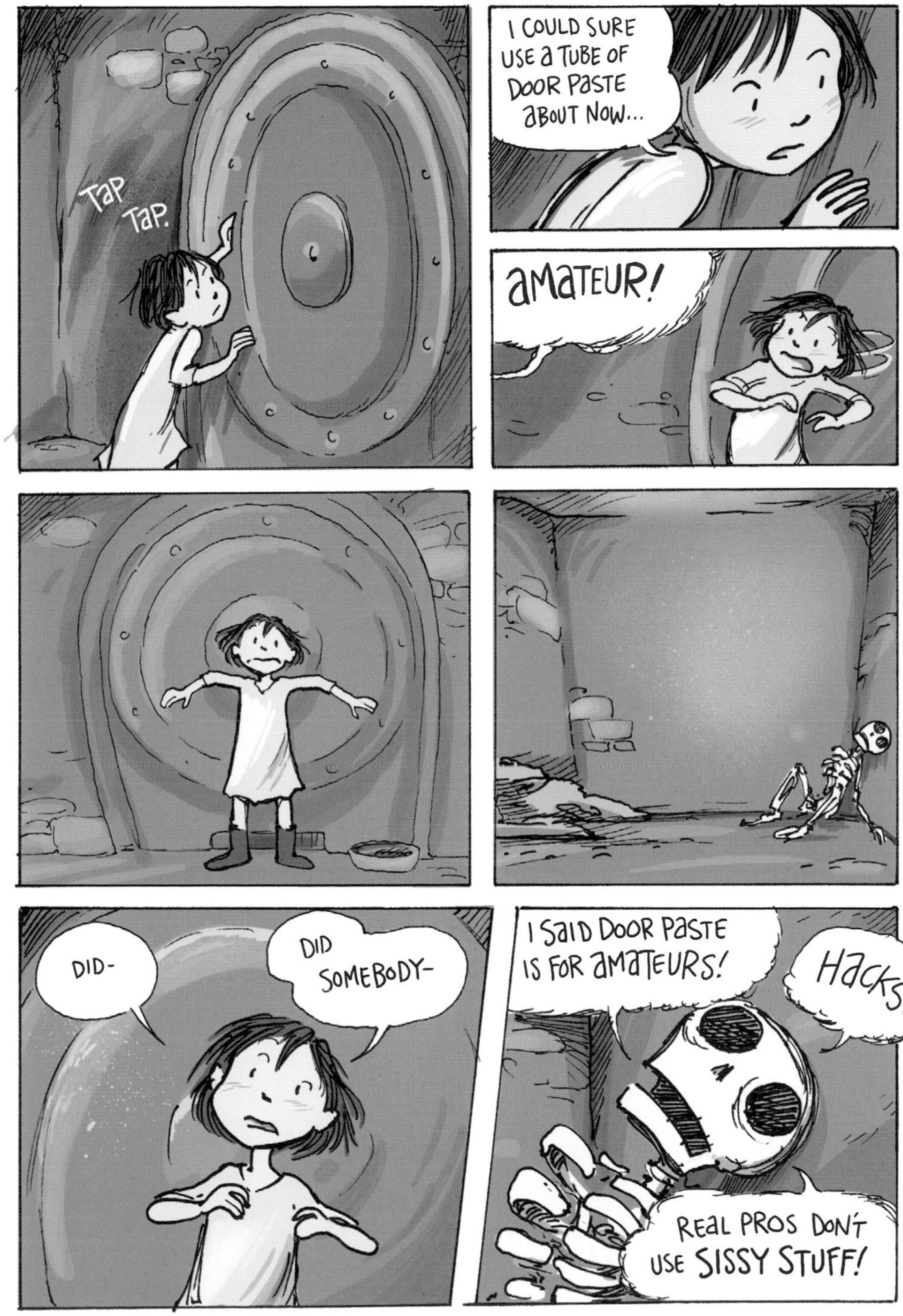
TAP TAP.
I COULD SURE USE A TUBE OF DOOR PASTE ABOUT NOW...
AMATEUR!
DID-
DID SOMEBODY-
I SAID DOOR PASTE IS FOR AMATEURS!
HACKS!
REAL PROS DON'T USE SISSY STUFF!

You can talk?

OF **COURSE** I can **TALK!**

I'm sorry. I didn't mean to upset you.

BAH.

AH, DON'T MIND OL' **FEMUR.**

HE'S JUS' TRYIN' TO **IMPRESS** YOU.

WE AIN'T NEVER HAD A CELLMATE B'FORE.

YOU'RE A LIVING— A LIVING—

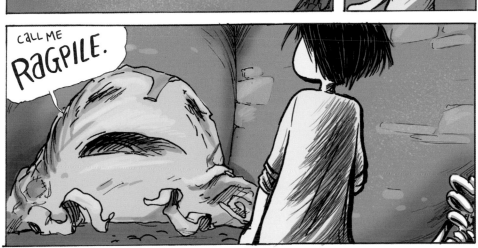

CALL ME RAGPILE.

RAGGY EVOLVED DOWN HERE. HE AIN'T NEVER SEEN THE WORLD OUTSIDE.

SAY! YOU WANNA PLAY EYE-SPY?

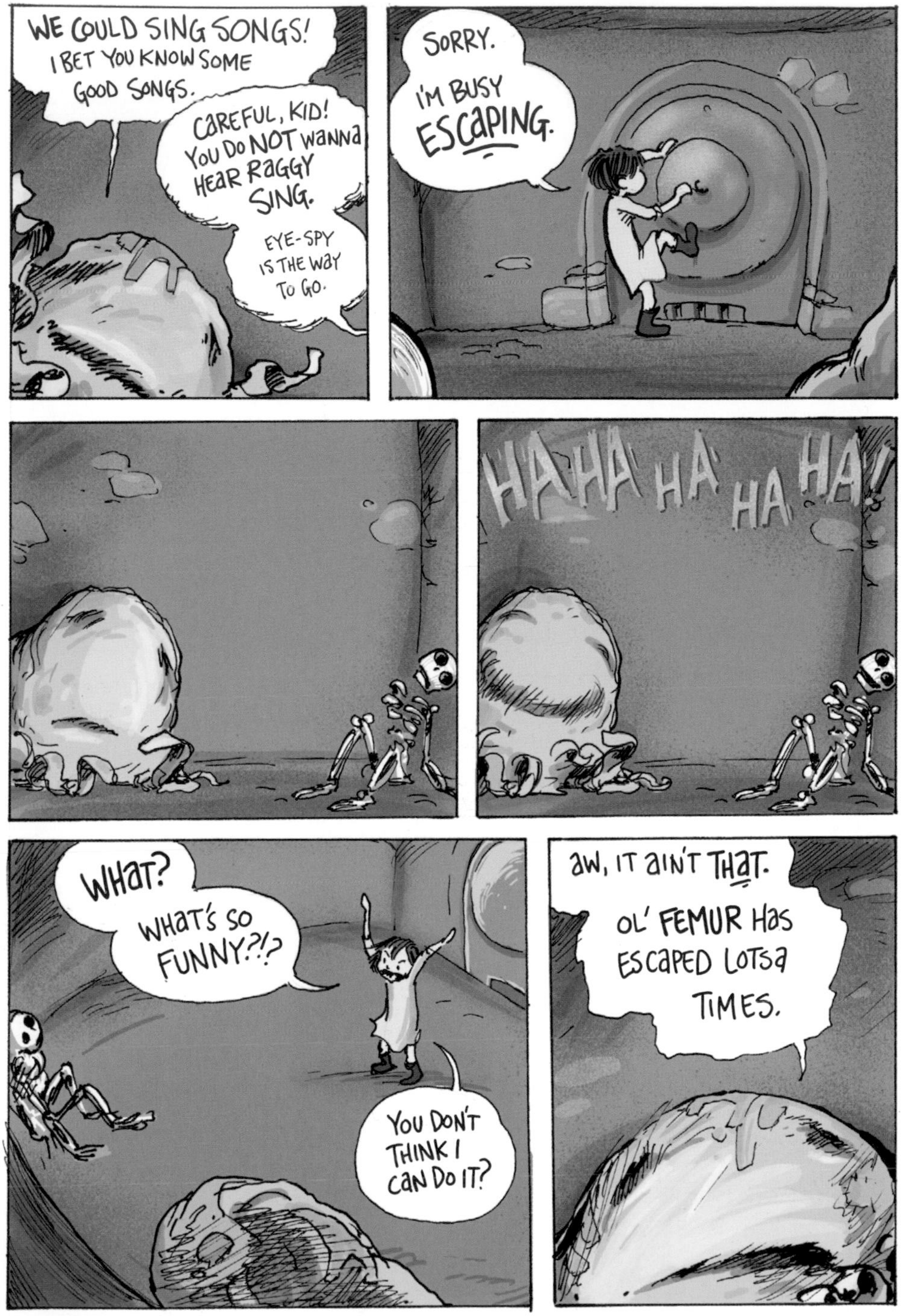
WE COULD SING SONGS! I BET YOU KNOW SOME GOOD SONGS.
CAREFUL, KID! YOU DO NOT WANNA HEAR RAGGY SING.
EYE-SPY IS THE WAY TO GO.
SORRY.
I'M BUSY ESCAPING.
HAHA HA HA HA!
WHAT?
WHAT'S SO FUNNY?!?
YOU DON'T THINK I CAN DO IT?
AW, IT AIN'T THAT.
OL' FEMUR HAS ESCAPED LOTSA TIMES.

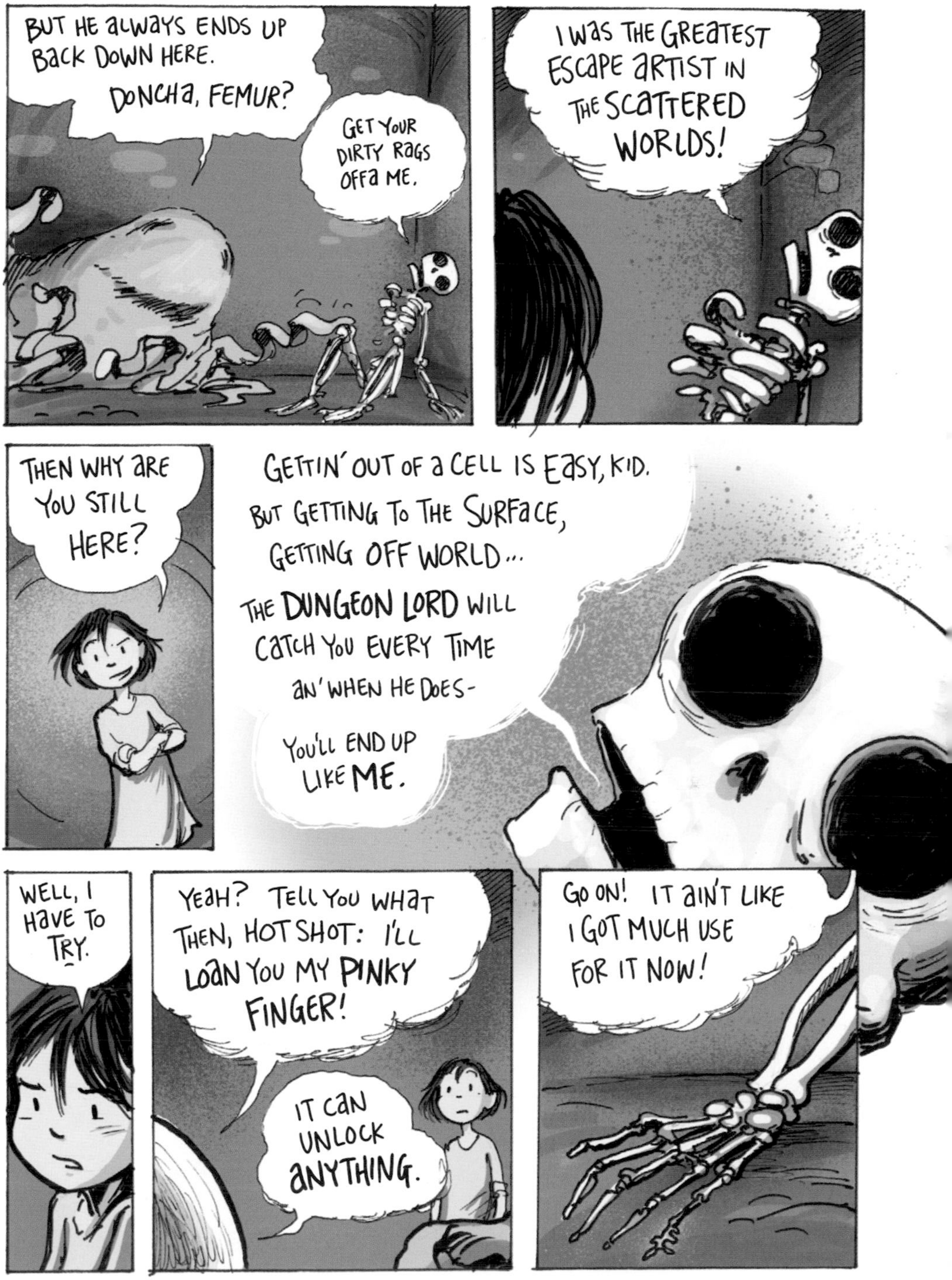
BUT HE ALWAYS ENDS UP BACK DOWN HERE.
DONCHA, FEMUR?
GET YOUR DIRTY RAGS OFFA ME.
I WAS THE GREATEST ESCAPE ARTIST IN THE SCATTERED WORLDS!
THEN WHY ARE YOU STILL HERE?
GETTIN' OUT OF A CELL IS EASY, KID.
BUT GETTING TO THE SURFACE, GETTING OFF WORLD...
THE DUNGEON LORD WILL CATCH YOU EVERY TIME AN' WHEN HE DOES-
YOU'LL END UP LIKE ME.
WELL, I HAVE TO TRY.
YEAH? TELL YOU WHAT THEN, HOT SHOT: I'LL LOAN YOU MY PINKY FINGER!
IT CAN UNLOCK ANYTHING.
GO ON! IT AIN'T LIKE I GOT MUCH USE FOR IT NOW!

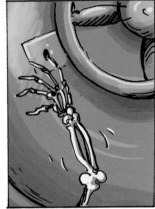

CHAK.

HEY! DON'T TAKE THE WHOLE ARM!

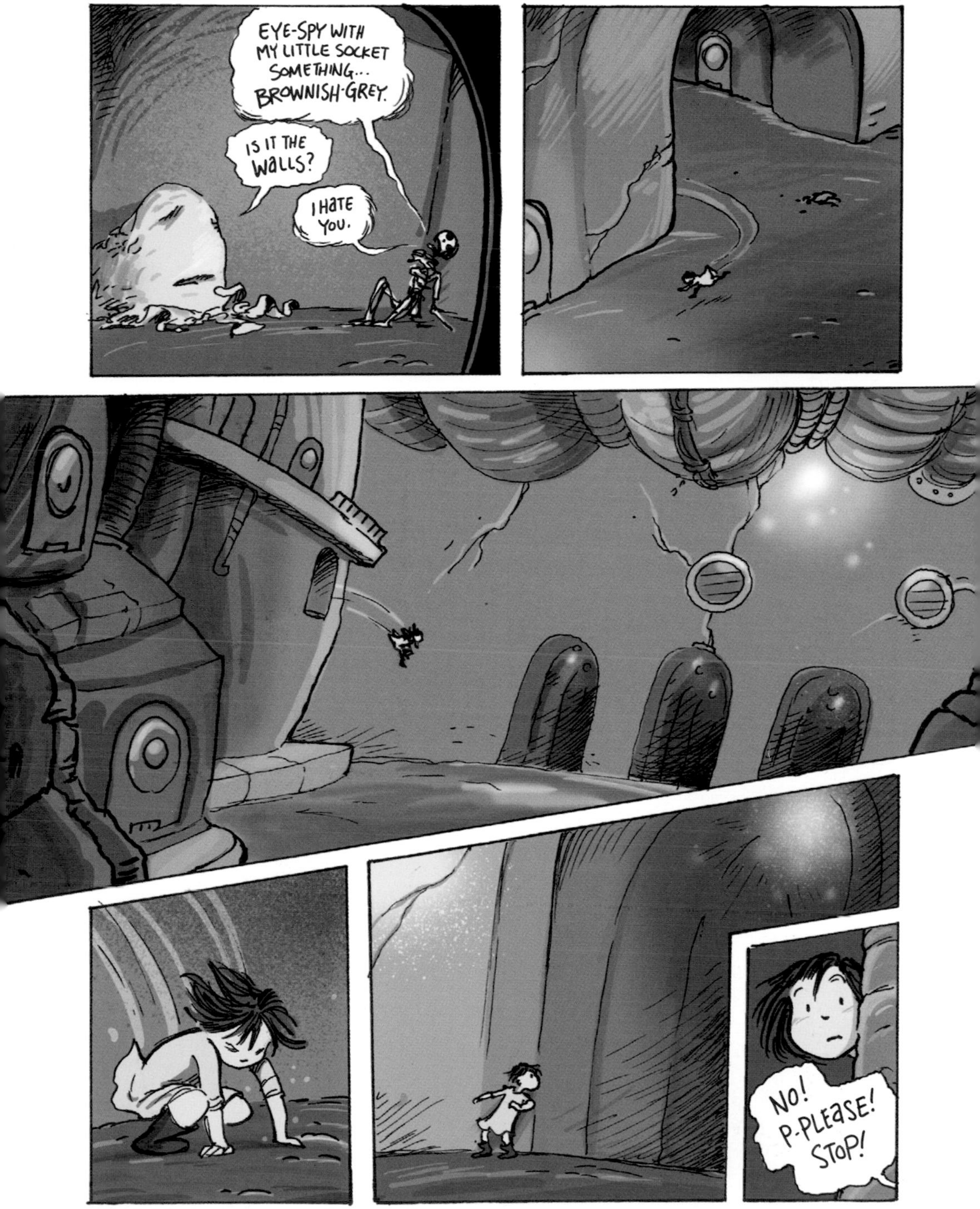
EYE-SPY WITH MY LITTLE SOCKET SOMETHING... BROWNISH-GREY.
IS IT THE WALLS?
I HATE YOU.
NO! P-PLEASE! STOP!

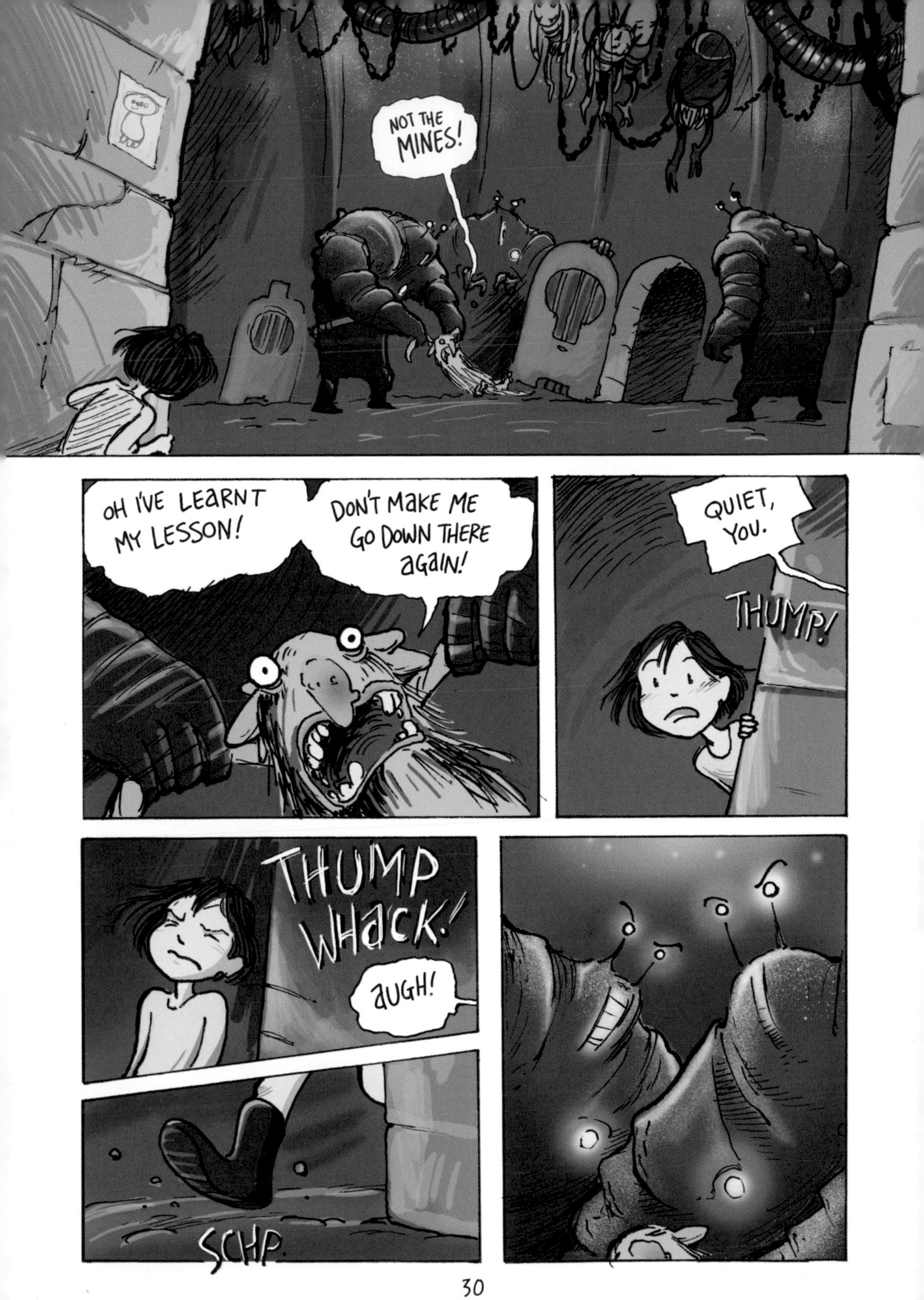
NOT THE MINES!
OH I'VE LEARNT MY LESSON!
DON'T MAKE ME GO DOWN THERE AGAIN!
QUIET, YOU.
THUMP!
THUMP WHACK!
AUGH!
SCHP.

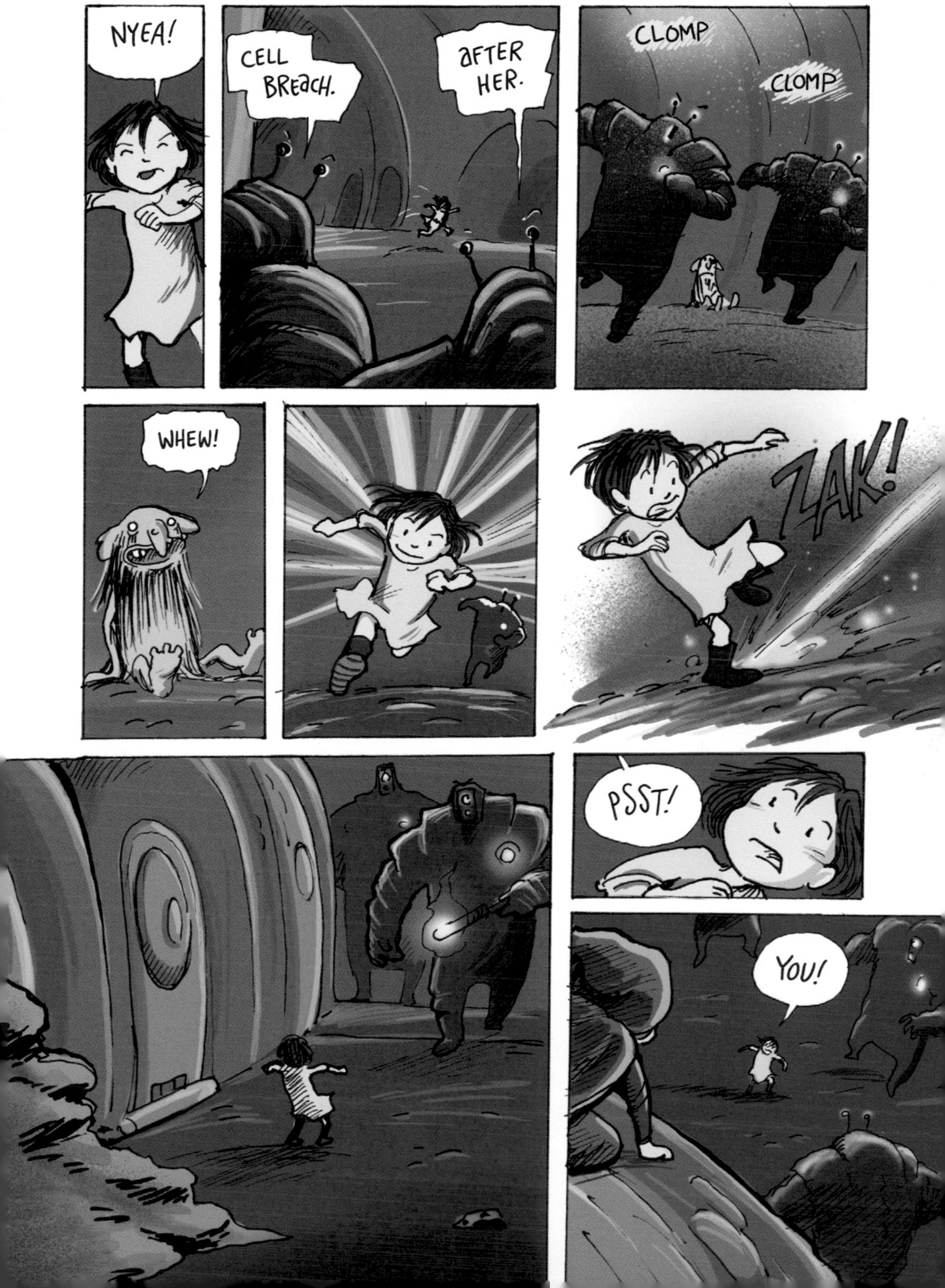
NYEA!
CELL BREACH.
AFTER HER.
CLOMP
CLOMP
WHEW!
ZAK!
PSST!
YOU!

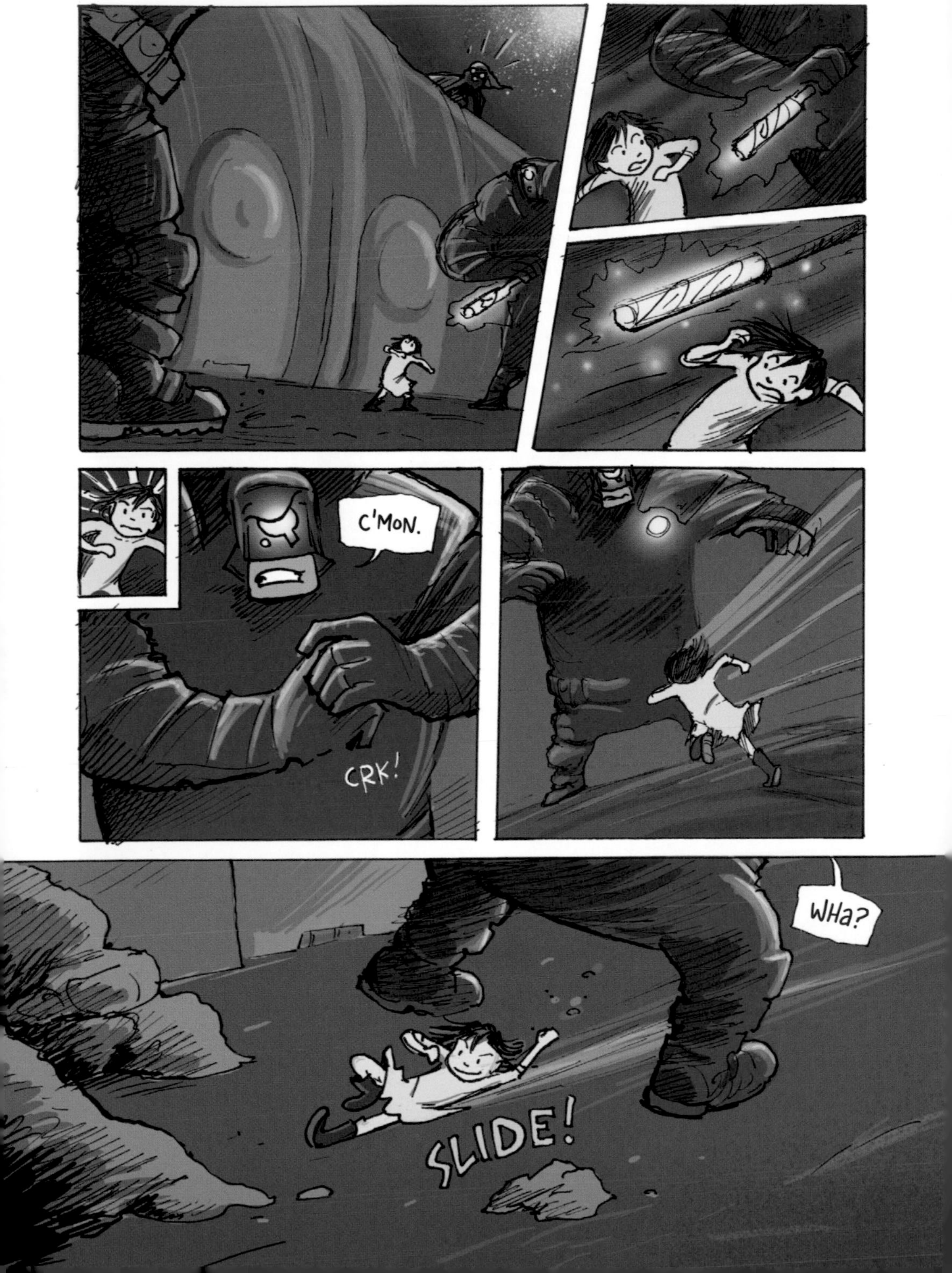
C'MON.
CRK!
WHa?
SLIDE!

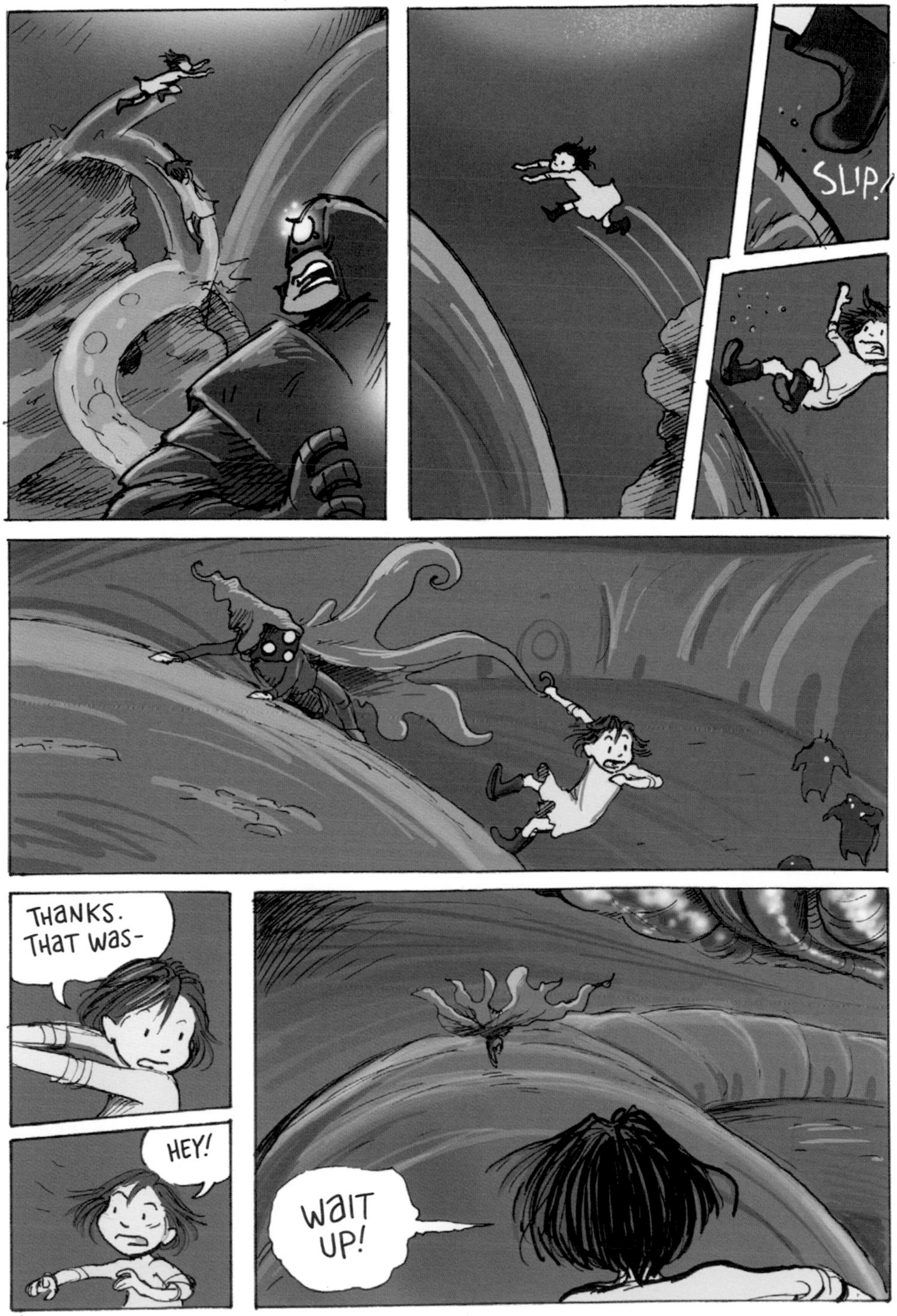
SLIP!
THANKS. THAT WAS-
HEY!
WAIT UP!

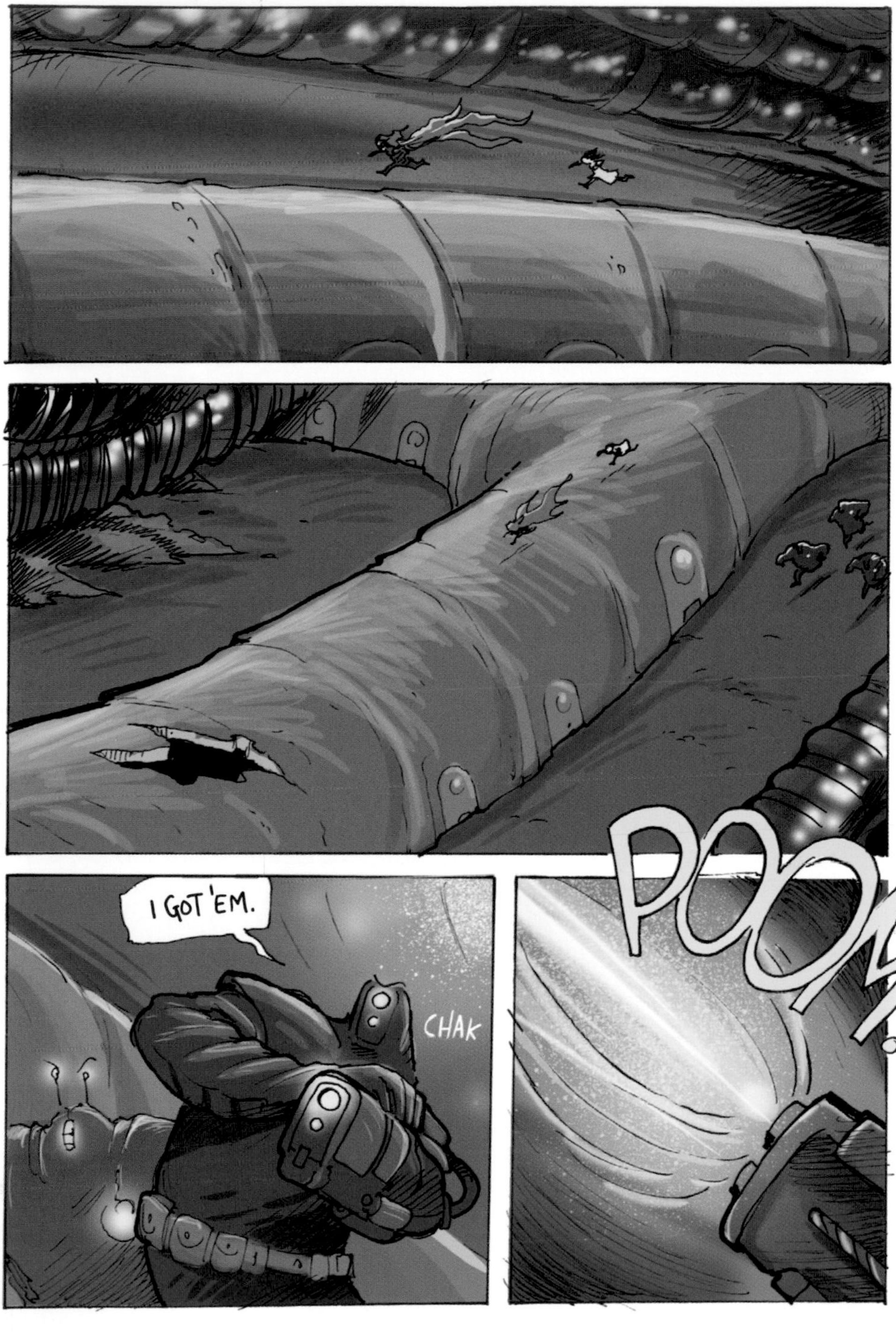
I GOT 'EM.
CHAK
POOM!

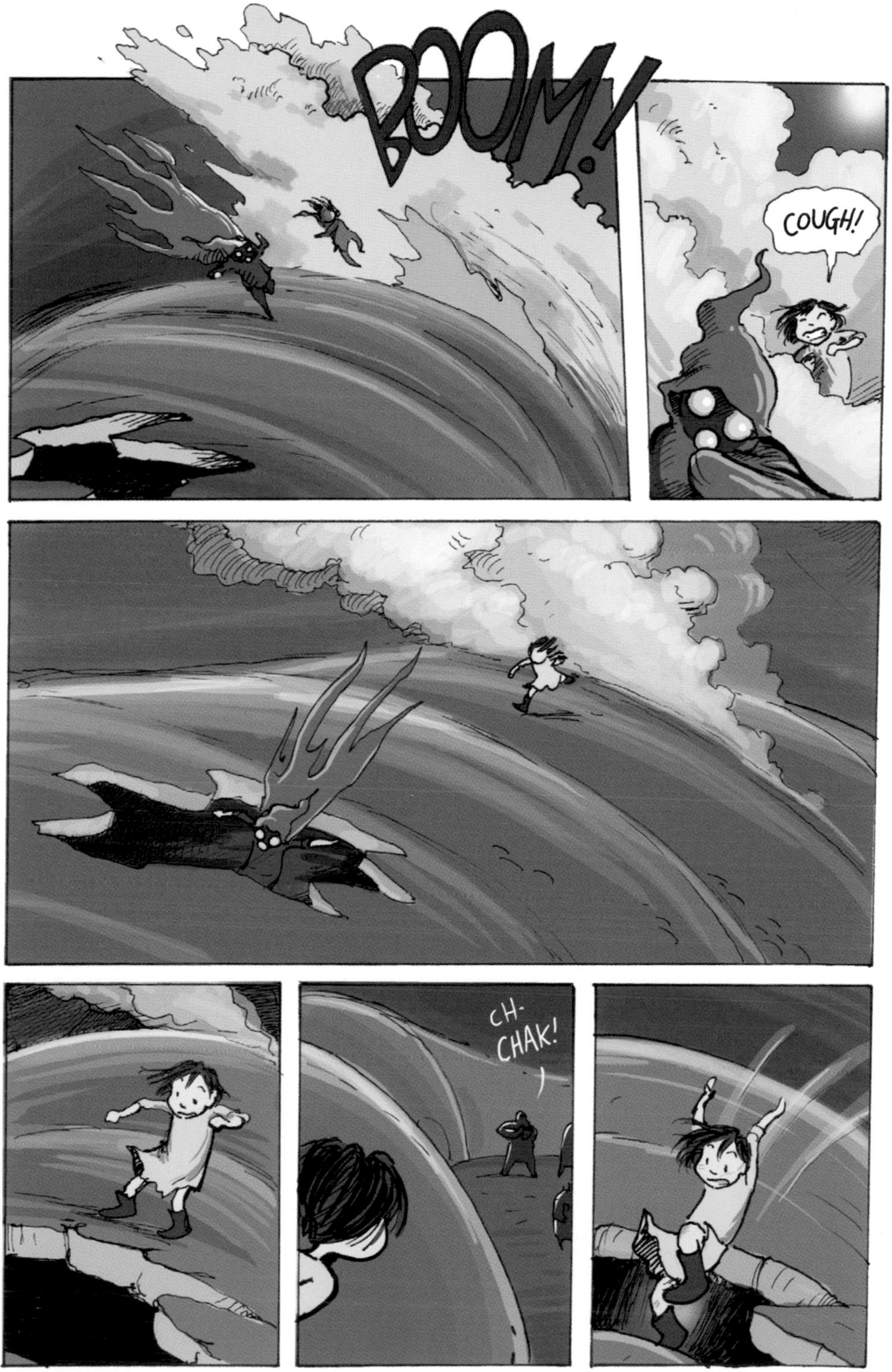
BOOM!
COUGH!
CH-CHAK!

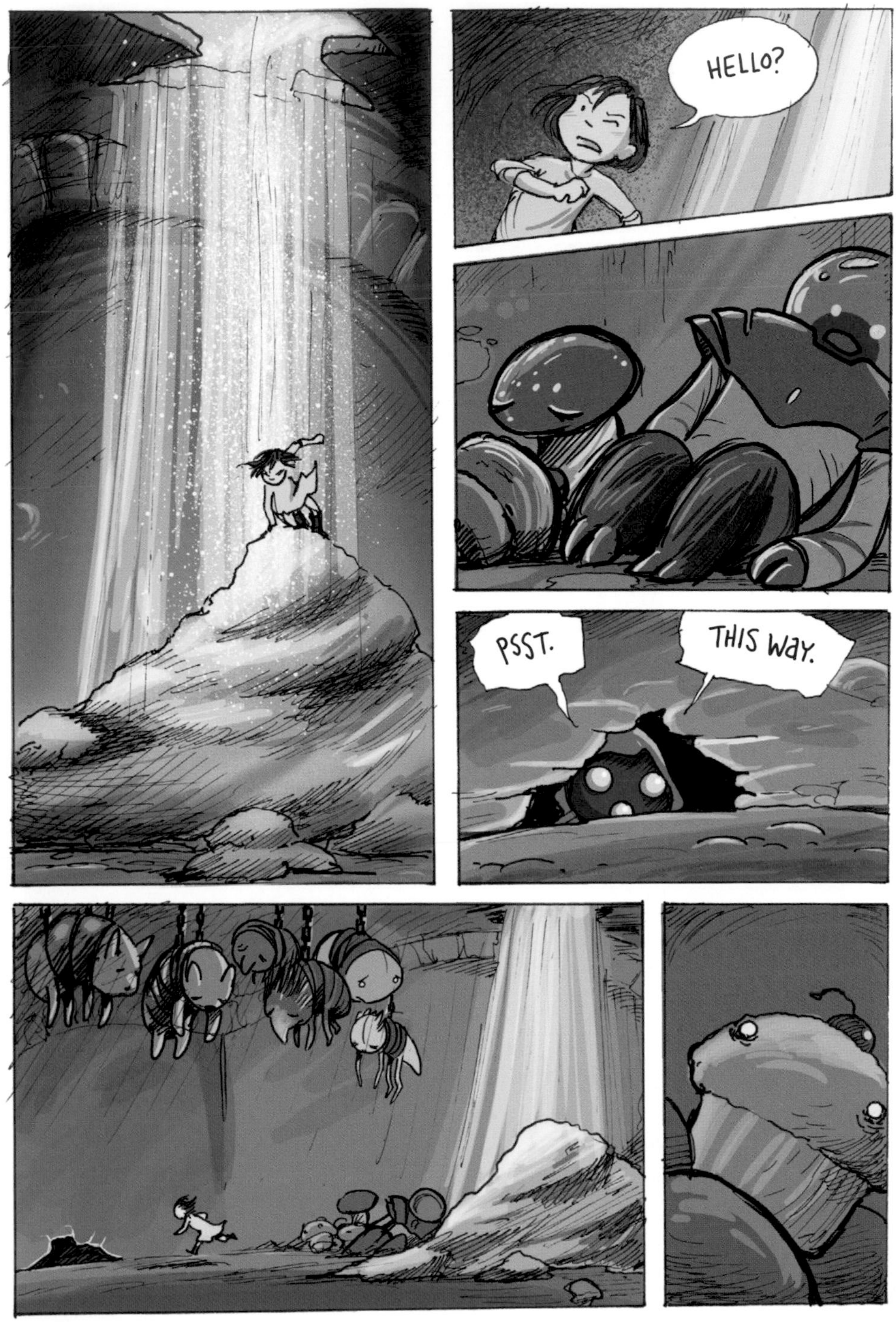
HELLO?
PSST.
THIS WAY.

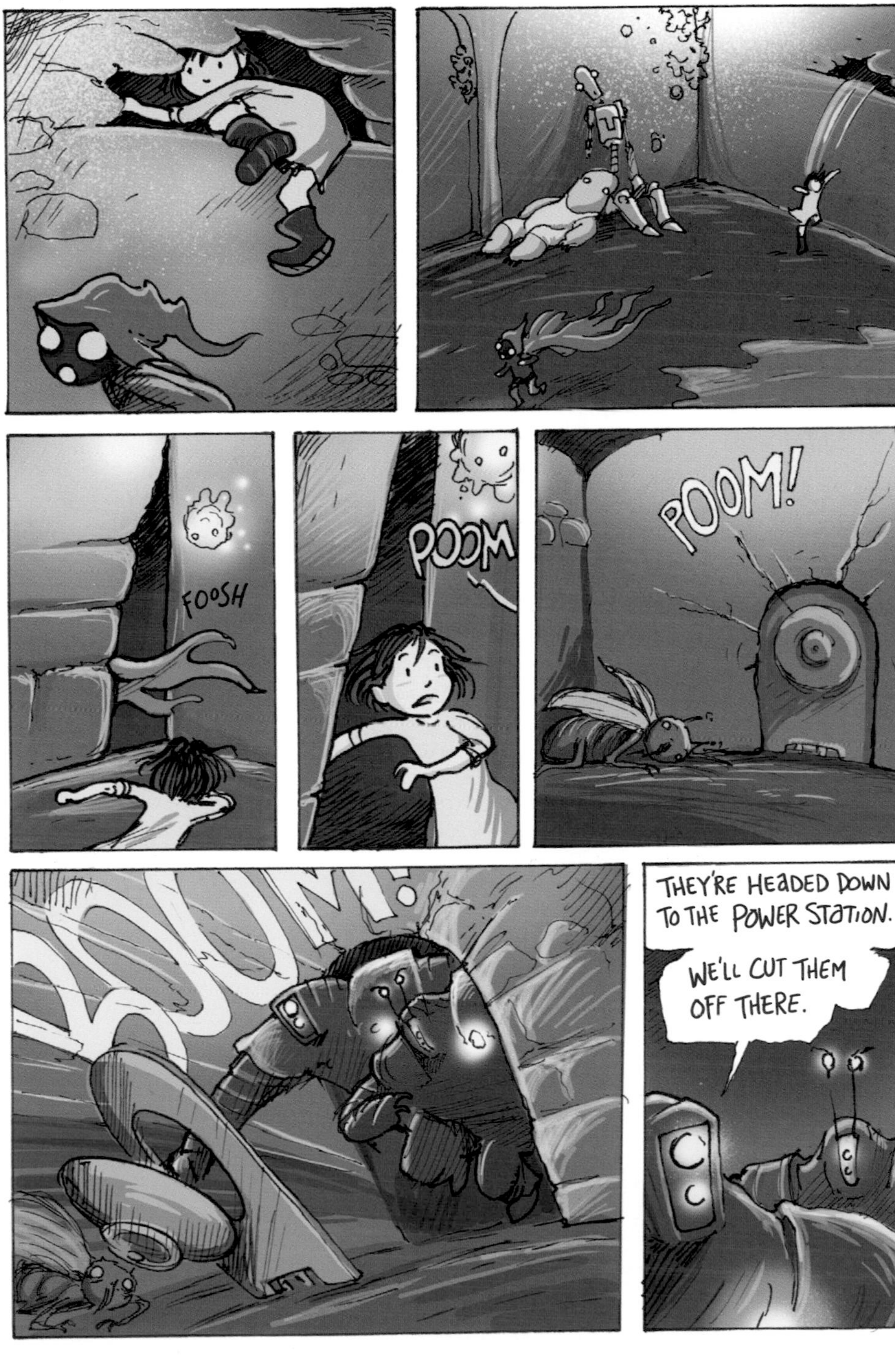
FOOSH
POOM
POOM!
BOOOM!
THEY'RE HEADED DOWN TO THE POWER STATION.
WE'LL CUT THEM OFF THERE.

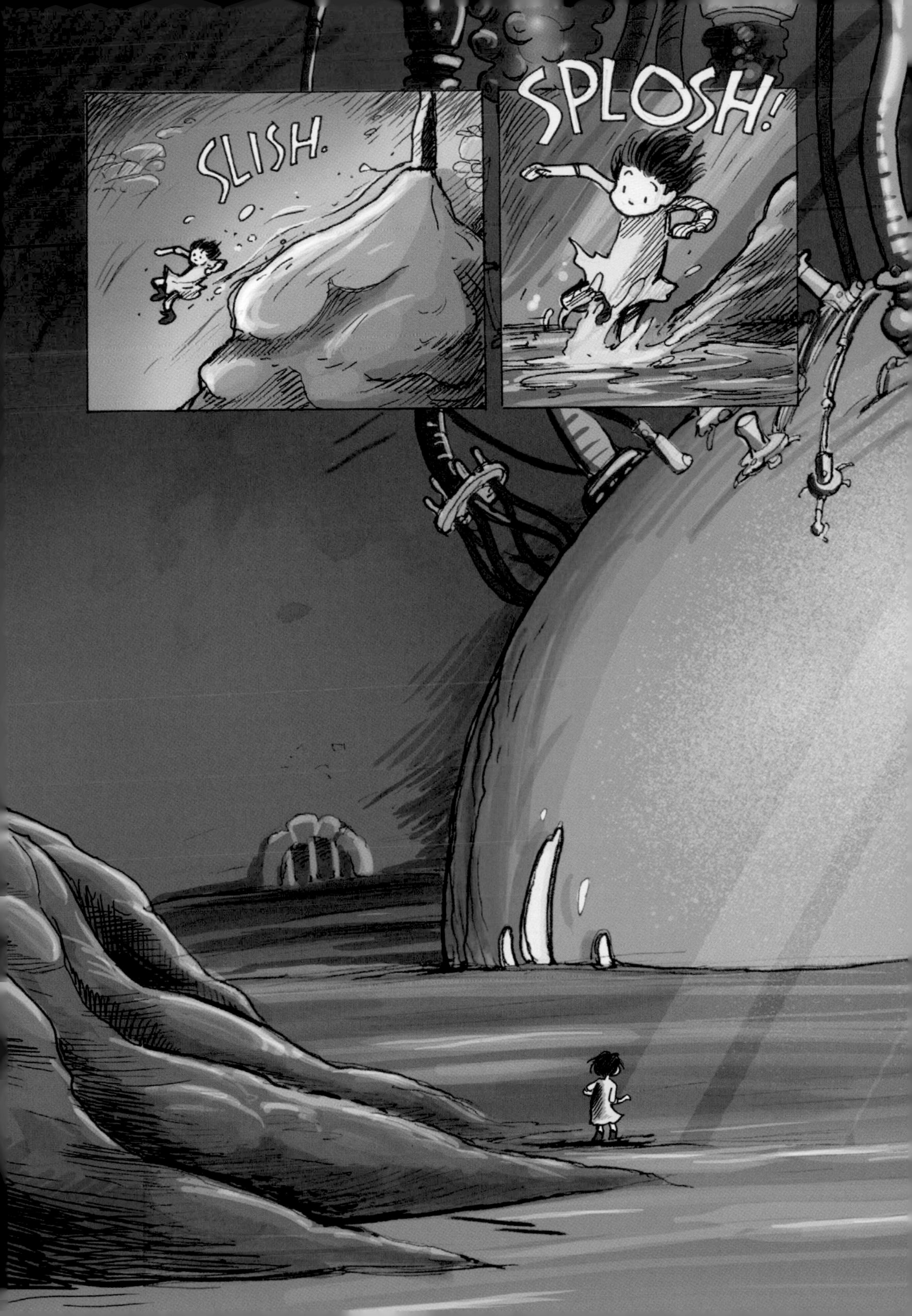
SLISH.
SPLOSH!

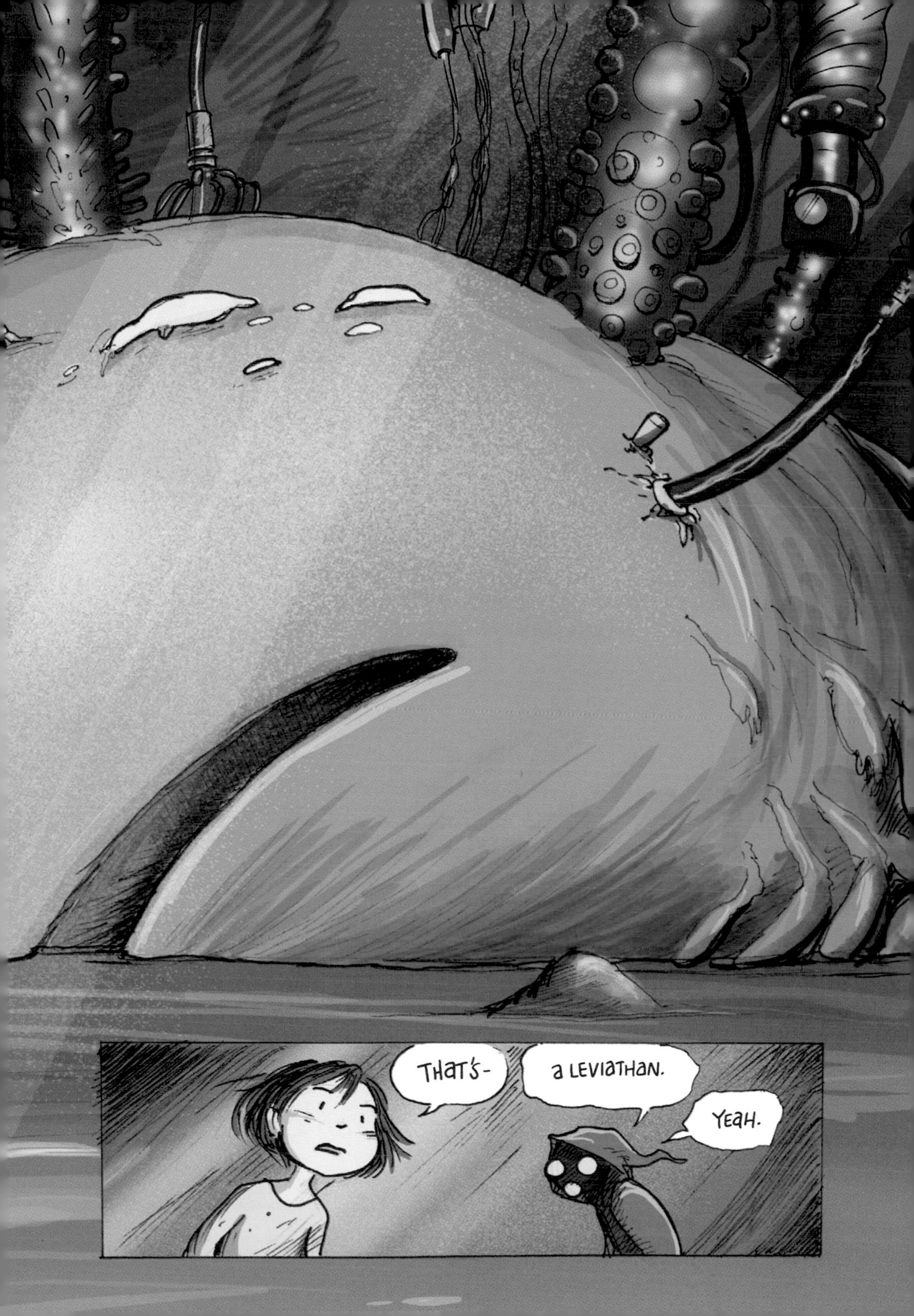
THAT'S-
a LEVIATHAN.
YEAH.

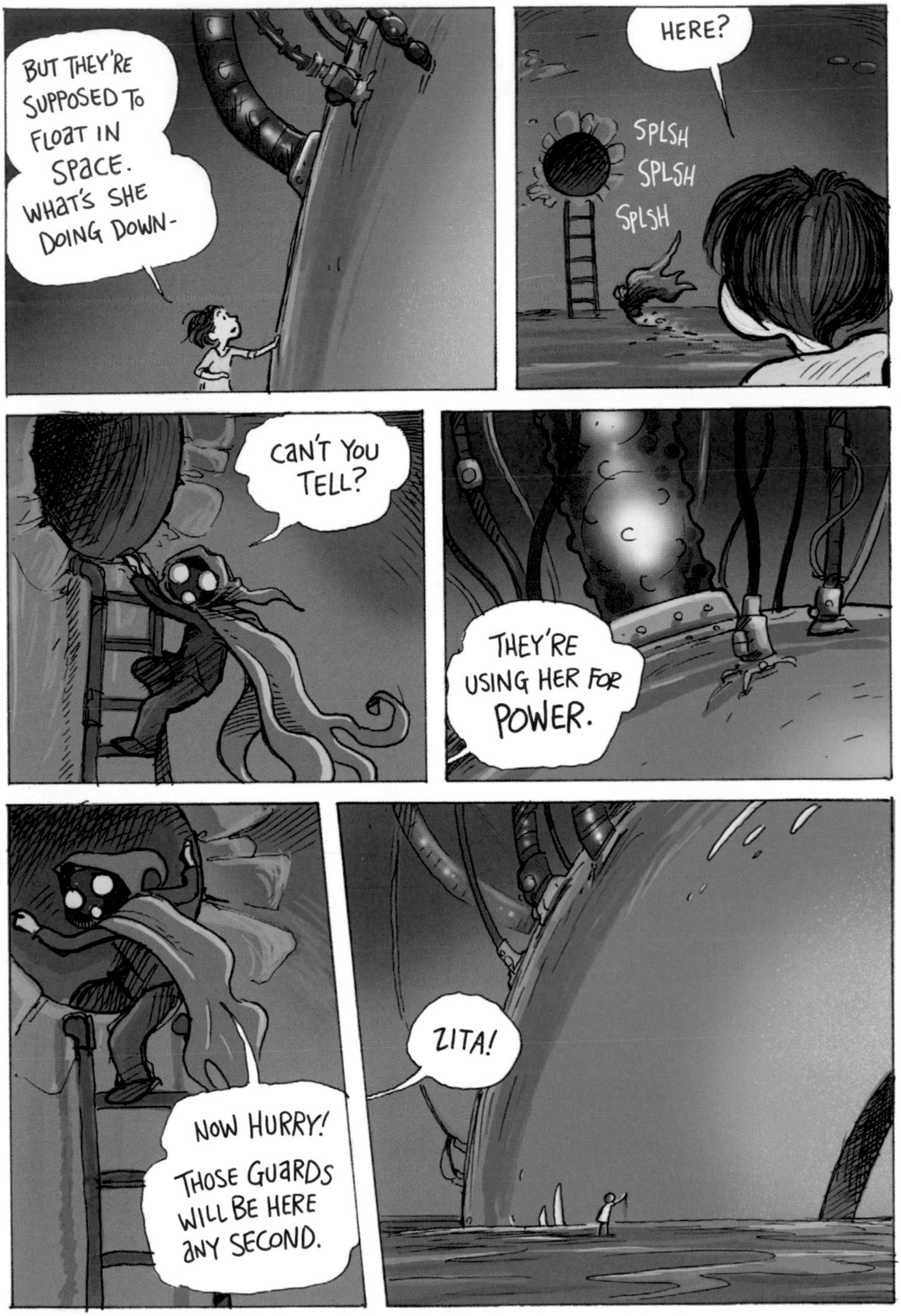
BUT THEY'RE SUPPOSED TO FLOAT IN SPACE. WHAT'S SHE DOING DOWN-
HERE?
SPLSH
SPLSH
SPLSH
CAN'T YOU TELL?
THEY'RE USING HER FOR POWER.
NOW HURRY!
THOSE GUARDS WILL BE HERE ANY SECOND.
ZITA!

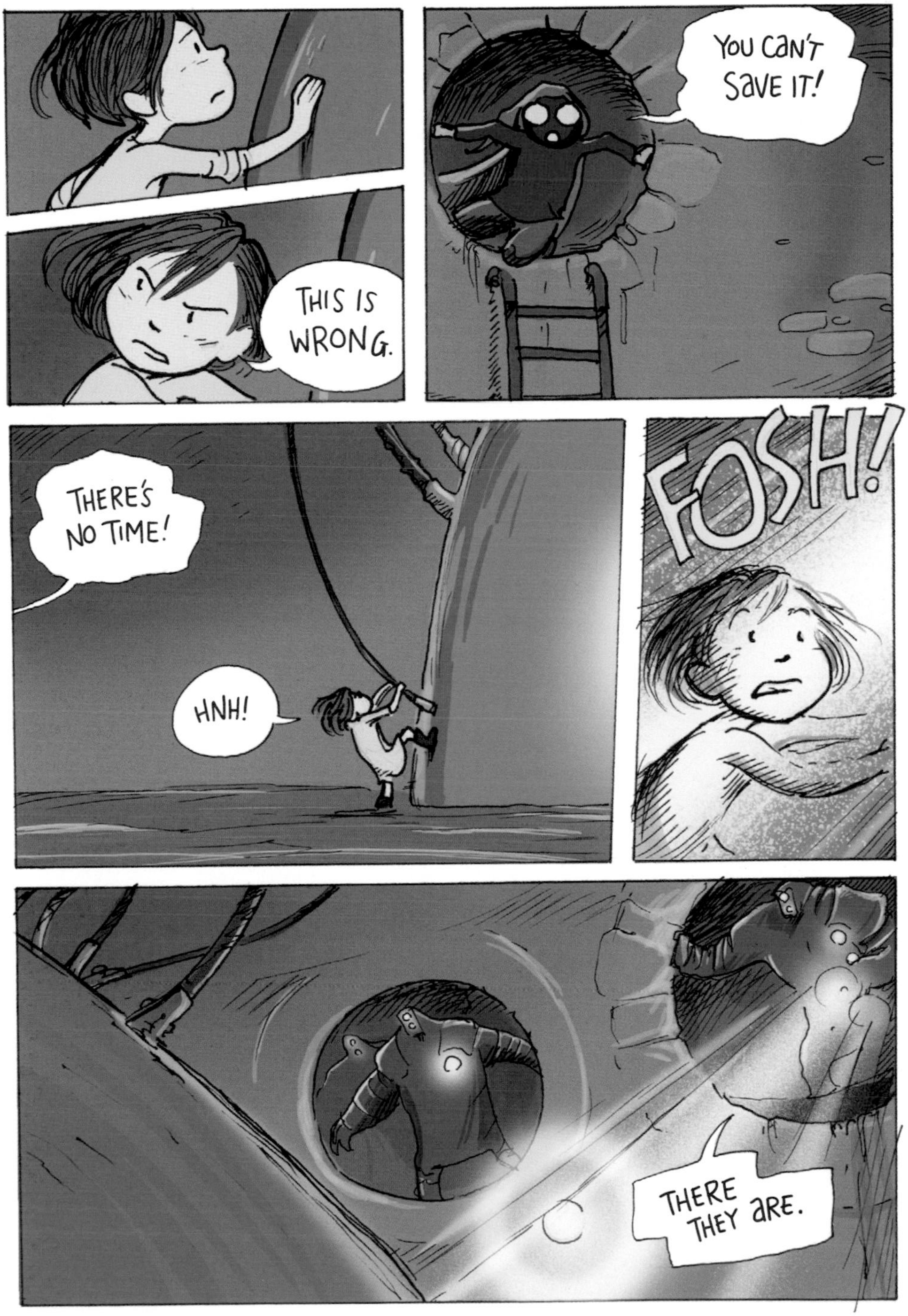
THIS IS WRONG.
YOU CAN'T SAVE IT!
THERE'S NO TIME!
HNH!
FOSH!
THERE THEY ARE.

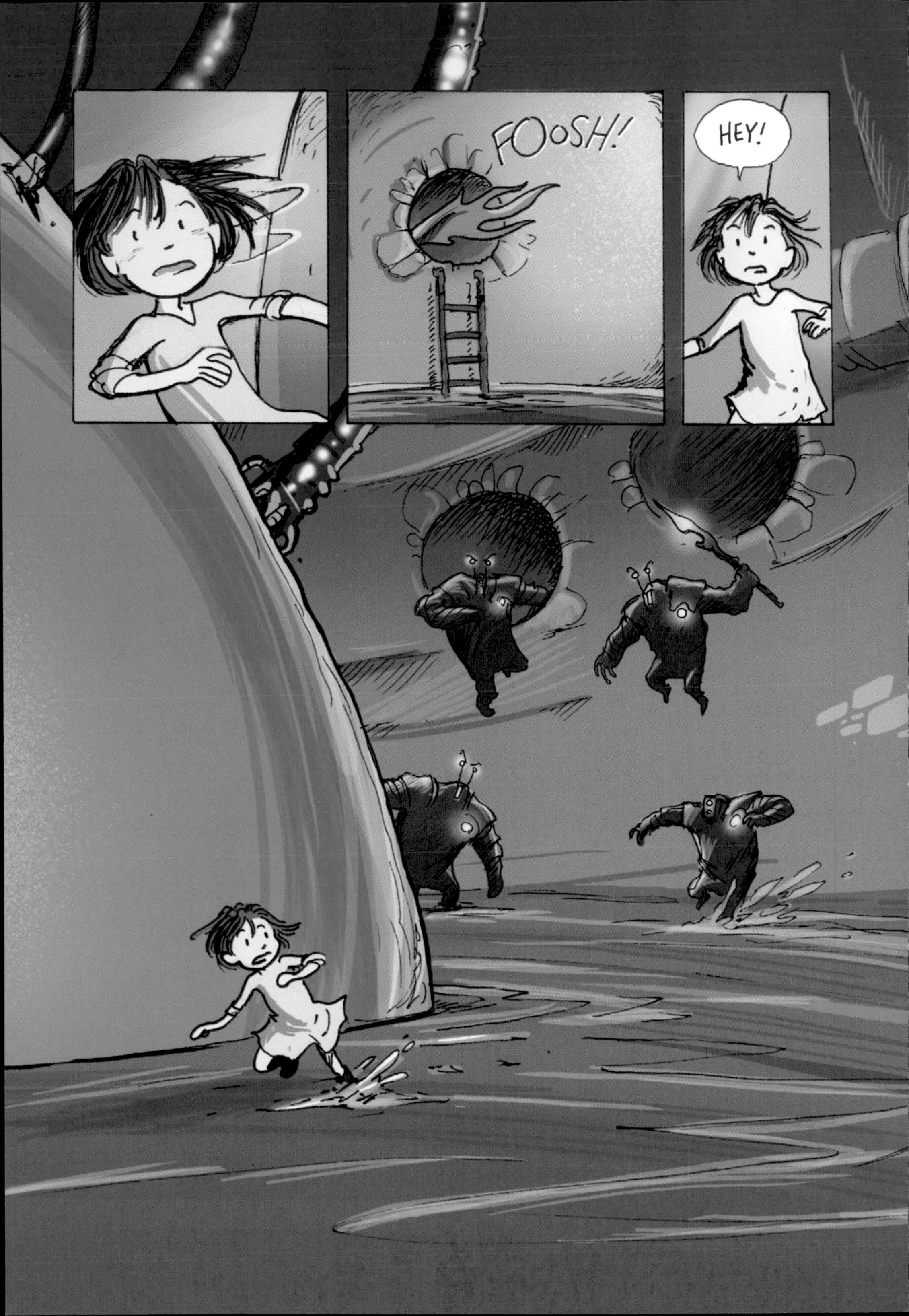
FOOSH!
HEY!

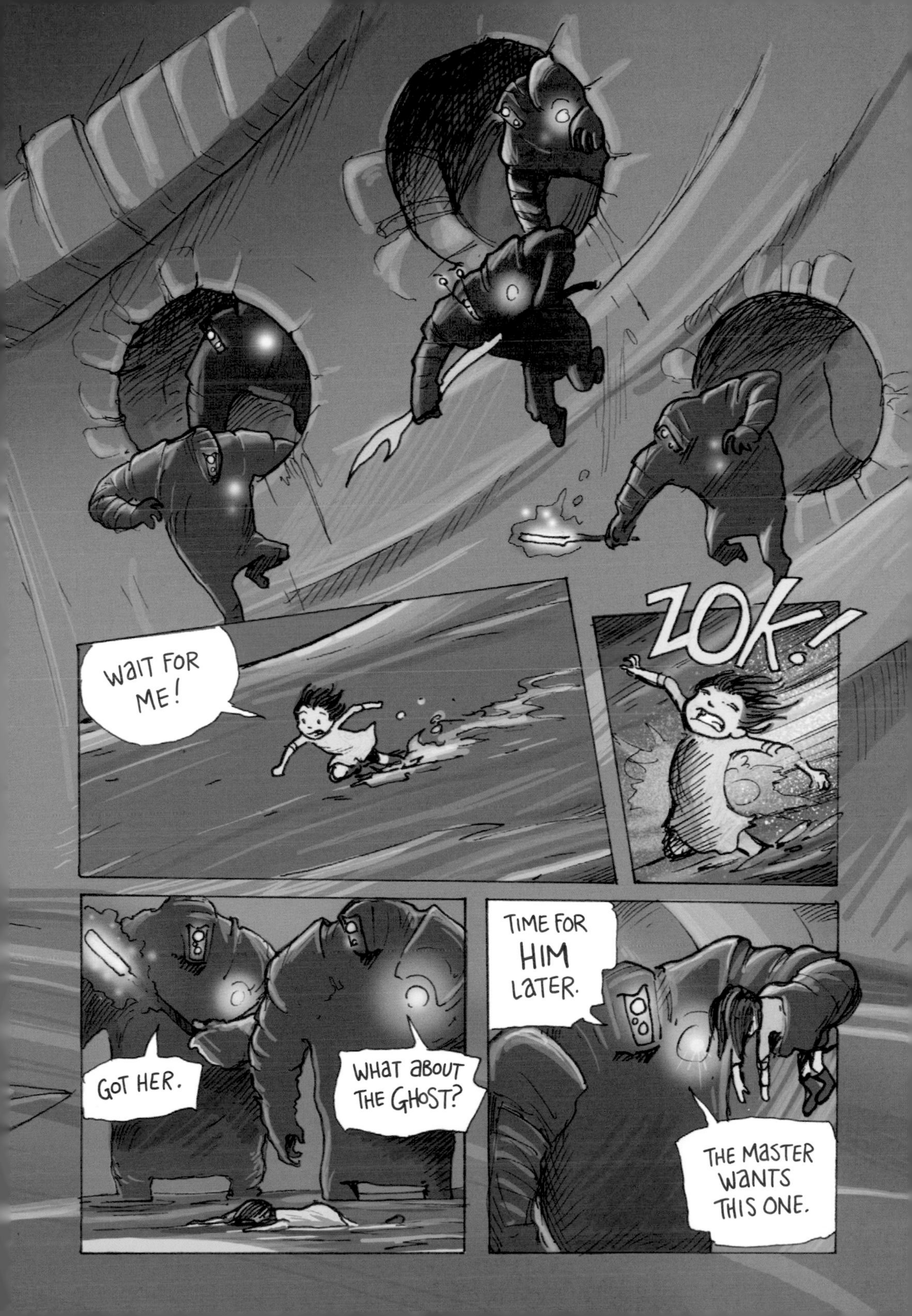
WAIT FOR ME!
ZOK!
GOT HER.
WHAT ABOUT THE GHOST?
TIME FOR HIM LATER.
THE MASTER WANTS THIS ONE.

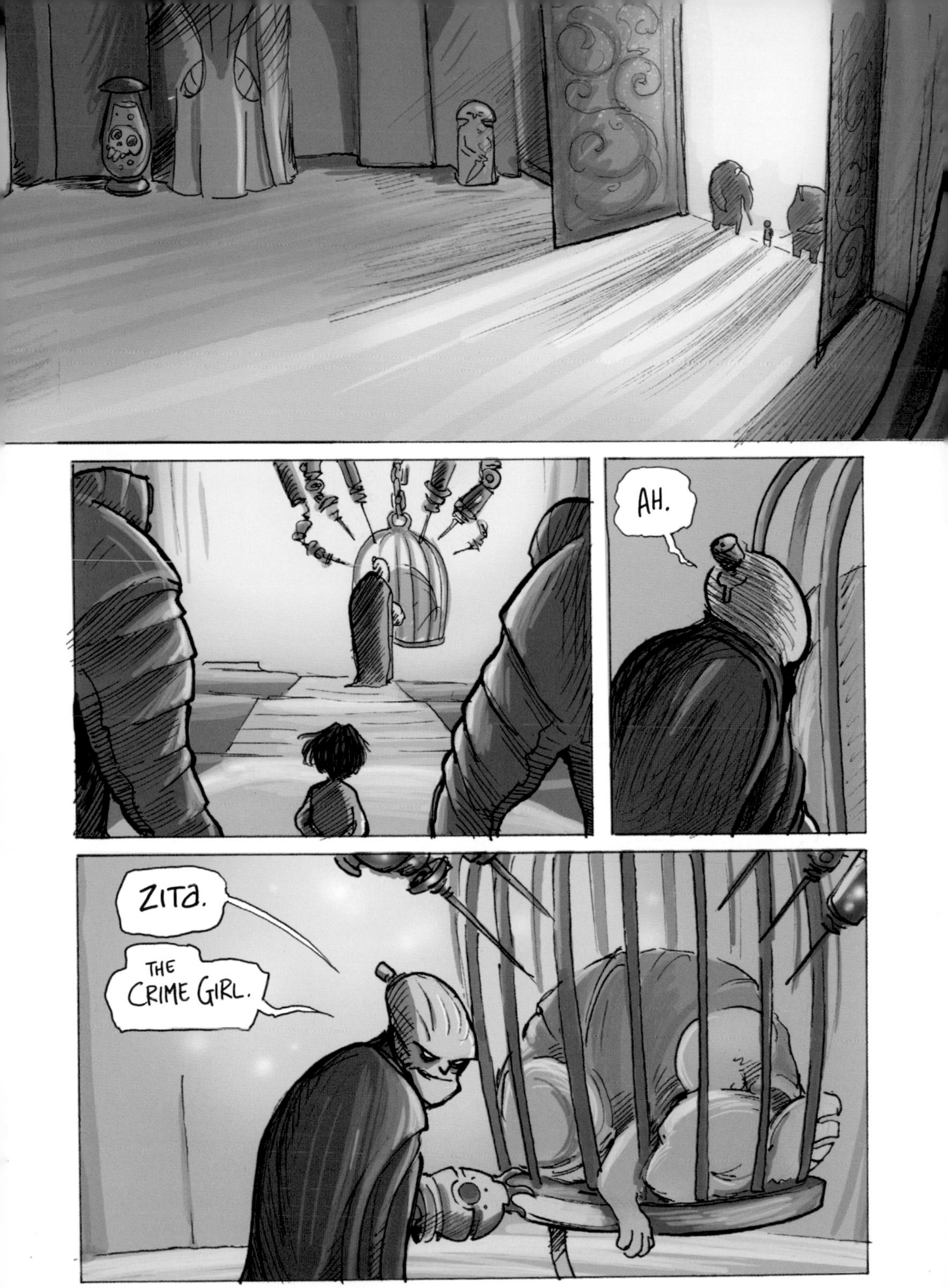
AH.
ZITA.
THE CRIME GIRL.

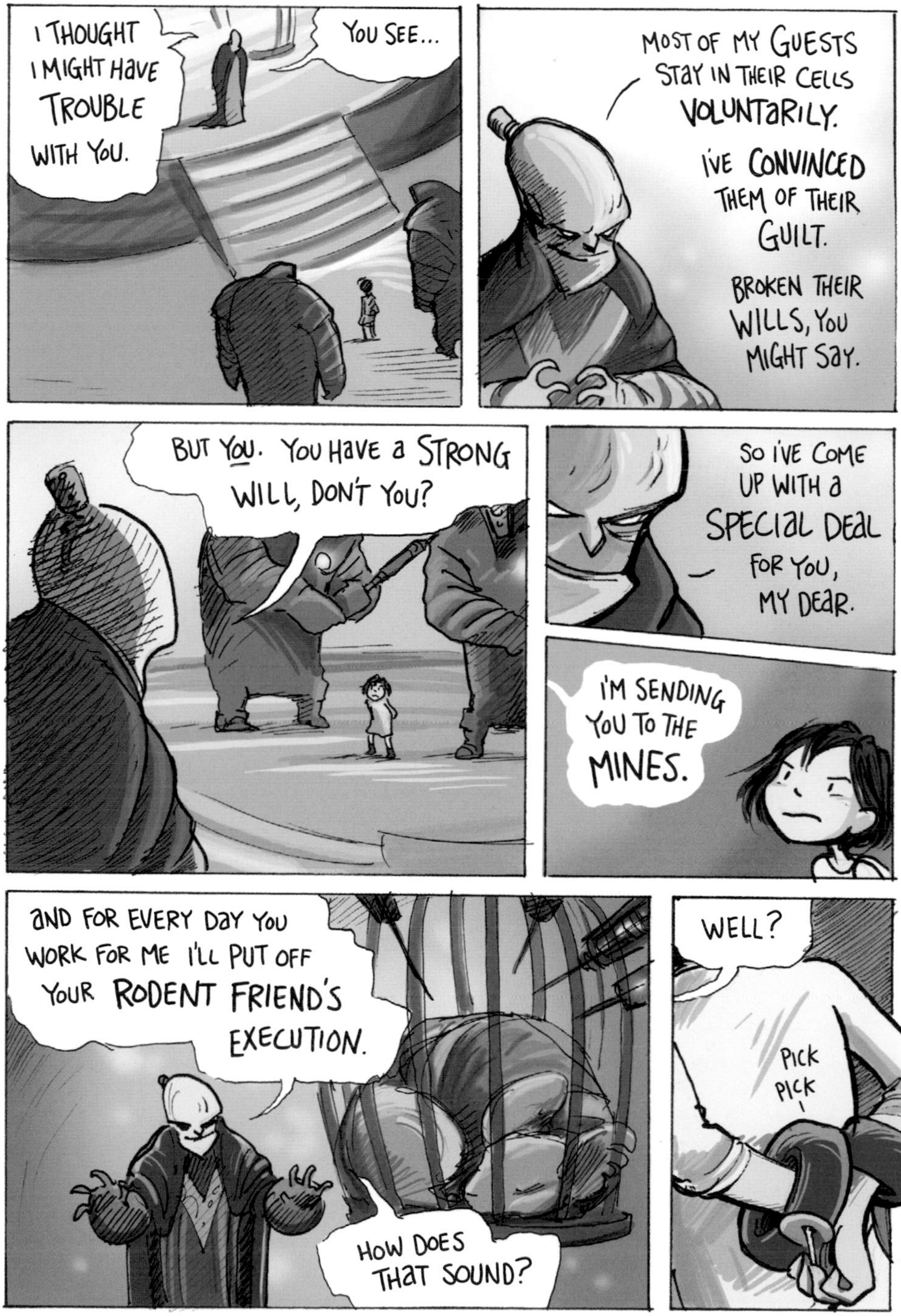
I THOUGHT I MIGHT HAVE TROUBLE WITH YOU.
YOU SEE...
MOST OF MY GUESTS STAY IN THEIR CELLS VOLUNTARILY.
I'VE CONVINCED THEM OF THEIR GUILT.
BROKEN THEIR WILLS, YOU MIGHT SAY.
BUT YOU. YOU HAVE A STRONG WILL, DON'T YOU?
SO I'VE COME UP WITH A SPECIAL DEAL FOR YOU, MY DEAR.
I'M SENDING YOU TO THE MINES.
AND FOR EVERY DAY YOU WORK FOR ME I'LL PUT OFF YOUR RODENT FRIEND'S EXECUTION.
HOW DOES THAT SOUND?
WELL?
PICK PICK

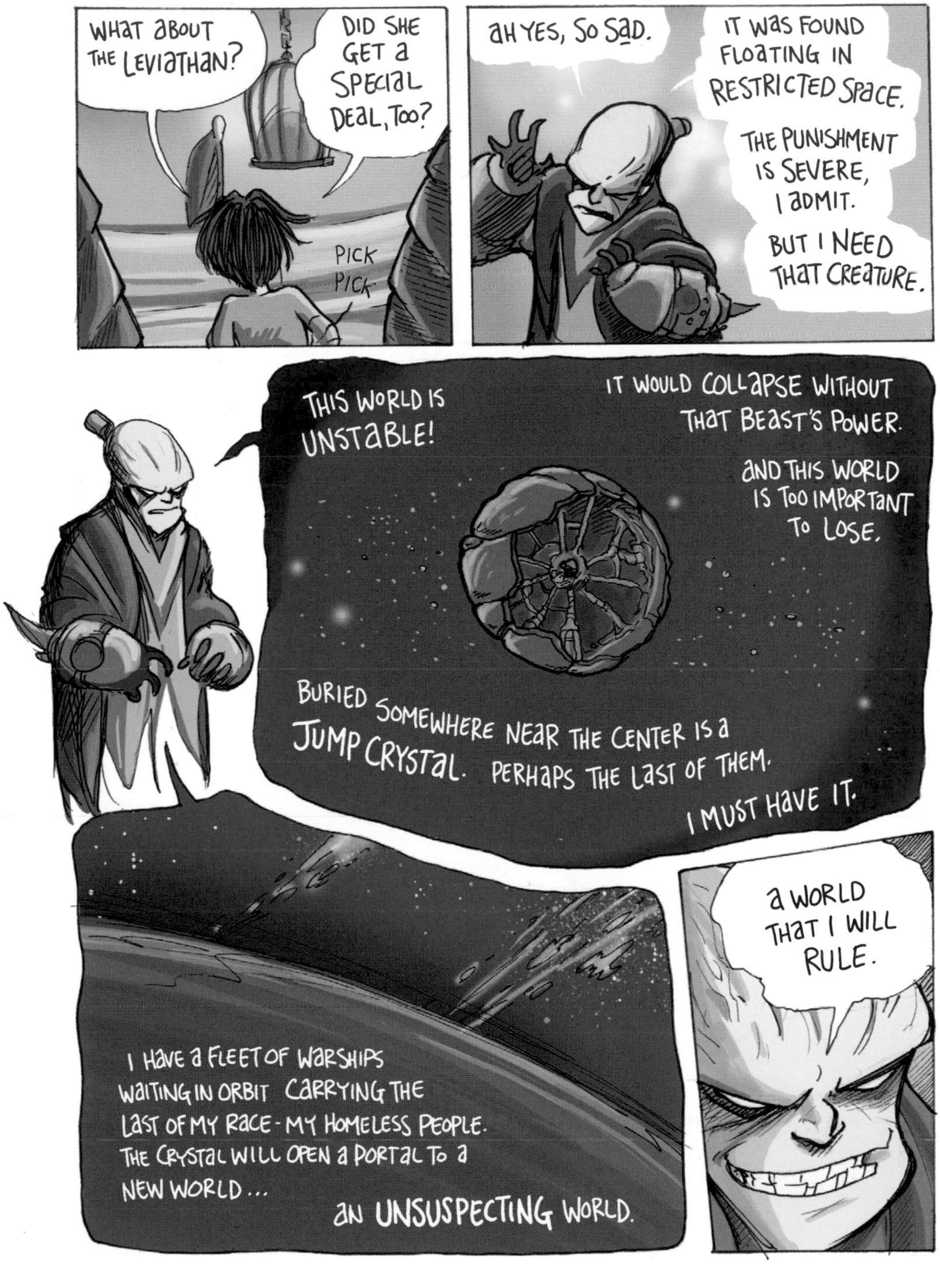
WHAT ABOUT THE LEVIATHAN?
DID SHE GET A SPECIAL DEAL, TOO?
PICK PICK
AH YES, SO SAD.
IT WAS FOUND FLOATING IN RESTRICTED SPACE.
THE PUNISHMENT IS SEVERE, I ADMIT.
BUT I NEED THAT CREATURE.
THIS WORLD IS UNSTABLE!
IT WOULD COLLAPSE WITHOUT THAT BEAST'S POWER.
AND THIS WORLD IS TOO IMPORTANT TO LOSE.
BURIED SOMEWHERE NEAR THE CENTER IS A JUMP CRYSTAL. PERHAPS THE LAST OF THEM.
I MUST HAVE IT.
I HAVE A FLEET OF WARSHIPS WAITING IN ORBIT CARRYING THE LAST OF MY RACE - MY HOMELESS PEOPLE. THE CRYSTAL WILL OPEN A PORTAL TO A NEW WORLD...
AN UNSUSPECTING WORLD.
A WORLD THAT I WILL RULE.

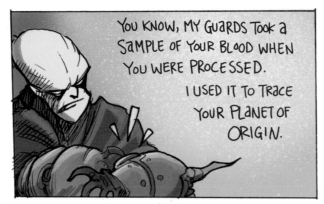

YOU KNOW, MY GUARDS TOOK A SAMPLE OF YOUR BLOOD WHEN YOU WERE PROCESSED. I USED IT TO TRACE YOUR PLANET OF ORIGIN.

...

AHH.

SUCH A PRETTY WORLD.

SUCH AN UNSUSPECTING WORLD...

CLICK

MONSTER!

SHE'S LOOSE!

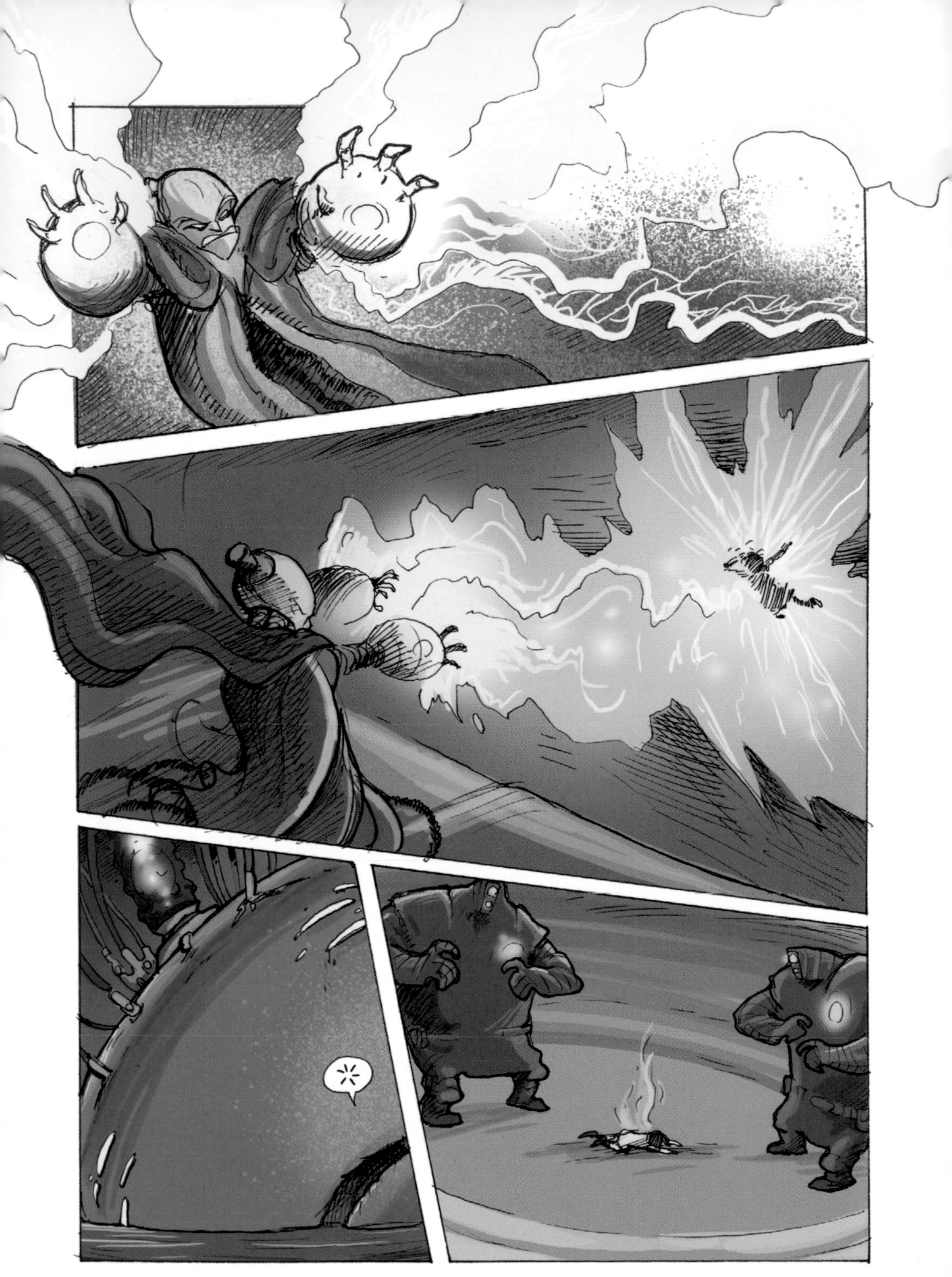

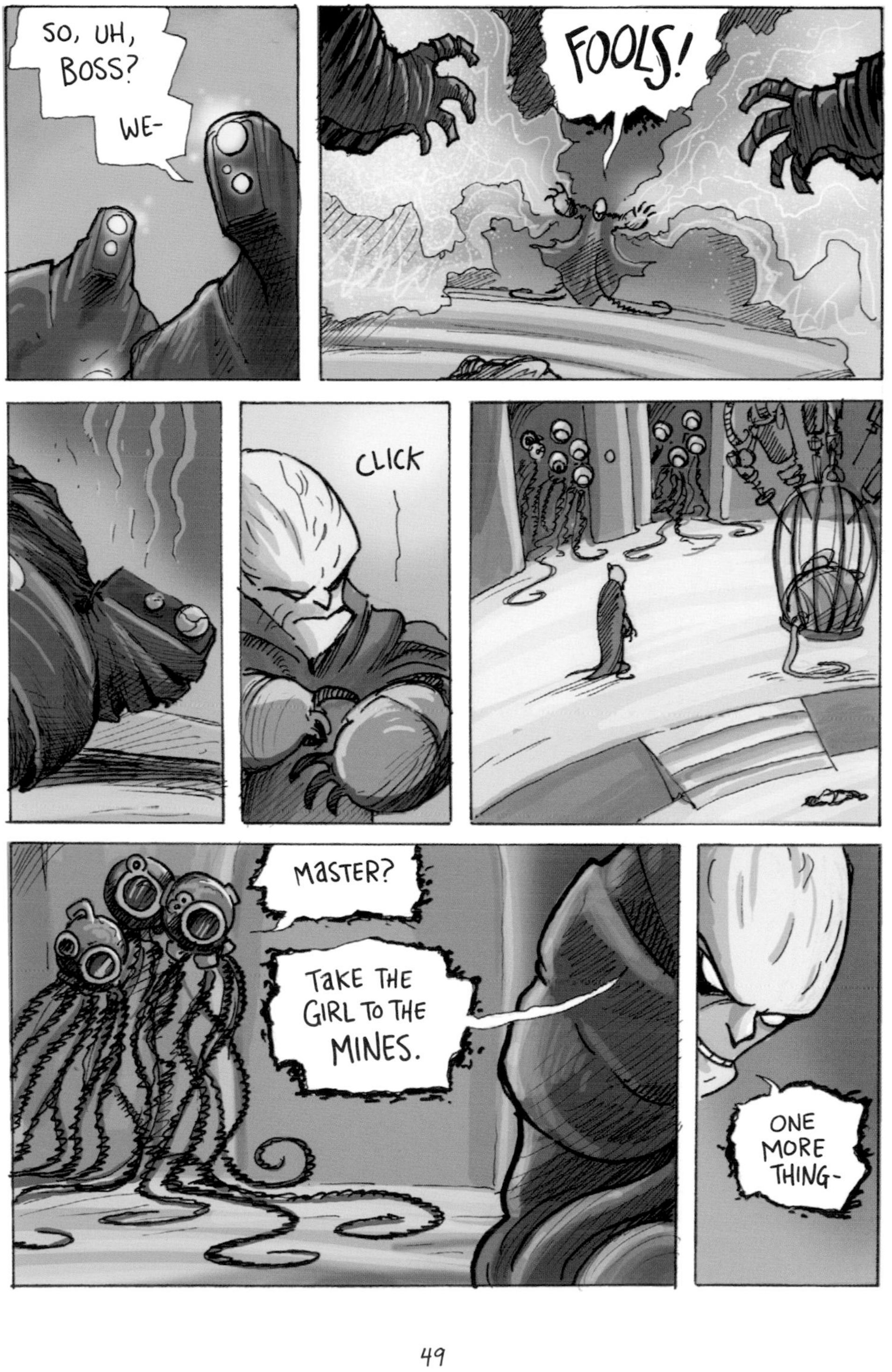
SO, UH, BOSS?
WE-
FOOLS!
CLICK
MASTER?
TAKE THE GIRL TO THE MINES.
ONE MORE THING-

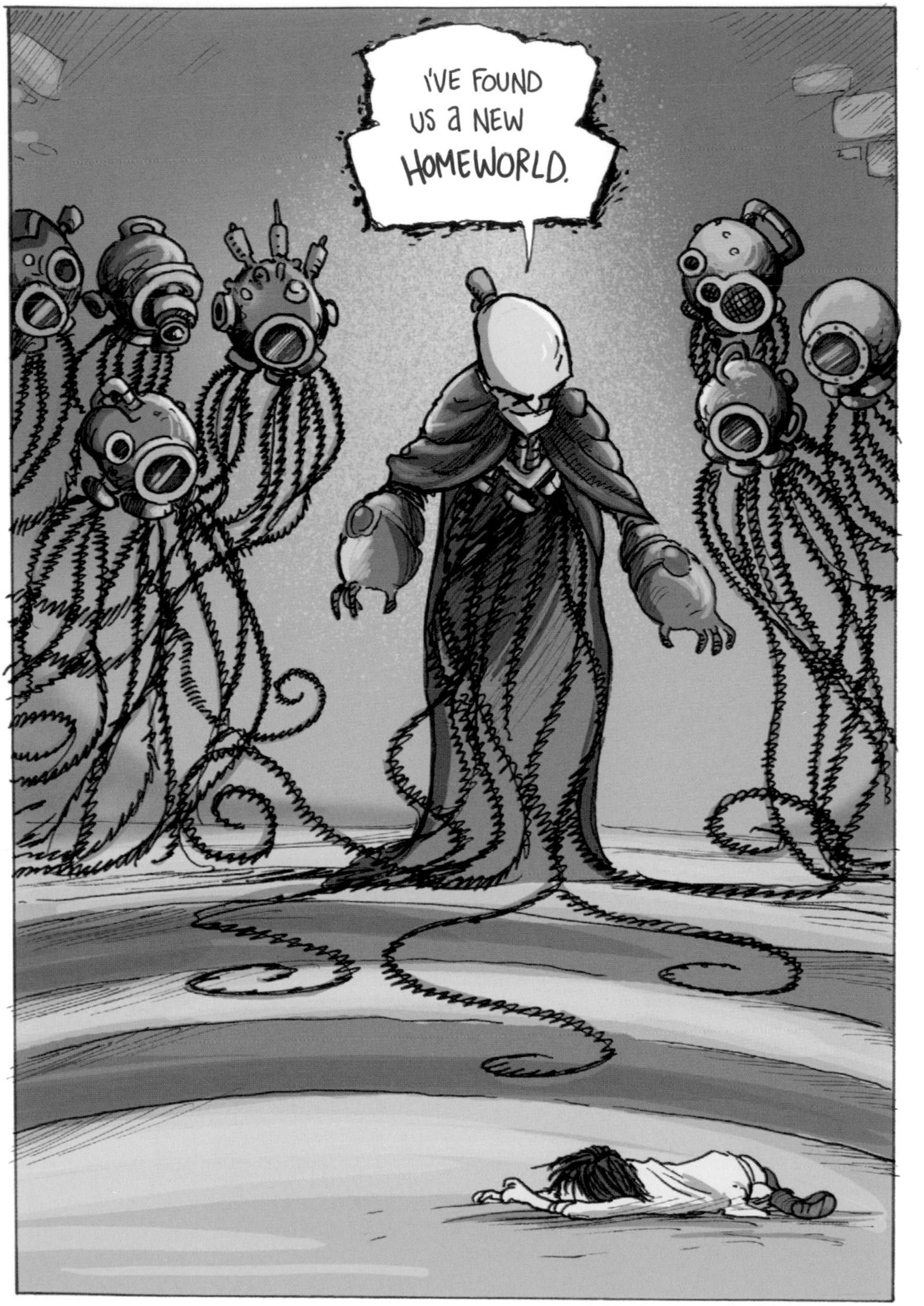
I'VE FOUND US A NEW HOMEWORLD.

Chapter
Three

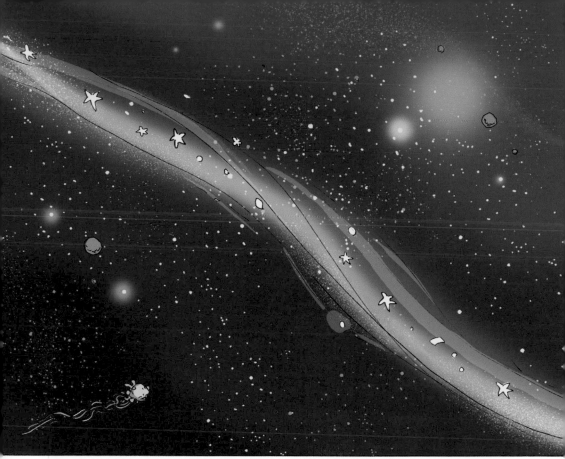

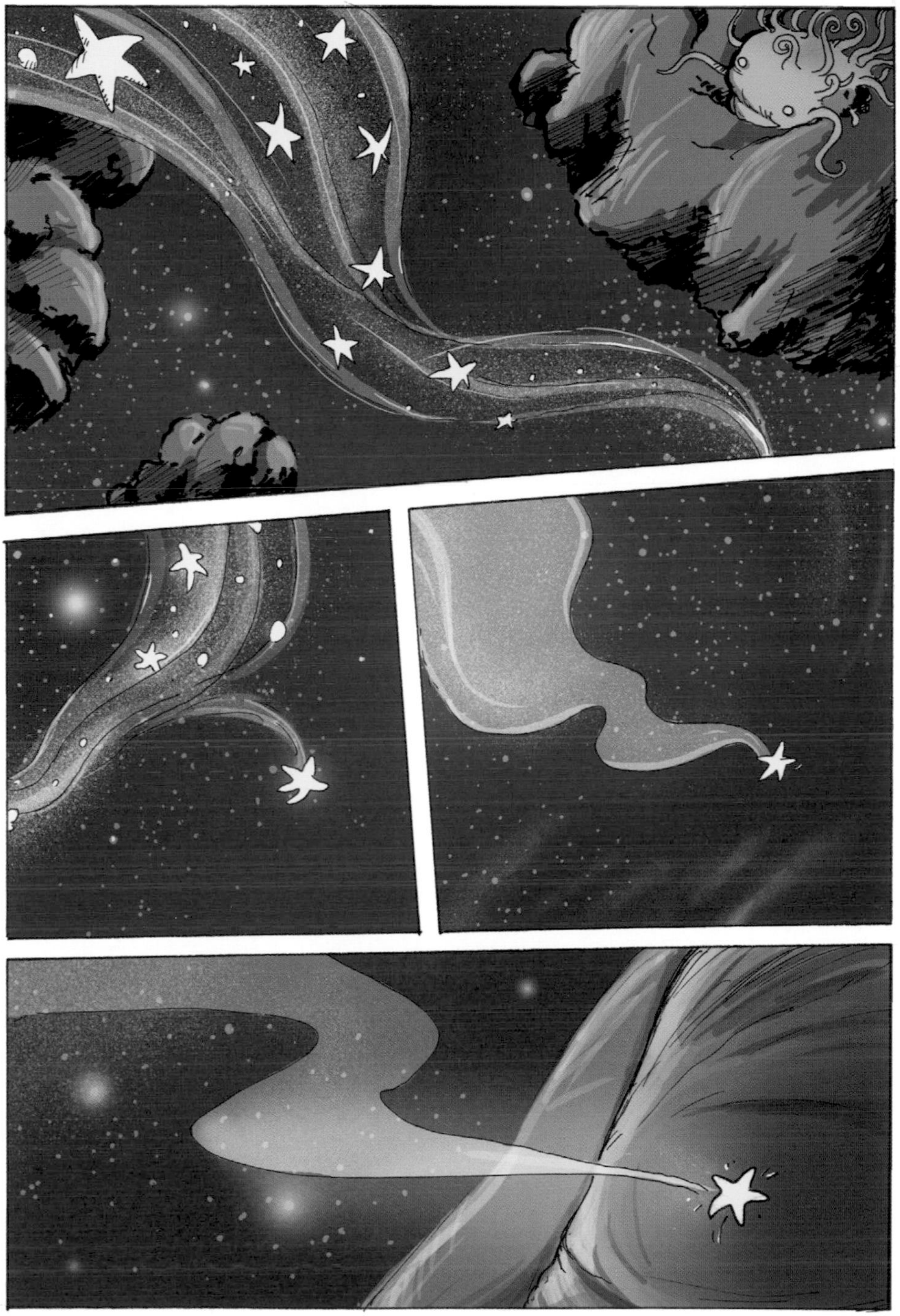

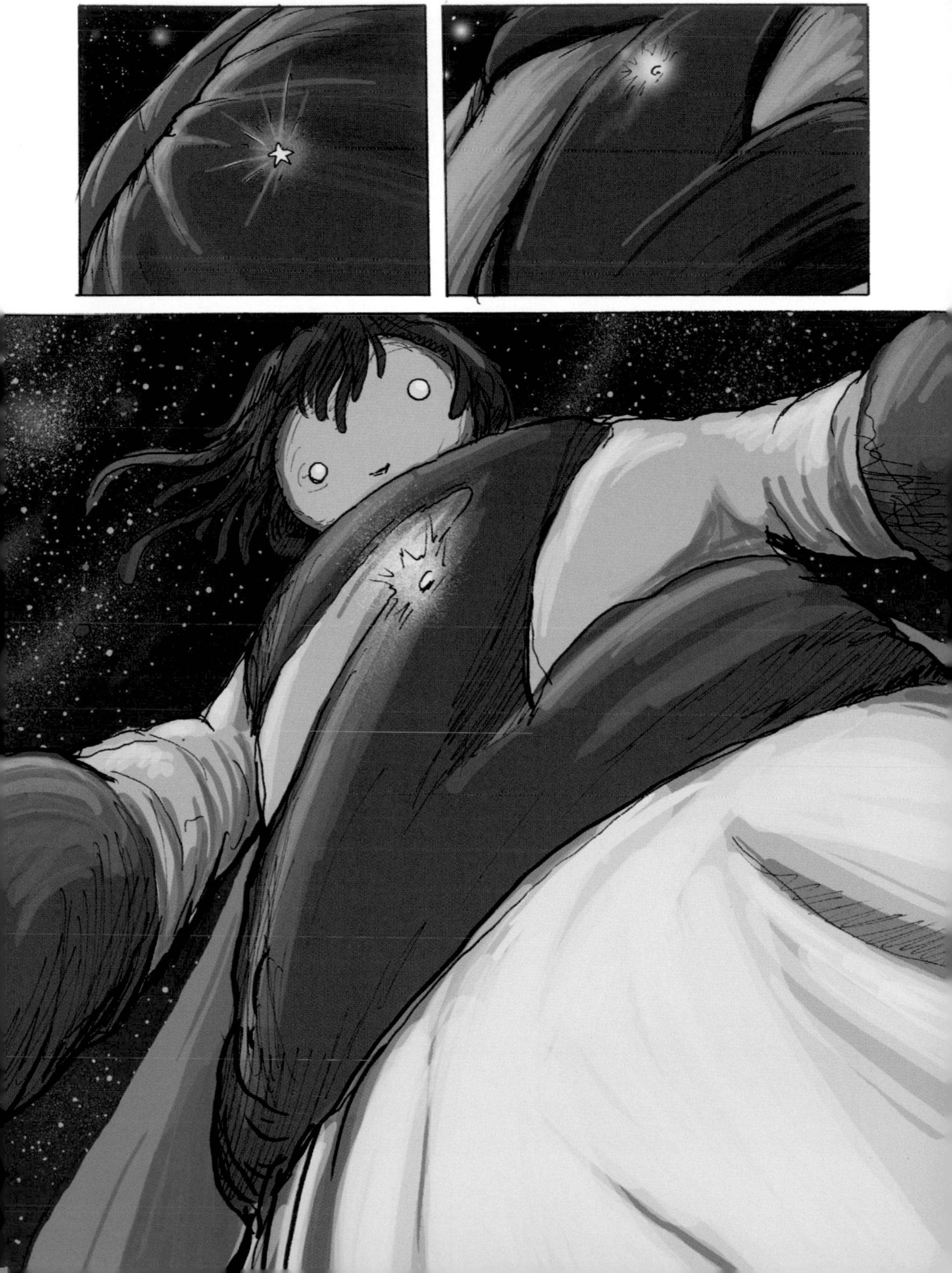

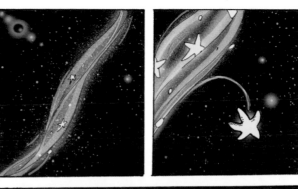

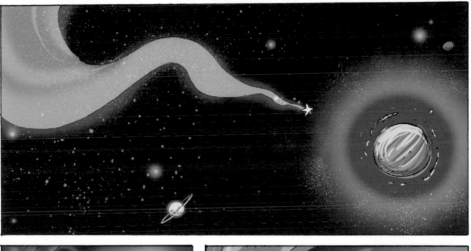

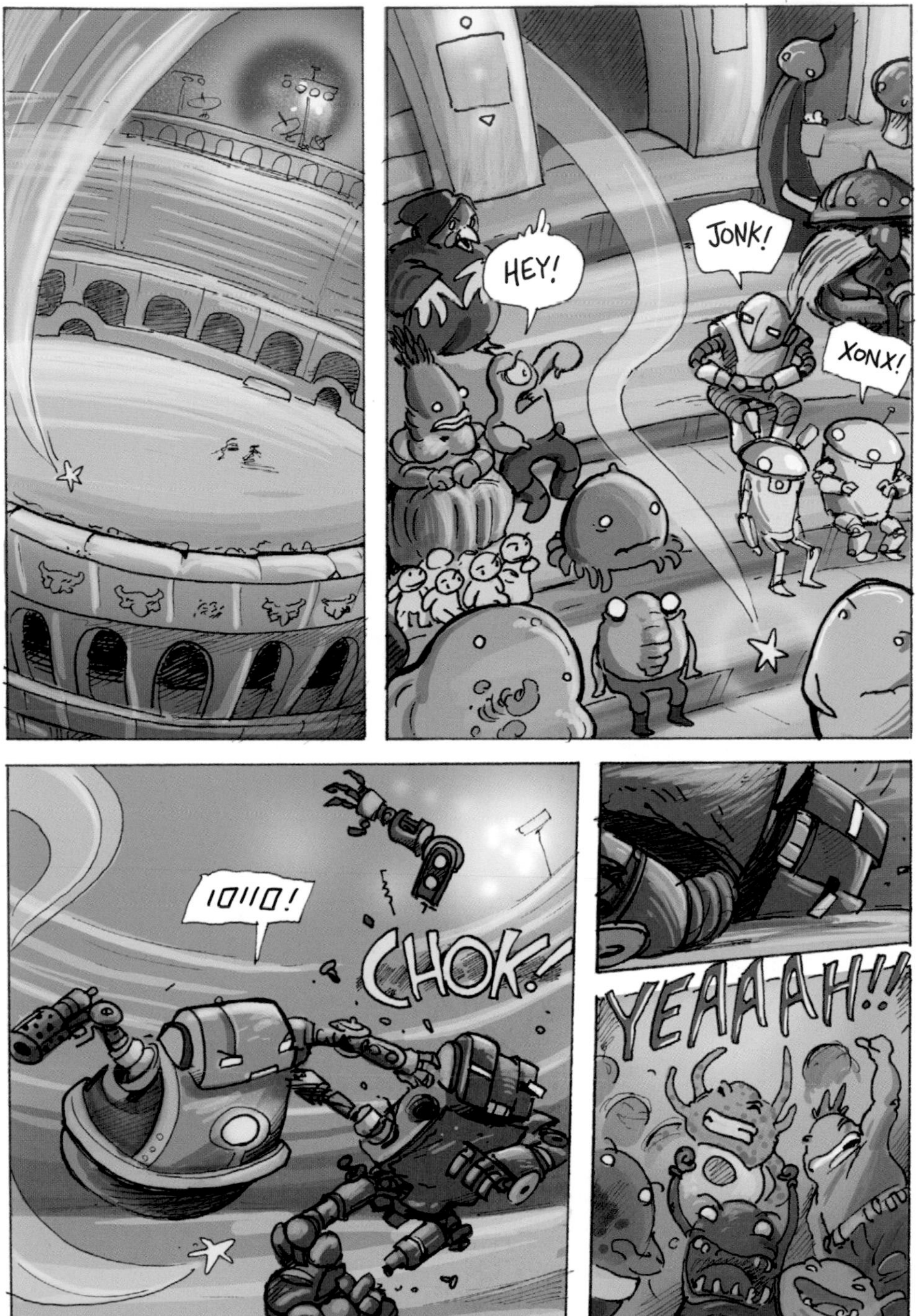
HEY!
JONK!
XONX!
10110!
CHOK!
YEAAAH!!!

SMEK

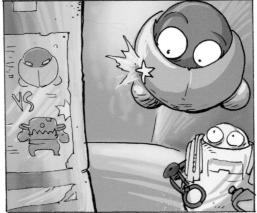

THE GIRL!

LADIES AND GENTLEMEN AND VARIATIONS THEREUPON! WELCOME TO OUR MAIN EVENT!

LET'S MAKE SOME NOISE FOR OUR REIGNING CHAMPION-

COMMANDANT CHOMPERS!

CHOMP CHOMP!

AND OUR (HEH HEH) CHALLENGER, A SCRAPPY OLD H·A·M·B·O· UNIT CALLED-

ONE!

EH?

57

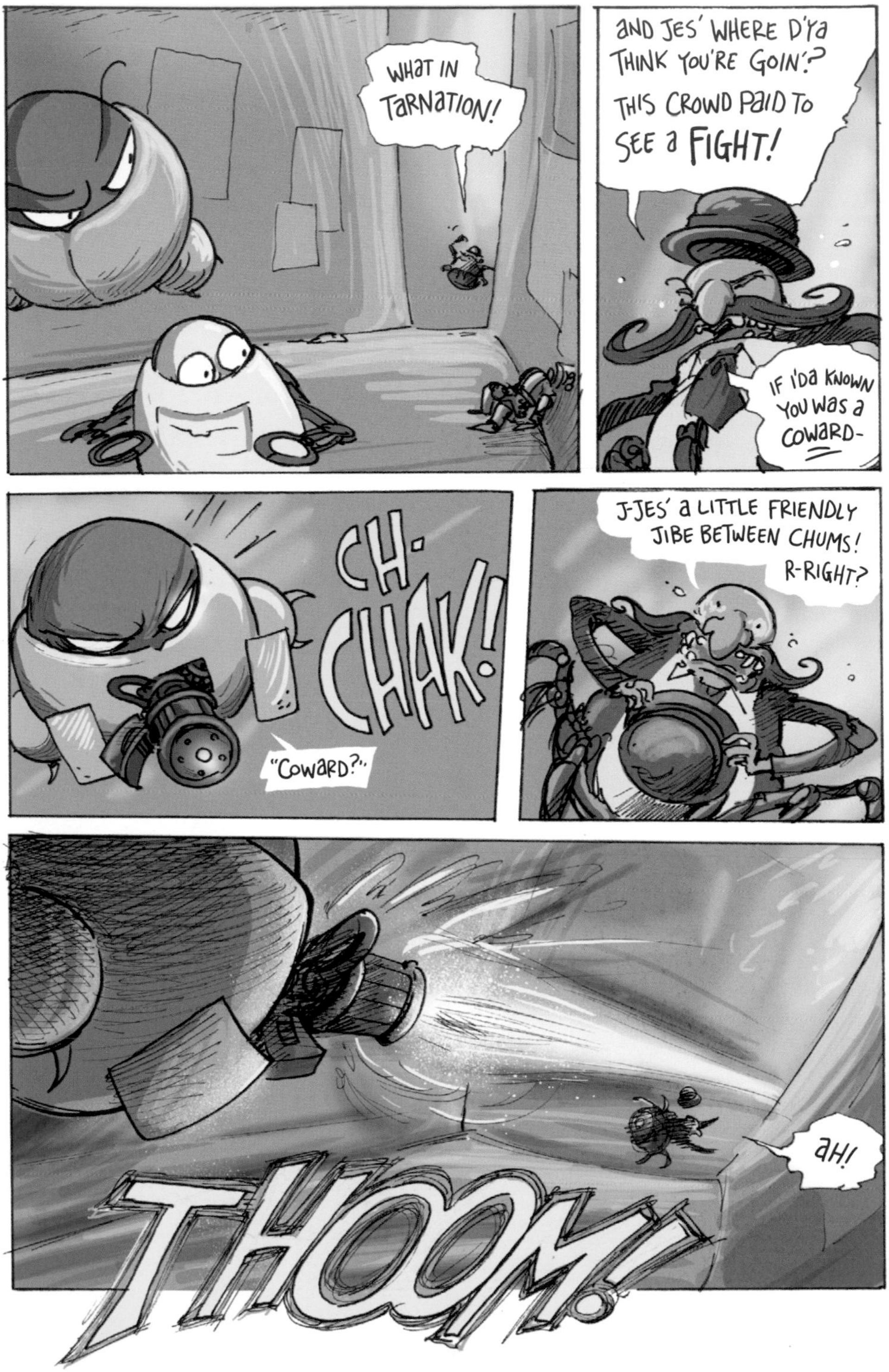

WHAT IN TARNATION!
AND JES' WHERE D'YA THINK YOU'RE GOIN'?
THIS CROWD PAID TO SEE A FIGHT!
IF I'DA KNOWN YOU WAS A COWARD-
CH-CHAK!
"COWARD?"
J-JES' A LITTLE FRIENDLY JIBE BETWEEN CHUMS!
R-RIGHT?
AH!
THOOM!

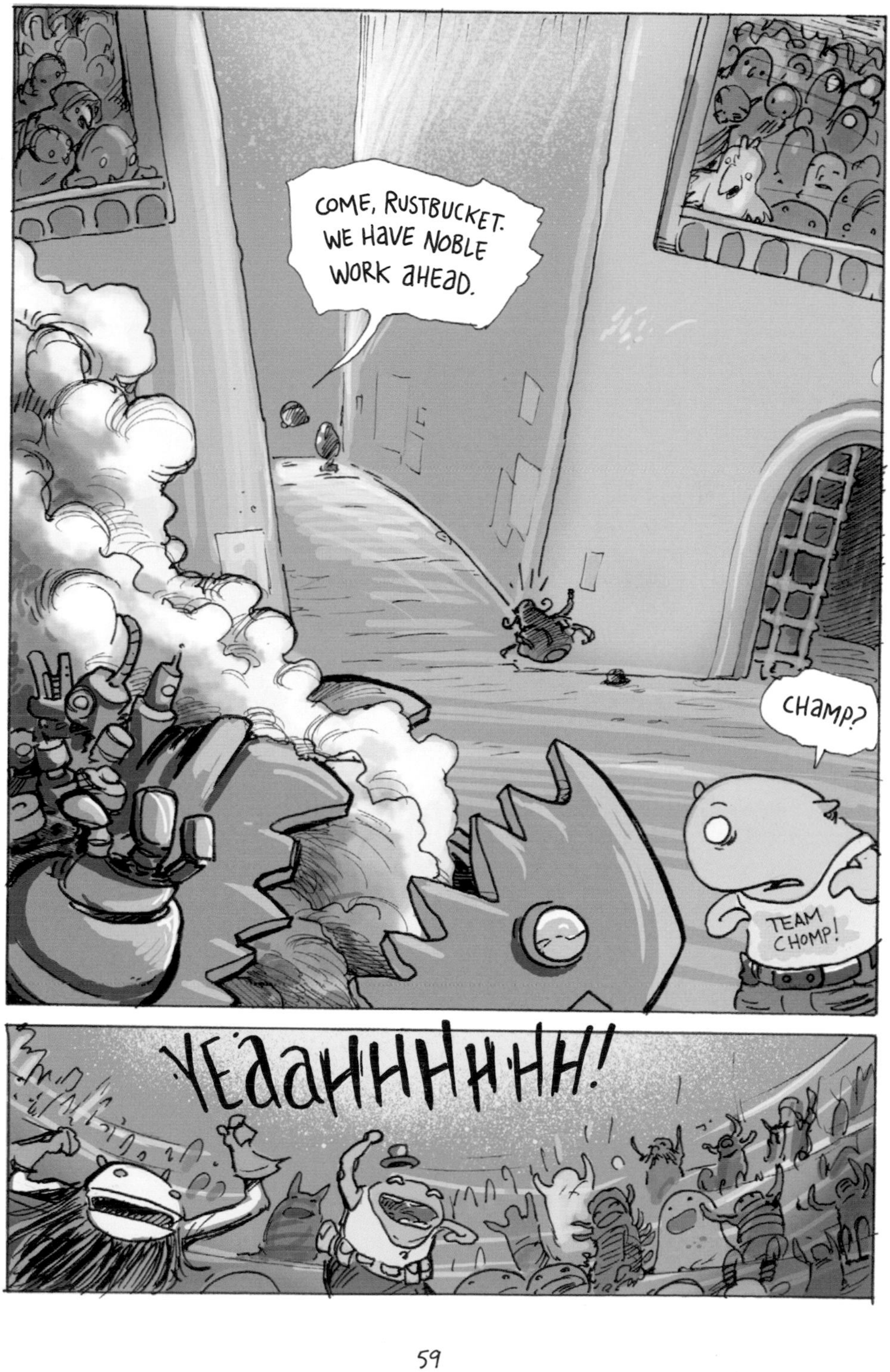
COME, RUSTBUCKET. WE HAVE NOBLE WORK AHEAD.
CHAMP?
TEAM CHOMP!
YEAAHHHHHHH!

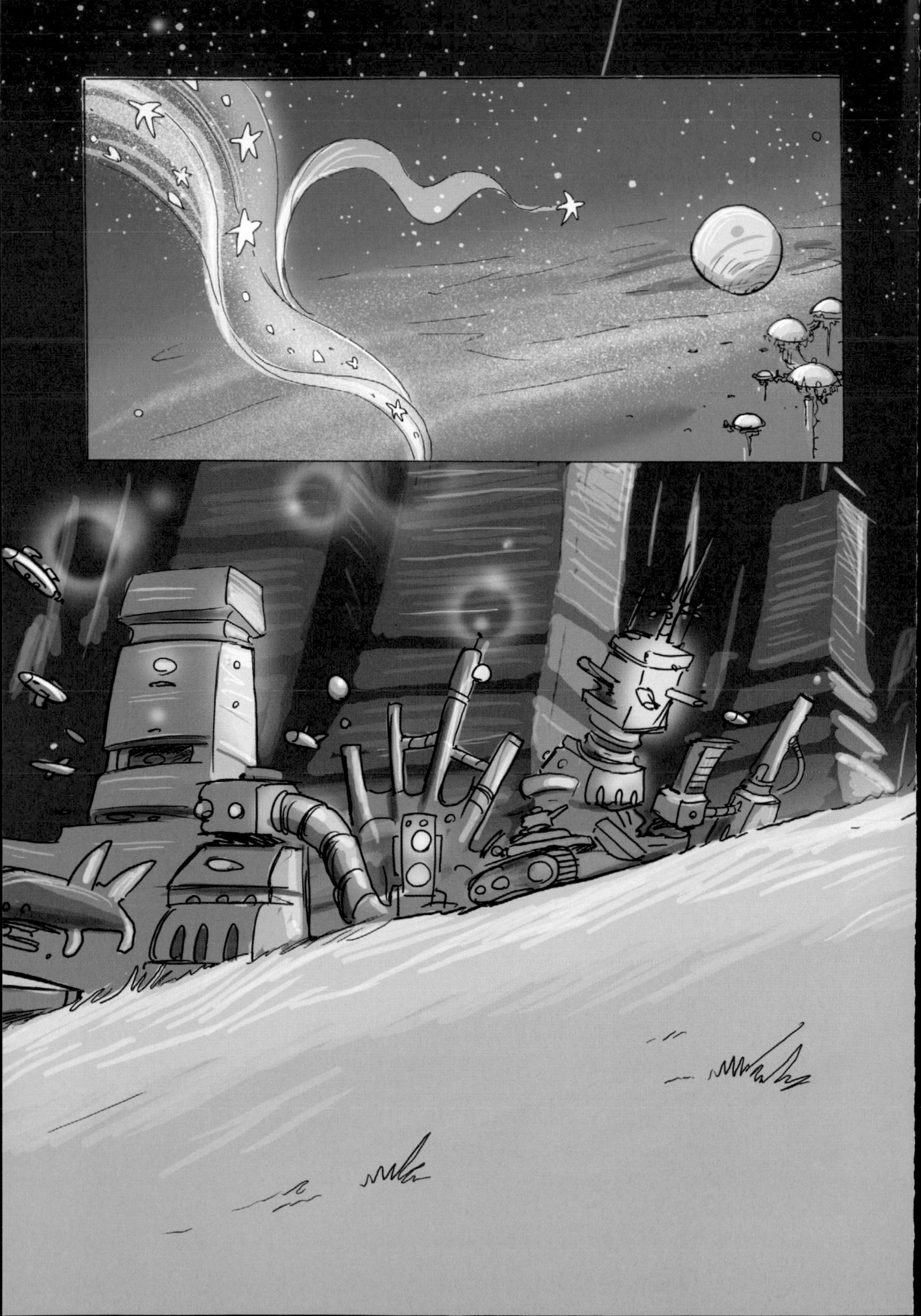

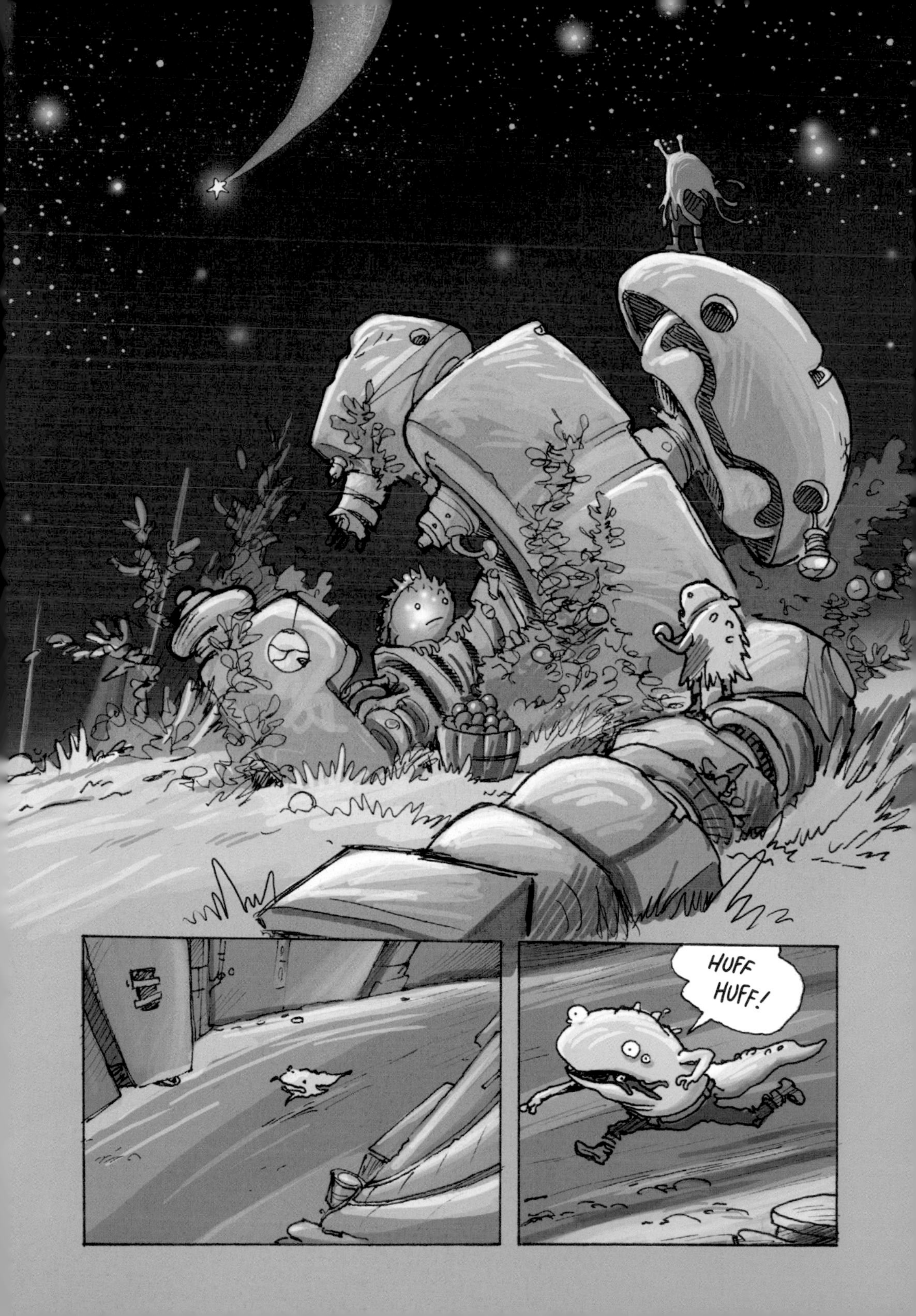
HUFF HUFF!

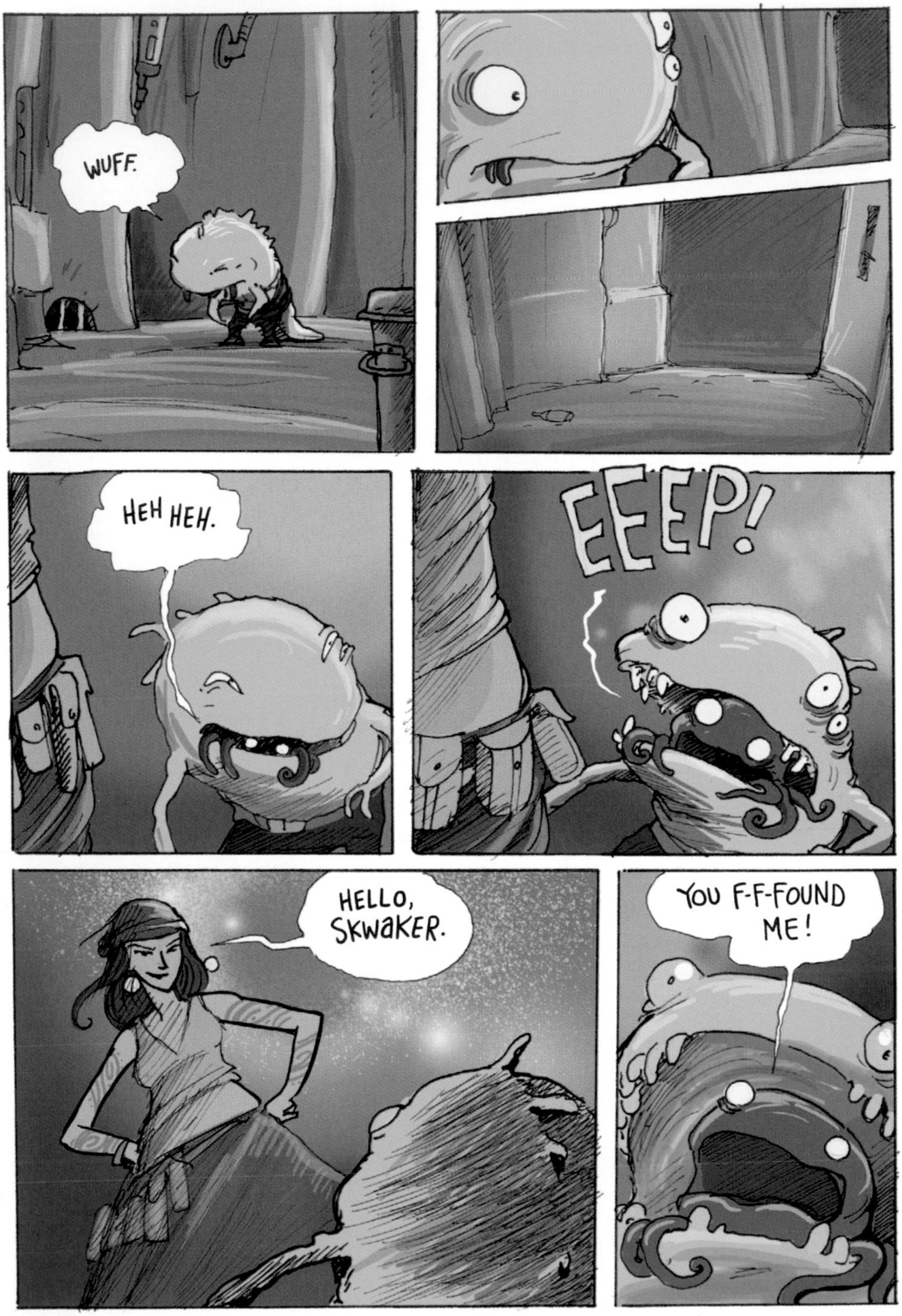
WUFF.
HEH HEH.
EEEP!
HELLO, SKWAKER.
YOU F-F-FOUND ME!

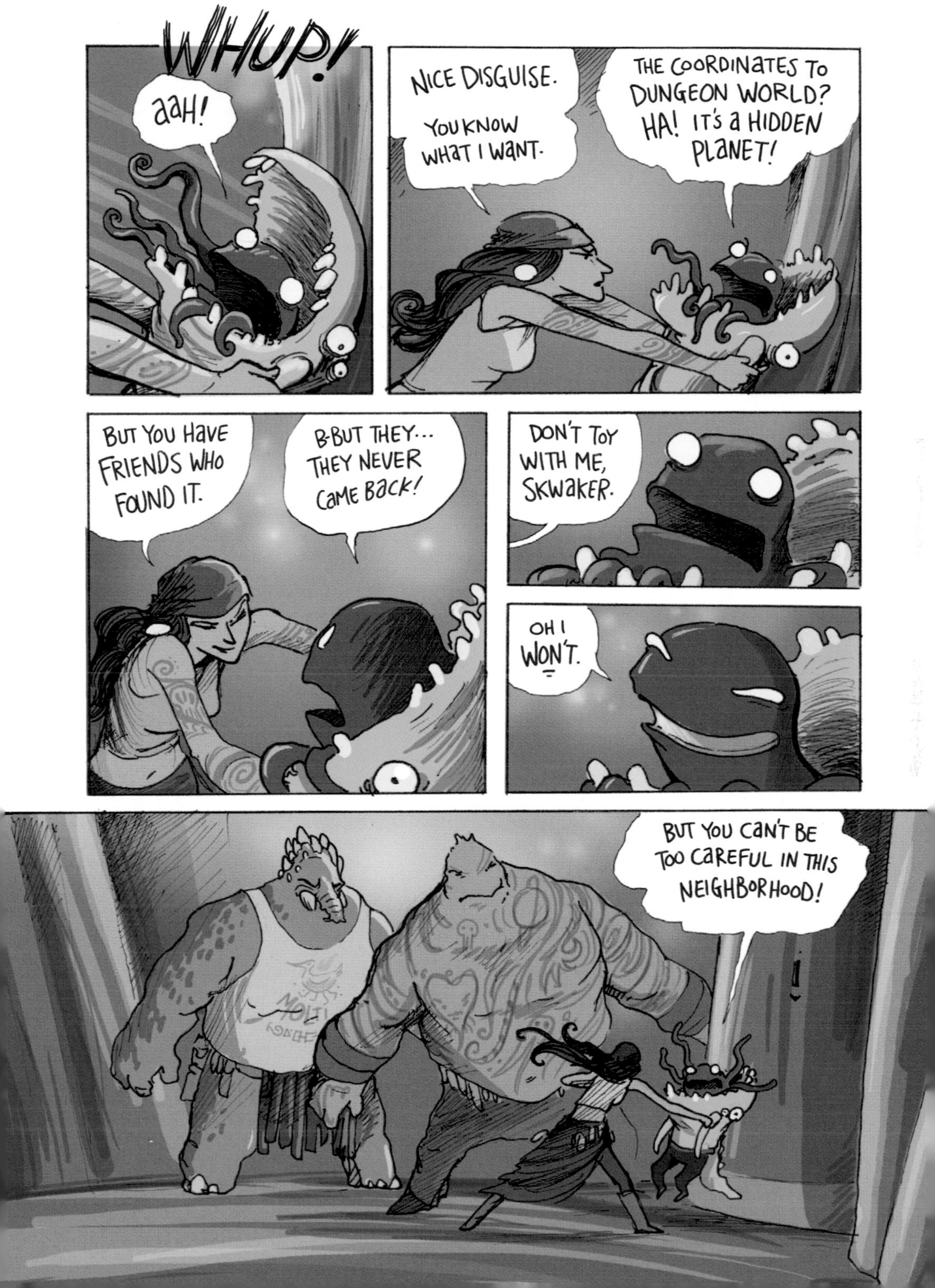
WHUP!
aaH!
NICE DISGUISE.
YOU KNOW WHAT I WANT.
THE COORDINATES TO DUNGEON WORLD? HA! IT'S a HIDDEN PLANET!
BUT YOU HaVE FRIENDS WHO FOUND IT.
B-BUT THEY... THEY NEVER CaME BaCK!
DON'T TOY WITH ME, SKWaKER.
OH I WON'T.
BUT YOU CaN'T BE TOO CaREFUL IN THIS NEIGHBORHOOD!

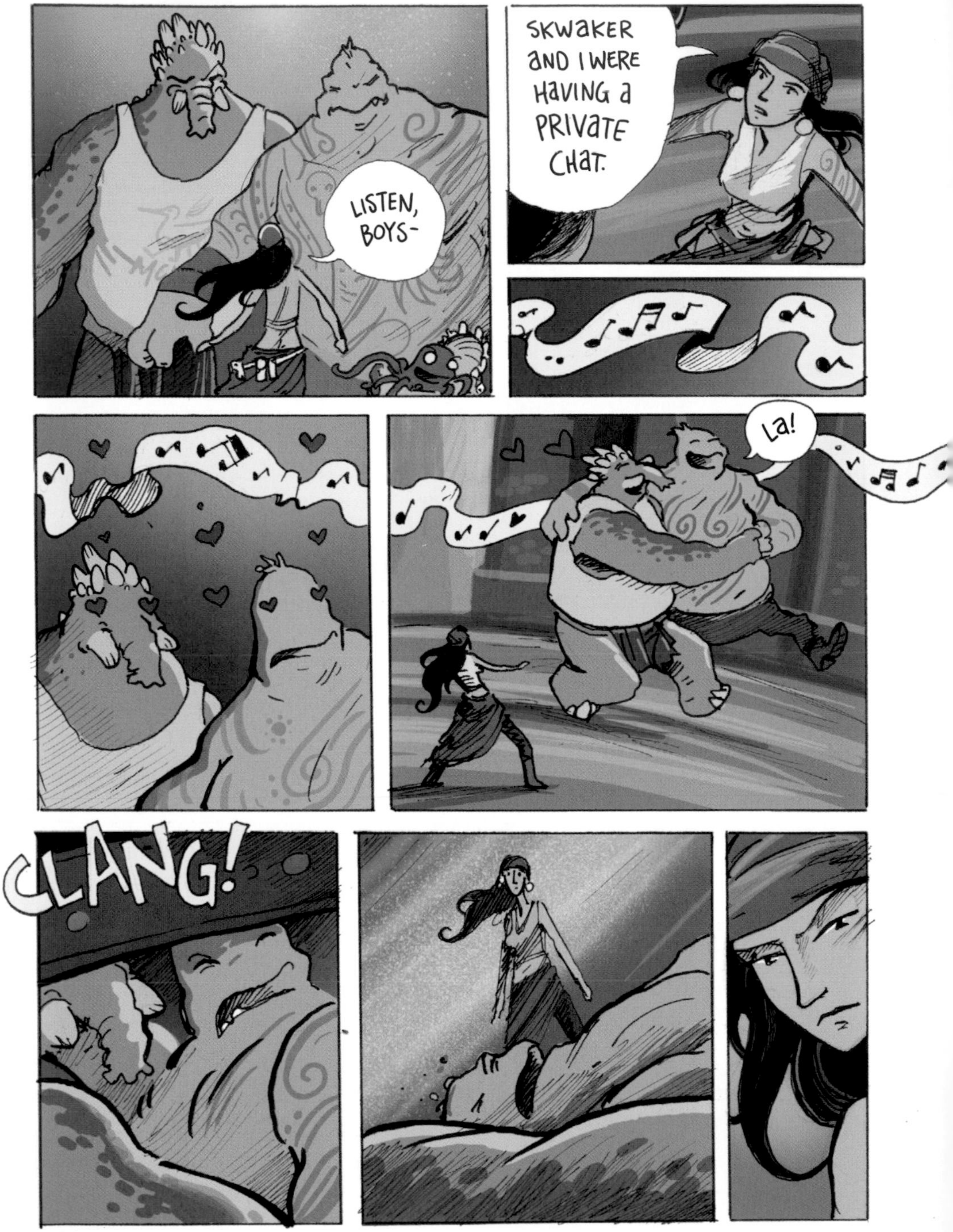
LISTEN, BOYS-
SKWAKER AND I WERE HAVING A PRIVATE CHAT.
LA!
CLANG!

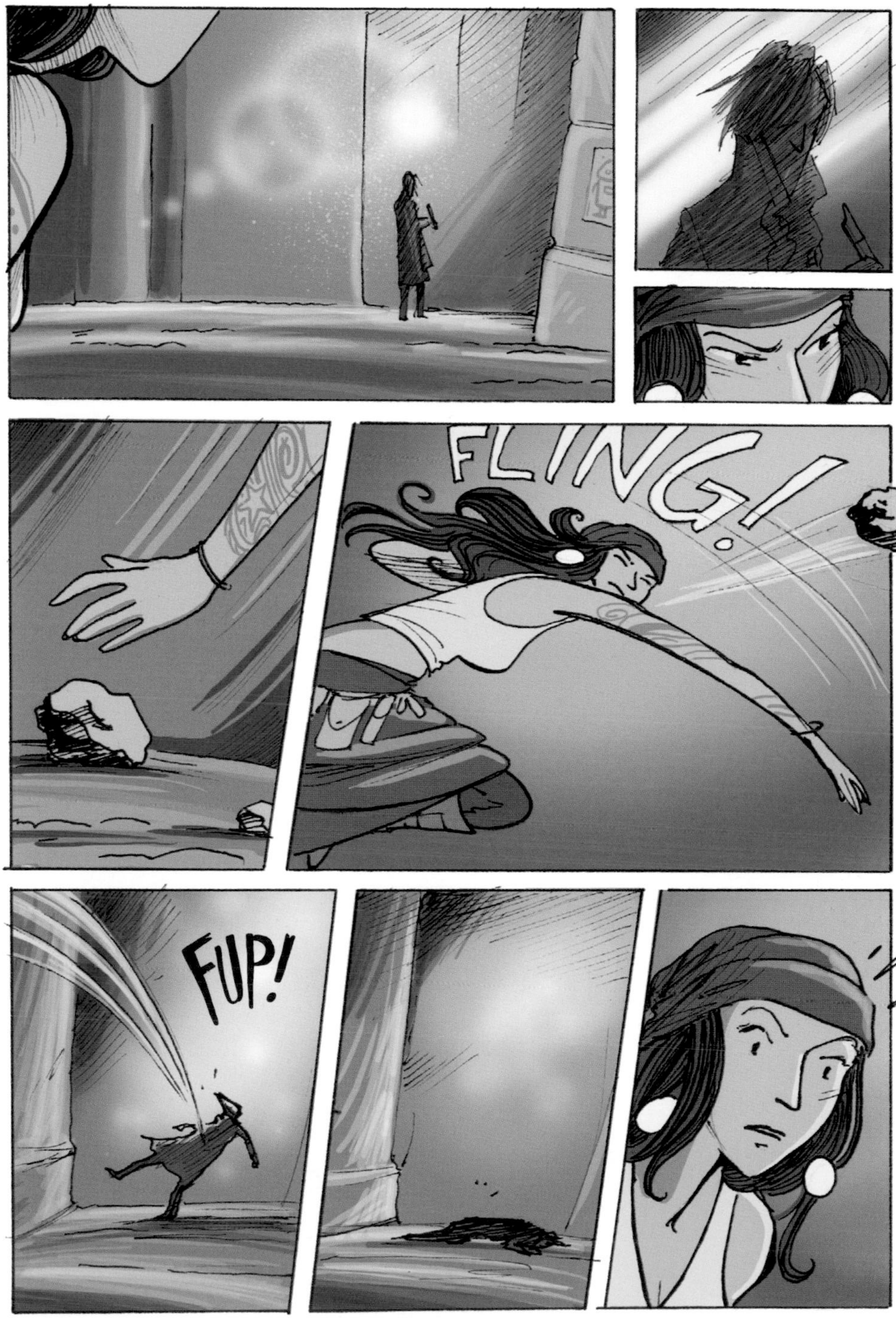
FLING!
FUP!

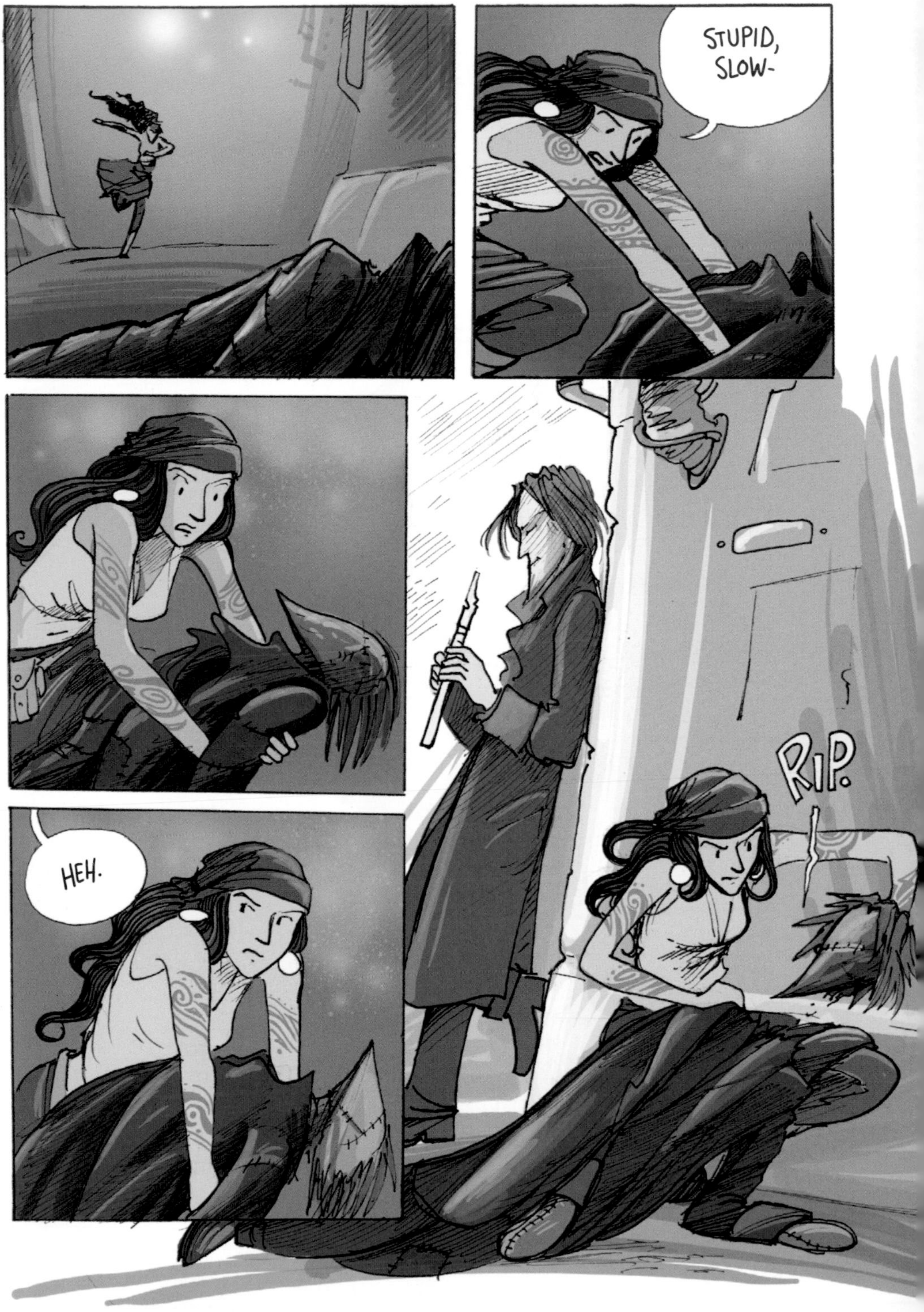
STUPID, SLOW-
HEH.
RIP.

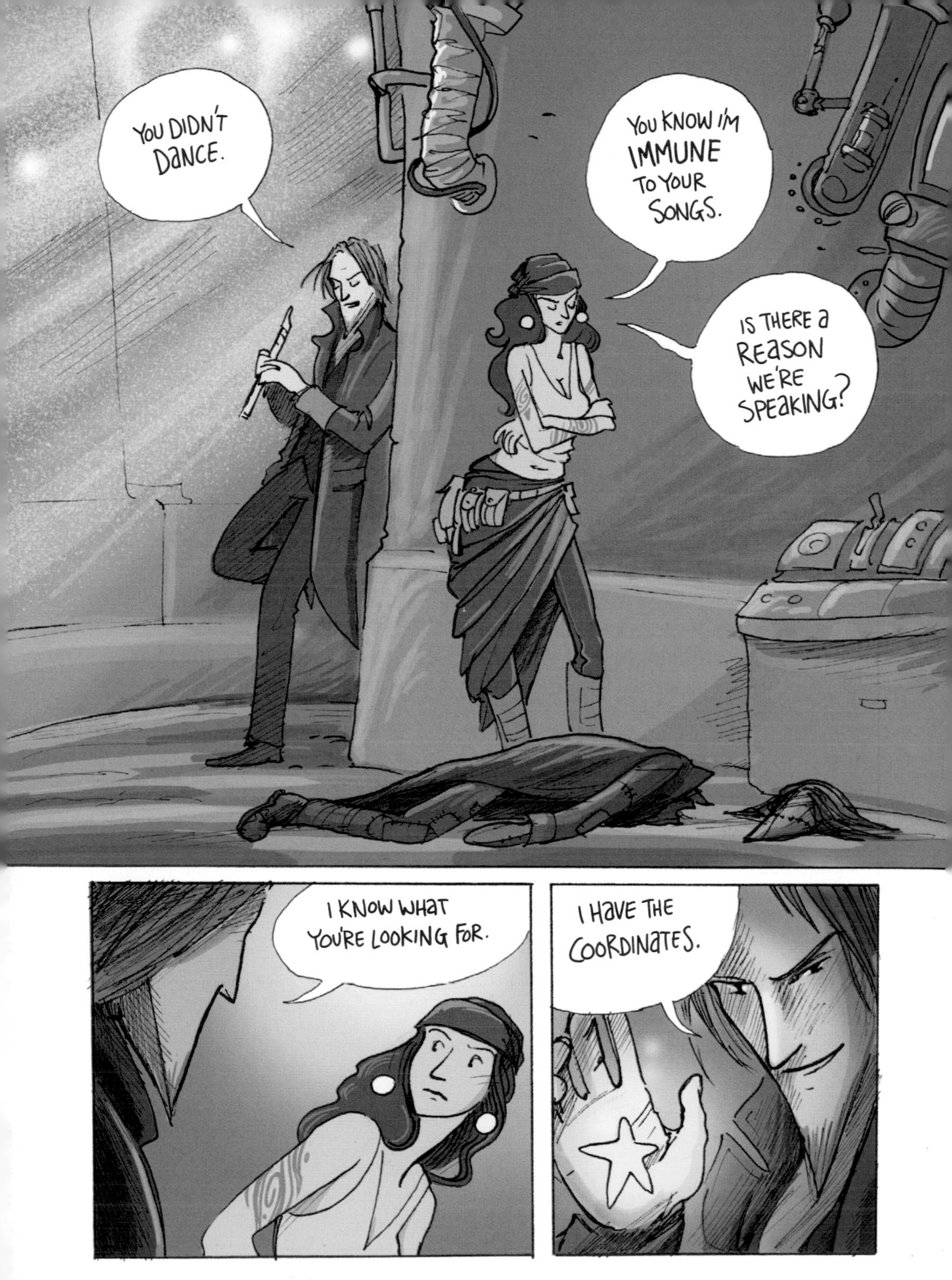

YOU DIDN'T DANCE.
YOU KNOW I'M IMMUNE TO YOUR SONGS.
IS THERE a REASON WE'RE SPEAKING?
I KNOW WHAT YOU'RE LOOKING FOR.
I HAVE THE COORDINATES.

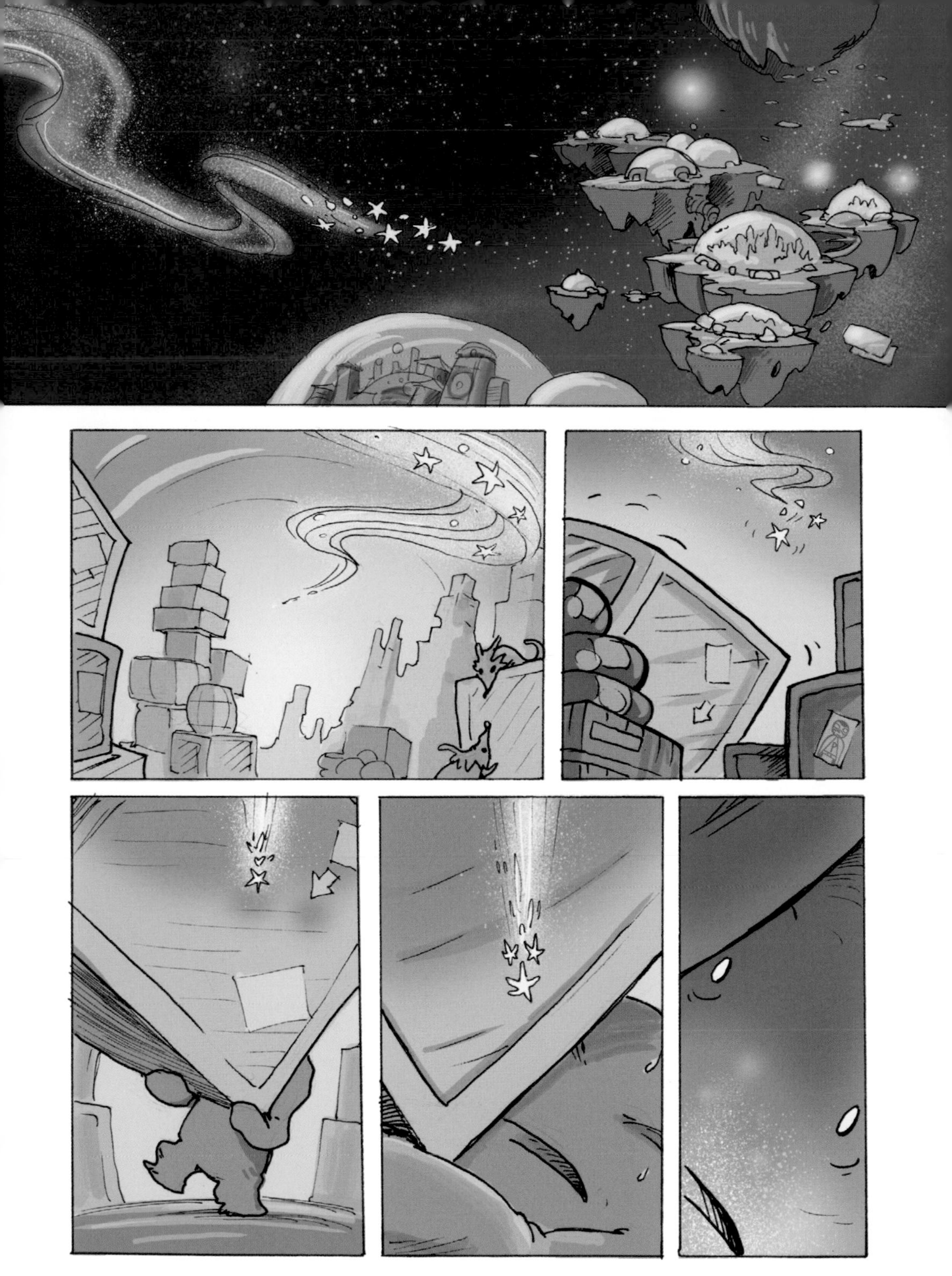

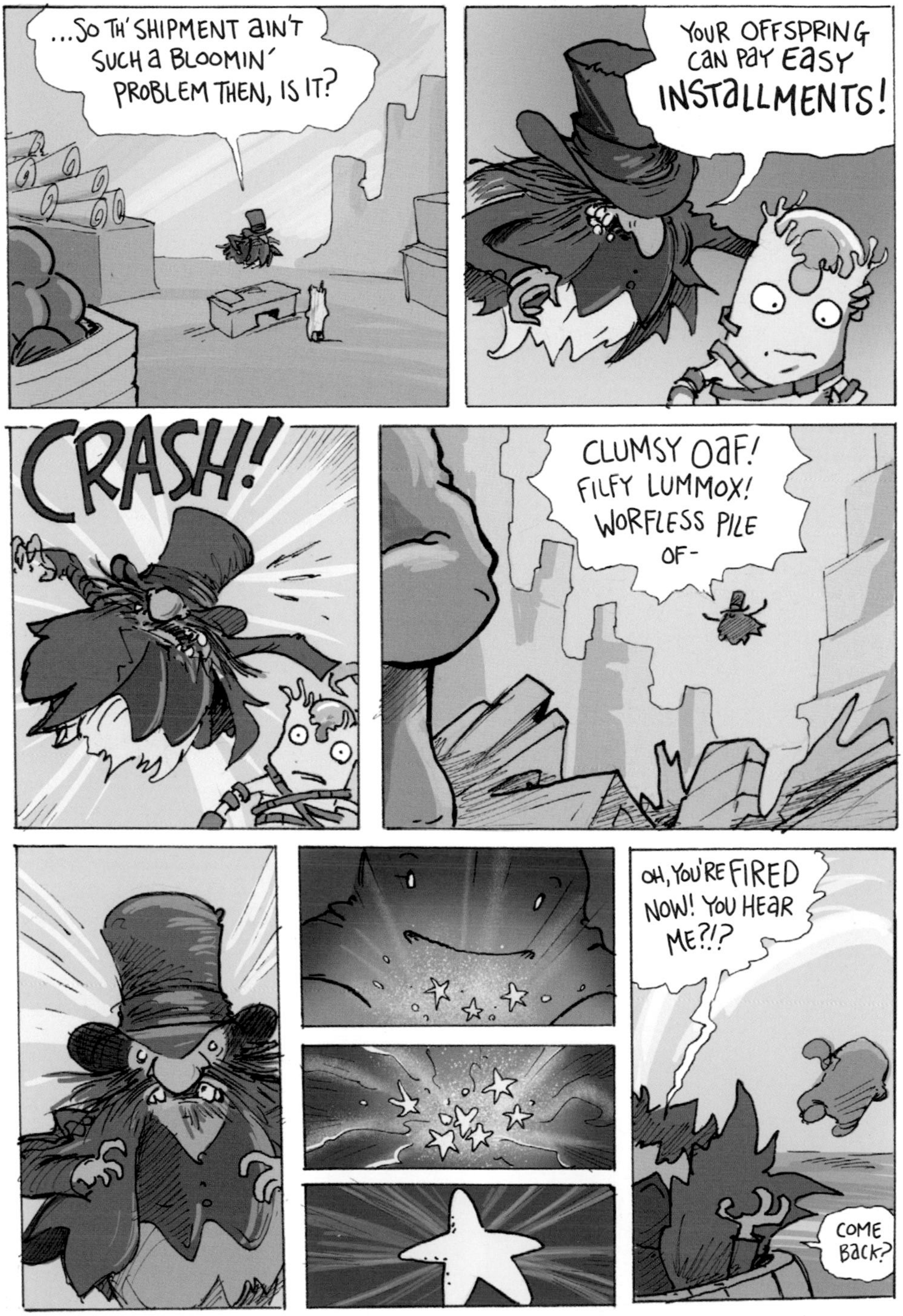
...SO TH' SHIPMENT AIN'T SUCH A BLOOMIN' PROBLEM THEN, IS IT?
YOUR OFFSPRING CAN PAY EASY INSTALLMENTS!
CRASH!
CLUMSY OAF! FILFY LUMMOX! WORFLESS PILE OF-
OH, YOU'RE FIRED NOW! YOU HEAR ME?!?
COME BACK?

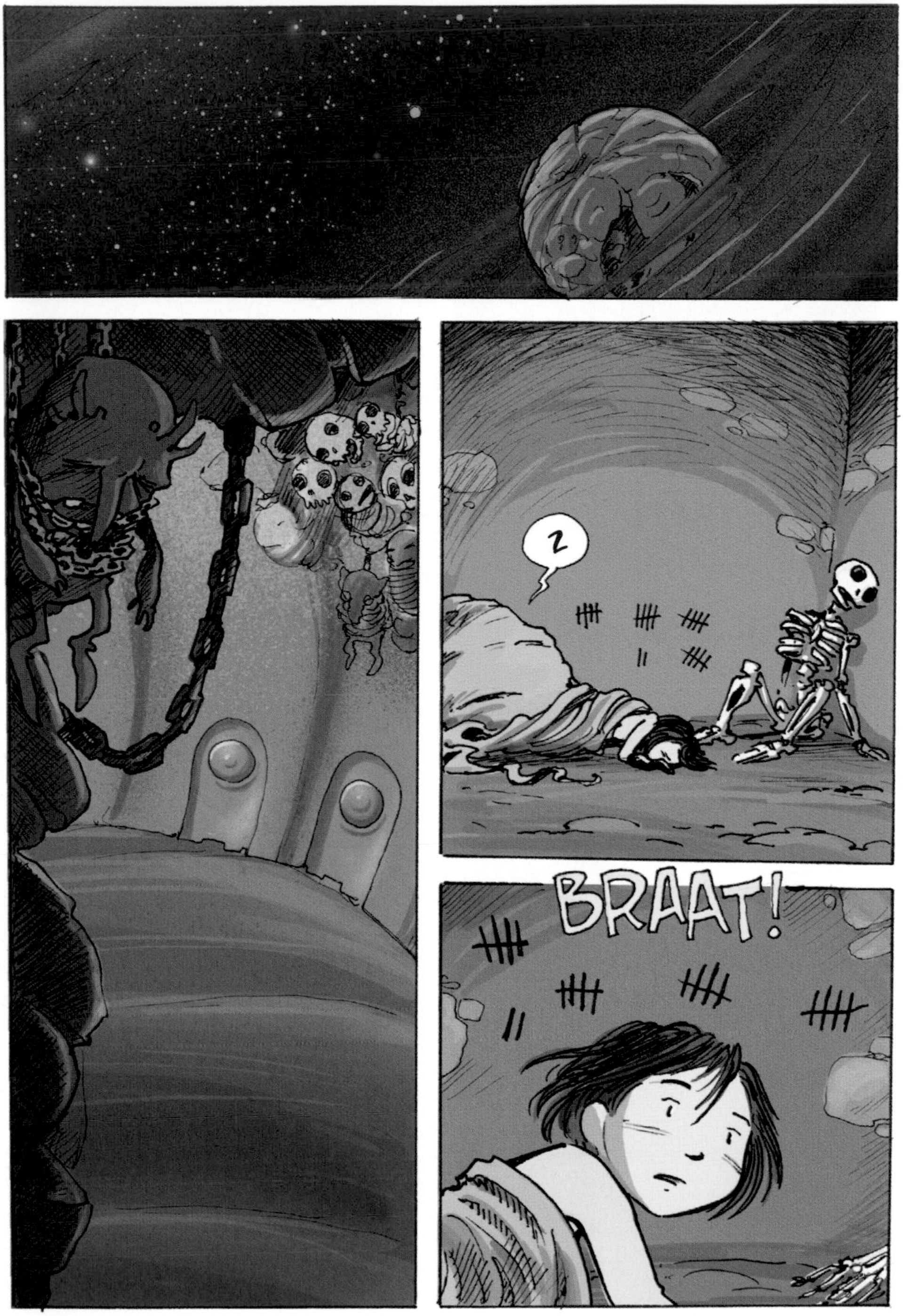
z
BRAAT!

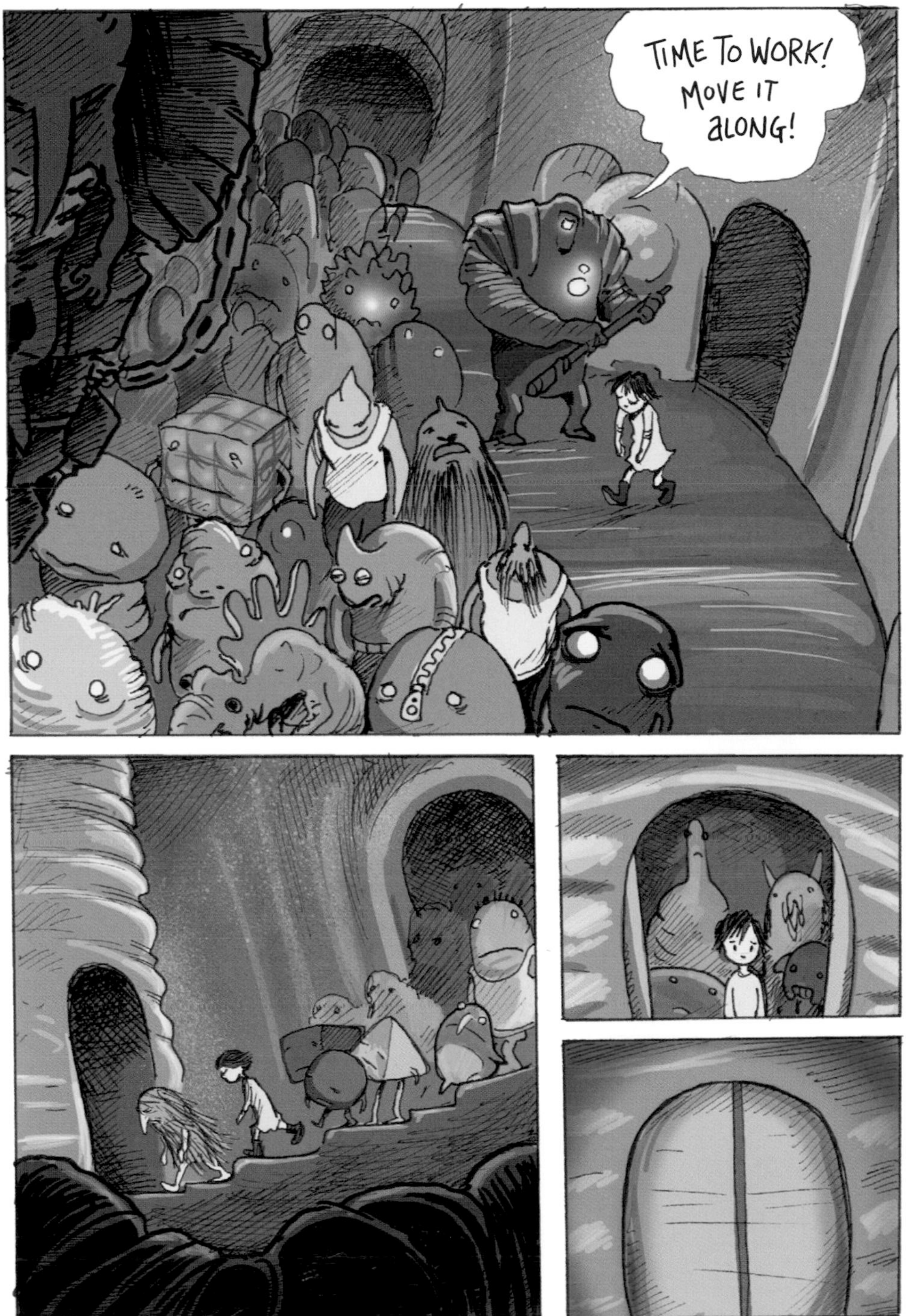
TIME TO WORK! MOVE IT ALONG!

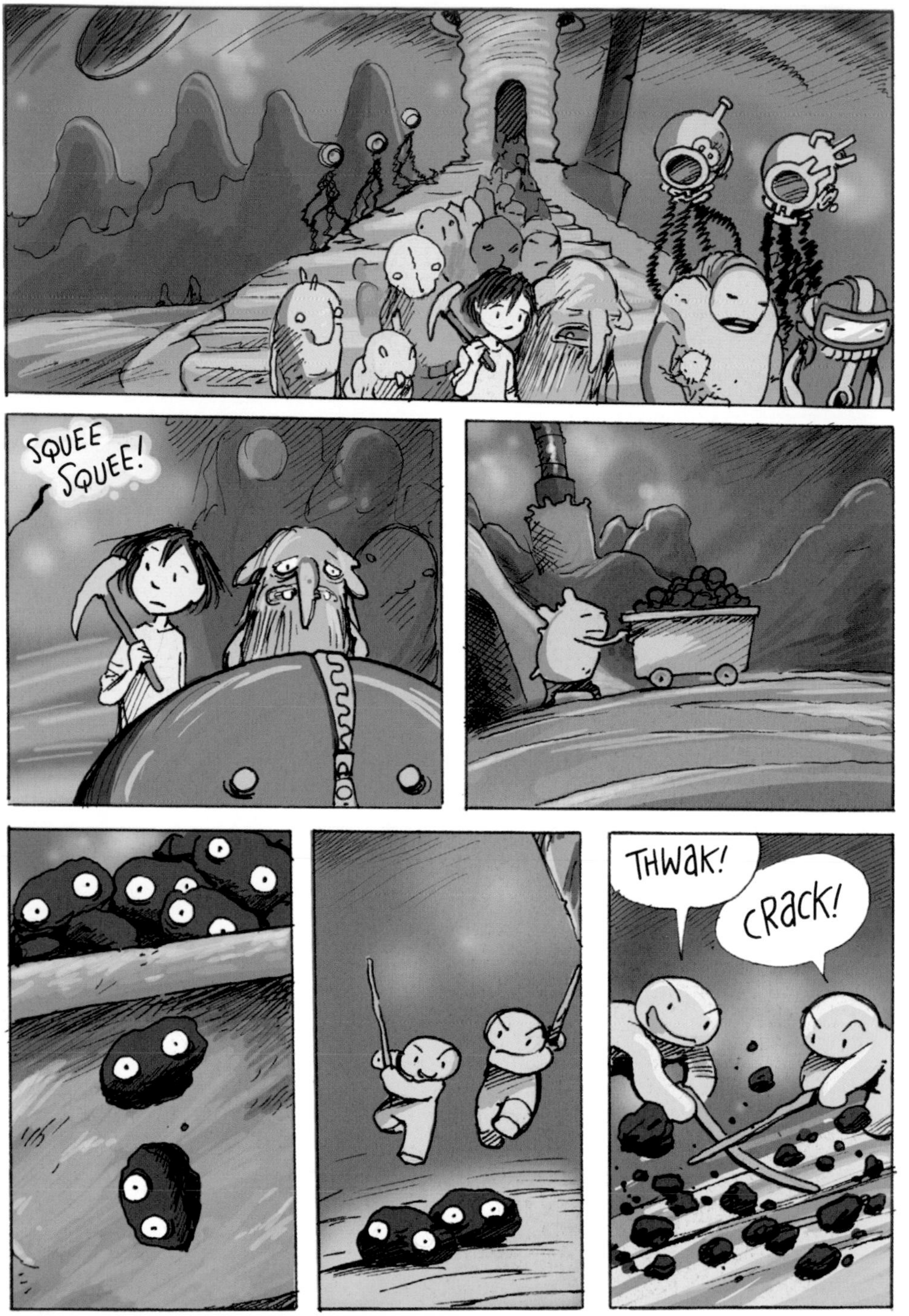
SQUEE SQUEE!
THWAK!
CRACK!

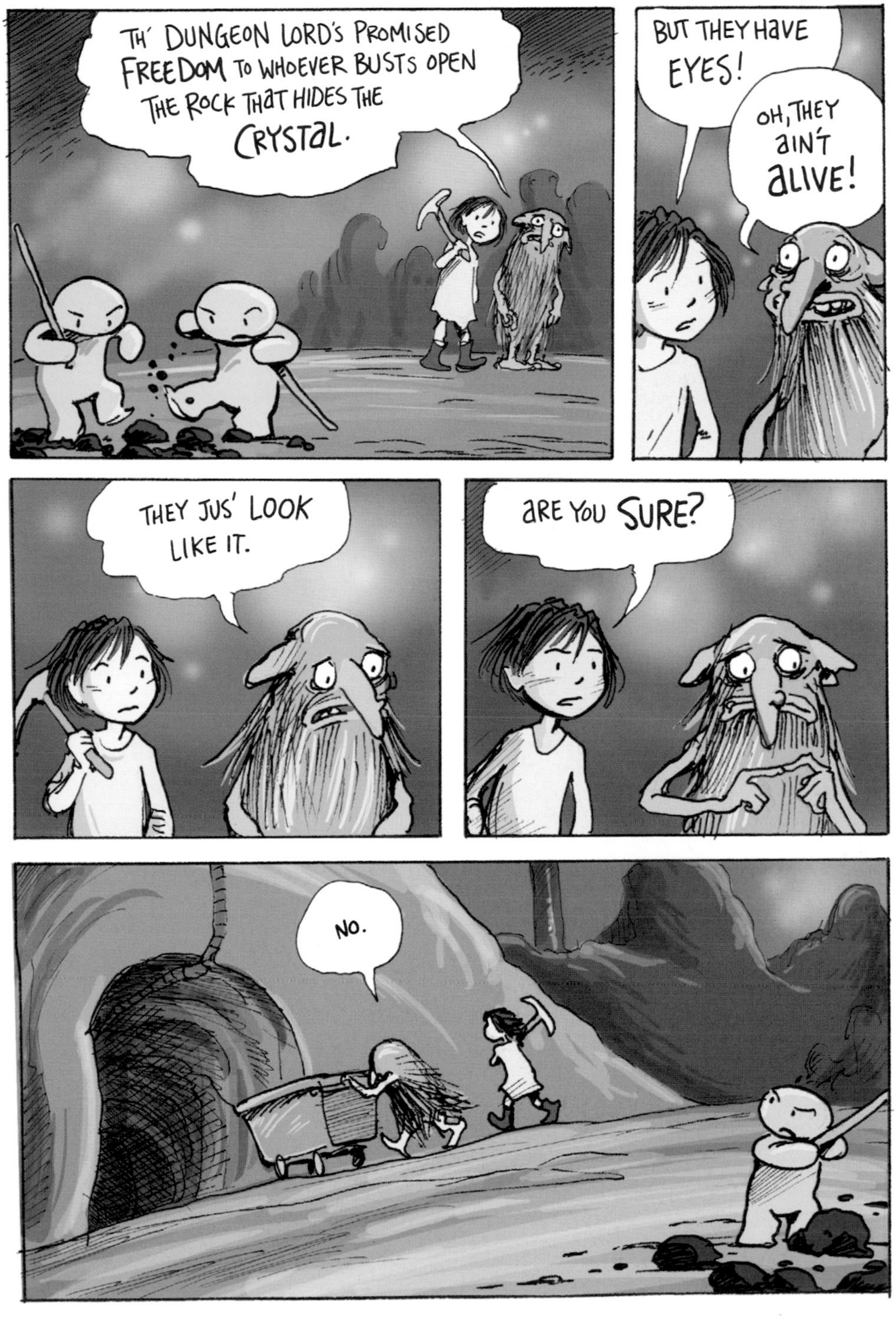
TH' DUNGEON LORD'S PROMISED FREEDOM TO WHOEVER BUSTS OPEN THE ROCK THAT HIDES THE CRYSTAL.
BUT THEY HAVE EYES!
OH, THEY AIN'T ALIVE!
THEY JUS' LOOK LIKE IT.
ARE YOU SURE?
NO.

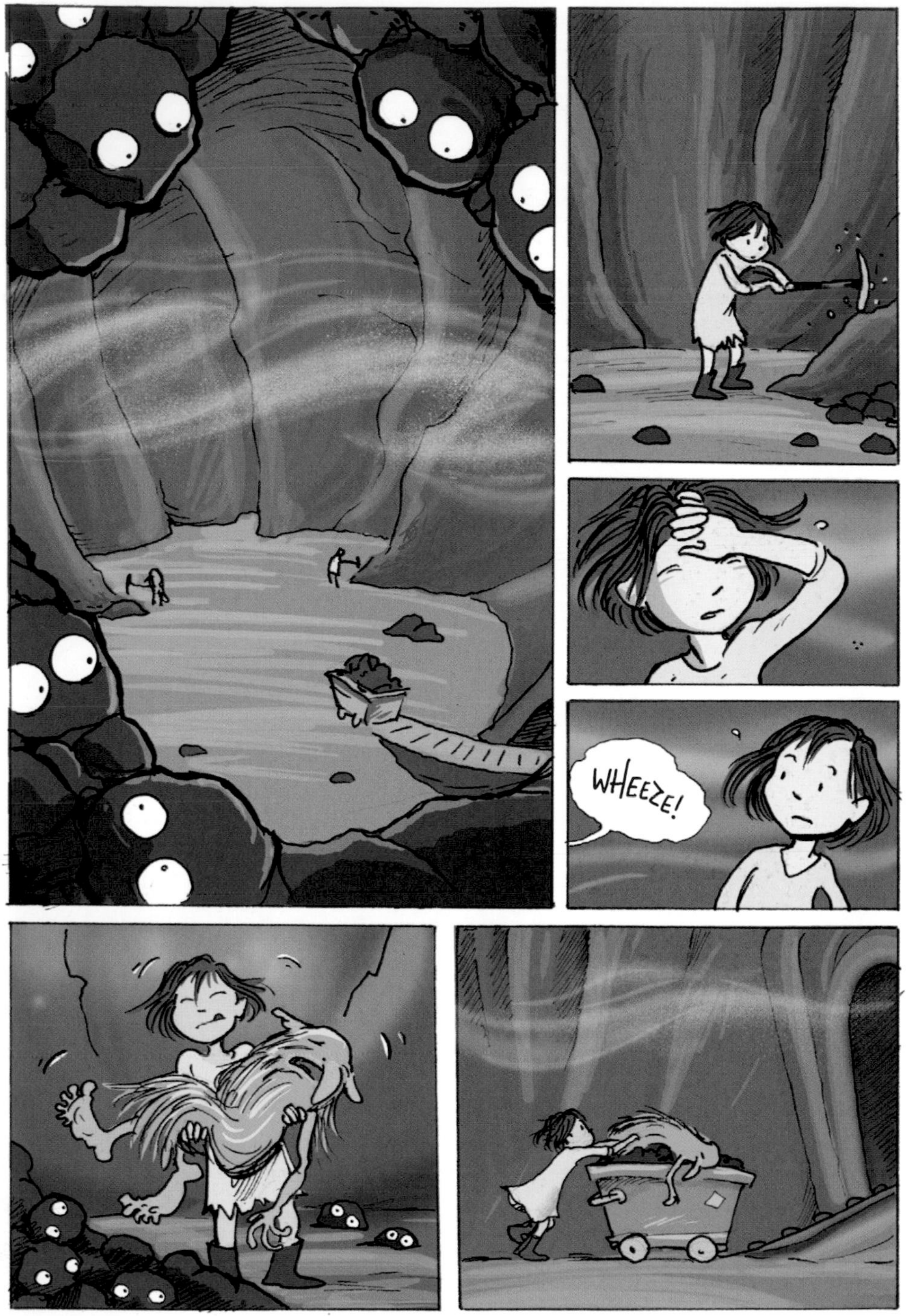
WHEEZE!

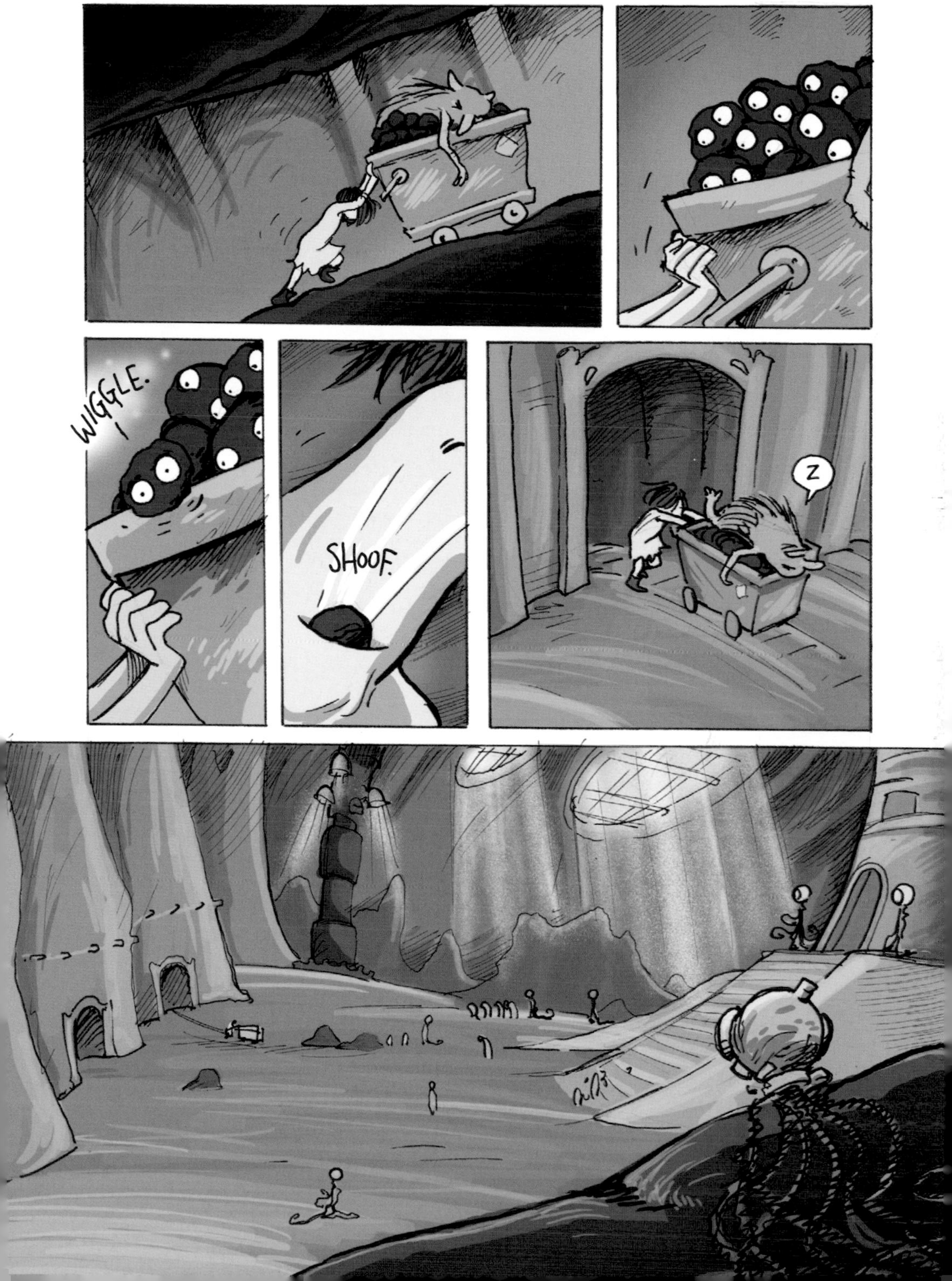
WIGGLE.
SHOOF.
Z

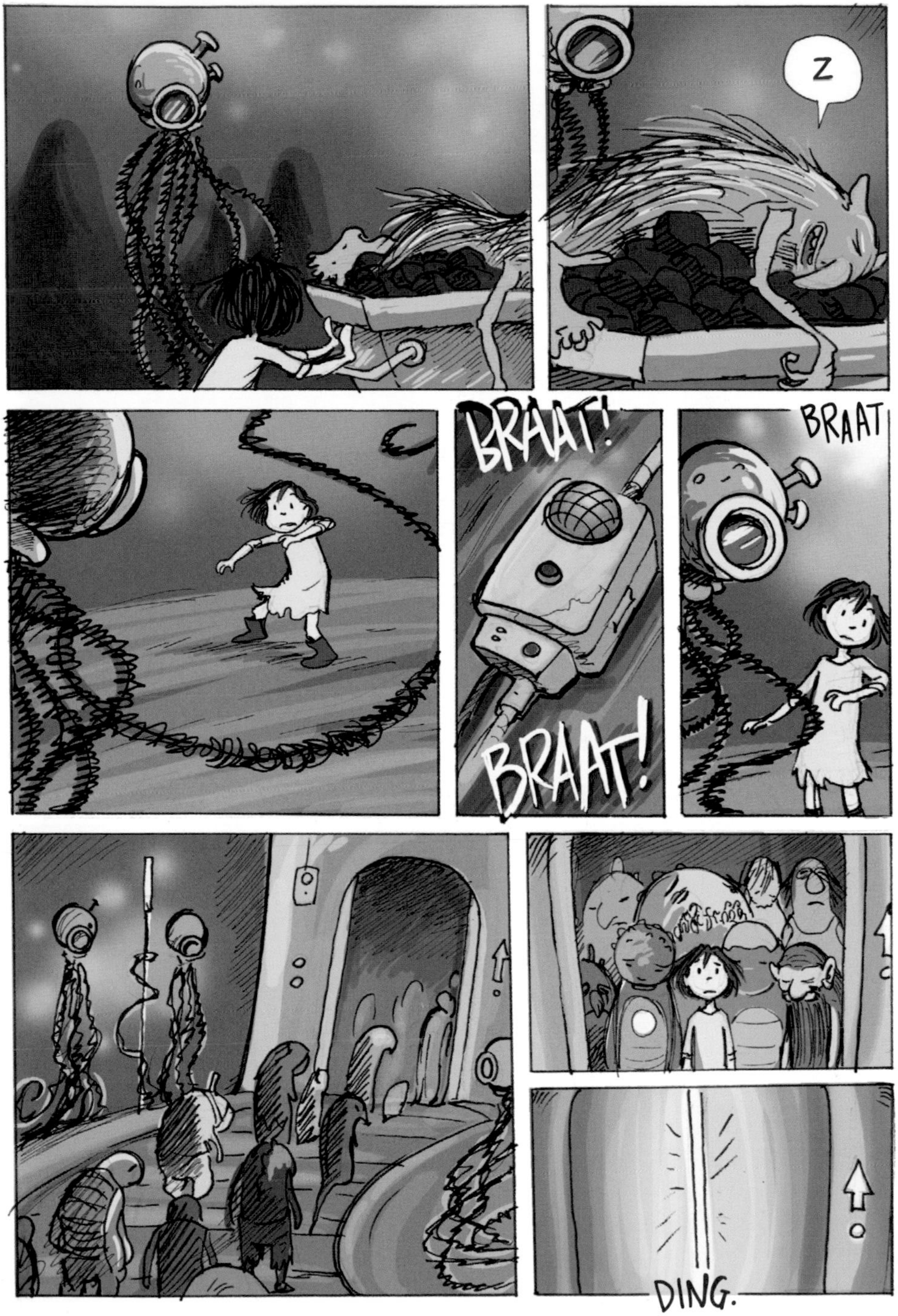
Z
BRAAT!
BRAAT!
BRAAT
DING.

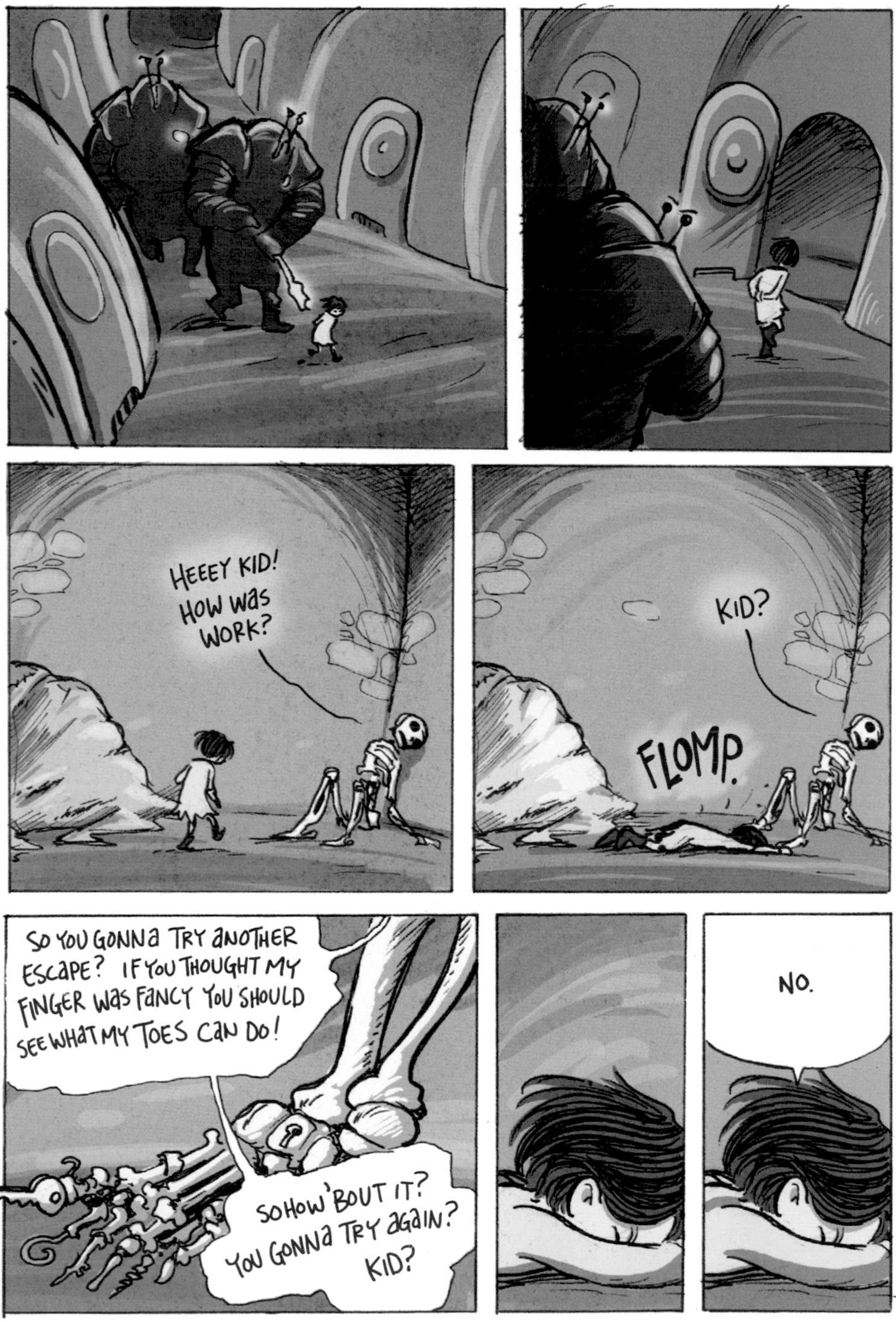
HEEEY KID! HOW WAS WORK?
KID?
FLOMP.
SO YOU GONNA TRY ANOTHER ESCAPE? IF YOU THOUGHT MY FINGER WAS FANCY YOU SHOULD SEE WHAT MY TOES CAN DO!
SO HOW 'BOUT IT? YOU GONNA TRY AGAIN? KID?
NO.

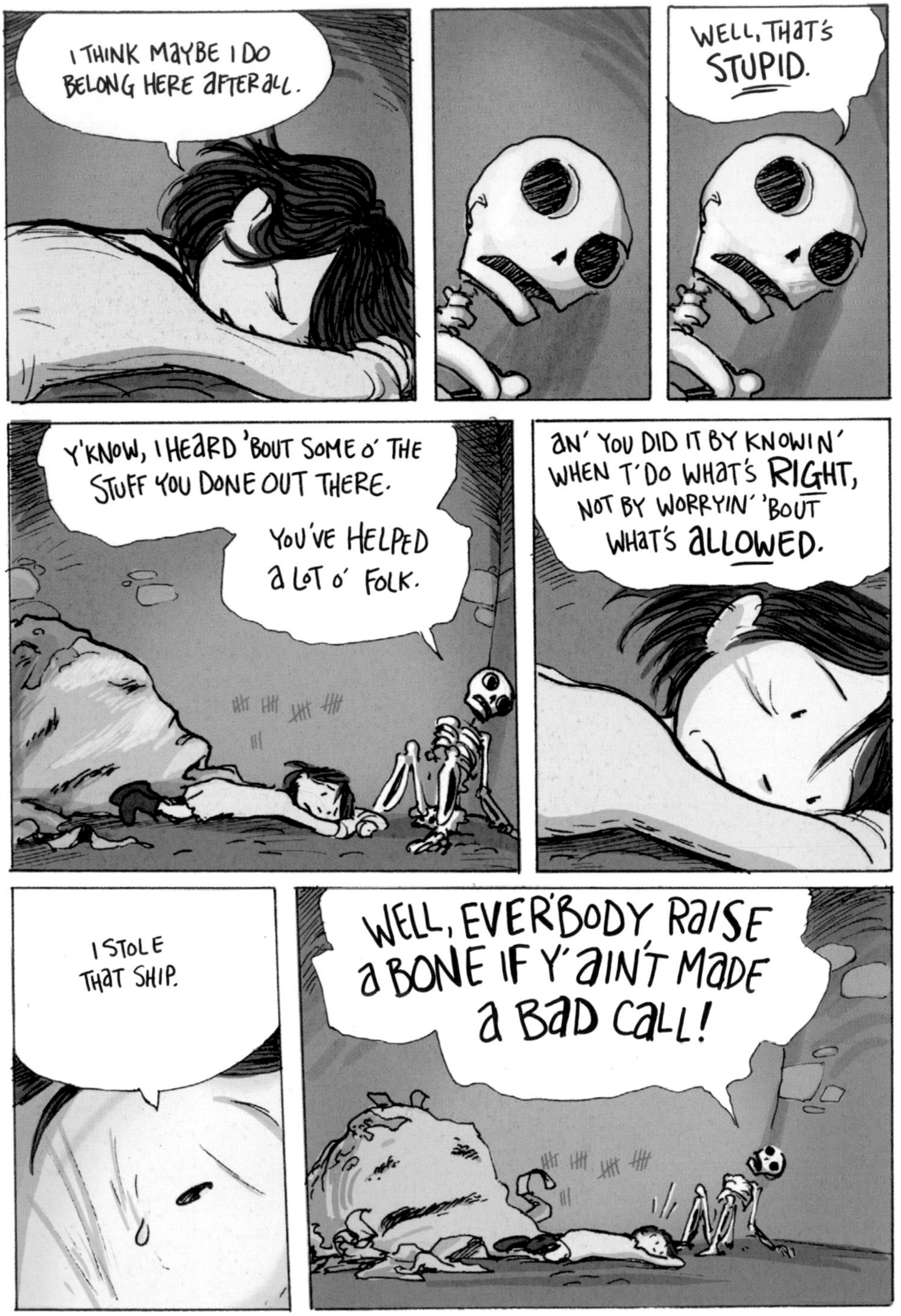
I THINK MAYBE I DO BELONG HERE AFTER ALL.
WELL, THAT'S STUPID.
Y'KNOW, I HEARD 'BOUT SOME O' THE STUFF YOU DONE OUT THERE.
YOU'VE HELPED A LOT O' FOLK.
AN' YOU DID IT BY KNOWIN' WHEN T'DO WHAT'S RIGHT, NOT BY WORRYIN' 'BOUT WHAT'S ALLOWED.
I STOLE THAT SHIP.
WELL, EVER'BODY RAISE A BONE IF Y'AIN'T MADE A BAD CALL!

ONLY WAY NOT T' MAKE MISTAKES IS T' STOP **LIVIN'**

LOOK AT ME AN' **RAGGY** - WE'RE **PATHETIC!**

I JUS' DON' GET OUT MUCH.

EVER'BODY KNOWS TH' DUNGEON LORD JUS' MAKES TH' LAWS AS HE GOES TO KEEP US WORKIN' THAT **MINE** O' HIS.

RATTLE.

HE TRUMP'D UP YOUR CHARGES!

LISTEN, KID, YOU GET ANOTHER CHANCE TO ESCAPE YOU GOTTA PROMISE ME YOU'LL TAKE IT!

WE NEED YOU OUT THERE.

RATTLE

YOU GIVE US HOPE, YOU -

CON **SHARN** IT RAGGY, IF Y' DON'T STOP **SHAKIN'** ME I SWEAR I'LL -

Z

OH.

Z...

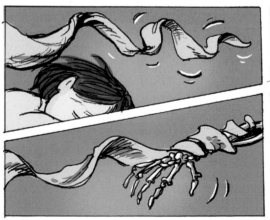

79

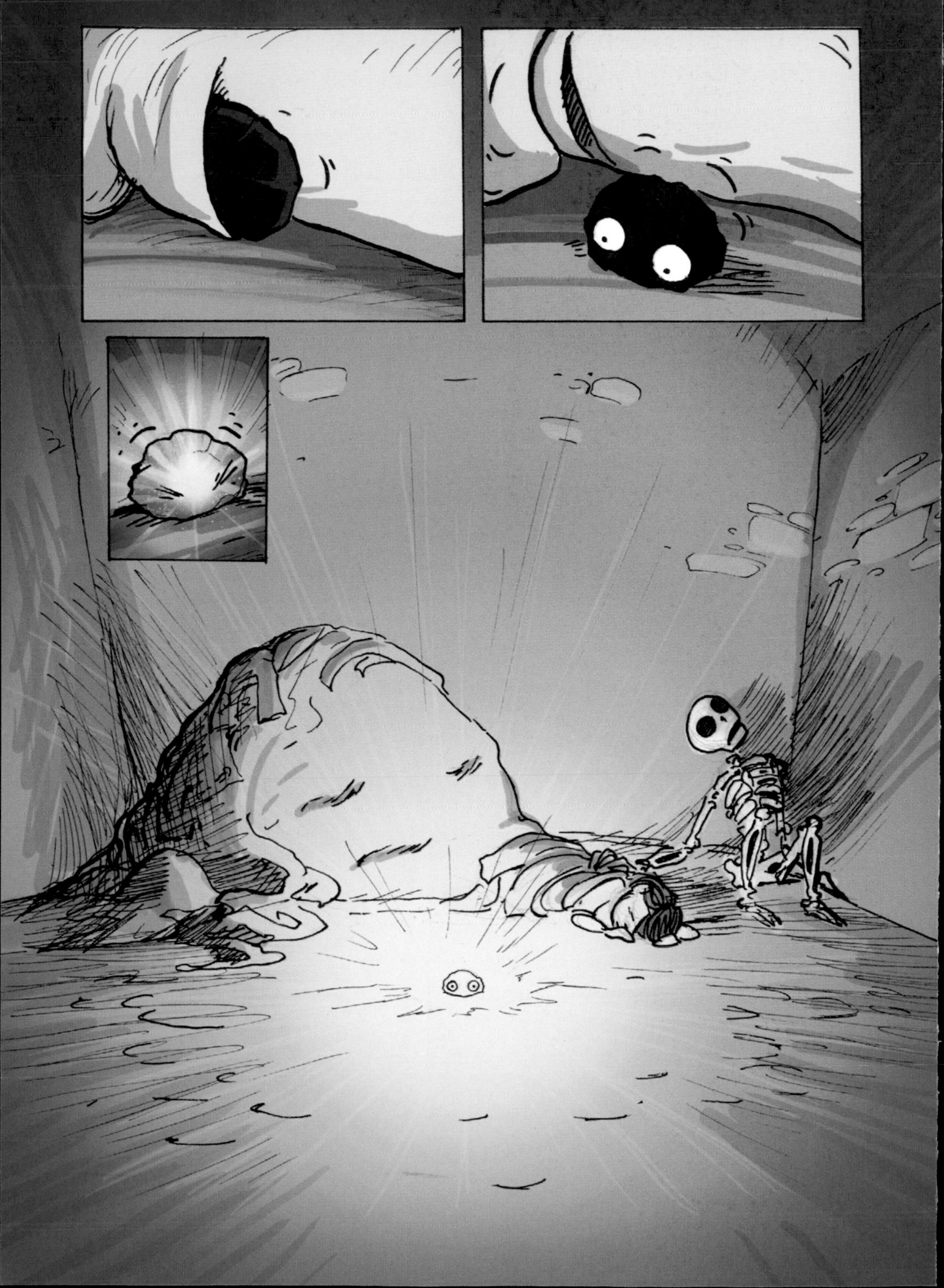

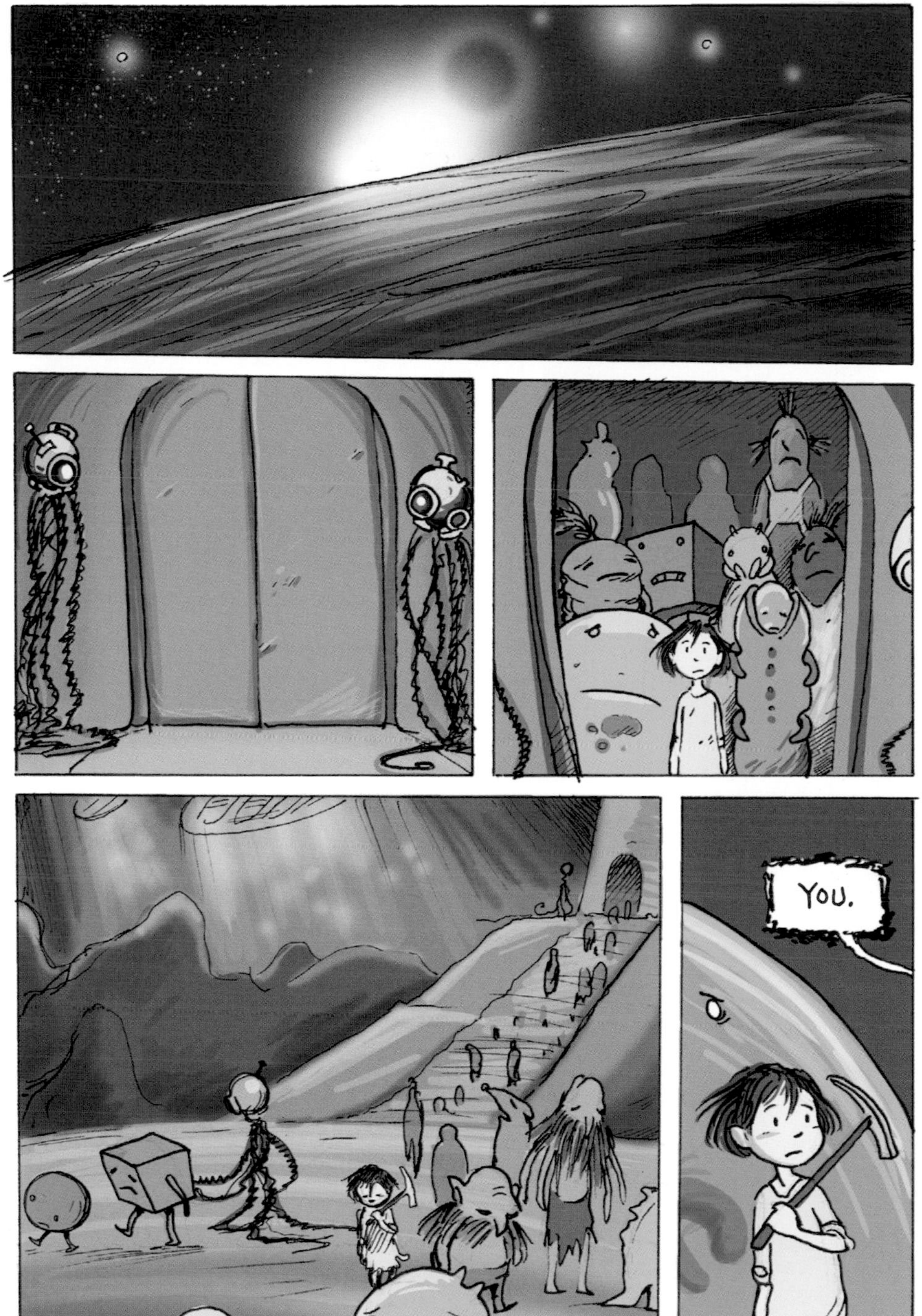
YOU.

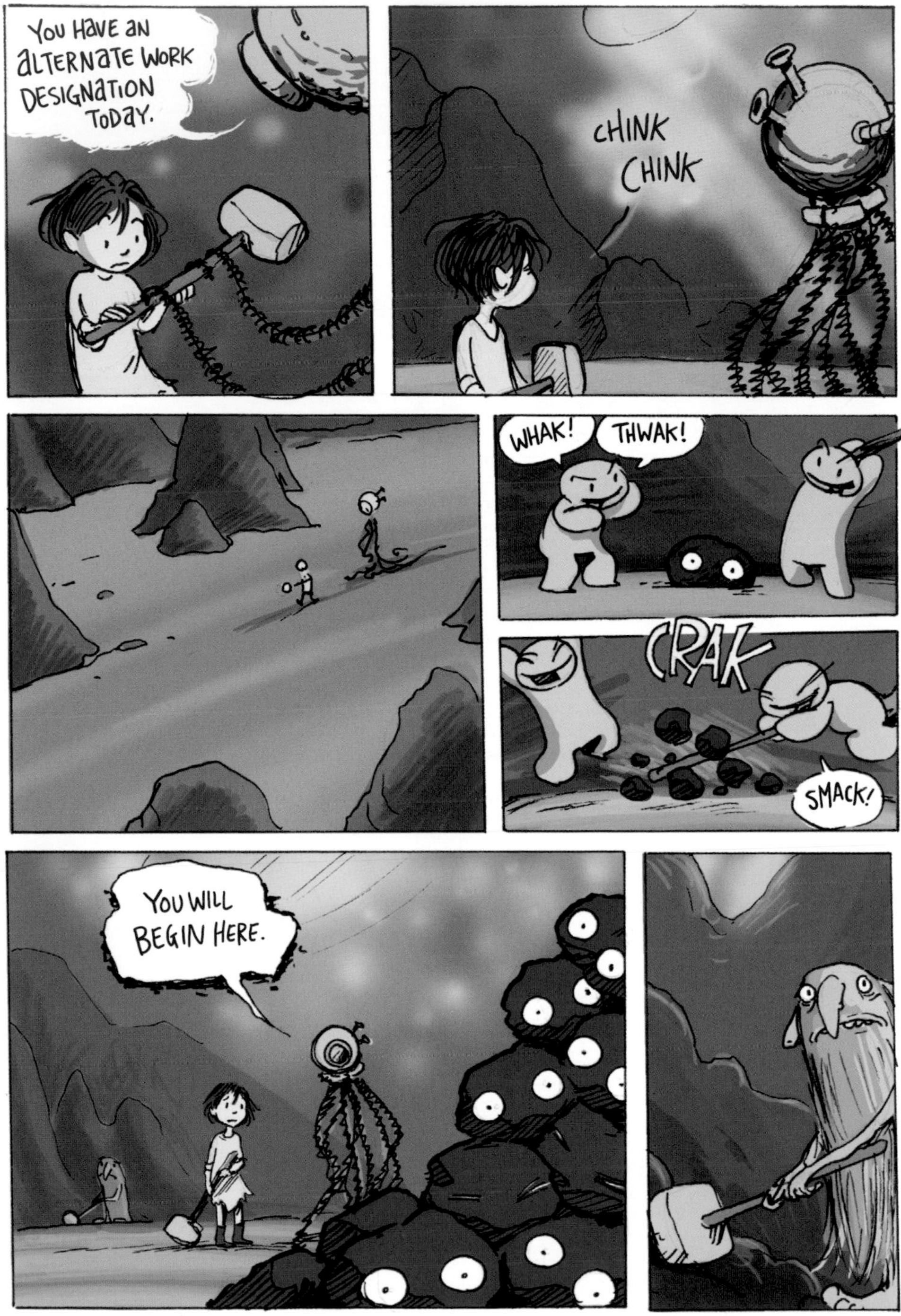
You have an alternate work designation today.
CHINK
CHINK
WHAK!
THWAK!
CRAK
SMACK!
You will begin here.

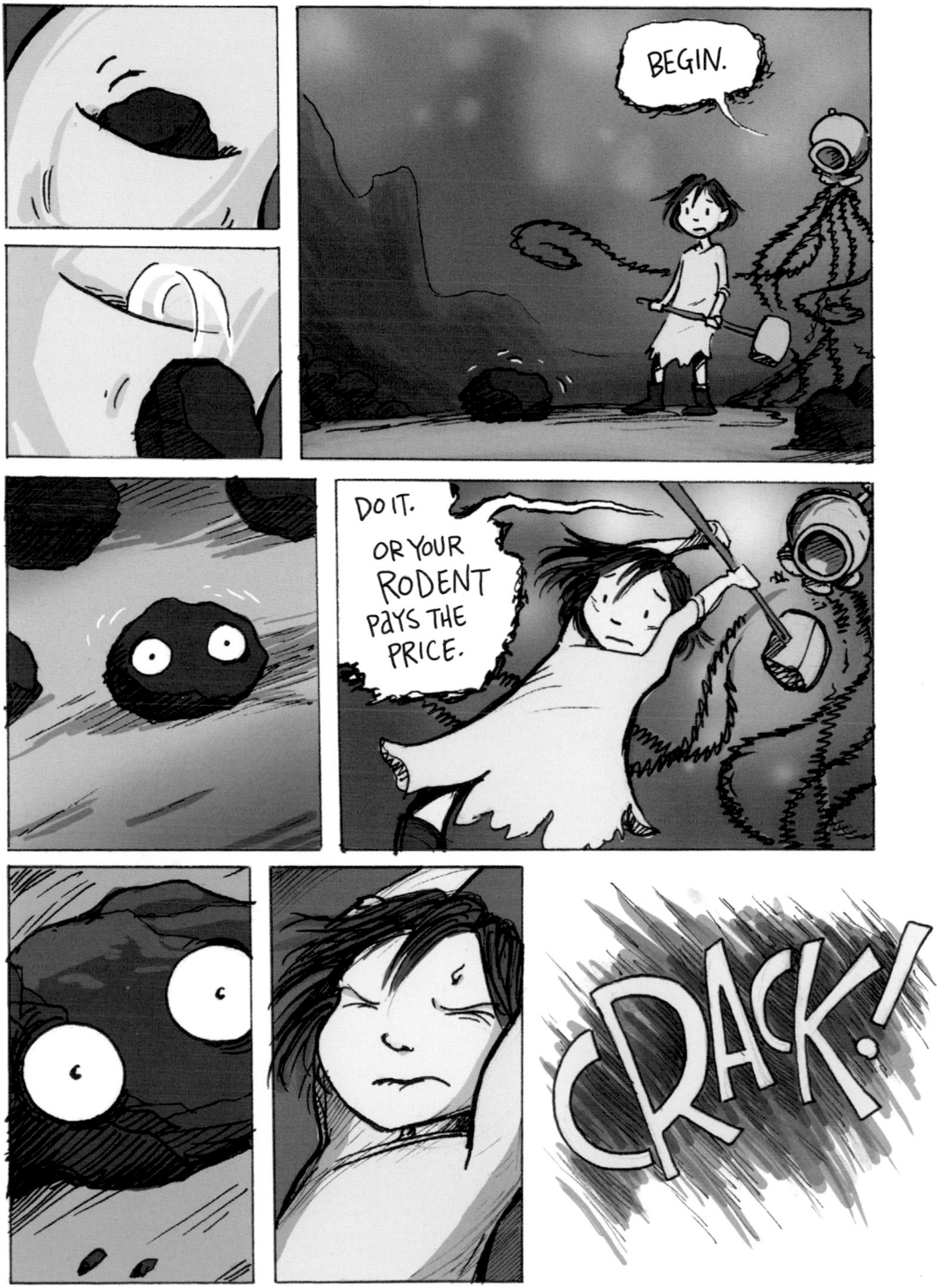
BEGIN.
DO IT.
OR YOUR RODENT PAYS THE PRICE.
CRACK!

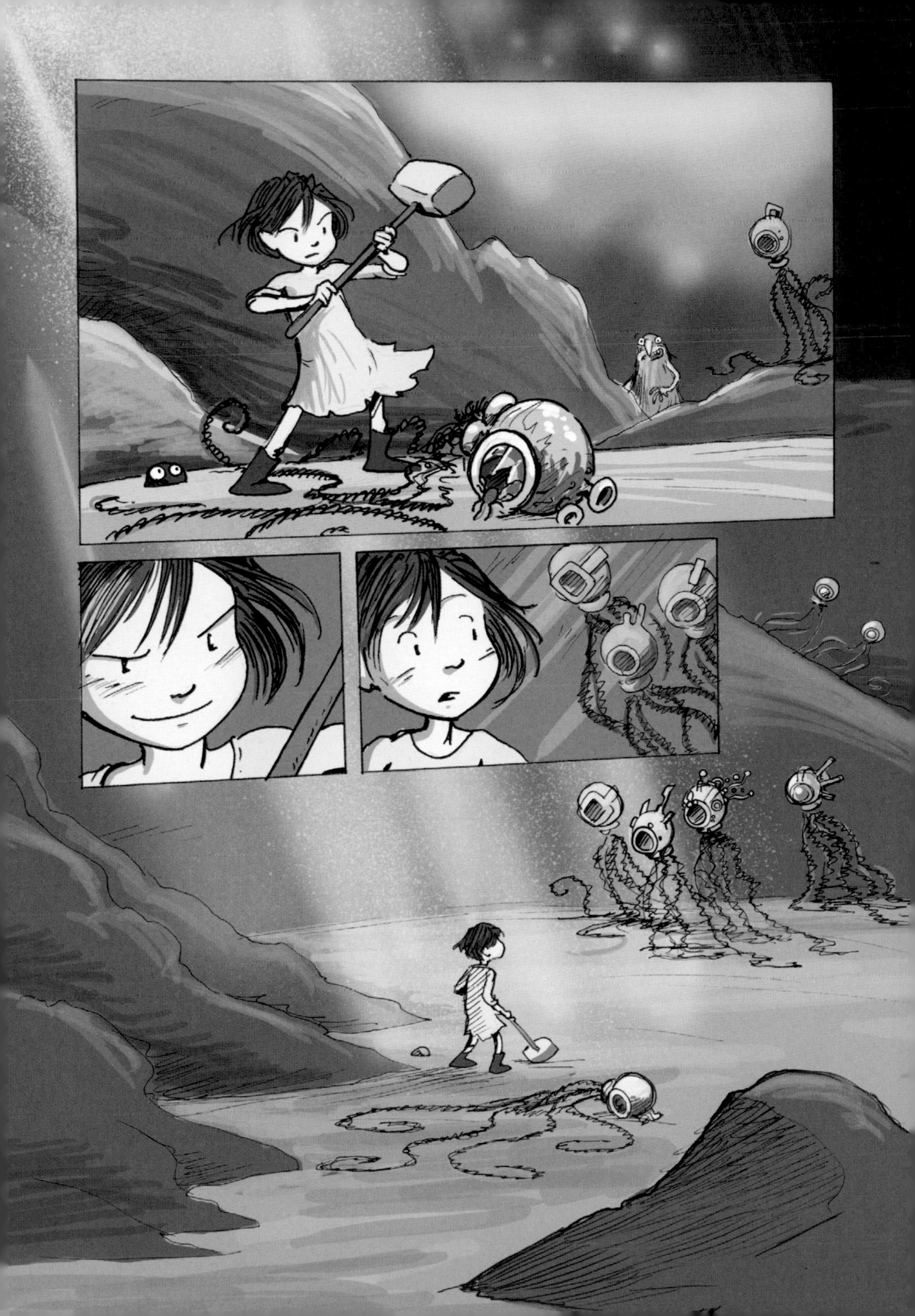

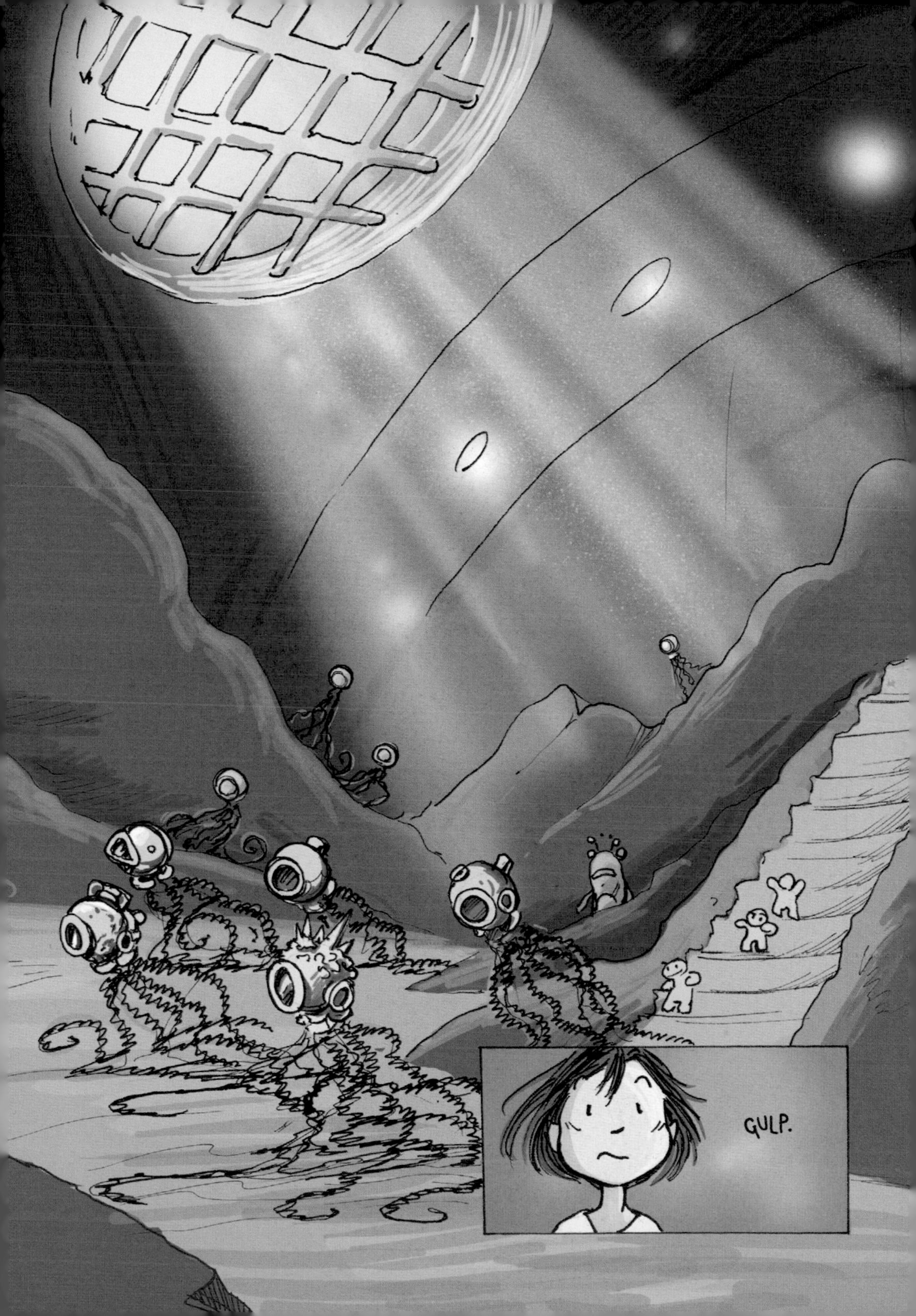
GULP.

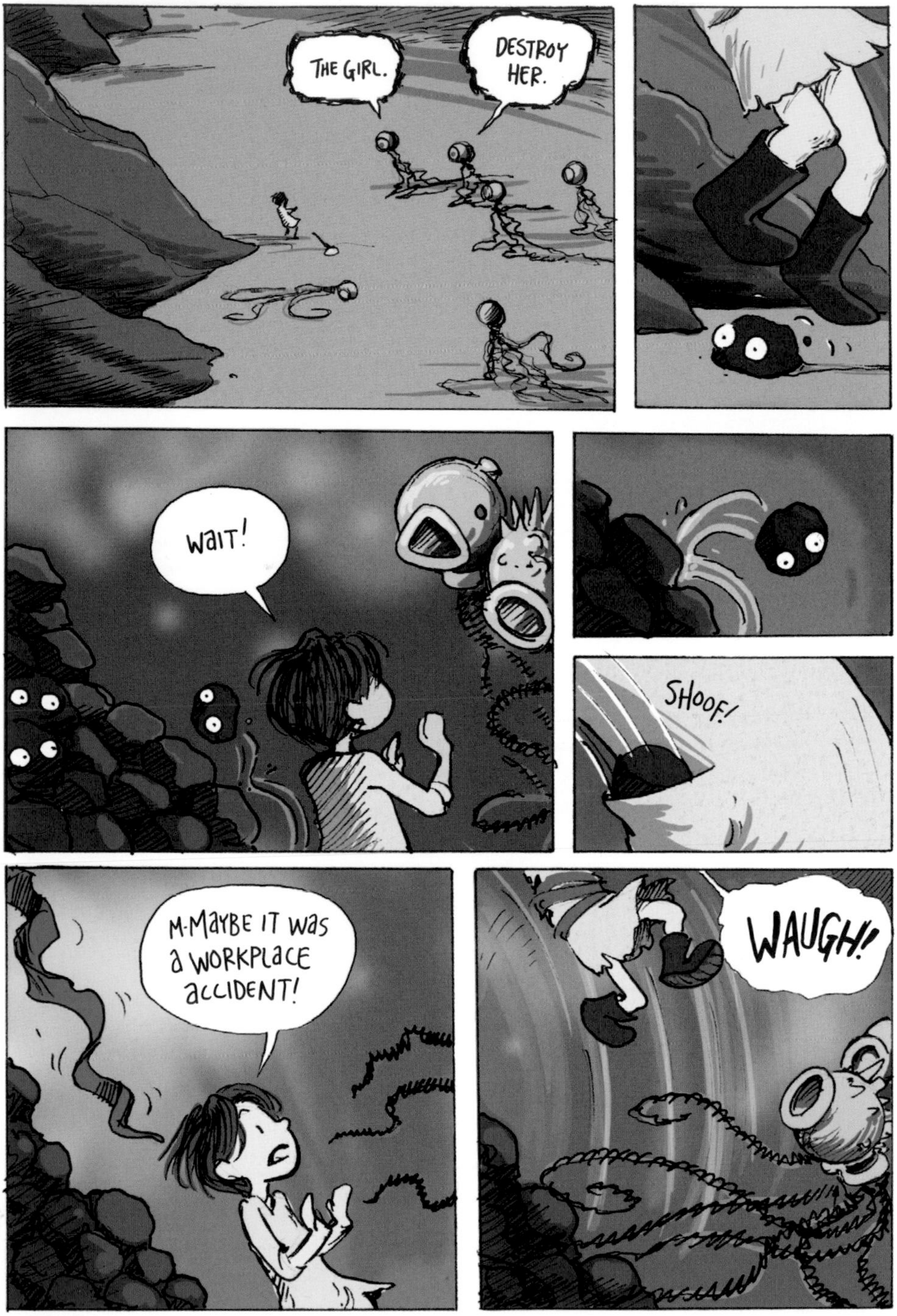
THE GIRL.
DESTROY HER.
WAIT!
SHOOF!
M-MAYBE IT WAS A WORKPLACE ACCIDENT!
WAUGH!

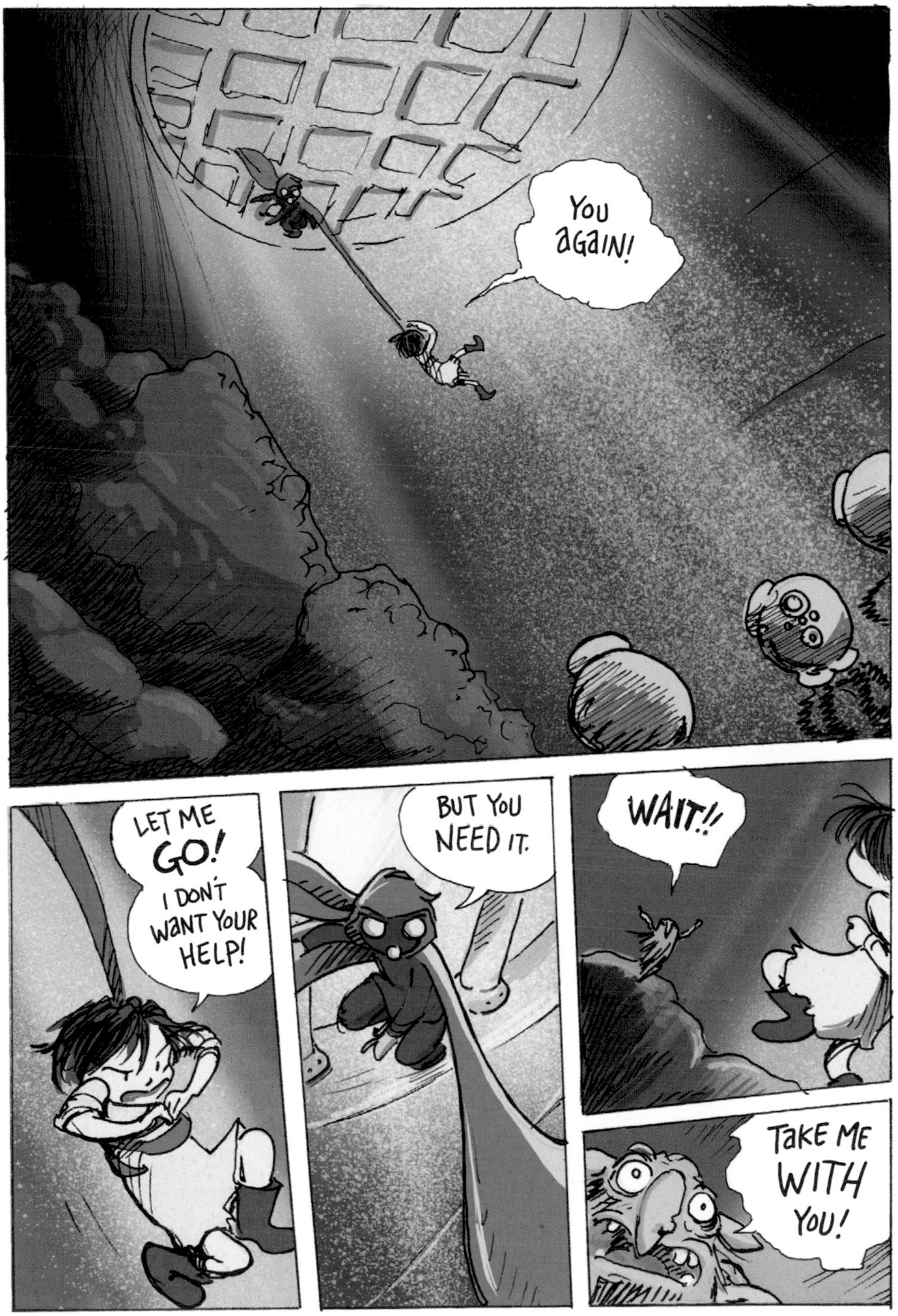
YOU AGAIN!
LET ME GO! I DON'T WANT YOUR HELP!
BUT YOU NEED IT.
WAIT!!
TAKE ME WITH YOU!

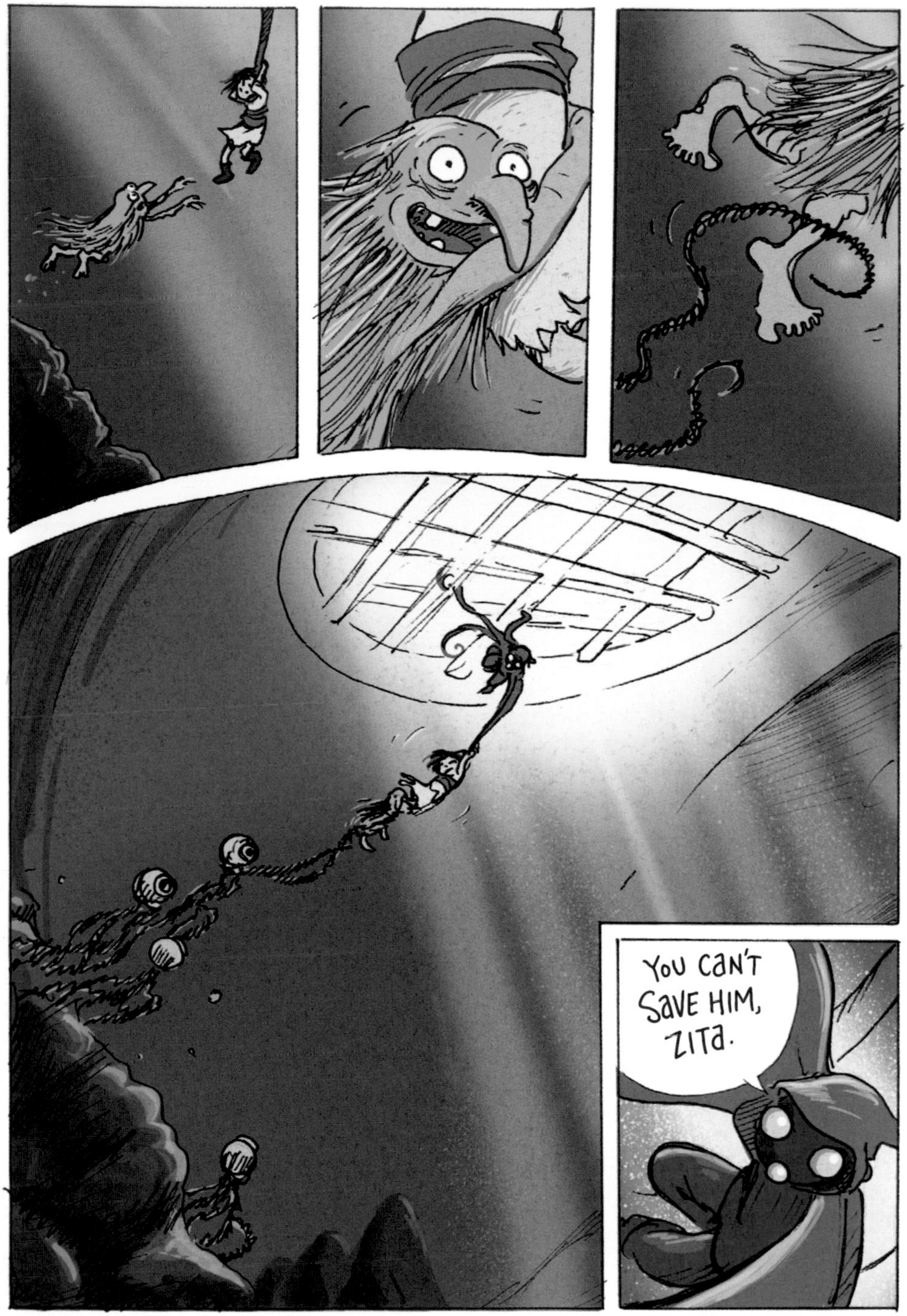
YOU CAN'T SAVE HIM, ZITA.

LET HIM GO!

I CAN SAVE ANYBODY I WANT! YOU DON'T KNOW ANYTHING!

NO!

SLIP.

LET HIM GO OR I'LL HAVE TO LET YOU GO.

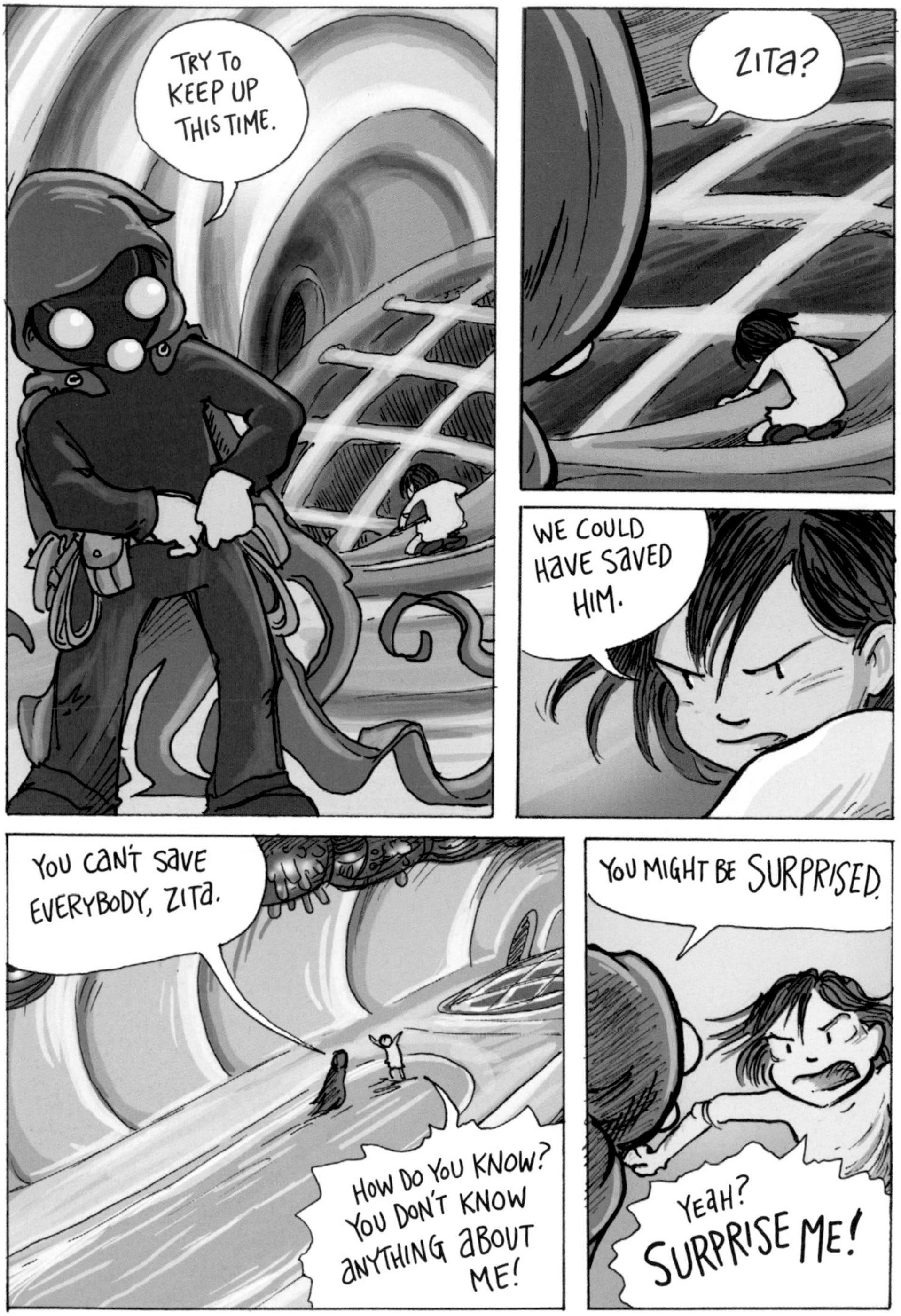
TRY TO KEEP UP THIS TIME.
ZITA?
WE COULD HAVE SAVED HIM.
YOU CAN'T SAVE EVERYBODY, ZITA.
HOW DO YOU KNOW? YOU DON'T KNOW ANYTHING ABOUT ME!
YOU MIGHT BE SURPRISED.
YEAH? SURPRISE ME!

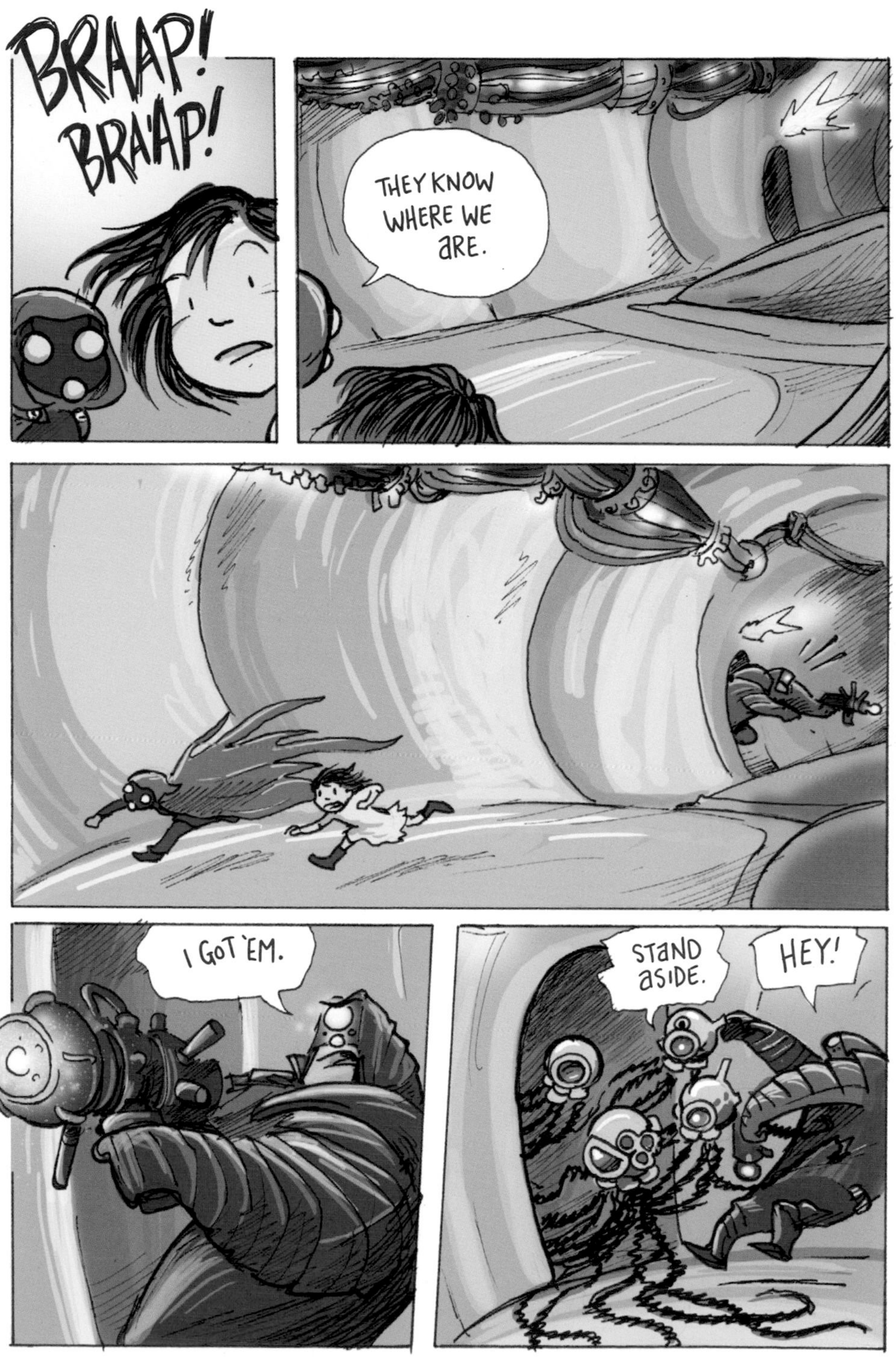
BRAAP! BRAAP!
THEY KNOW WHERE WE ARE.
I GOT 'EM.
STAND ASIDE.
HEY!

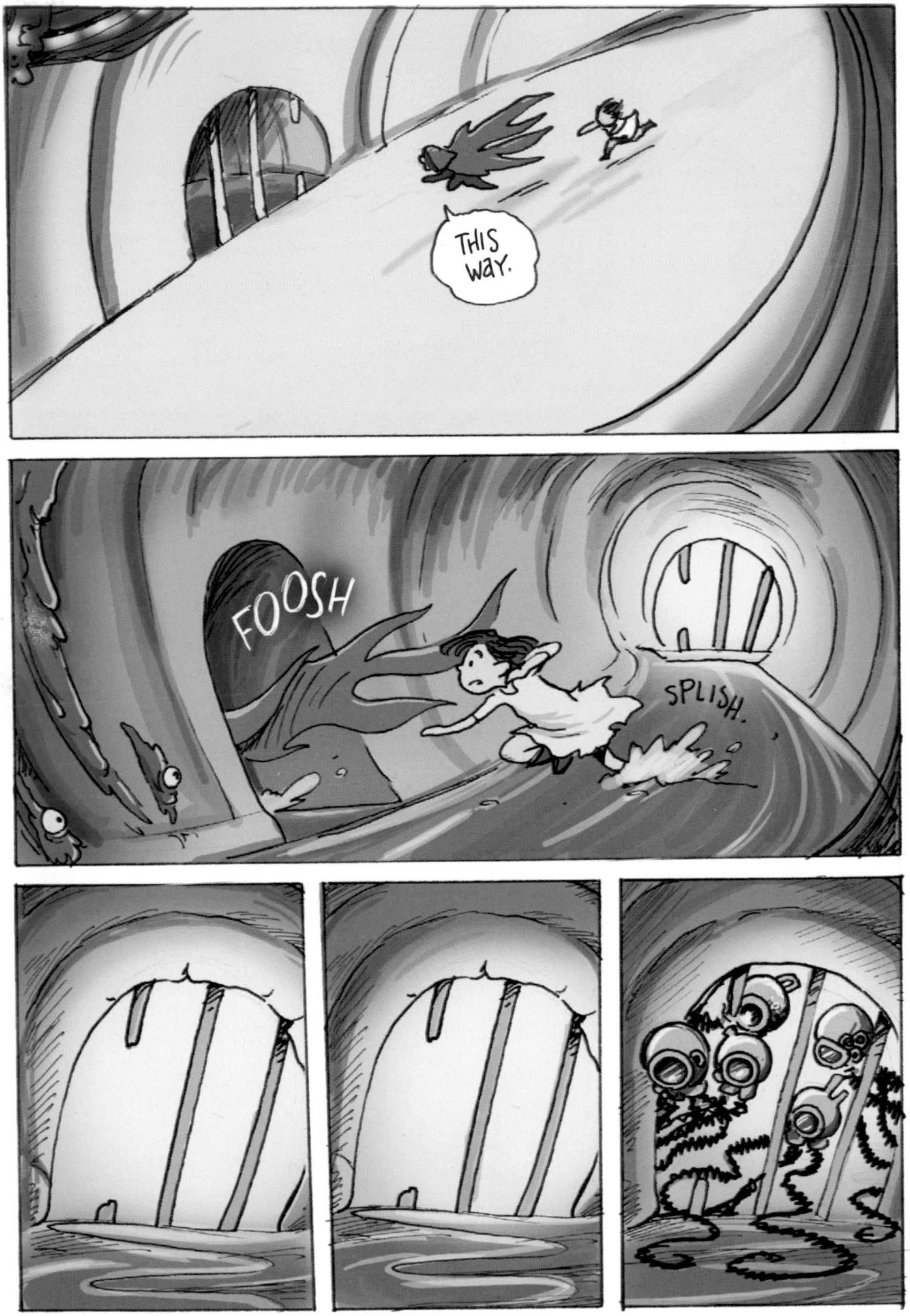
THIS WAY.
FOOSH
SPLISH.

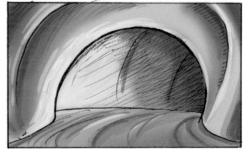

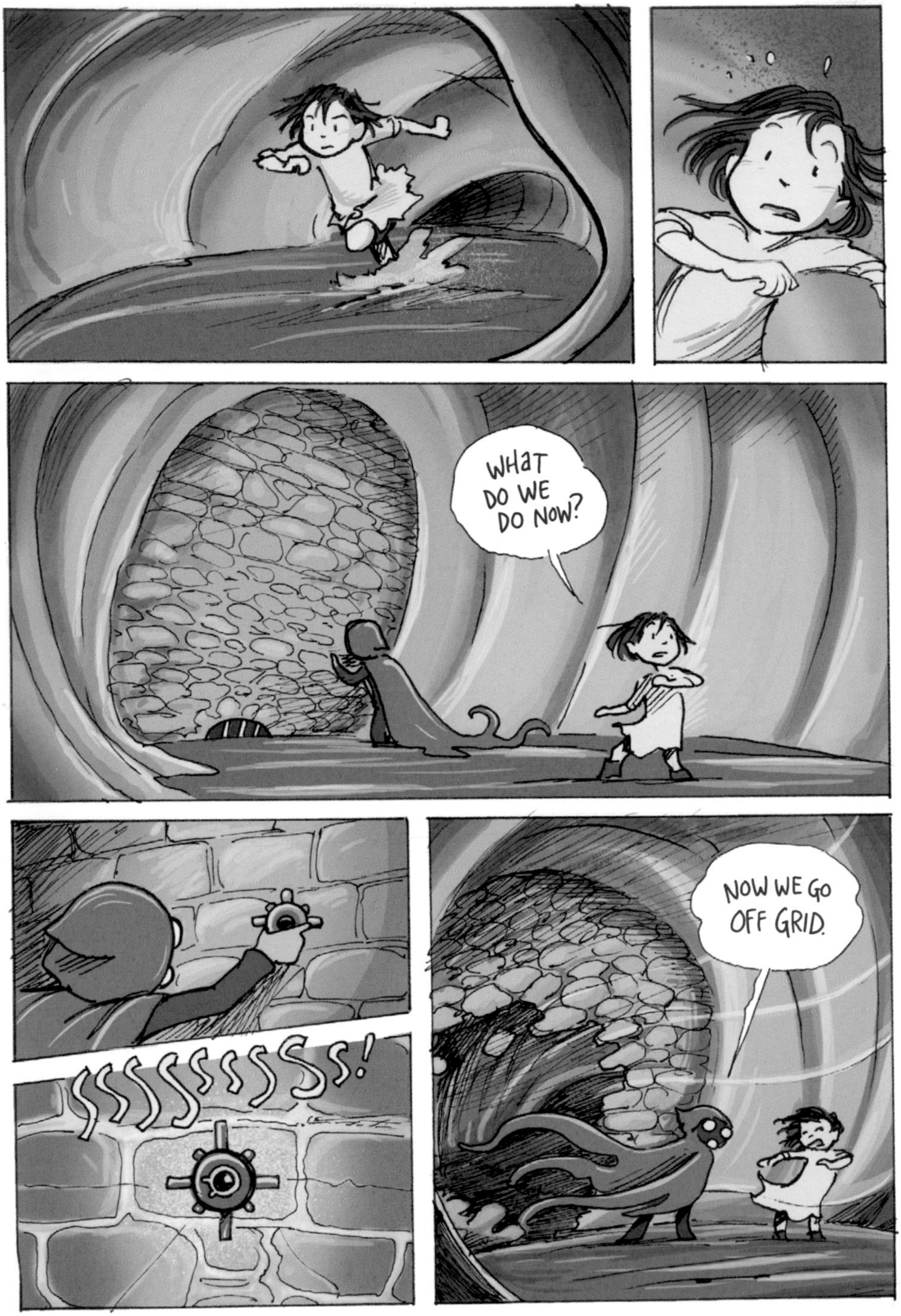
WHAT DO WE DO NOW?
SSSSSSSSSs!
NOW WE GO OFF GRID.

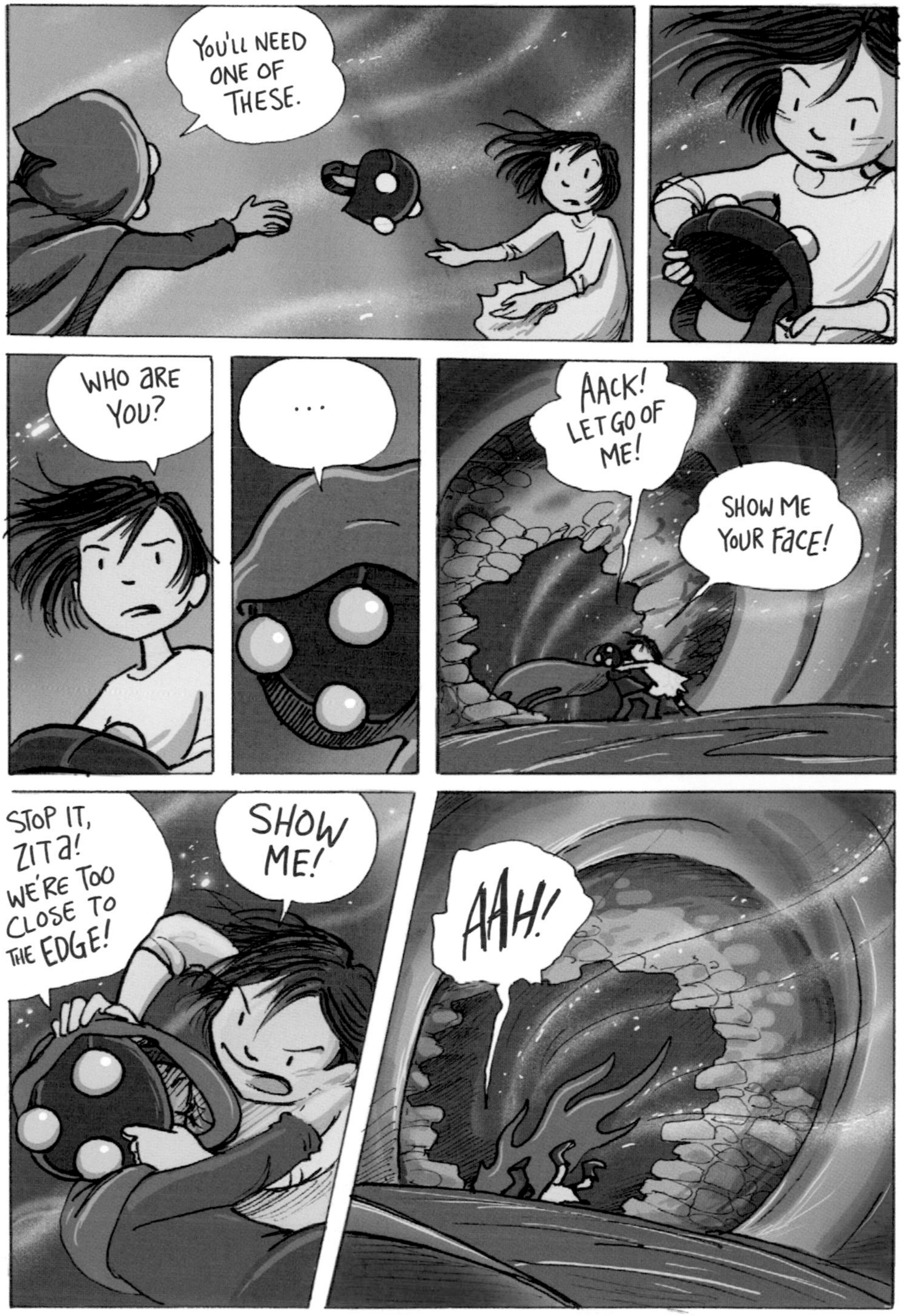
YOU'LL NEED ONE OF THESE.
WHO ARE YOU?
...
AACK! LET GO OF ME!
SHOW ME YOUR FACE!
STOP IT, ZITA! WE'RE TOO CLOSE TO THE EDGE!
SHOW ME!
AAH!

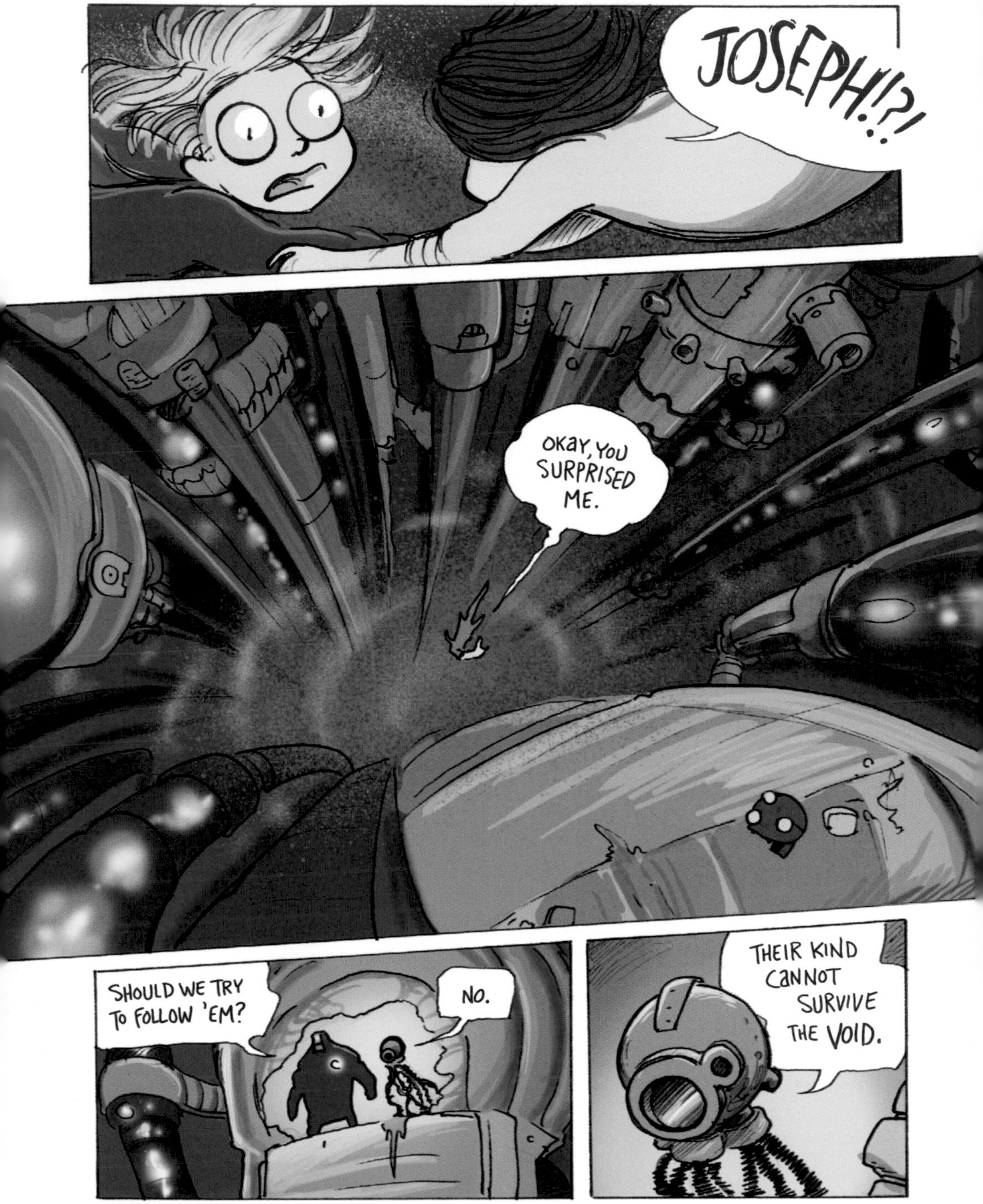
JOSEPH!?!
OKAY, YOU SURPRISED ME.
SHOULD WE TRY TO FOLLOW 'EM?
NO.
THEIR KIND CANNOT SURVIVE THE VOID.

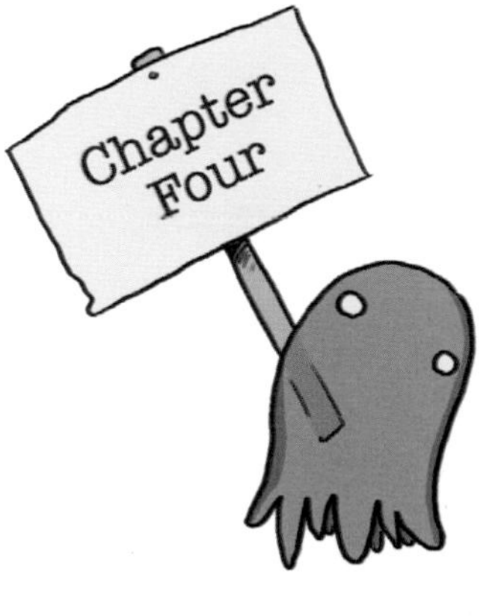
Chapter
Four

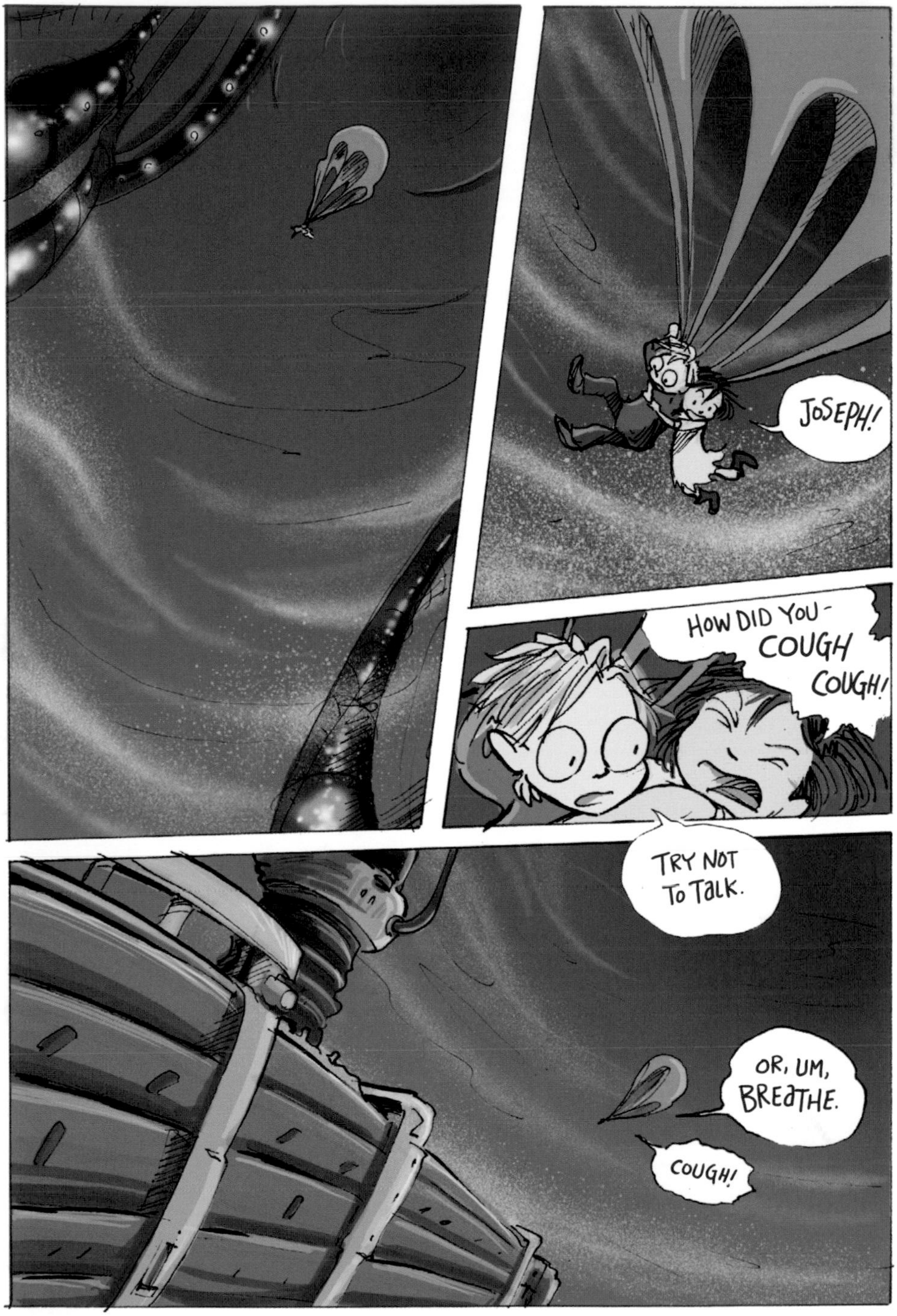

JOSEPH!
HOW DID YOU- COUGH COUGH!
TRY NOT TO TALK.
OR, UM, BREATHE.
COUGH!

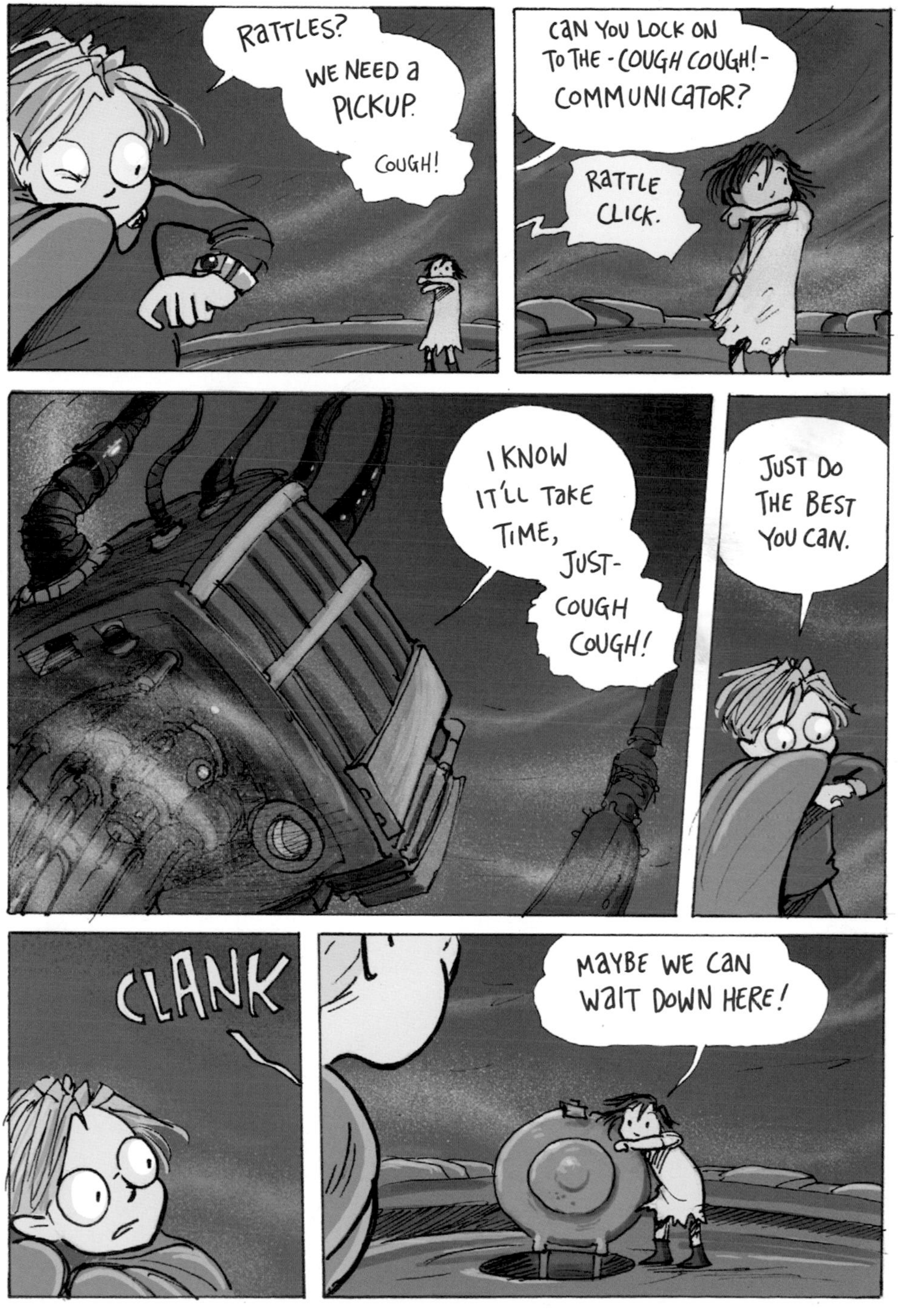
RATTLES?
WE NEED A PICKUP.
COUGH!
CAN YOU LOCK ON TO THE -COUGH COUGH!- COMMUNICATOR?
RATTLE CLICK.
I KNOW IT'LL TAKE TIME, JUST-
COUGH COUGH!
JUST DO THE BEST YOU CAN.
CLANK
MAYBE WE CAN WAIT DOWN HERE!

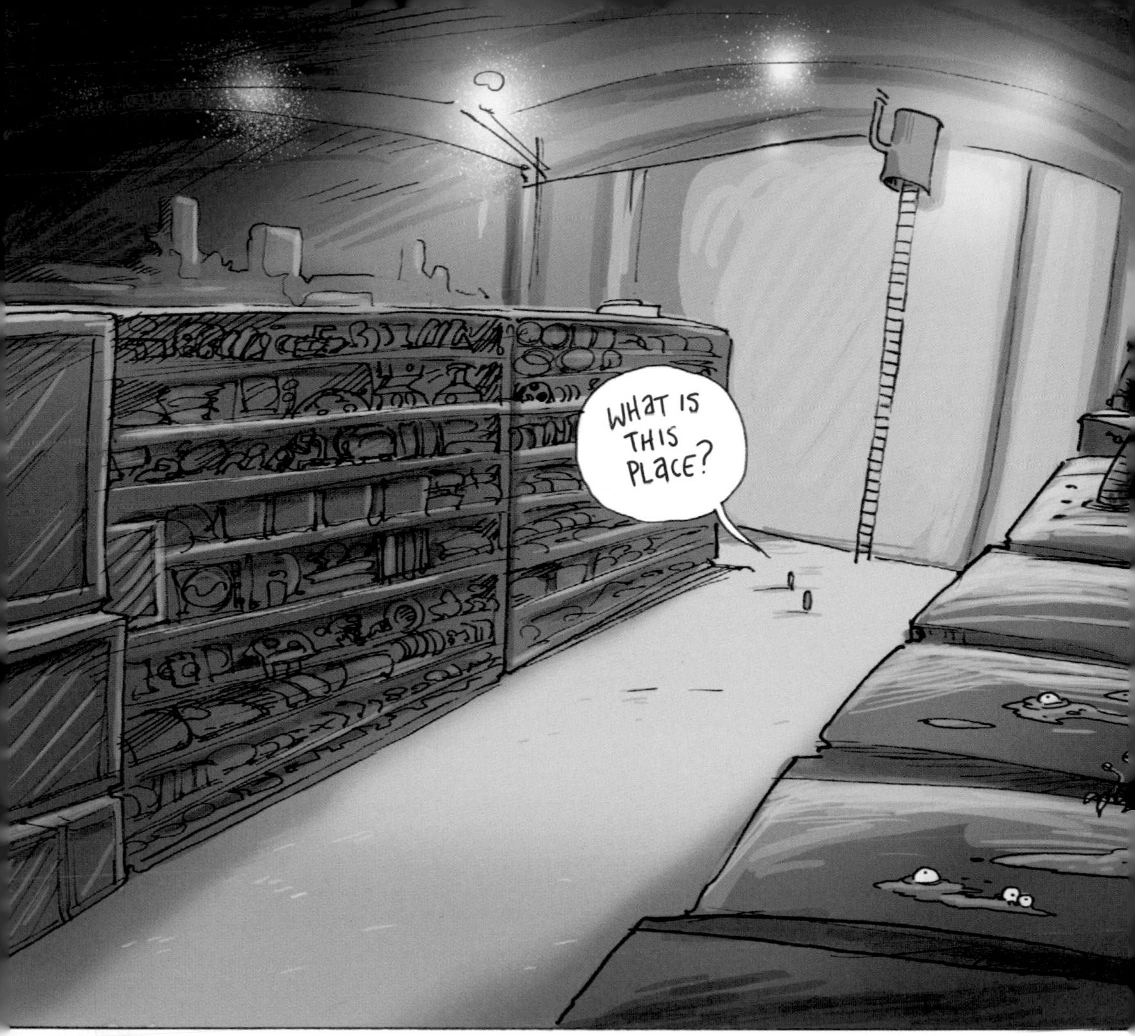
WHAT IS THIS PLACE?

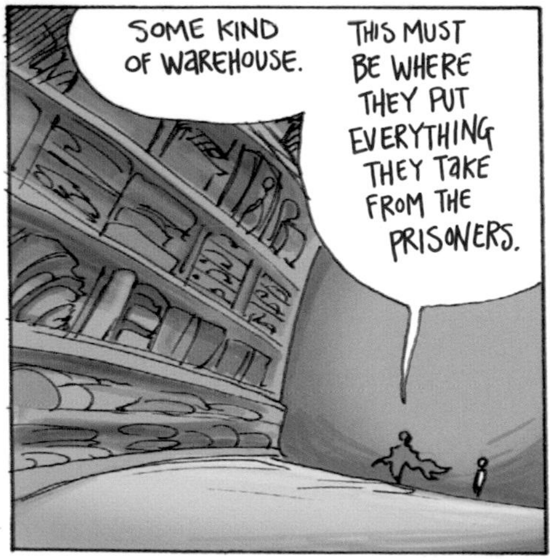
SOME KIND OF WAREHOUSE.
THIS MUST BE WHERE THEY PUT EVERYTHING THEY TAKE FROM THE PRISONERS.

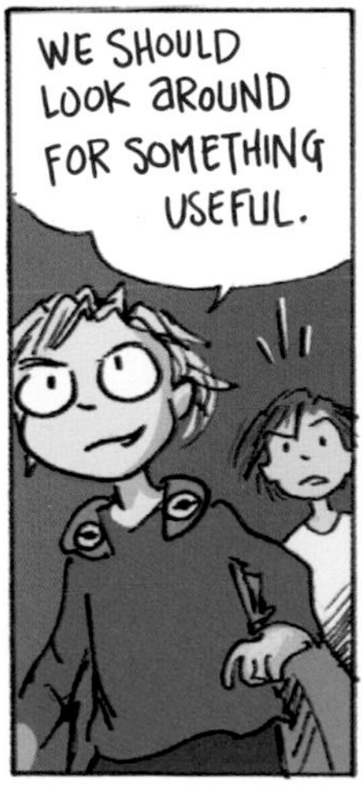
WE SHOULD LOOK AROUND FOR SOMETHING USEFUL.

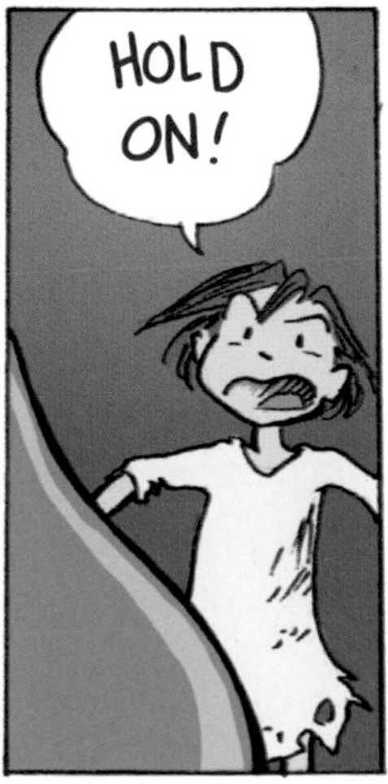
HOLD ON!

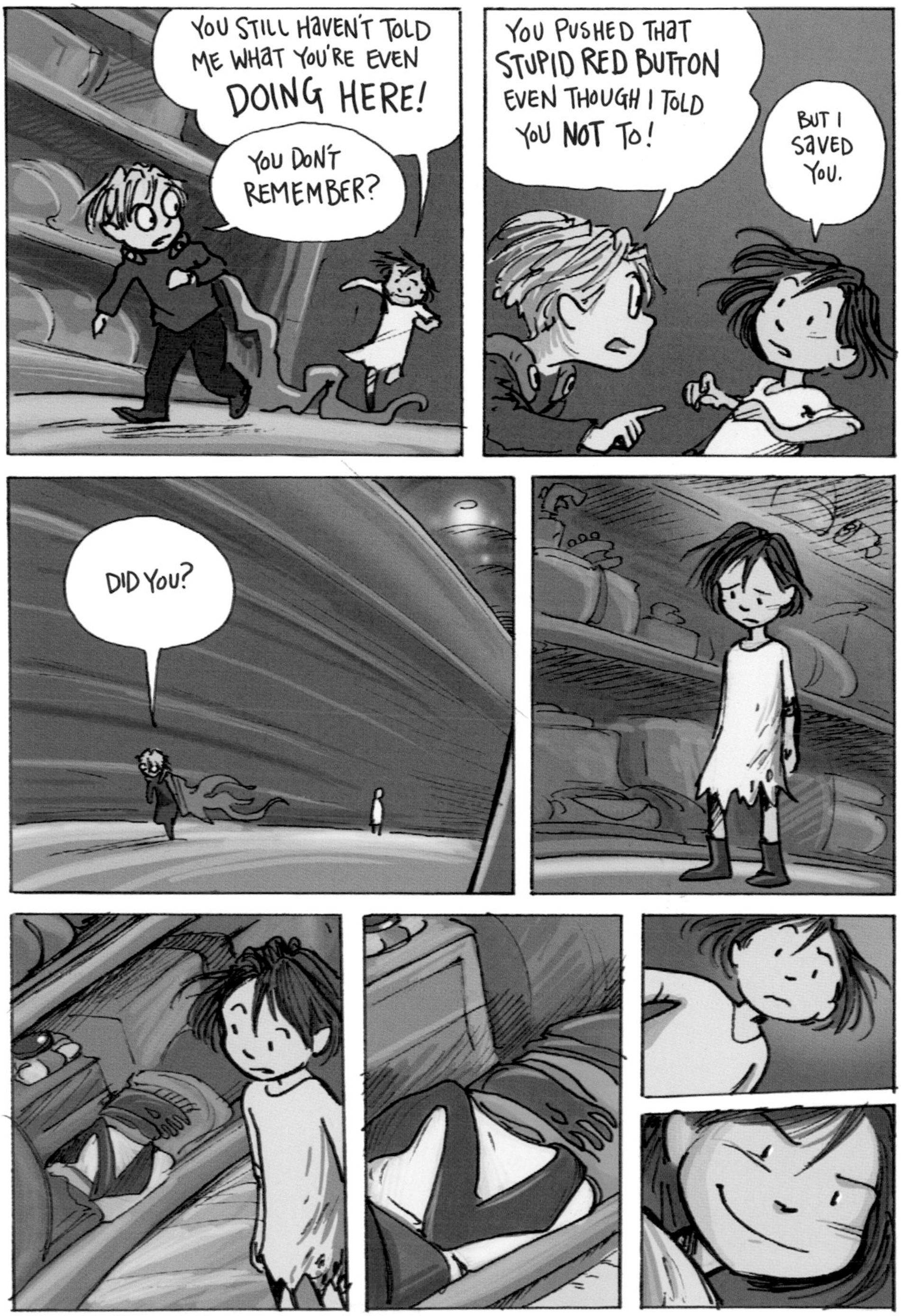

YOU STILL HAVEN'T TOLD ME WHAT YOU'RE EVEN DOING HERE!
YOU DON'T REMEMBER?
YOU PUSHED THAT STUPID RED BUTTON EVEN THOUGH I TOLD YOU NOT TO!
BUT I SAVED YOU.
DID YOU?

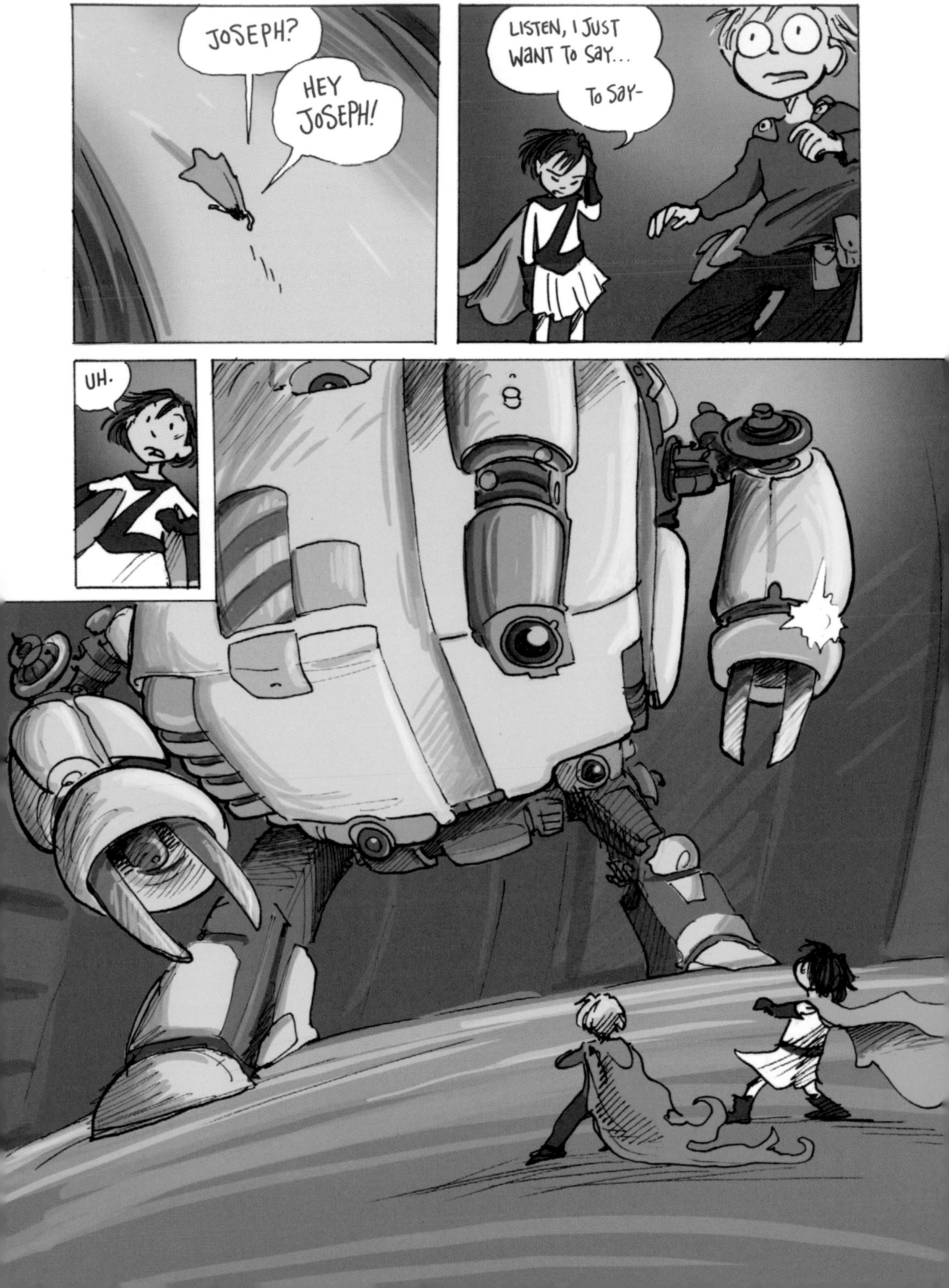
JOSEPH?
HEY JOSEPH!
LISTEN, I JUST WANT TO SAY...
TO SAY-
UH.

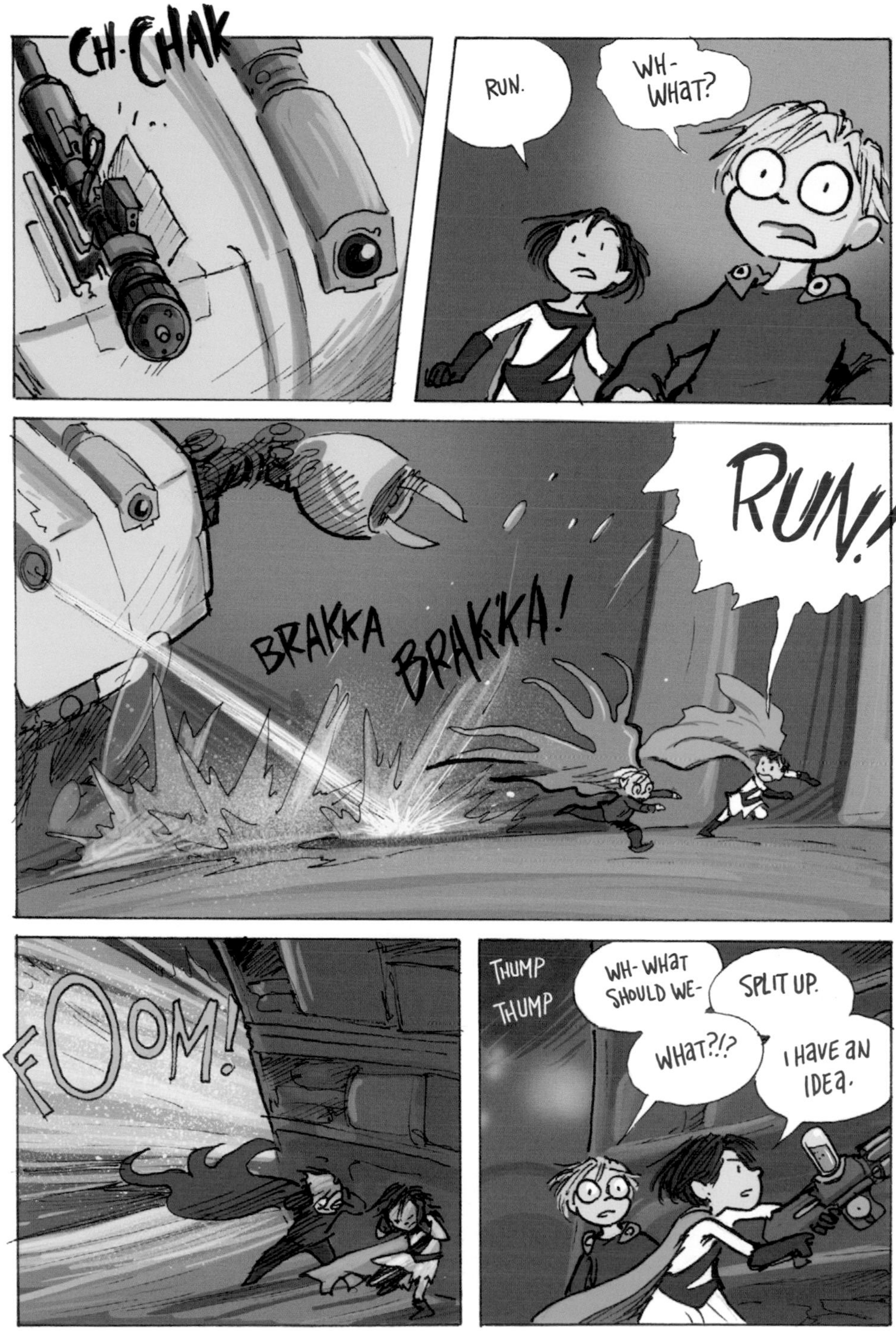
CH-CHAK
RUN.
WH- WHAT?
RUN!!
BRAKKA BRAKKA!
FOOM!
THUMP THUMP
WH- WHAT SHOULD WE-
SPLIT UP.
WHAT?!?
I HAVE AN IDEA.

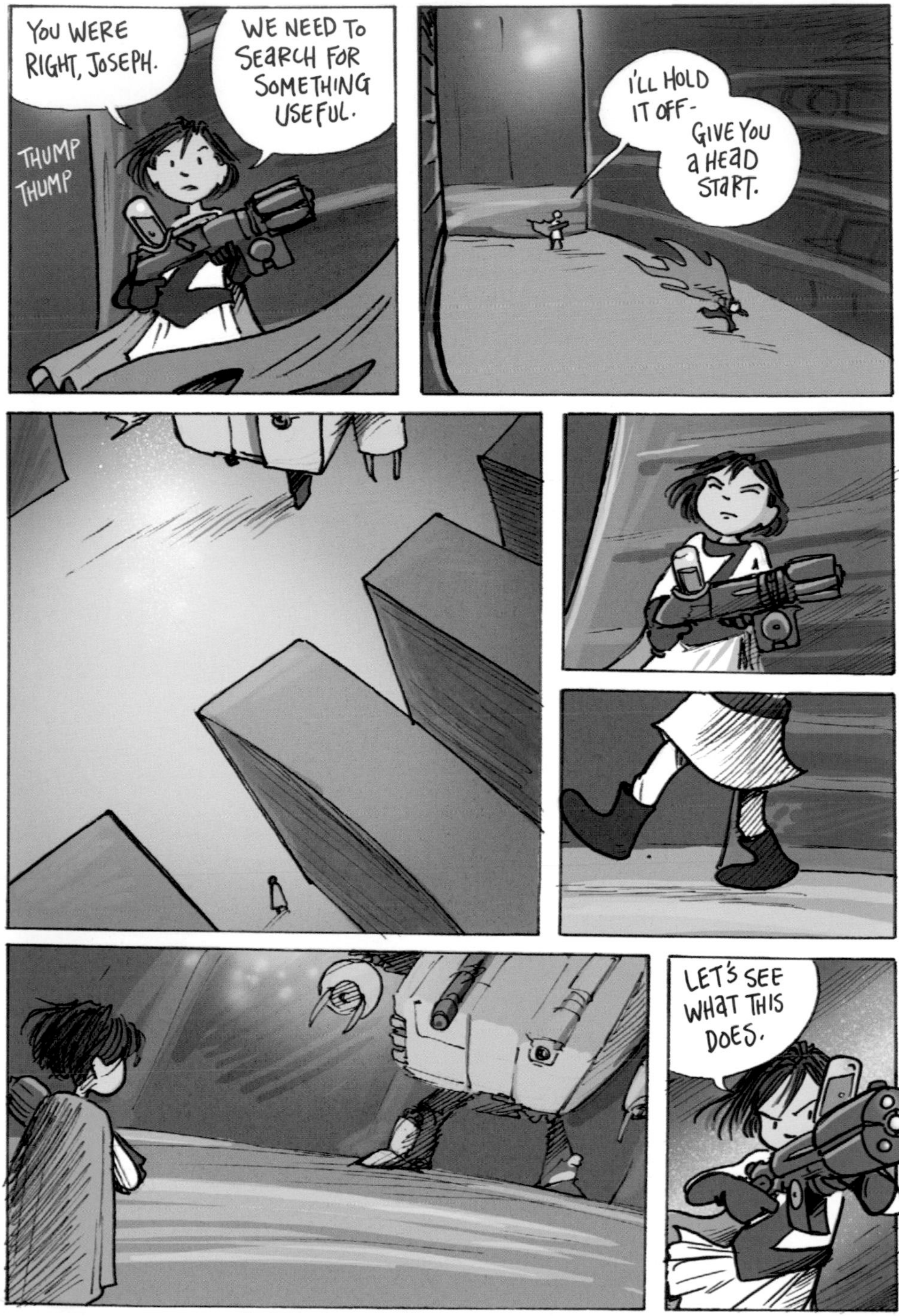

YOU WERE RIGHT, JOSEPH.
WE NEED TO SEARCH FOR SOMETHING USEFUL.
THUMP THUMP
I'LL HOLD IT OFF-
GIVE YOU A HEAD START.
LET'S SEE WHAT THIS DOES.

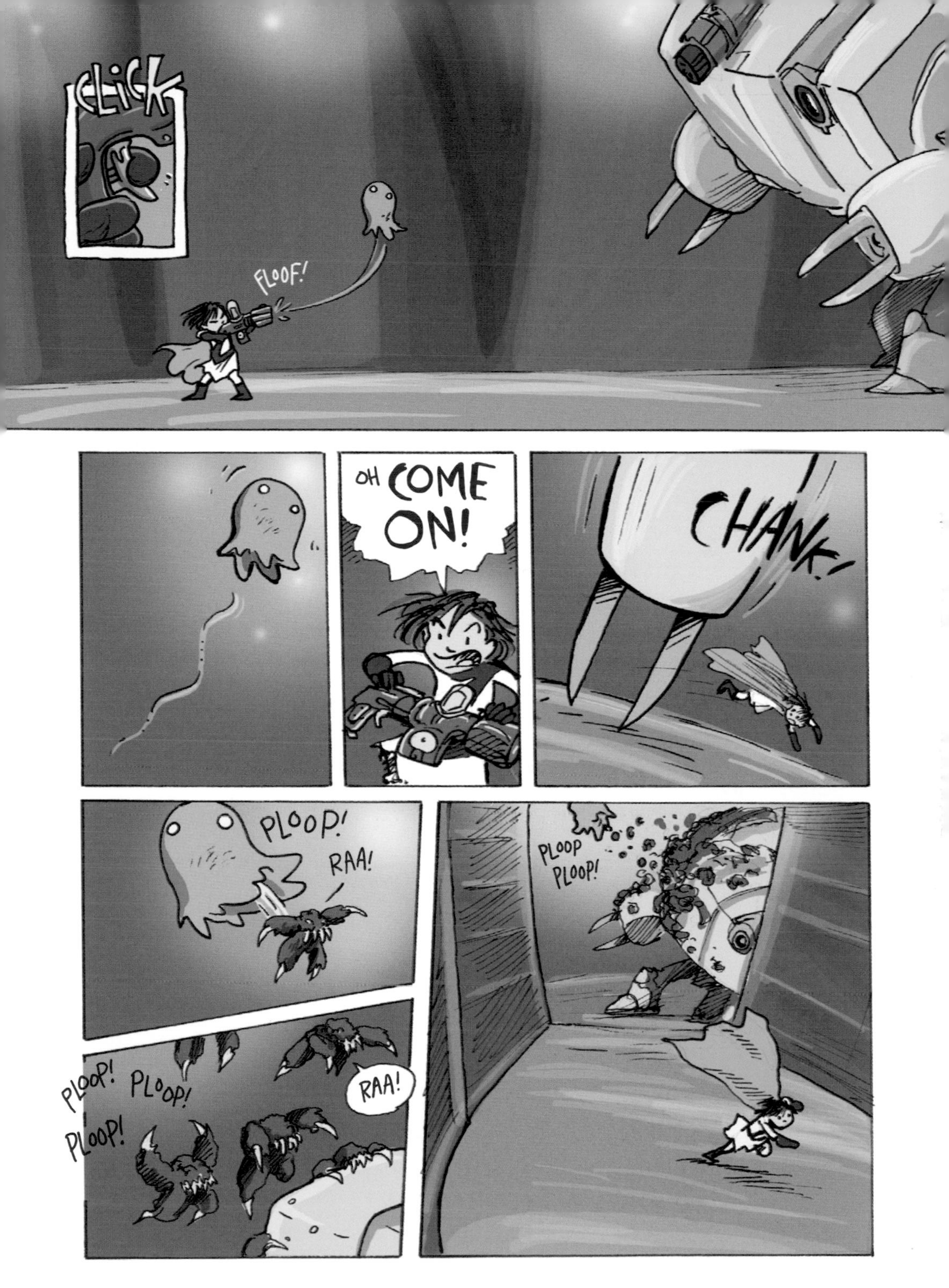
CLICK
FLOOF!
OH COME ON!
CHANK!
PLOOP!
RAA!
PLOOP PLOOP!
PLOOP!
PLOOP!
PLOOP!
RAA!

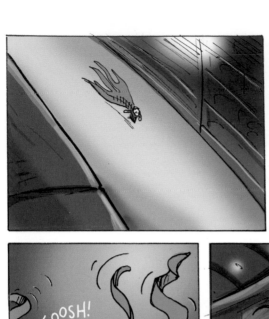

FOOSH!

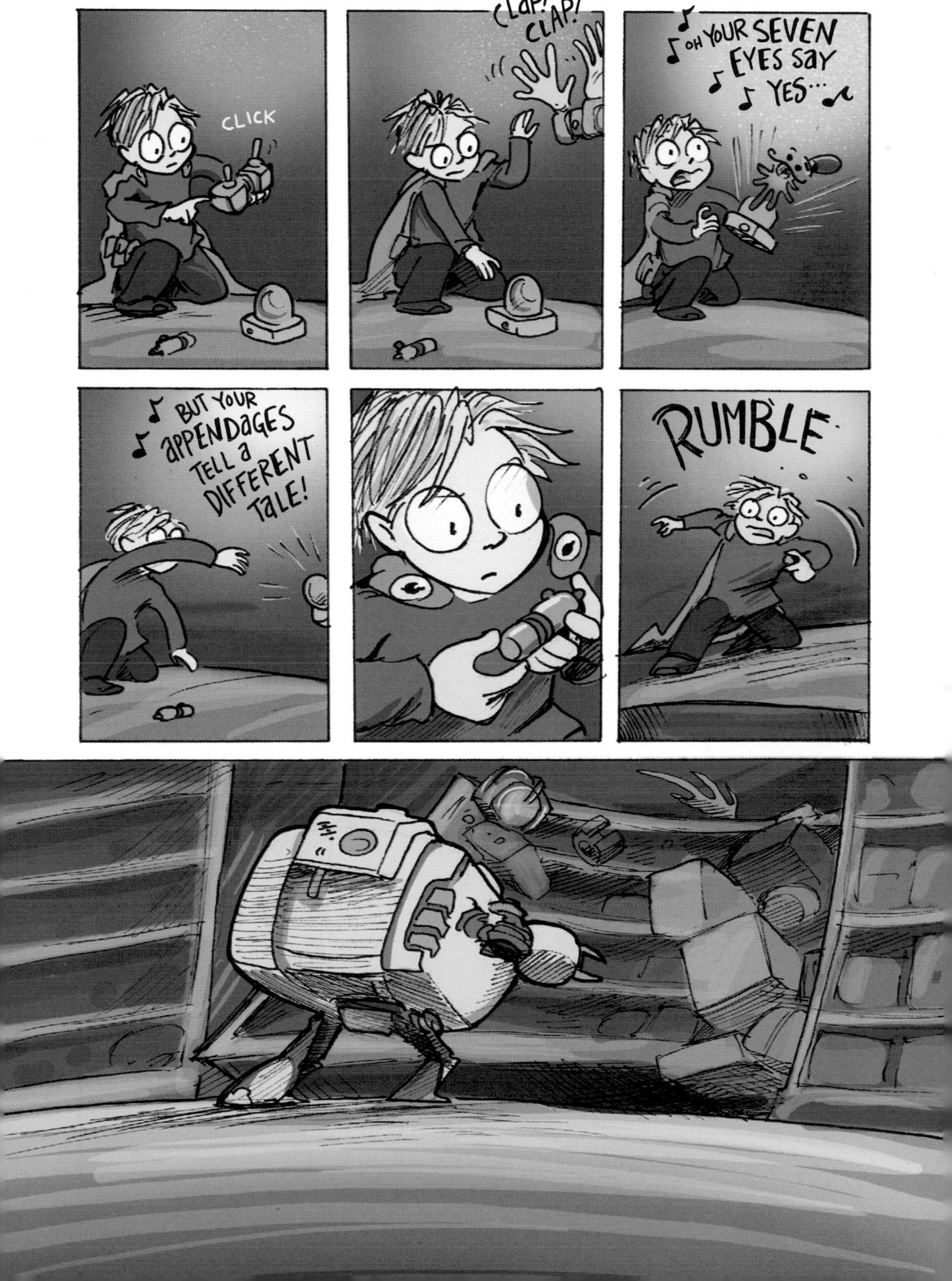
CLICK
CLAP! CLAP!
OH YOUR SEVEN EYES SAY YES...
BUT YOUR APPENDAGES TELL A DIFFERENT TALE!
RUMBLE

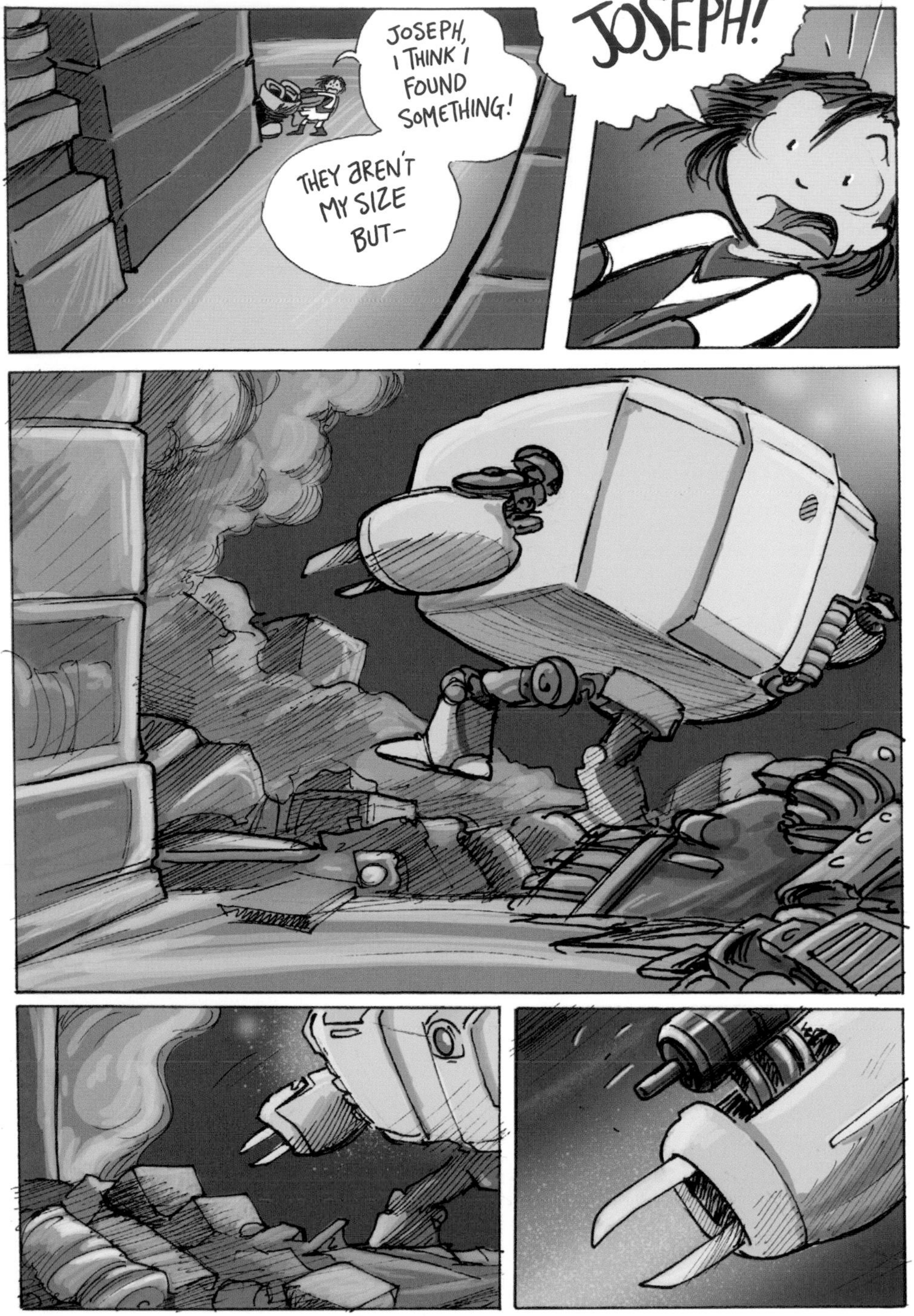
JOSEPH, I THINK I FOUND SOMETHING!
THEY aREN'T MY SIZE BUT-
JOSEPH!

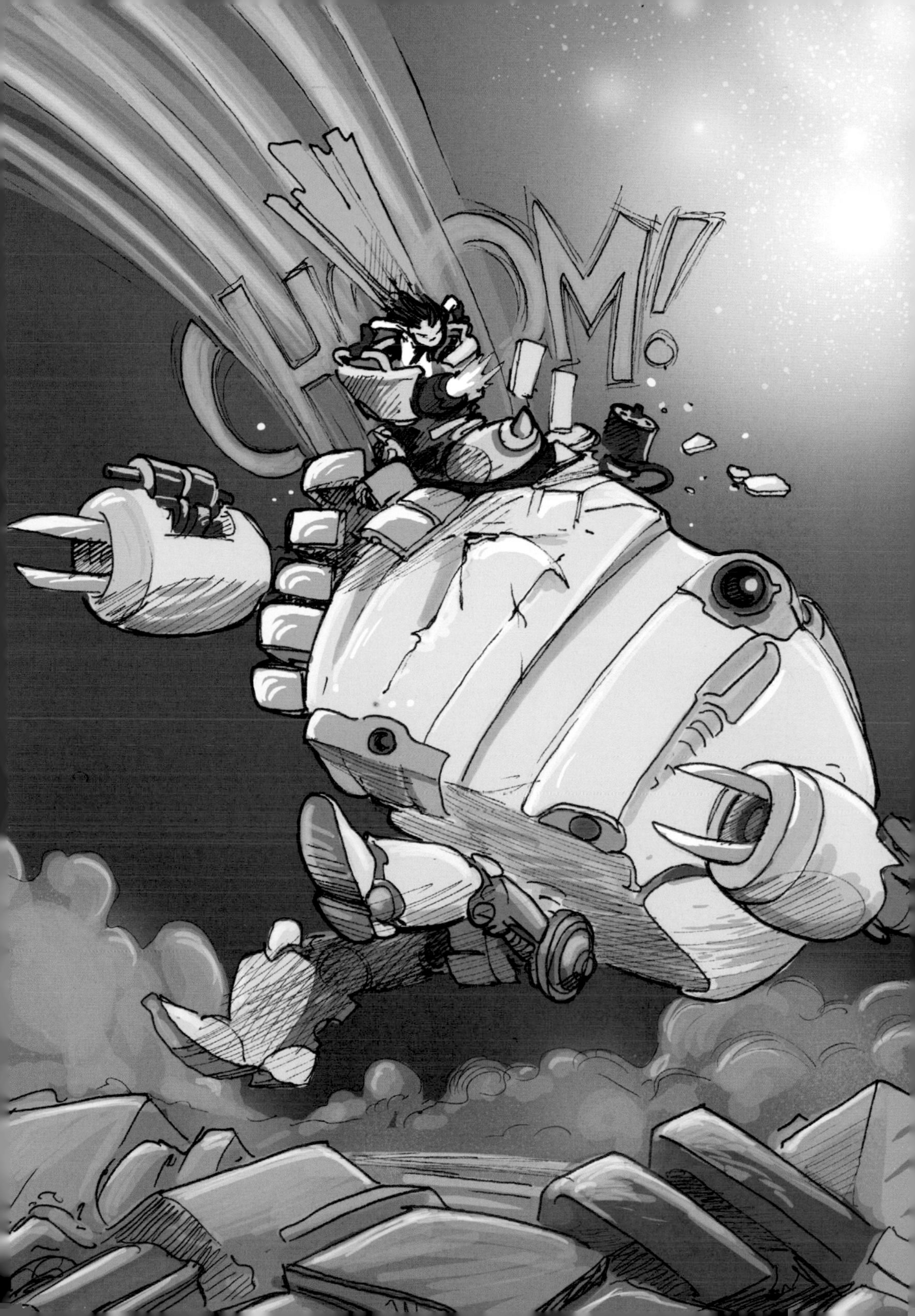
CHOOM!

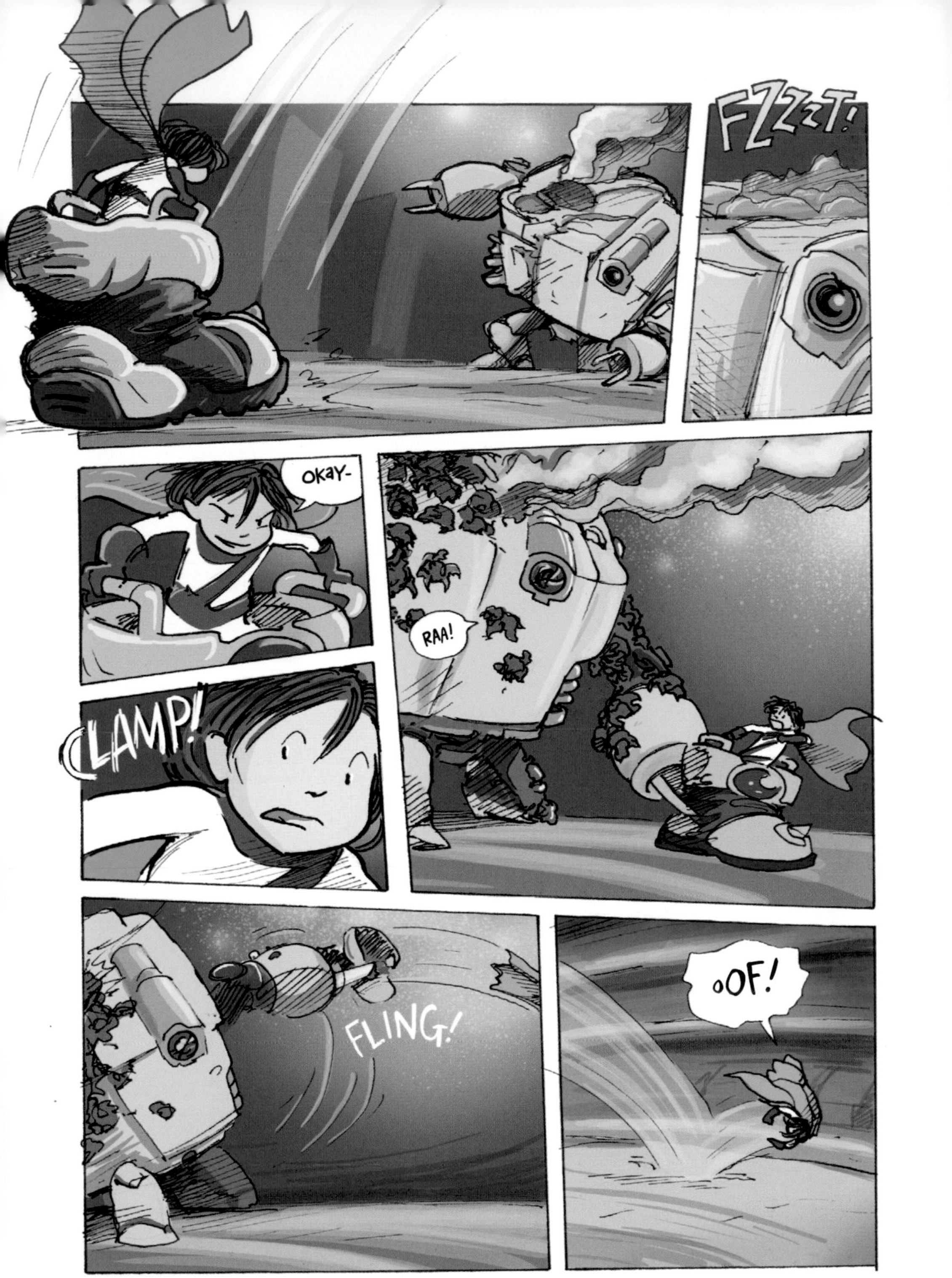
FZZZT!
OKAY-
RAA!
CLAMP!
FLING!
OOF!

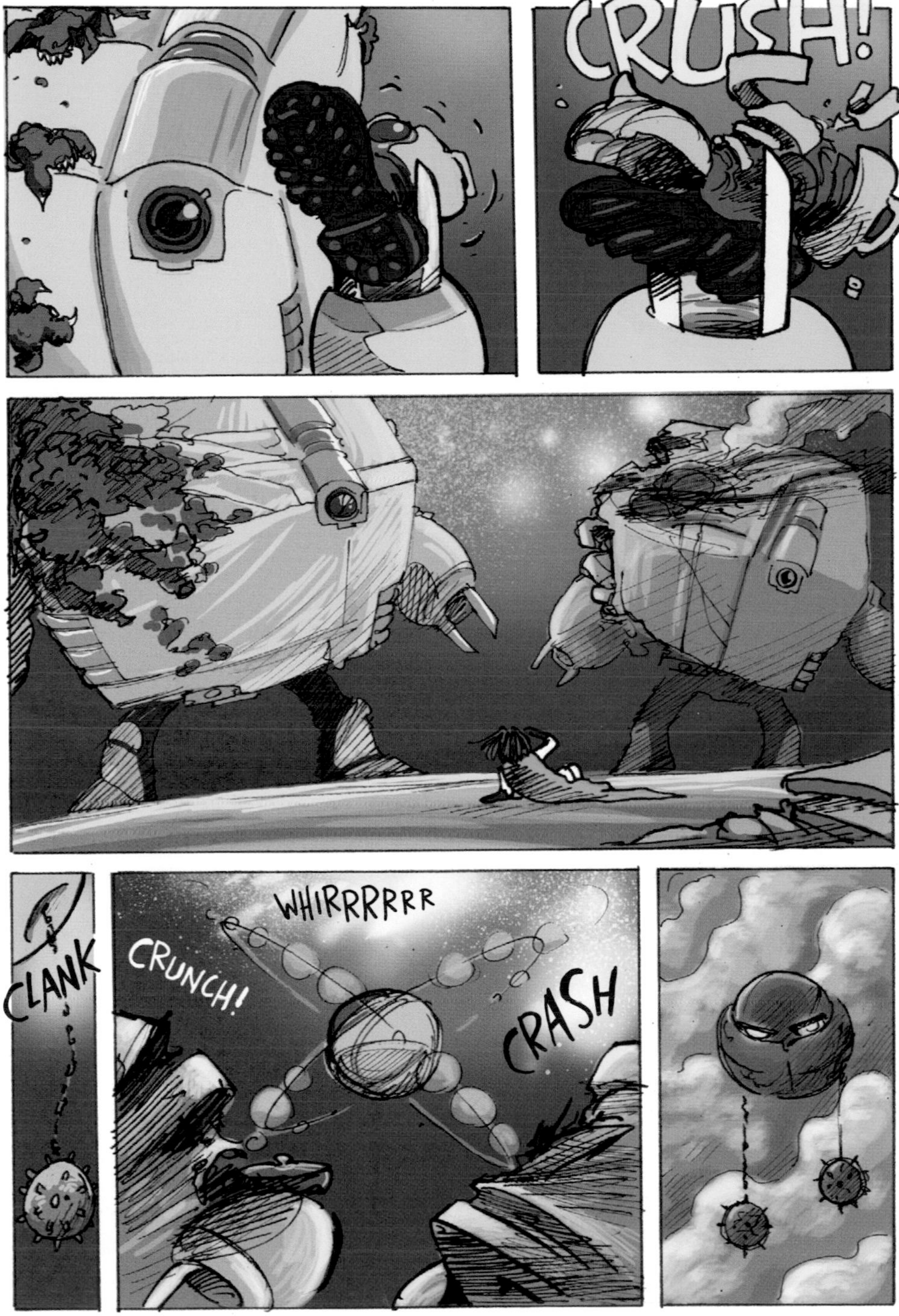
CRUSH!
CLANK
CRUNCH!
WHIRRRRRR
CRASH

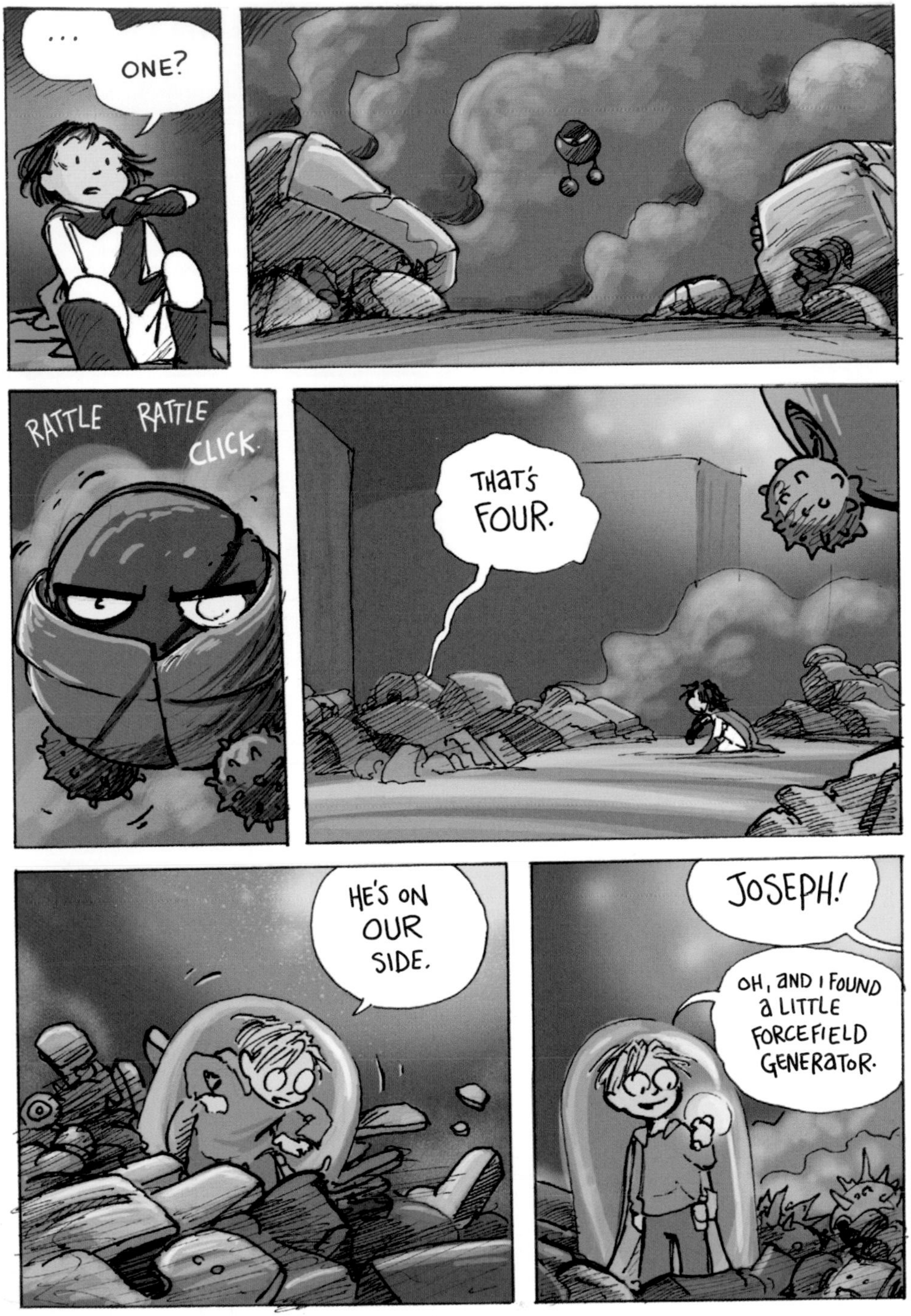
...
ONE?
RATTLE RATTLE
CLICK.
THAT'S FOUR.
HE'S ON OUR SIDE.
JOSEPH!
OH, AND I FOUND A LITTLE FORCEFIELD GENERATOR.

YOU'RE ALL RIGHT! I THOUGHT—

FOUR, DO WE HAVE A WAY OUT OF HERE?

RATTLE CLICK

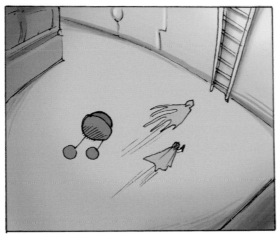

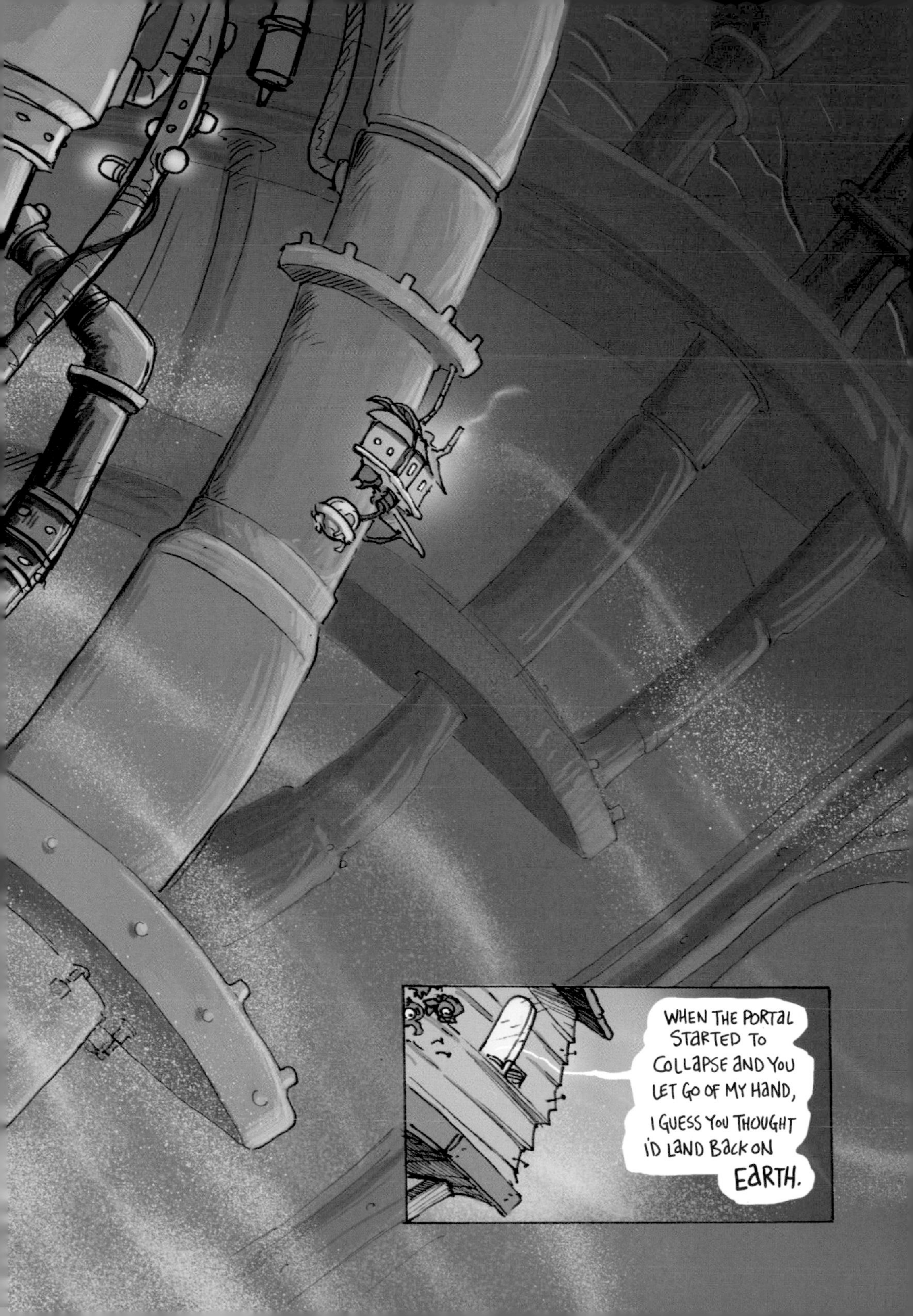
WHEN THE PORTAL STARTED TO COLLAPSE AND YOU LET GO OF MY HAND, I GUESS YOU THOUGHT I'D LAND BACK ON EARTH.

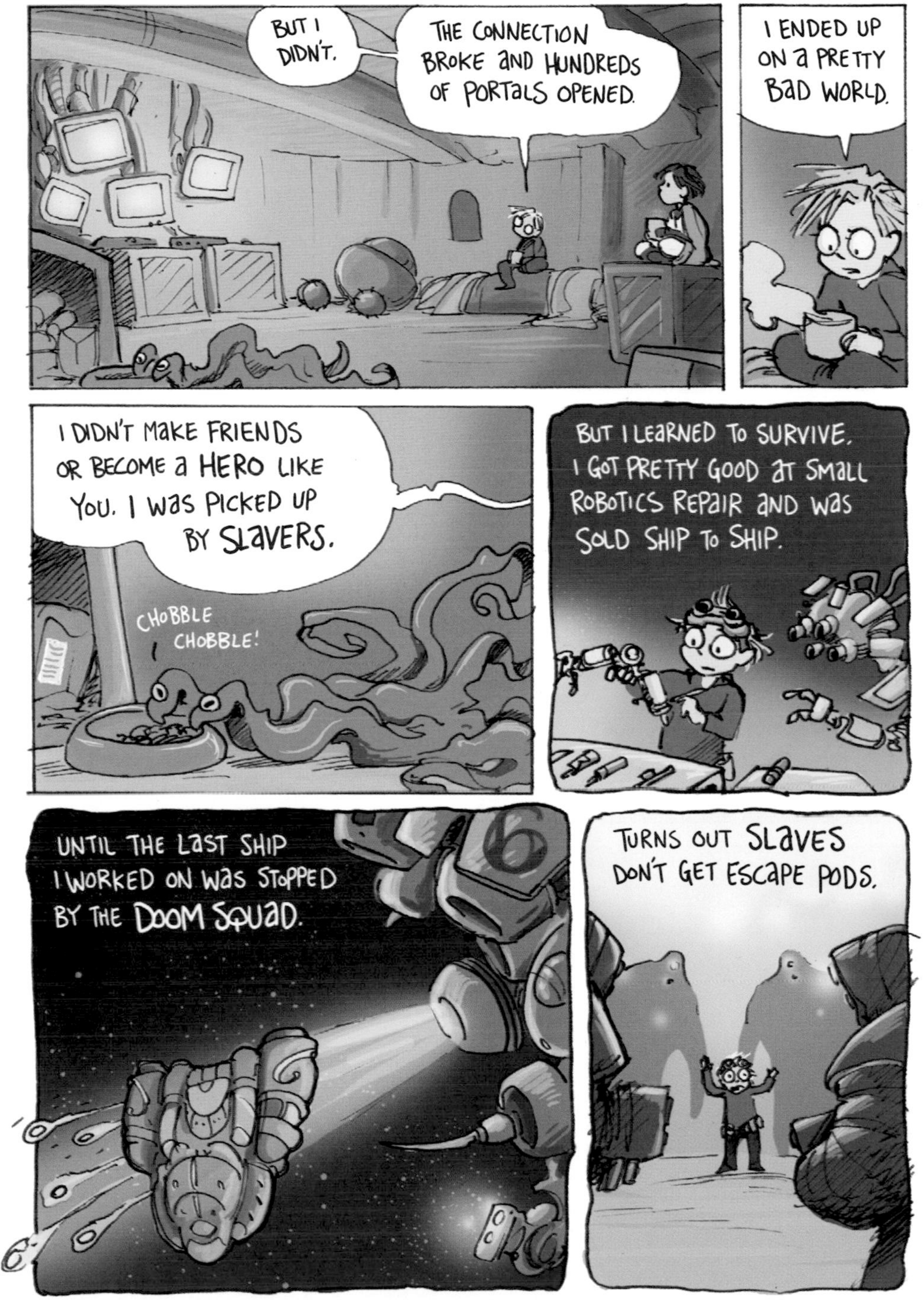

BUT I DIDN'T.
THE CONNECTION BROKE AND HUNDREDS OF PORTALS OPENED.
I ENDED UP ON A PRETTY BAD WORLD.
I DIDN'T MAKE FRIENDS OR BECOME A HERO LIKE YOU. I WAS PICKED UP BY SLAVERS.
CHOBBLE CHOBBLE!
BUT I LEARNED TO SURVIVE. I GOT PRETTY GOOD AT SMALL ROBOTICS REPAIR AND WAS SOLD SHIP TO SHIP.
UNTIL THE LAST SHIP I WORKED ON WAS STOPPED BY THE DOOM SQUAD.
TURNS OUT SLAVES DON'T GET ESCAPE PODS.

I ENDED UP IN ONE OF THE DEEP CELLS, AND THAT'S WHERE I FOUND FOUR.

OR WHAT WAS LEFT OF HIM.

AND THEN WHAT? HOW DID YOU GET—

YAWN!

JOSEPH?

Z

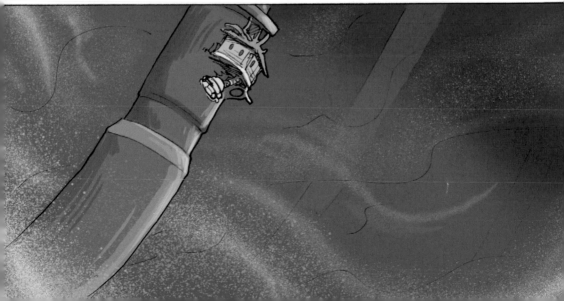

Chapter
Five

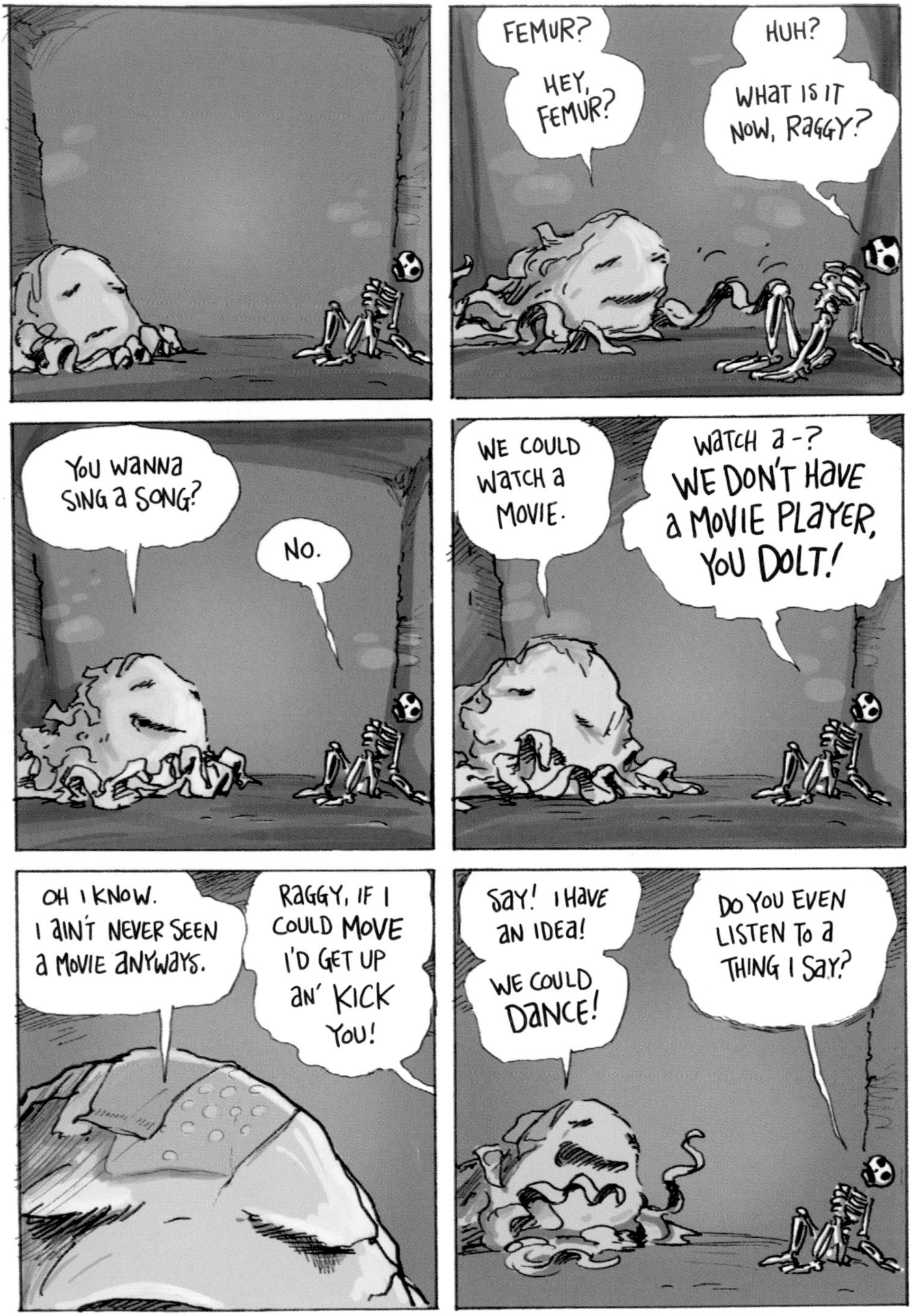
FEMUR?
HEY, FEMUR?
HUH?
WHAT IS IT NOW, RAGGY?
YOU WANNA SING A SONG?
NO.
WE COULD WATCH A MOVIE.
WATCH A -? WE DON'T HAVE A MOVIE PLAYER, YOU DOLT!
OH I KNOW. I AIN'T NEVER SEEN A MOVIE ANYWAYS.
RAGGY, IF I COULD MOVE I'D GET UP AN' KICK YOU!
SAY! I HAVE AN IDEA!
WE COULD DANCE!
DO YOU EVEN LISTEN TO A THING I SAY?

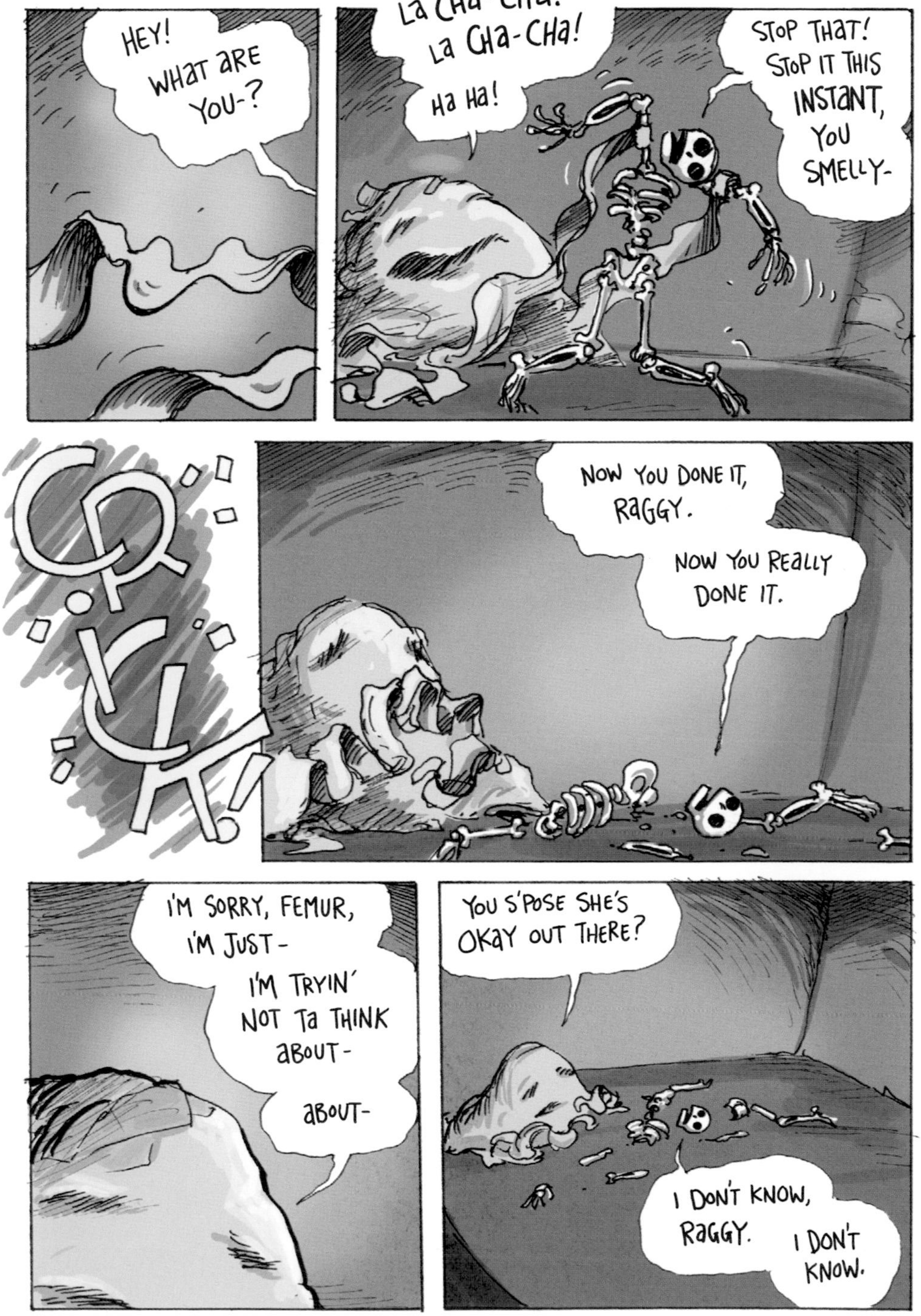
HEY! WHAT ARE YOU-?
LA CHA-CHA! LA CHA-CHA!
HA HA!
STOP THAT! STOP IT THIS INSTANT, YOU SMELLY-
CRICK!
NOW YOU DONE IT, RAGGY.
NOW YOU REALLY DONE IT.
I'M SORRY, FEMUR, I'M JUST-
I'M TRYIN' NOT TA THINK ABOUT-
ABOUT-
YOU S'POSE SHE'S OKAY OUT THERE?
I DON'T KNOW, RAGGY.
I DON'T KNOW.

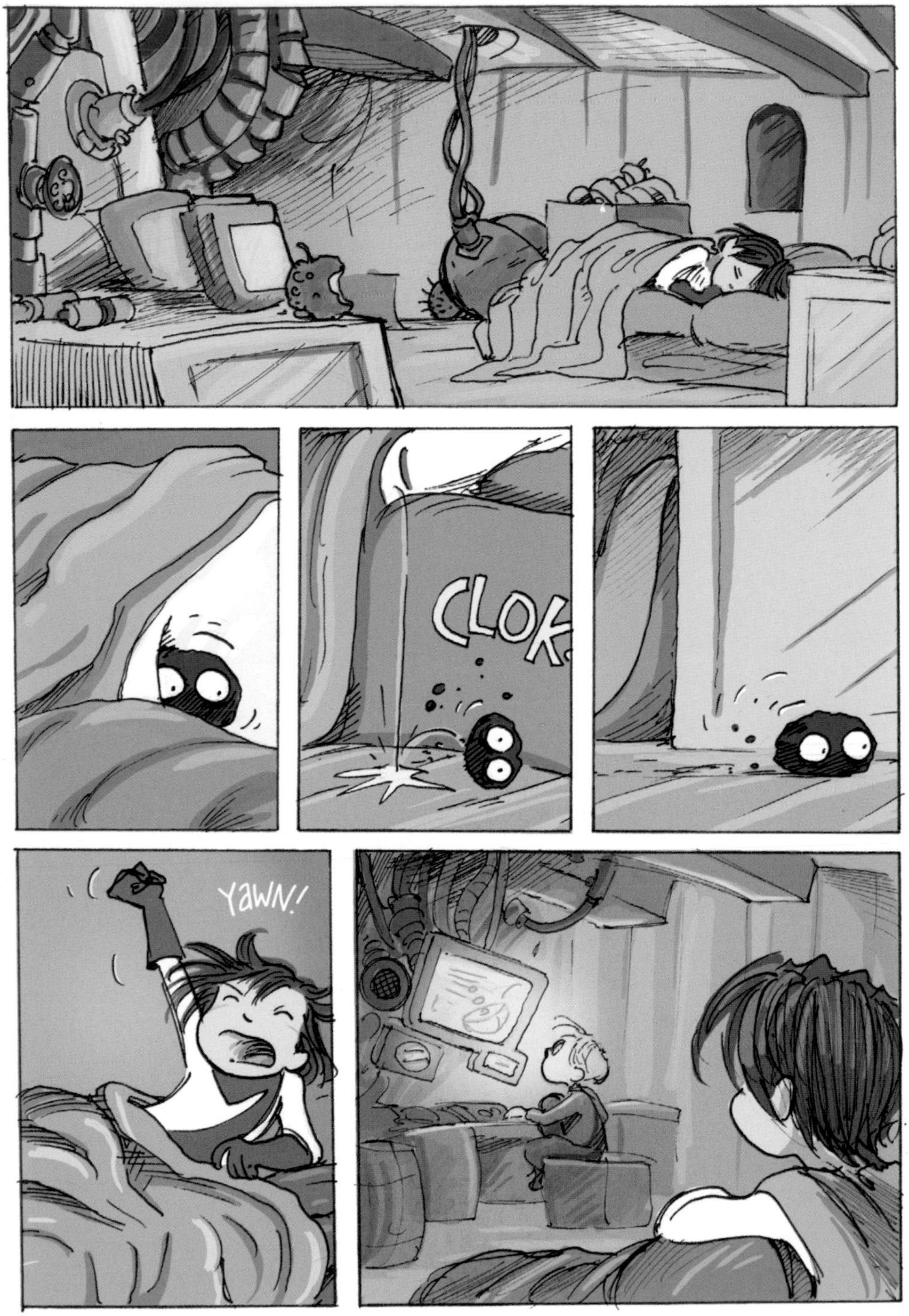
CLOK
YAWN!

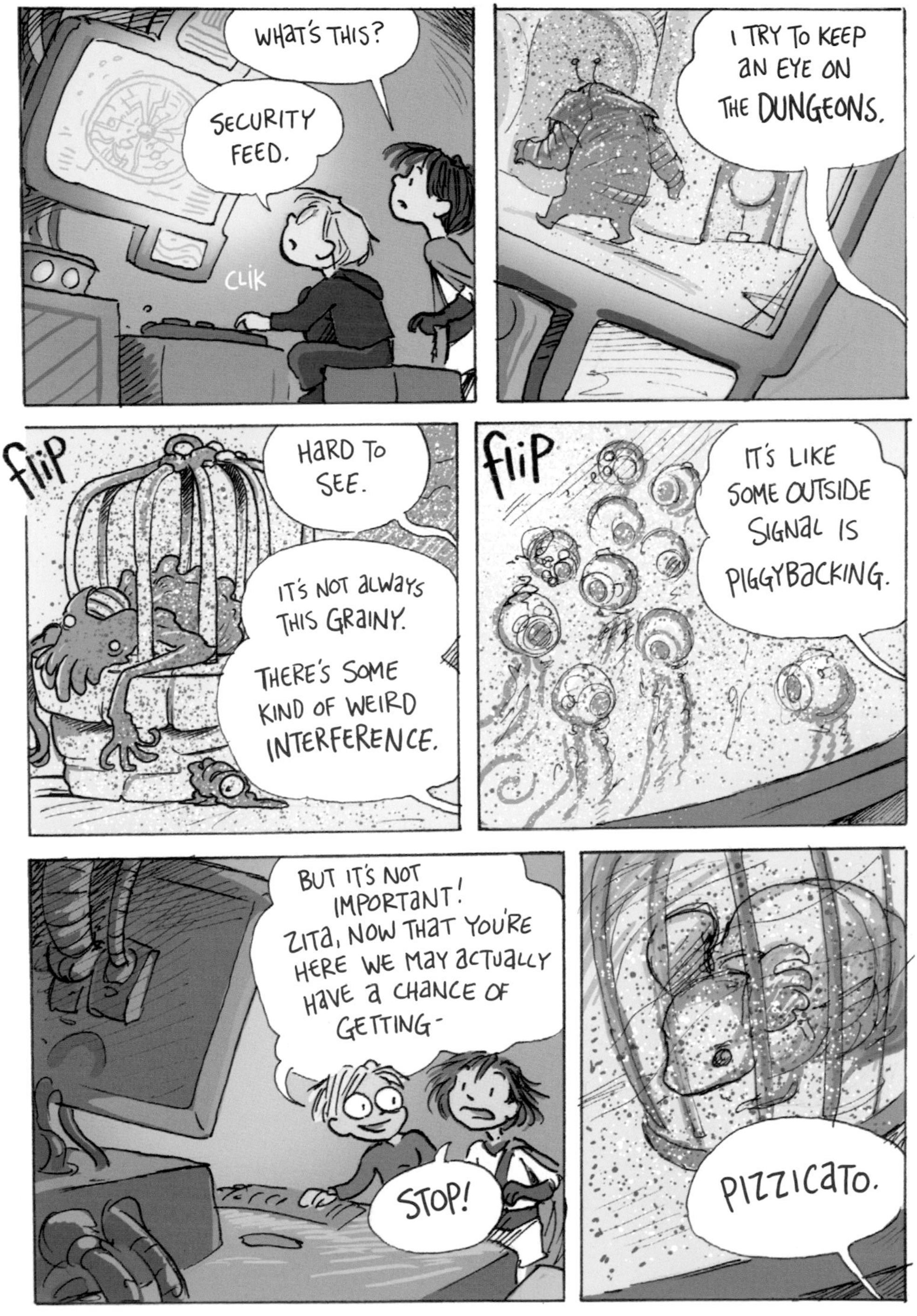
WHAT'S THIS?
SECURITY FEED.
CLIK
I TRY TO KEEP AN EYE ON THE DUNGEONS.
FLIP
HARD TO SEE.
IT'S NOT ALWAYS THIS GRAINY.
THERE'S SOME KIND OF WEIRD INTERFERENCE.
FLIP
IT'S LIKE SOME OUTSIDE SIGNAL IS PIGGYBACKING.
BUT IT'S NOT IMPORTANT! ZITA, NOW THAT YOU'RE HERE WE MAY ACTUALLY HAVE A CHANCE OF GETTING-
STOP!
PIZZICATO.

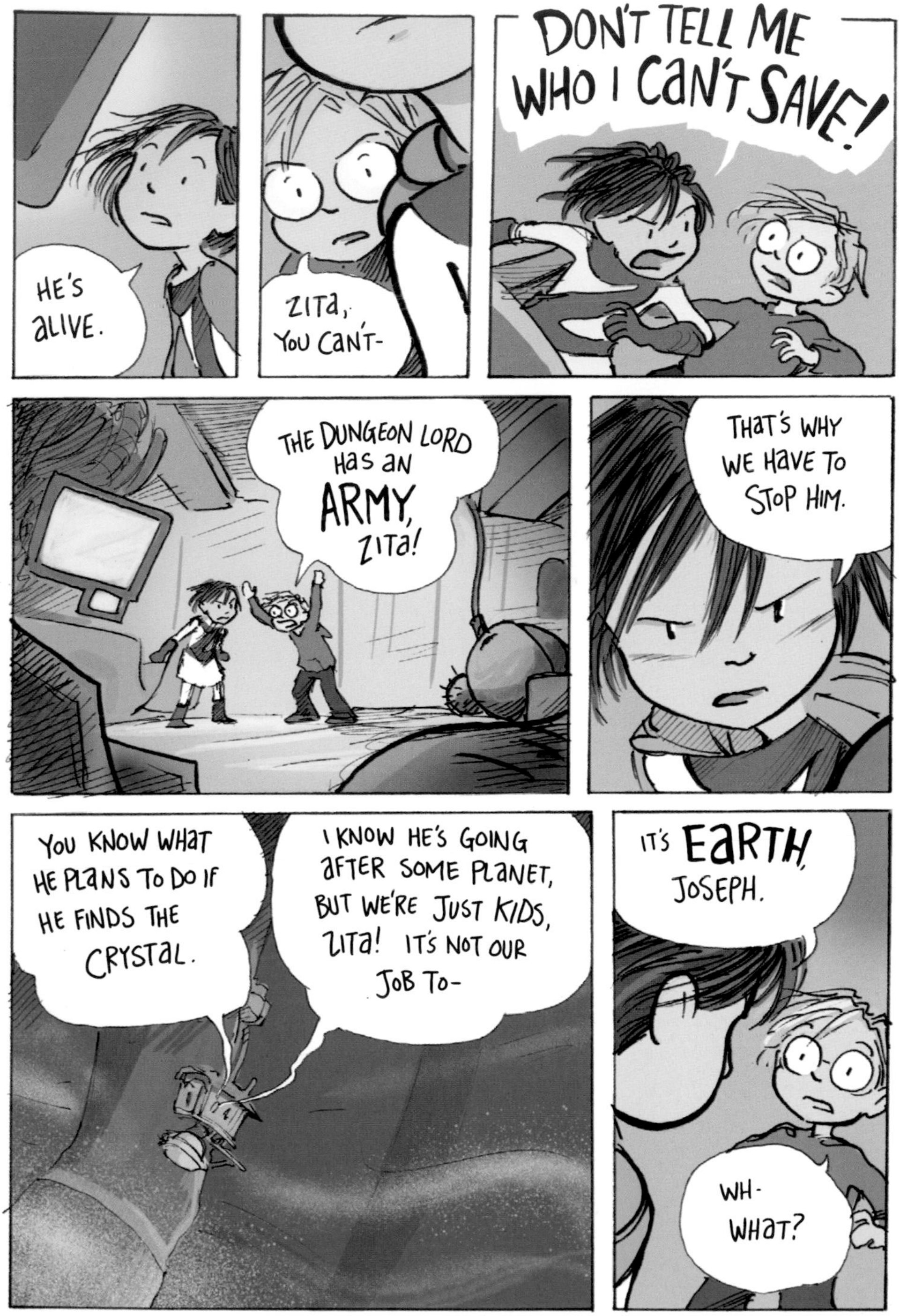
HE'S ALIVE.
ZITA, YOU CAN'T-
DON'T TELL ME WHO I CAN'T SAVE!
THE DUNGEON LORD HAS AN ARMY, ZITA!
THAT'S WHY WE HAVE TO STOP HIM.
YOU KNOW WHAT HE PLANS TO DO IF HE FINDS THE CRYSTAL.
I KNOW HE'S GOING AFTER SOME PLANET, BUT WE'RE JUST KIDS, ZITA! IT'S NOT OUR JOB TO-
IT'S EARTH, JOSEPH.
WH- WHAT?

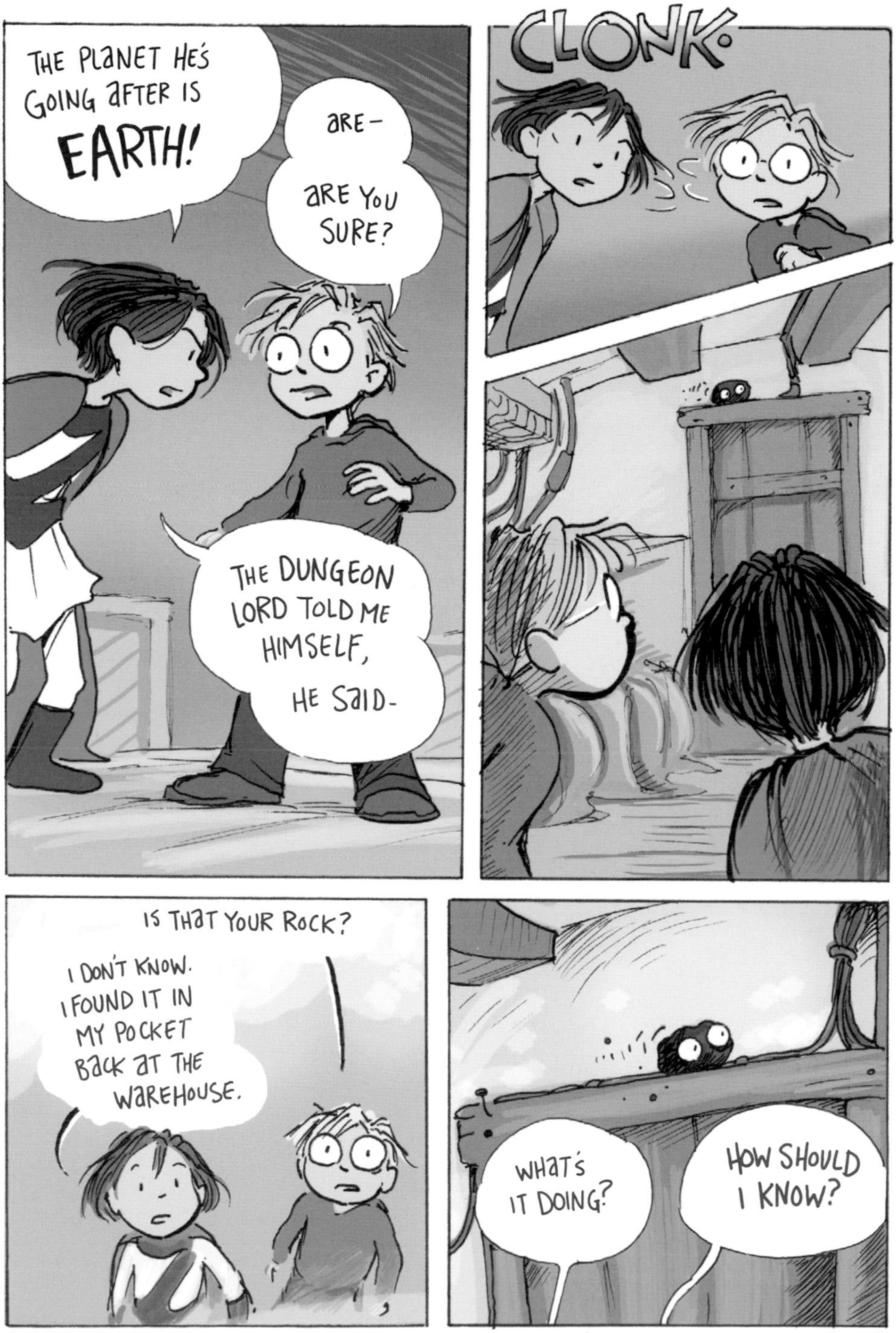
THE PLANET HE'S GOING AFTER IS EARTH!
ARE-
ARE YOU SURE?
THE DUNGEON LORD TOLD ME HIMSELF,
HE SAID-
CLONK.
IS THAT YOUR ROCK?
I DON'T KNOW. I FOUND IT IN MY POCKET BACK AT THE WAREHOUSE.
WHAT'S IT DOING?
HOW SHOULD I KNOW?

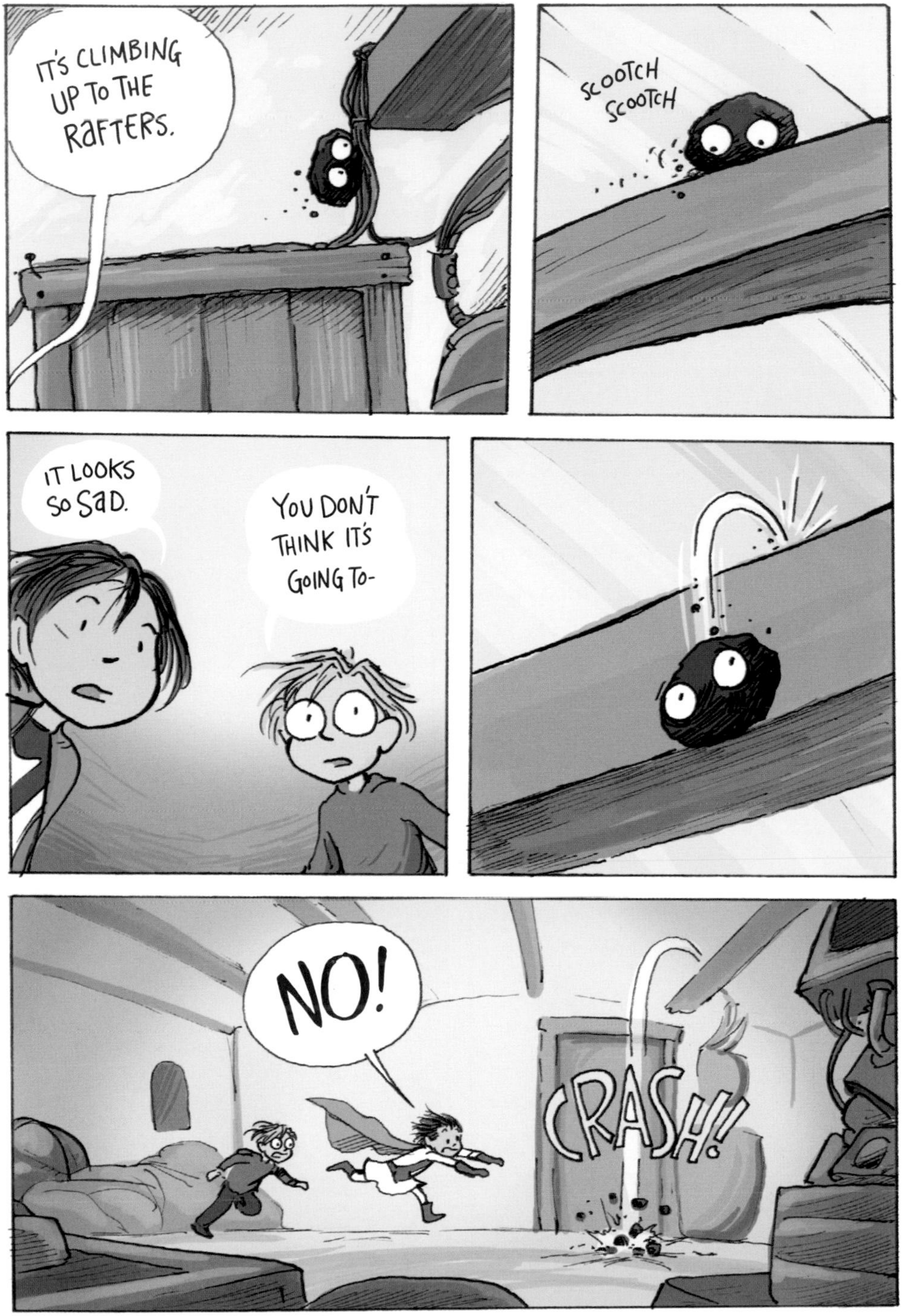
IT'S CLIMBING UP TO THE RAFTERS.
SCOOTCH SCOOTCH
IT LOOKS SO SAD.
YOU DON'T THINK IT'S GOING TO-
NO!
CRASH!

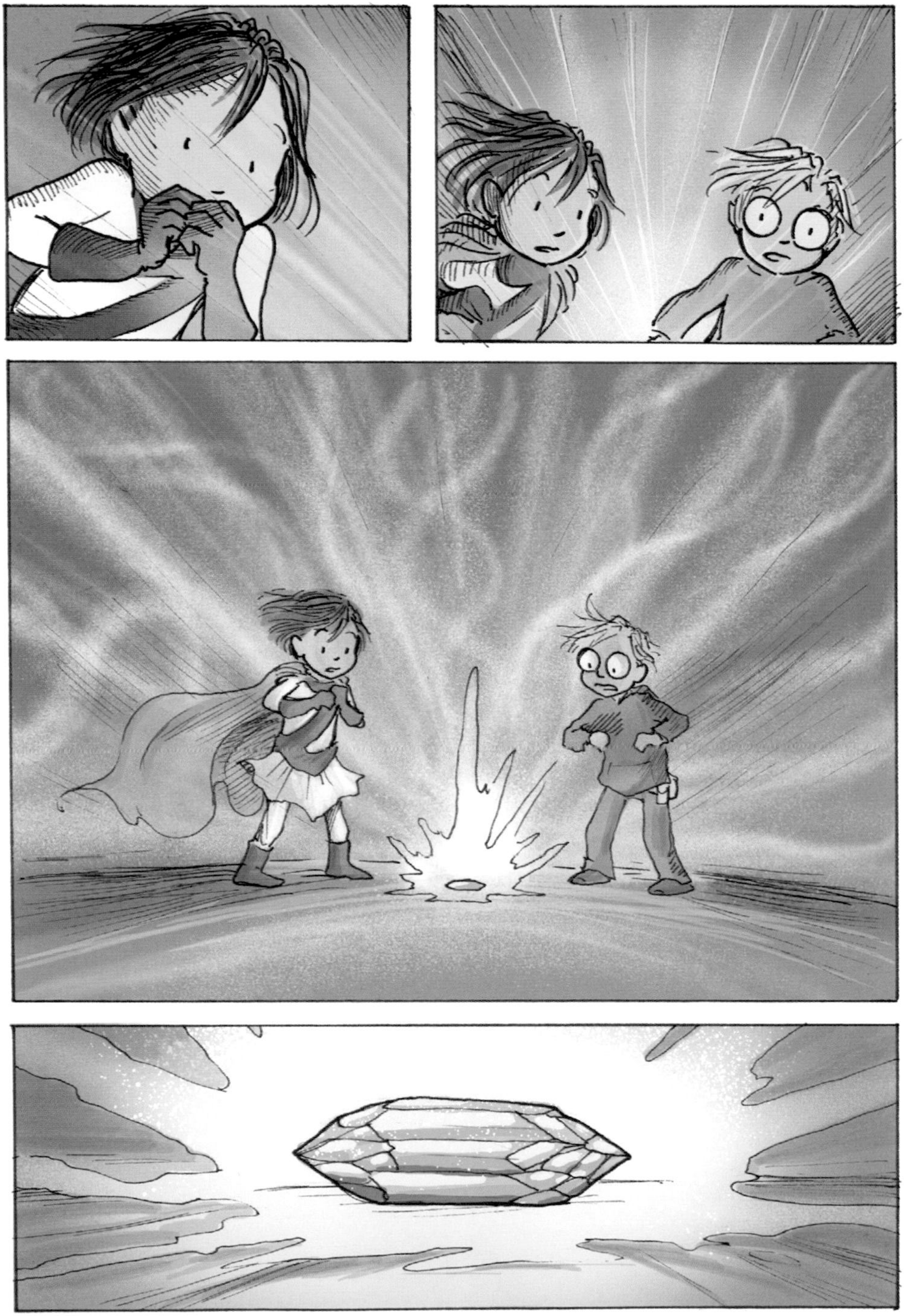

IT MUST HAVE SLIPPED ITSELF INTO MY POCKET.

I THINK IT CHOSE ME.

DO YOU KNOW WHAT THIS MEANS?

WE CAN GO HOME! WE CAN GO RIGHT NOW AND THE DUNGEON LORD WON'T BE ABLE TO FOLLOW!

WAS IT BECAUSE I TRIED TO HELP THAT OTHER PRISONER?

OR—

BECAUSE I WAS TRYING TO SAVE—

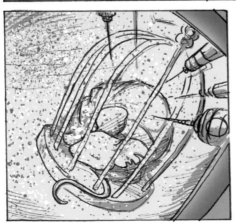

NO.

WHAT?

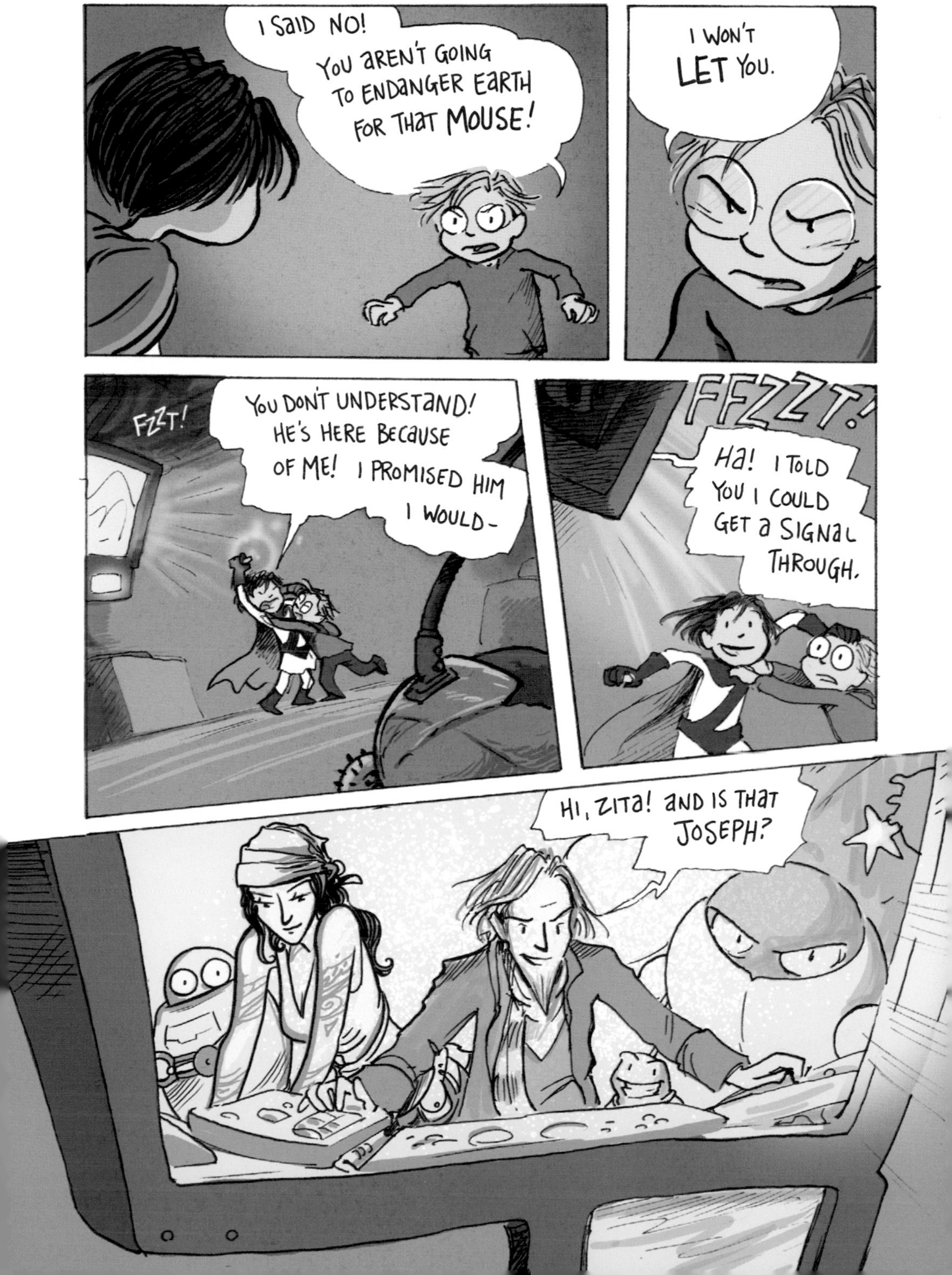
I SaID NO!
YOU aREN'T GOING TO ENDaNGER EaRTH FOR THaT MOUSE!
I WON'T LET YOU.
FZZT!
YOU DON'T UNDERSTaND! HE'S HERE BECaUSE OF ME! I PROMISED HIM I WOULD-
FFZZZT!
Ha! I TOLD YOU I COULD GET a SIGNaL THROUGH.
HI, ZITa! aND IS THaT JOSEPH?

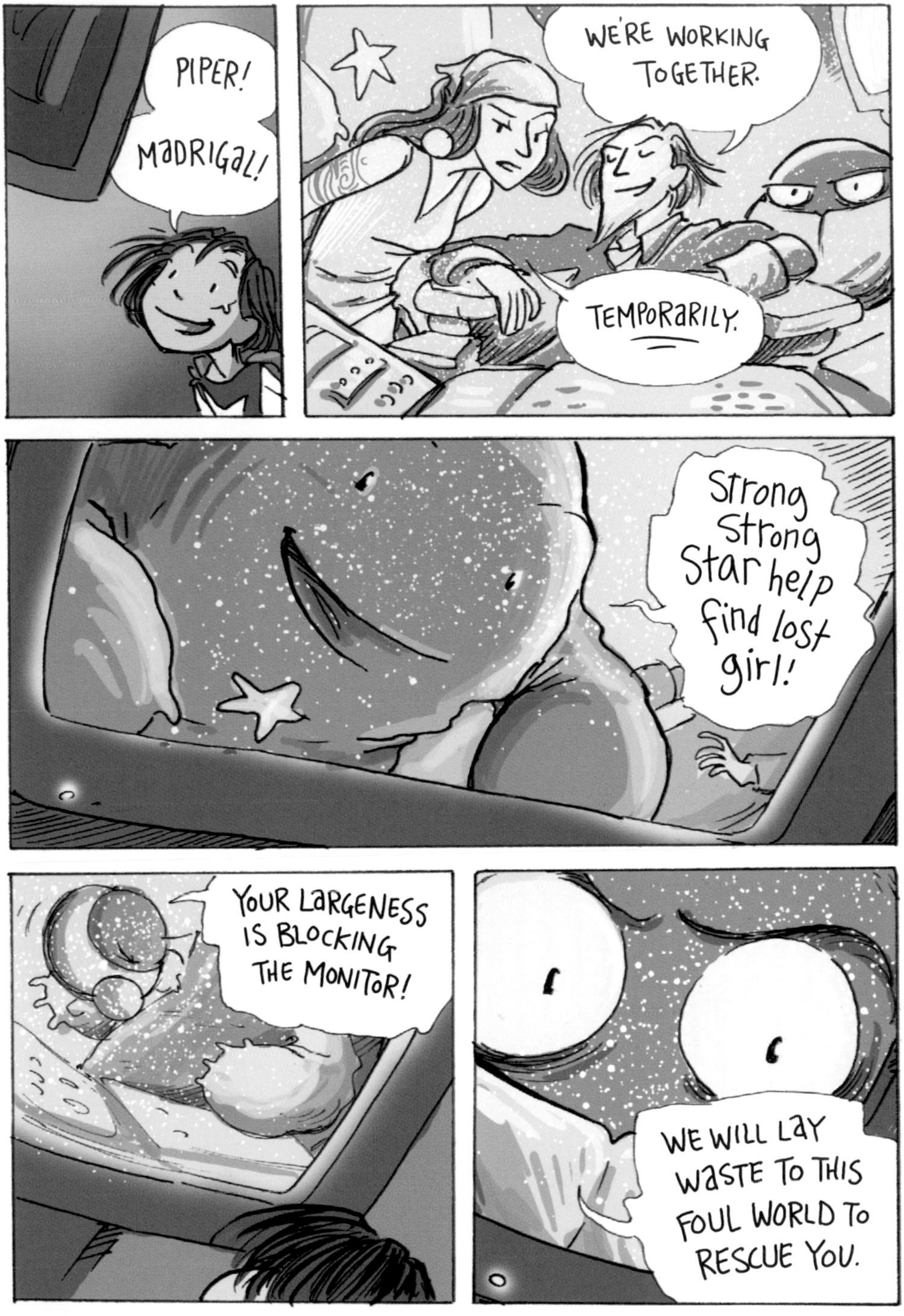
PIPER!
MADRIGAL!
WE'RE WORKING TOGETHER.
TEMPORARILY.
Strong Strong Star help find lost girl!
YOUR LARGENESS IS BLOCKING THE MONITOR!
WE WILL LAY WASTE TO THIS FOUL WORLD TO RESCUE YOU.

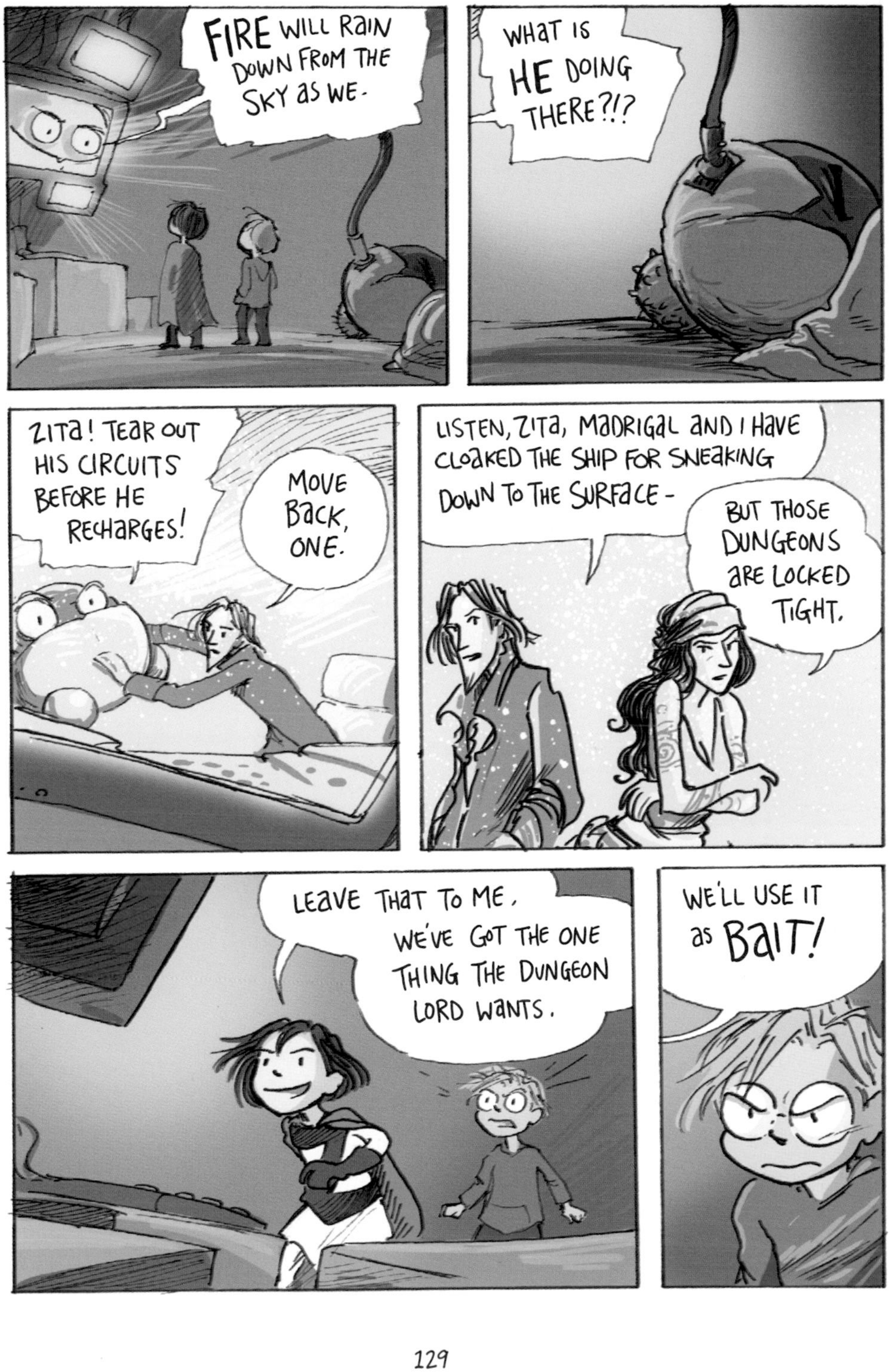
FIRE WILL RAIN DOWN FROM THE SKY AS WE-
WHAT IS HE DOING THERE?!?
ZITA! TEAR OUT HIS CIRCUITS BEFORE HE RECHARGES!
MOVE BACK, ONE.
LISTEN, ZITA, MADRIGAL AND I HAVE CLOAKED THE SHIP FOR SNEAKING DOWN TO THE SURFACE-
BUT THOSE DUNGEONS ARE LOCKED TIGHT.
LEAVE THAT TO ME.
WE'VE GOT THE ONE THING THE DUNGEON LORD WANTS.
WE'LL USE IT AS BAIT!

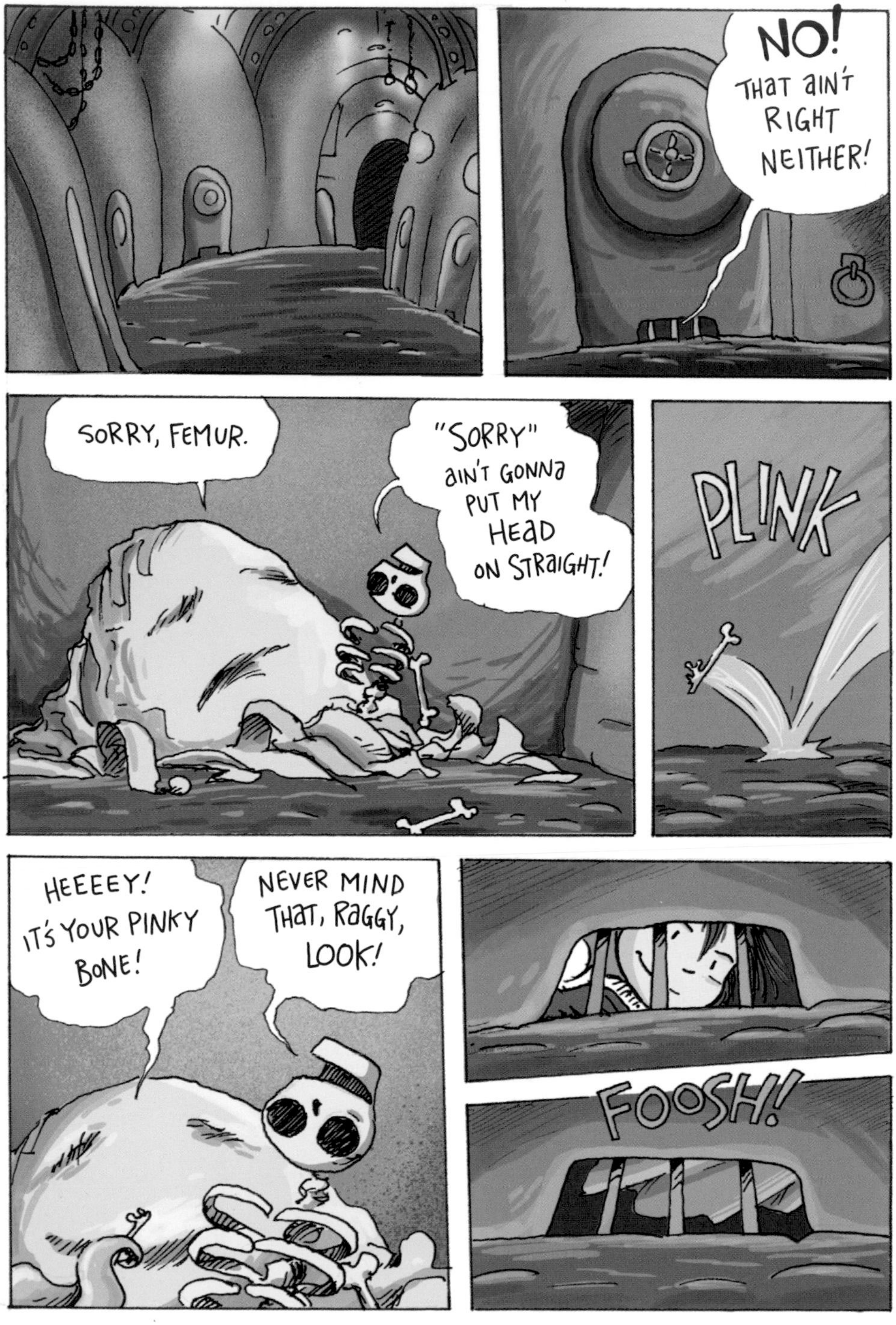
NO! THAT AIN'T RIGHT NEITHER!
SORRY, FEMUR.
"SORRY" AIN'T GONNA PUT MY HEAD ON STRAIGHT!
PLINK
HEEEEY! IT'S YOUR PINKY BONE!
NEVER MIND THAT, RAGGY, LOOK!
FOOSH!

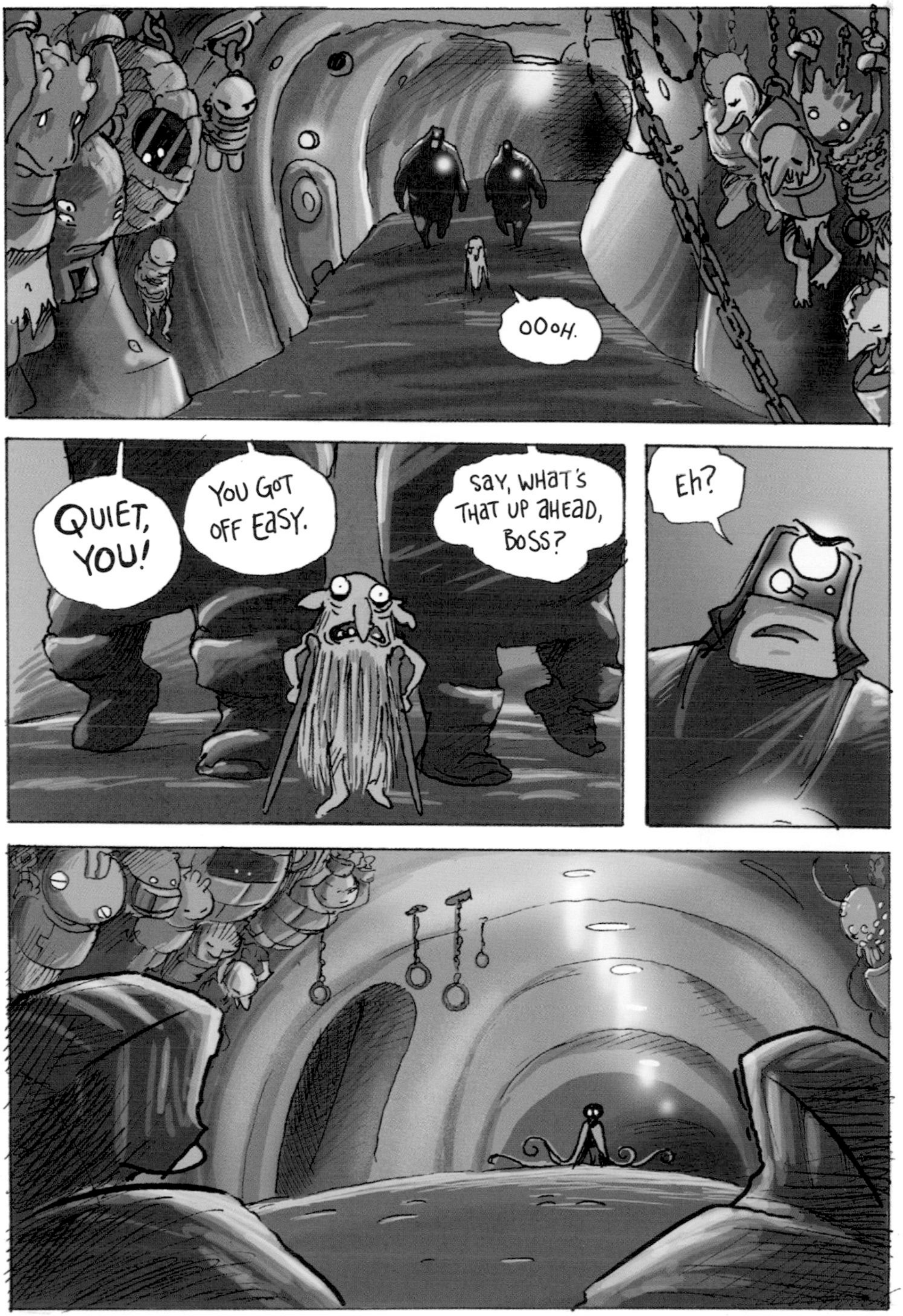
OOOH.
QUIET, YOU!
YOU GOT OFF EASY.
SAY, WHAT'S THAT UP AHEAD, BOSS?
EH?

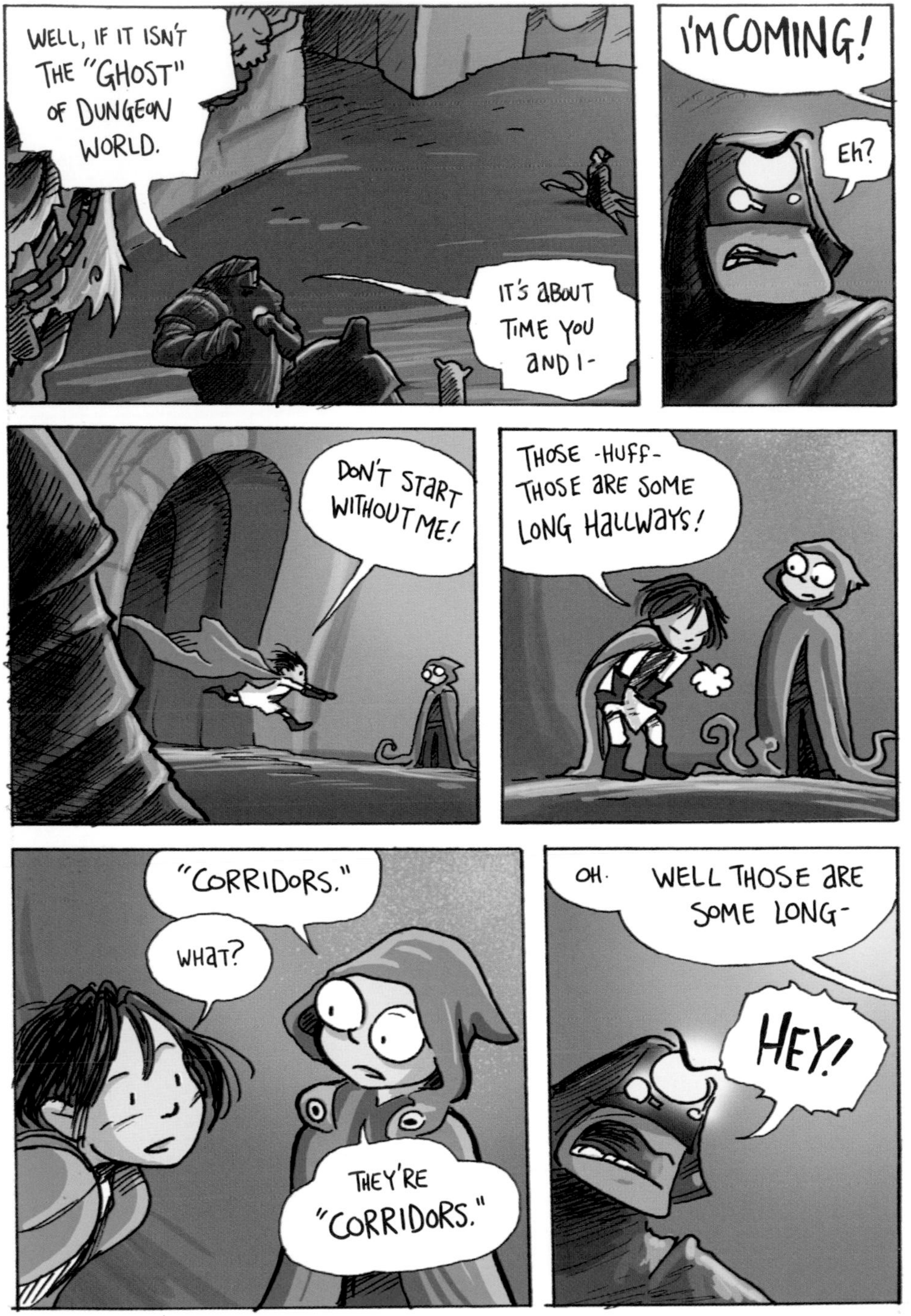

WELL, IF IT ISN'T THE "GHOST" OF DUNGEON WORLD.
IT'S ABOUT TIME YOU AND I-
I'M COMING!
EH?
DON'T START WITHOUT ME!
THOSE -HUFF- THOSE ARE SOME LONG HALLWAYS!
"CORRIDORS."
WHAT?
THEY'RE "CORRIDORS."
OH.
WELL THOSE ARE SOME LONG-
HEY!

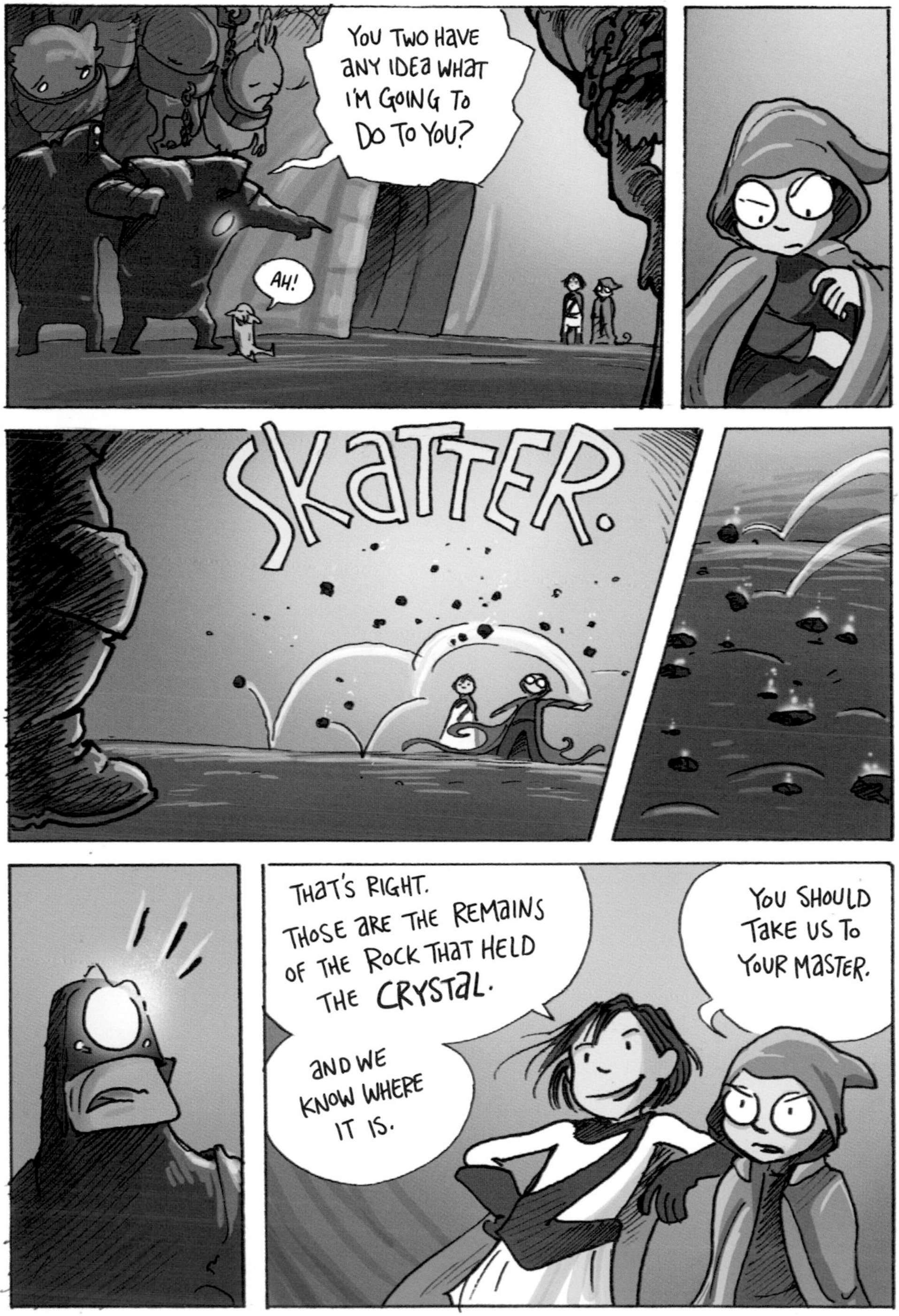
YOU TWO HAVE ANY IDEA WHAT I'M GOING TO DO TO YOU?
AH!
SKATTER.
THAT'S RIGHT. THOSE ARE THE REMAINS OF THE ROCK THAT HELD THE CRYSTAL.
AND WE KNOW WHERE IT IS.
YOU SHOULD TAKE US TO YOUR MASTER.

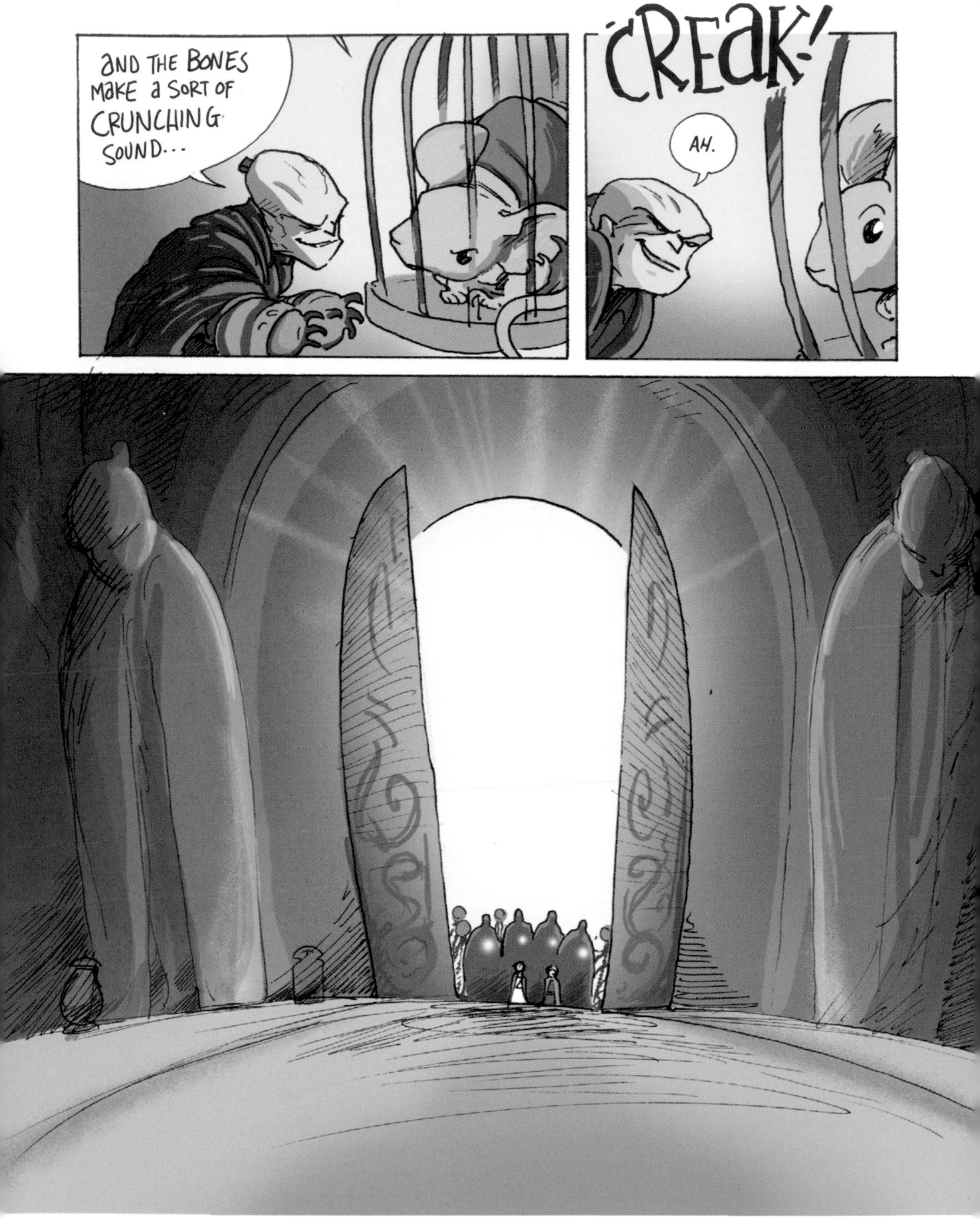
AND THE BONES MAKE A SORT OF CRUNCHING SOUND...
CREAK!
AH.

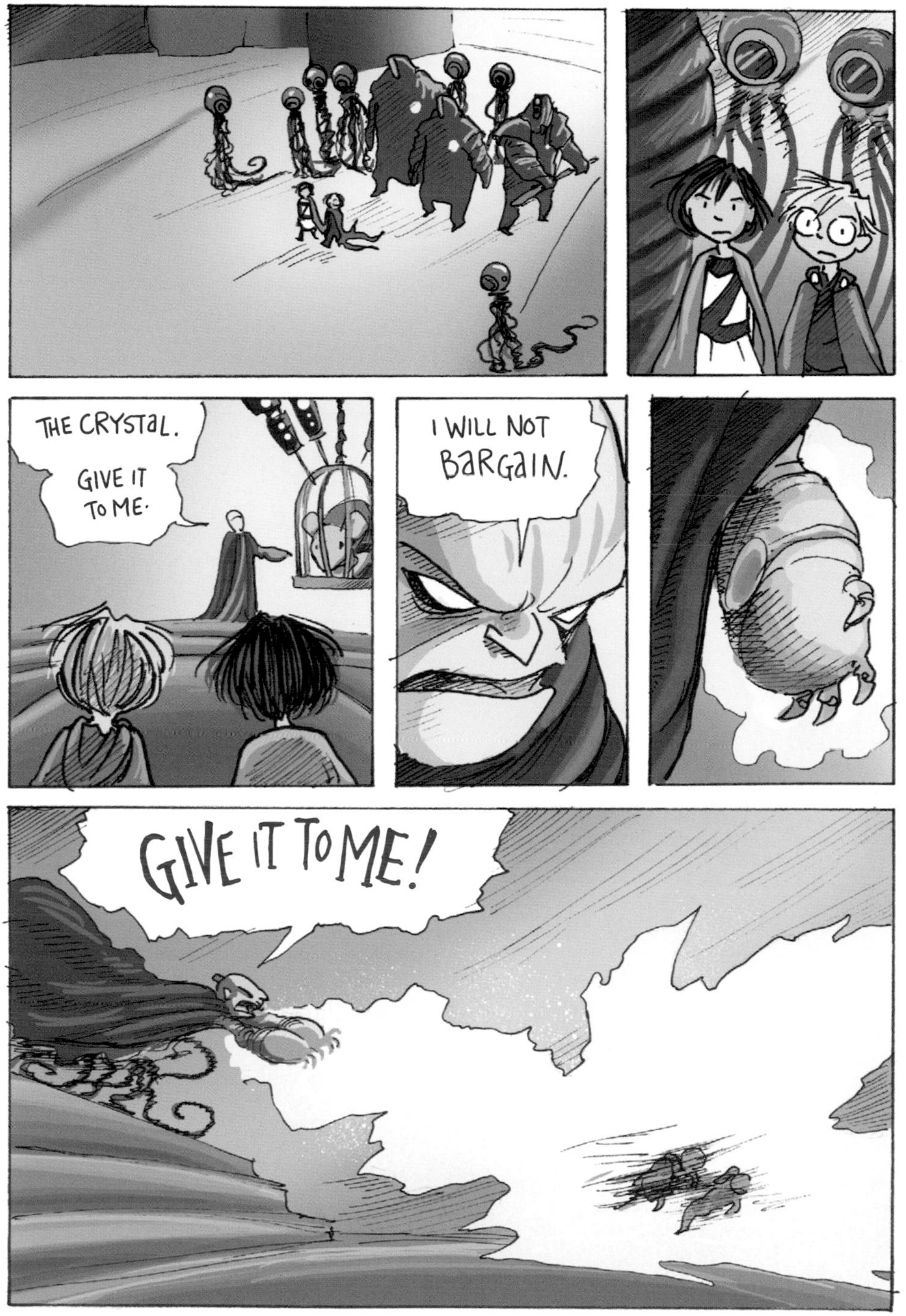
THE CRYSTAL.
GIVE IT TO ME.
I WILL NOT BARGAIN.
GIVE IT TO ME!

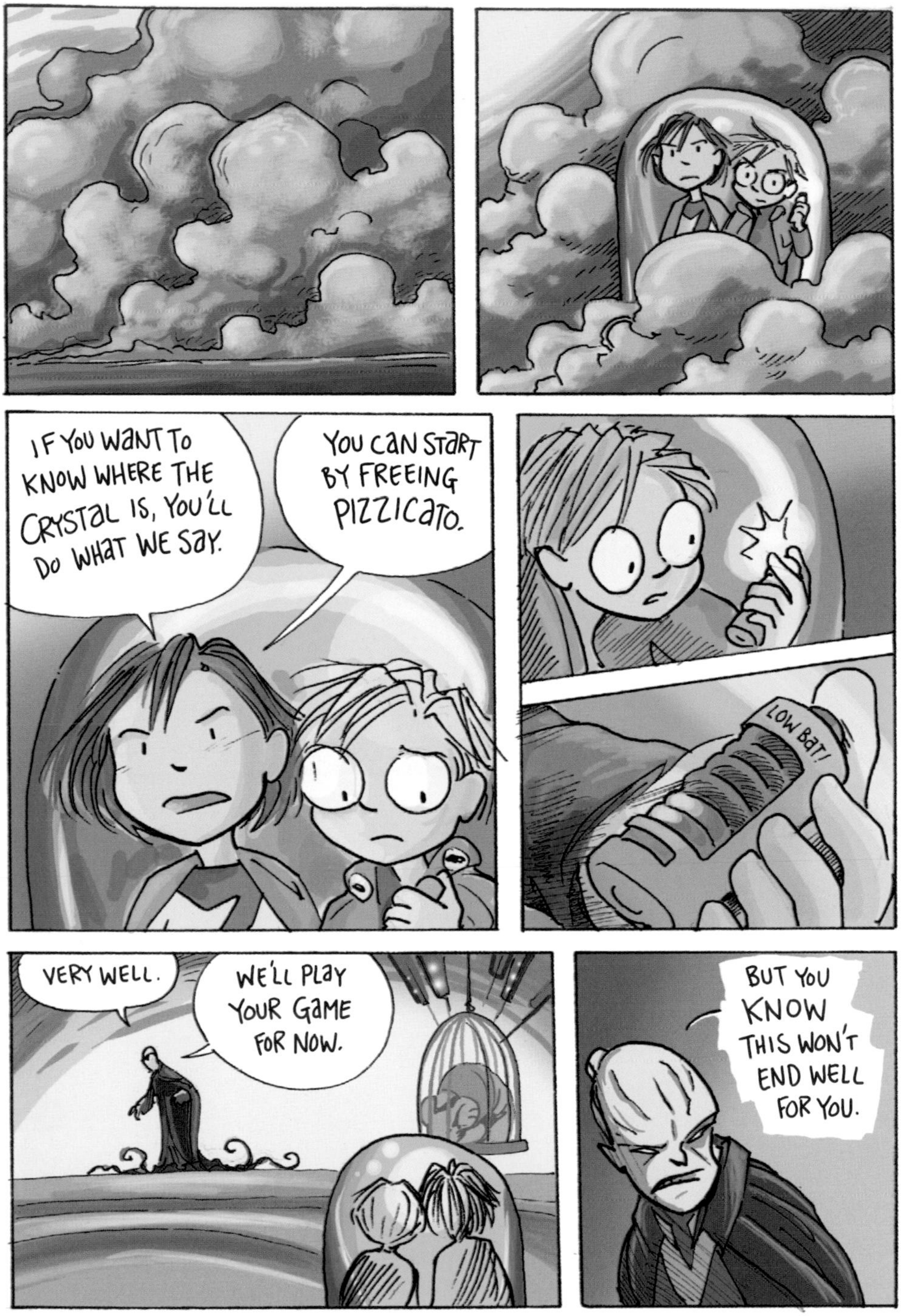
IF YOU WANT TO KNOW WHERE THE CRYSTAL IS, YOU'LL DO WHAT WE SAY.
YOU CAN START BY FREEING PIZZICATO.
LOW BAT!
VERY WELL.
WE'LL PLAY YOUR GAME FOR NOW.
BUT YOU KNOW THIS WON'T END WELL FOR YOU.

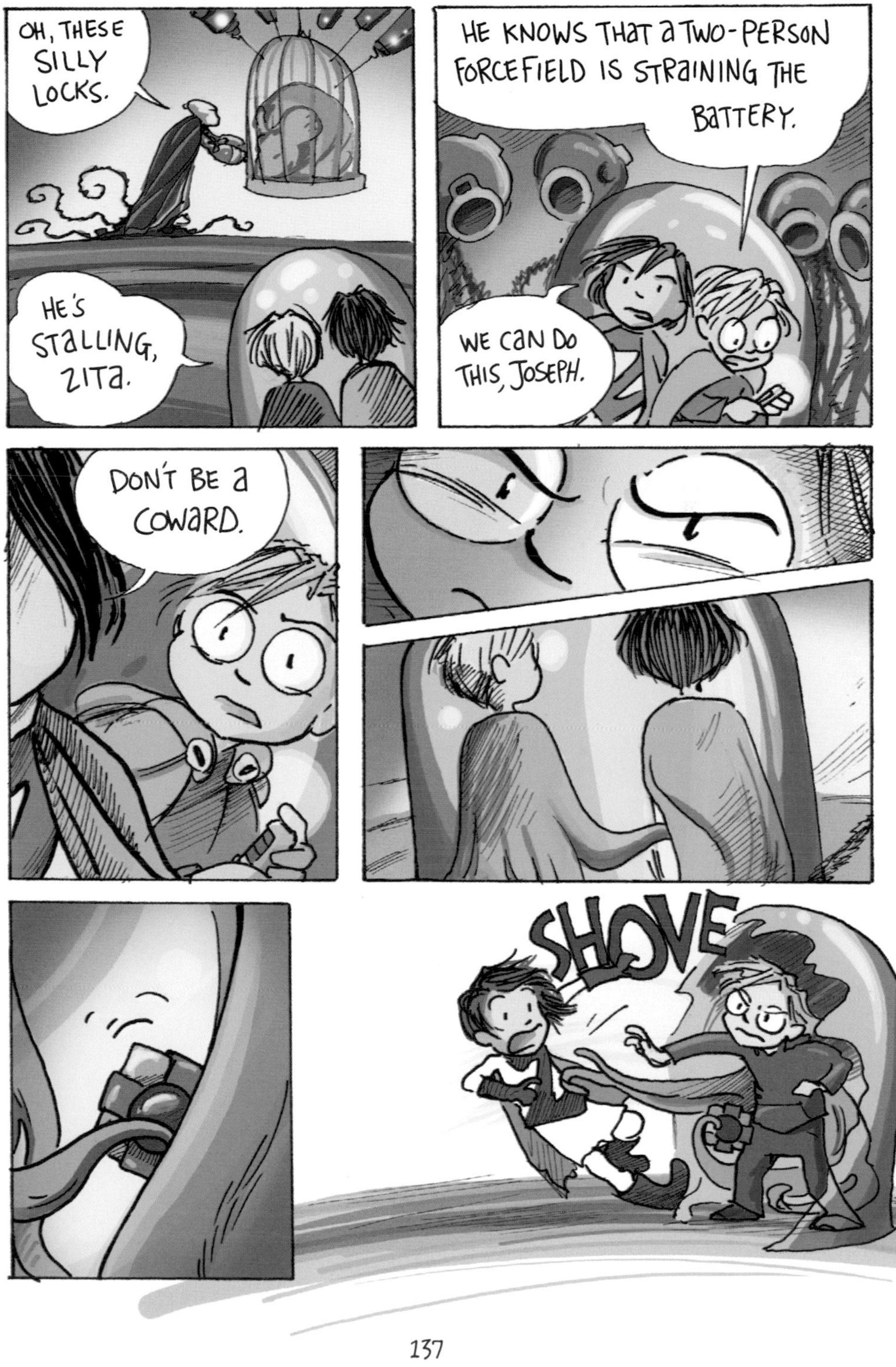
OH, THESE SILLY LOCKS.
HE'S STALLING, ZITA.
HE KNOWS THAT A TWO-PERSON FORCEFIELD IS STRAINING THE BATTERY.
WE CAN DO THIS, JOSEPH.
DON'T BE A COWARD.
SHOVE

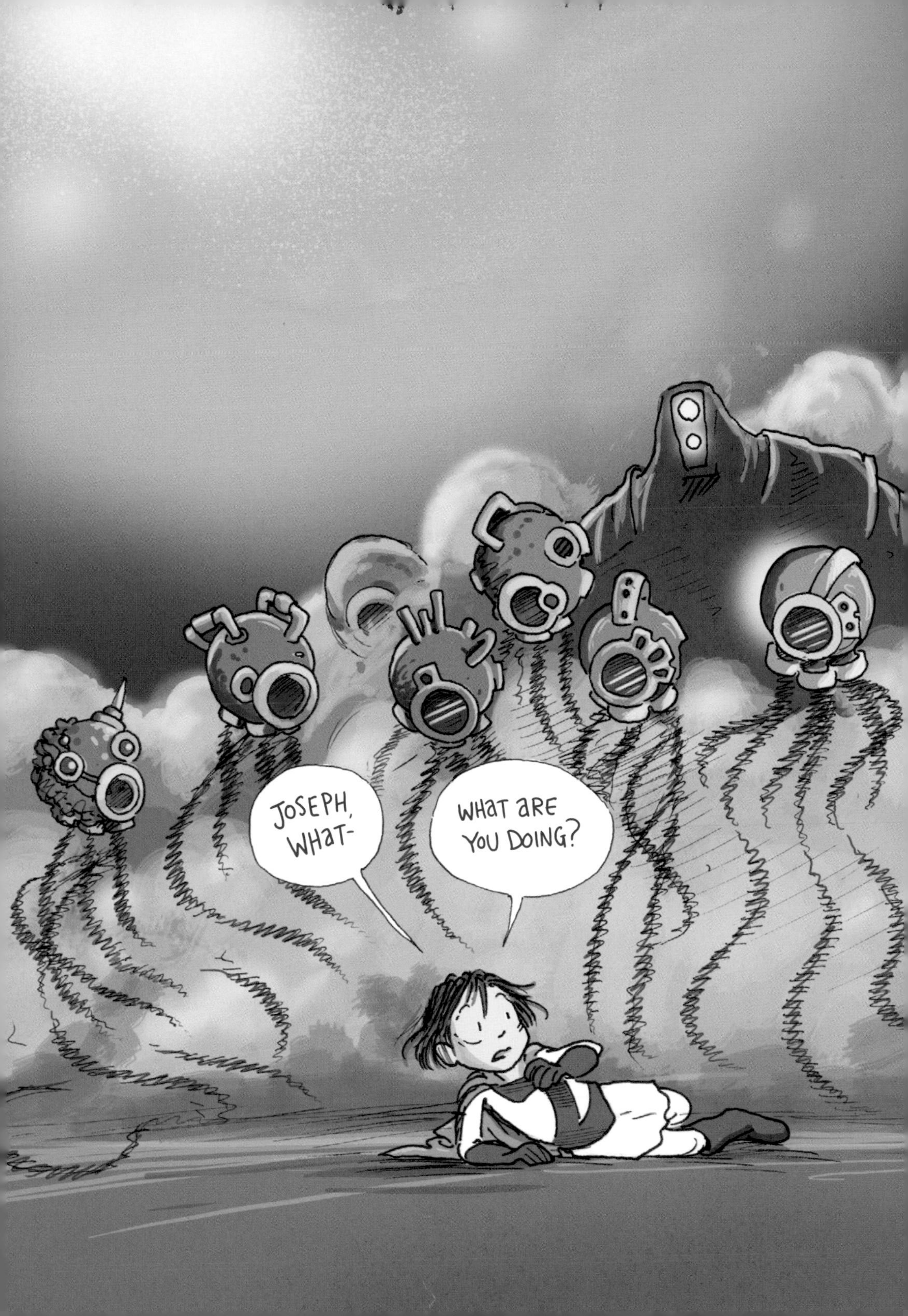
JOSEPH, WHAT-
WHAT ARE YOU DOING?

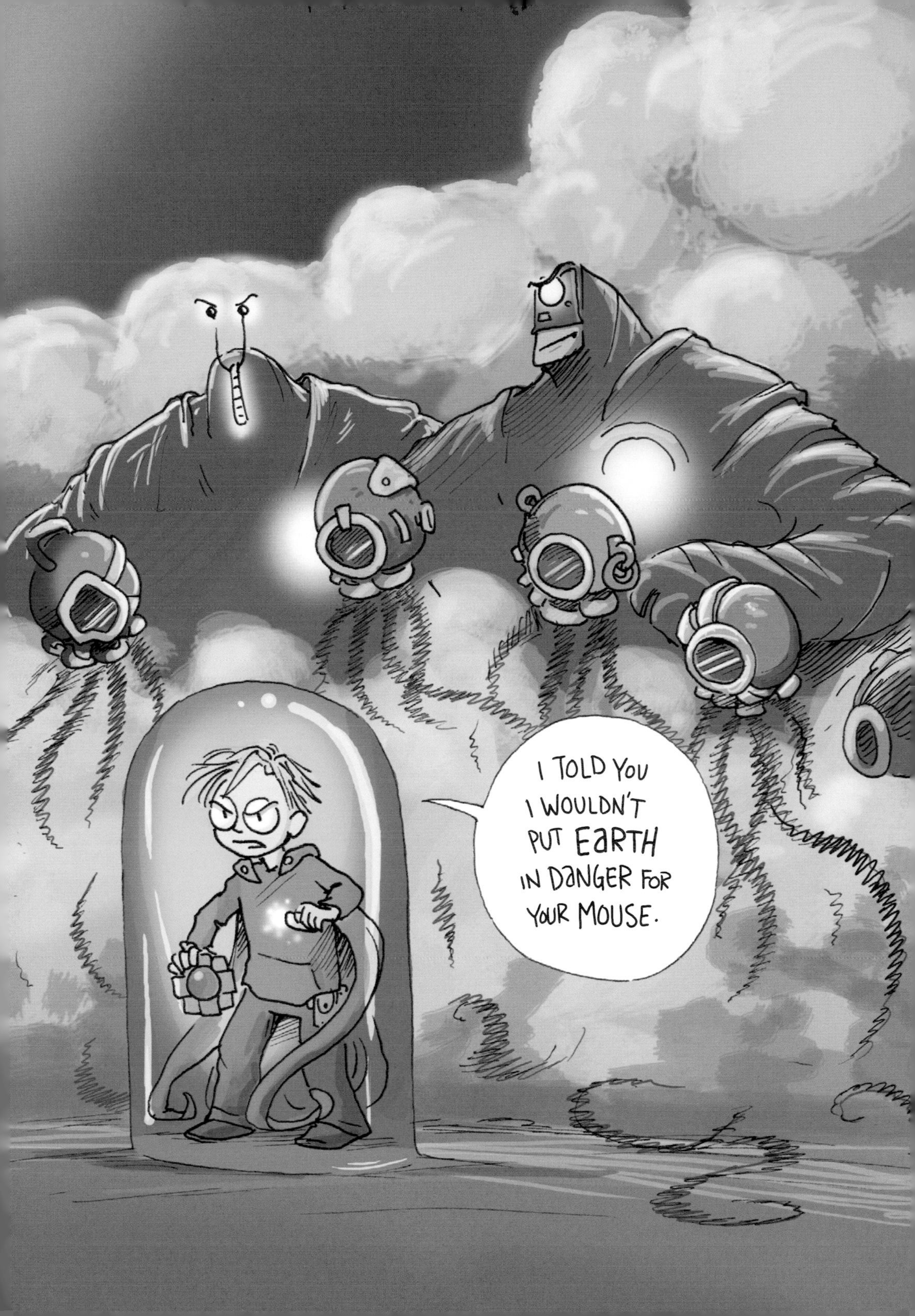
I TOLD YOU I WOULDN'T PUT EARTH IN DANGER FOR YOUR MOUSE.

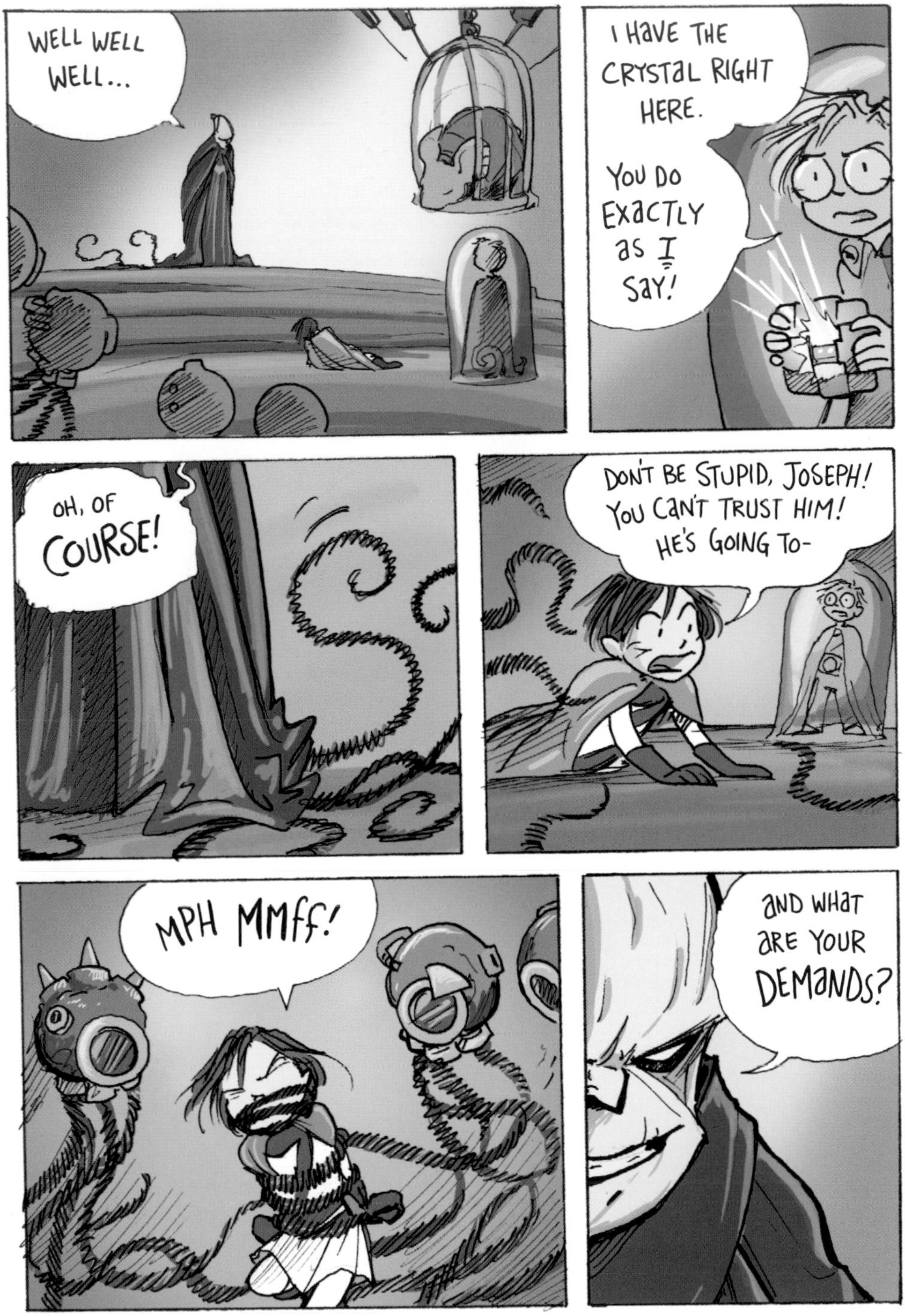
WELL WELL WELL...
I HAVE THE CRYSTAL RIGHT HERE.
YOU DO EXACTLY AS I SAY!
OH, OF COURSE!
DON'T BE STUPID, JOSEPH! YOU CAN'T TRUST HIM! HE'S GOING TO-
MPH MMFF!
AND WHAT ARE YOUR DEMANDS?

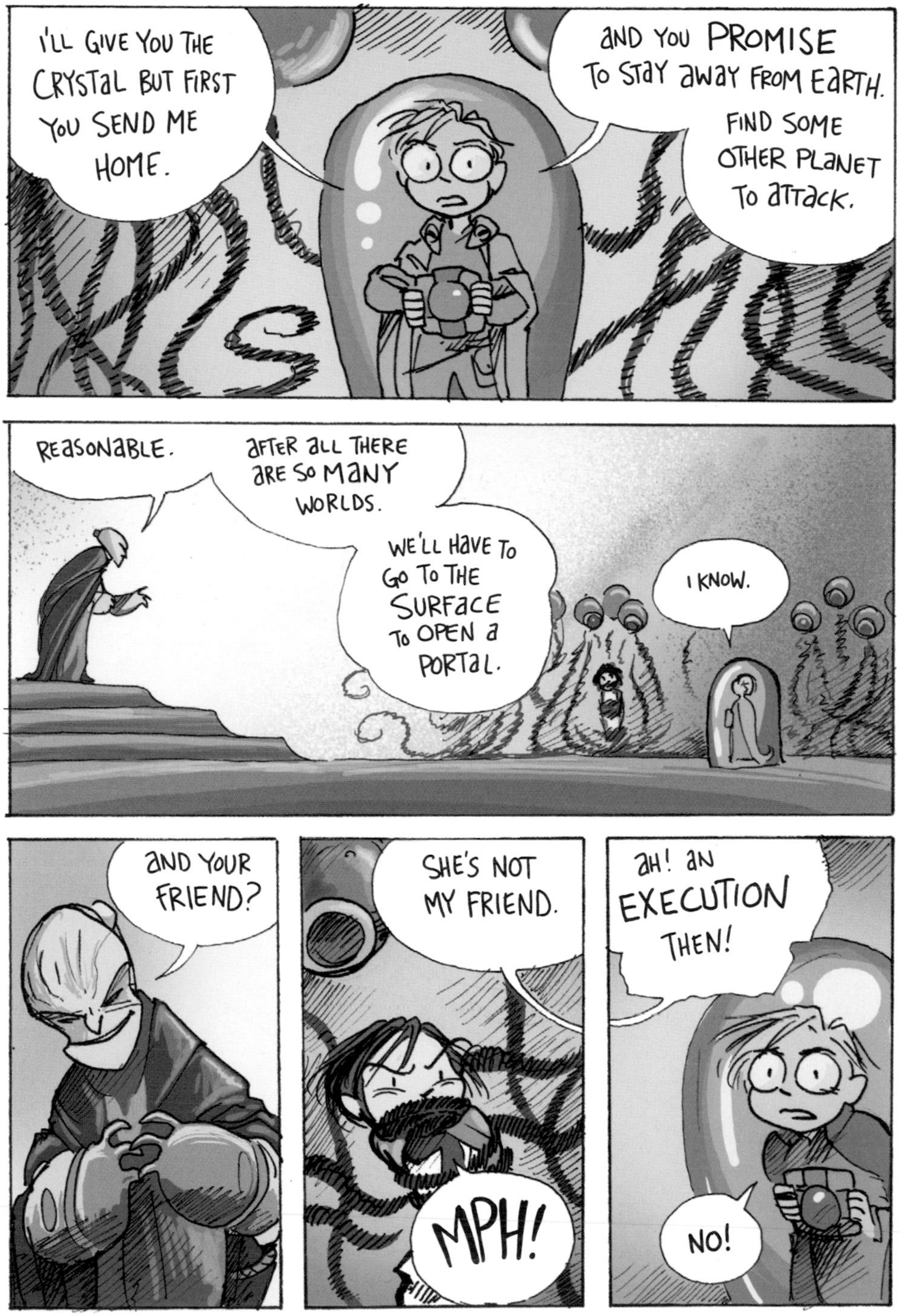
I'LL GIVE YOU THE CRYSTAL BUT FIRST YOU SEND ME HOME.
AND YOU PROMISE TO STAY AWAY FROM EARTH.
FIND SOME OTHER PLANET TO ATTACK.
REASONABLE.
AFTER ALL THERE ARE SO MANY WORLDS.
WE'LL HAVE TO GO TO THE SURFACE TO OPEN A PORTAL.
I KNOW.
AND YOUR FRIEND?
SHE'S NOT MY FRIEND.
MPH!
AH! AN EXECUTION THEN!
NO!

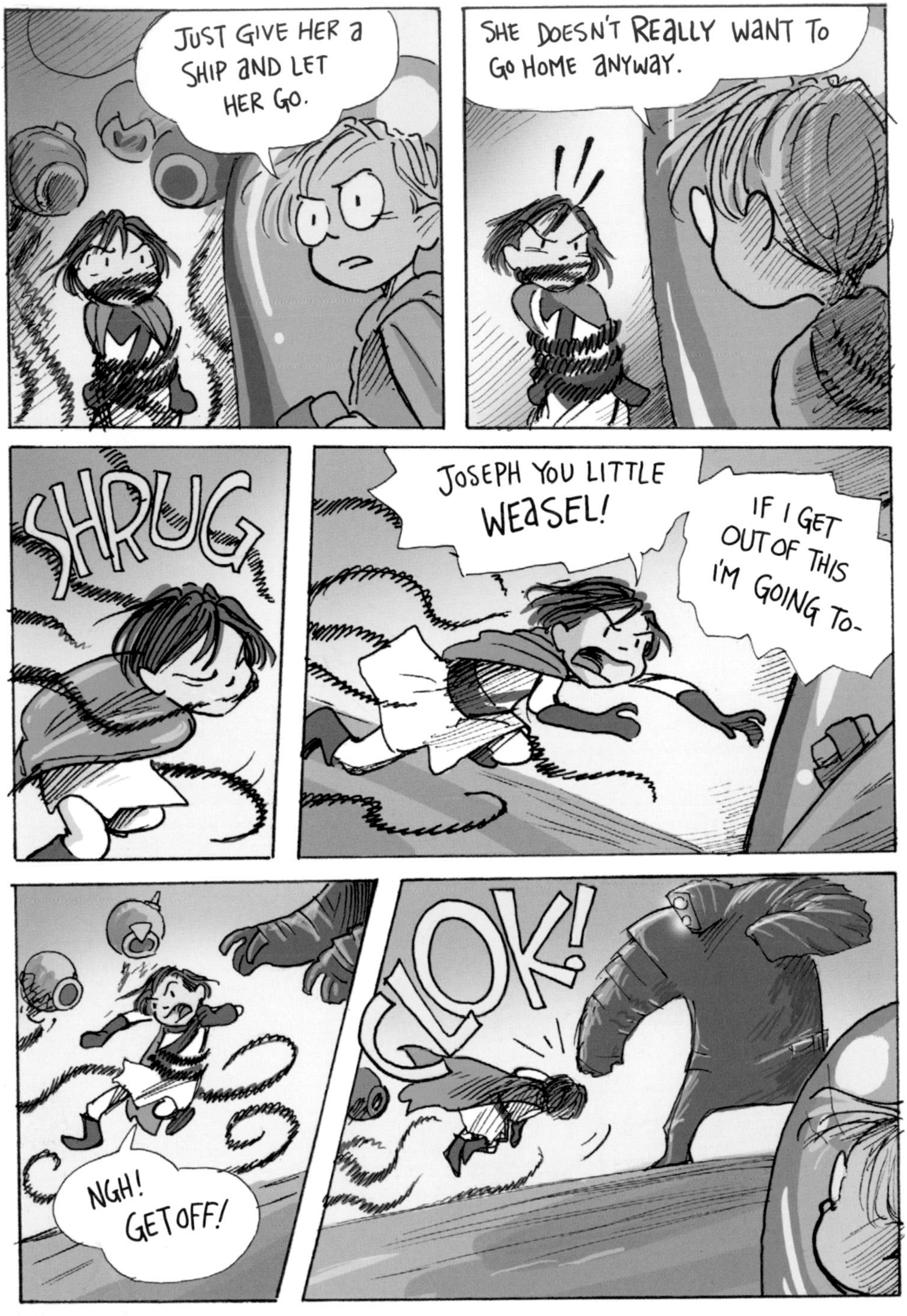
JUST GIVE HER A SHIP AND LET HER GO.
SHE DOESN'T REALLY WANT TO GO HOME ANYWAY.
SHRUG
JOSEPH YOU LITTLE WEASEL!
IF I GET OUT OF THIS I'M GOING TO-
NGH! GET OFF!
CLOK!

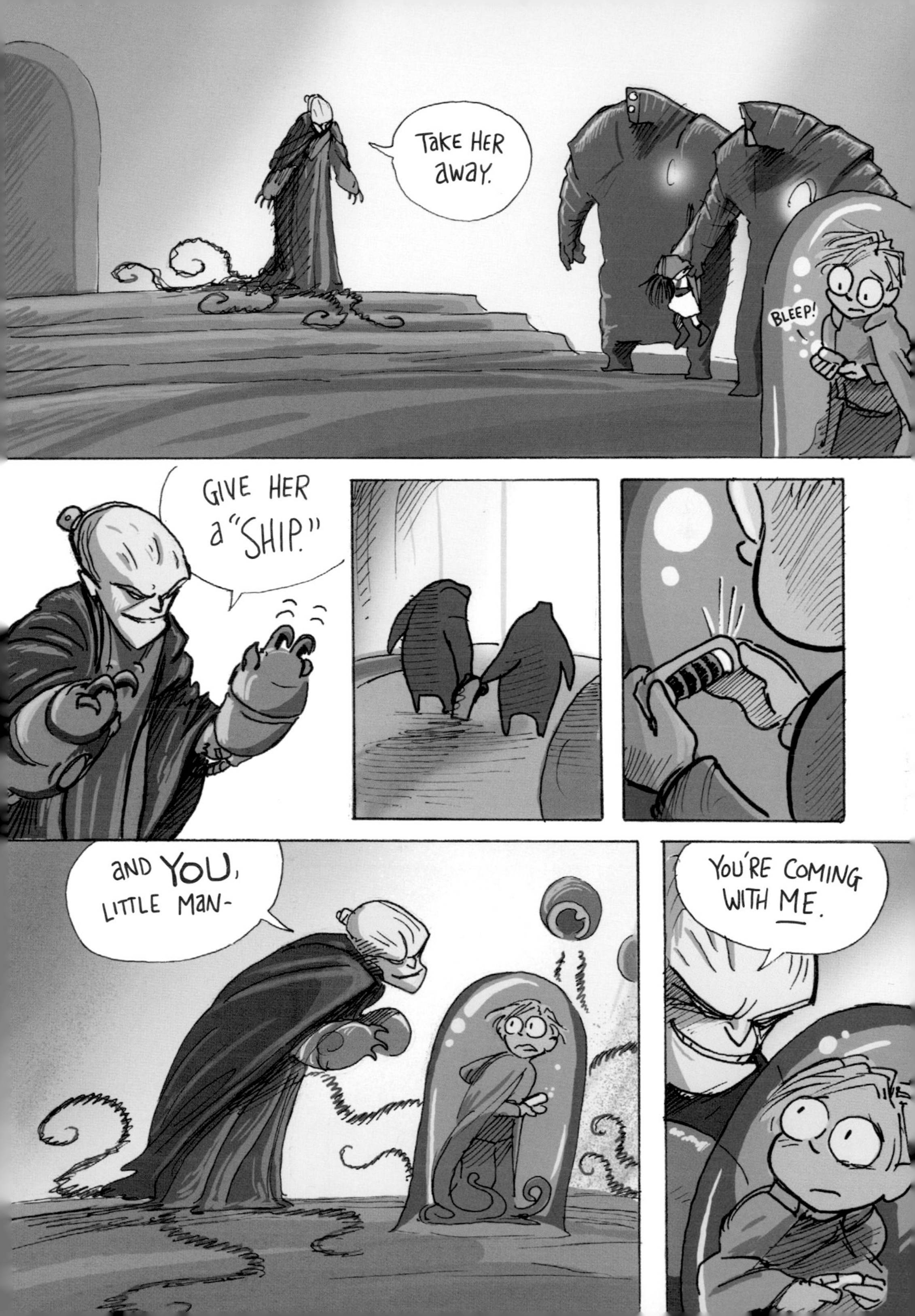
TAKE HER away.
BLEEP!
GIVE HER a "SHIP."
and YOU, LITTLE MAN-
YOU'RE COMING WITH ME.

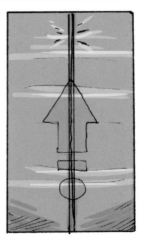

Chapter
Six

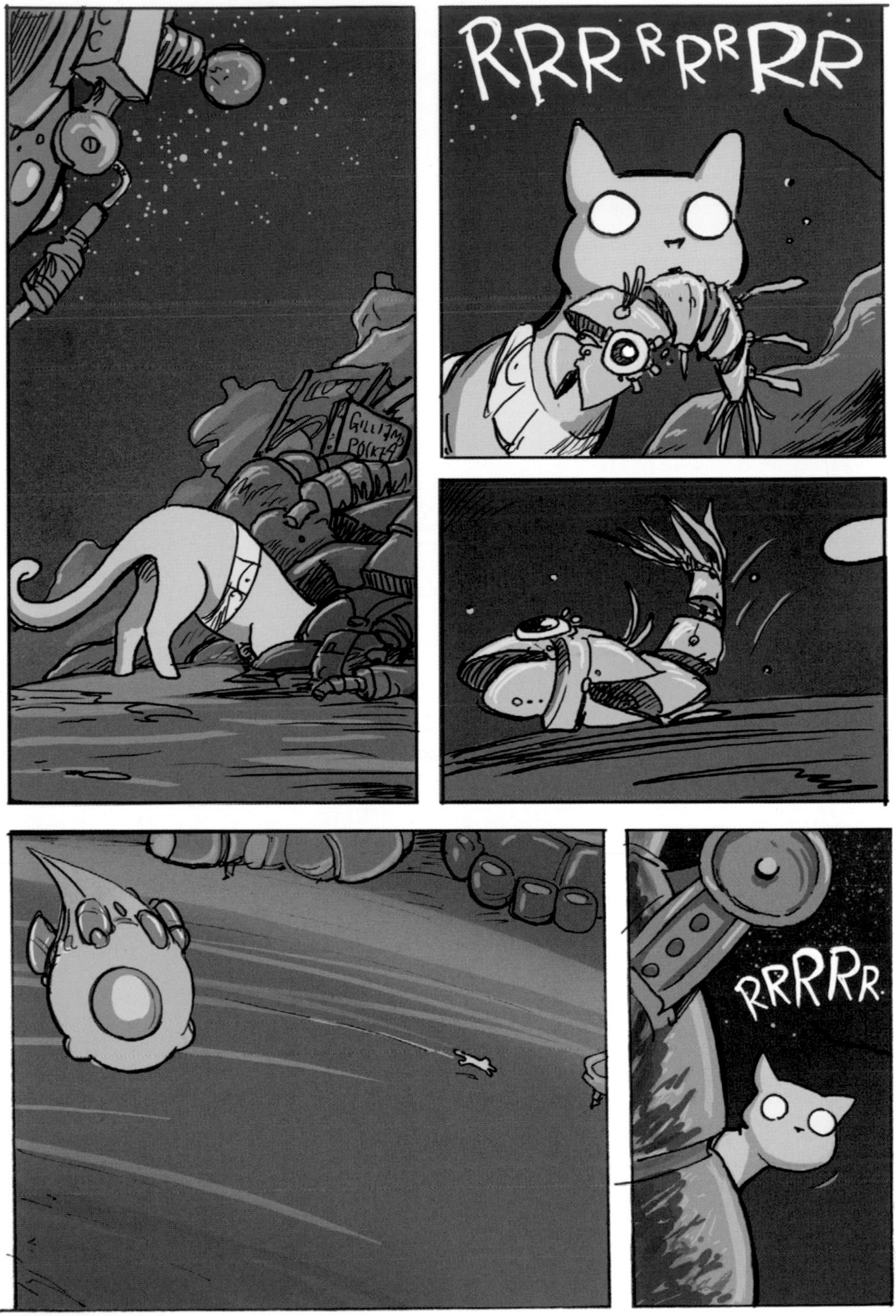
RRRRRRR
RRRRR.

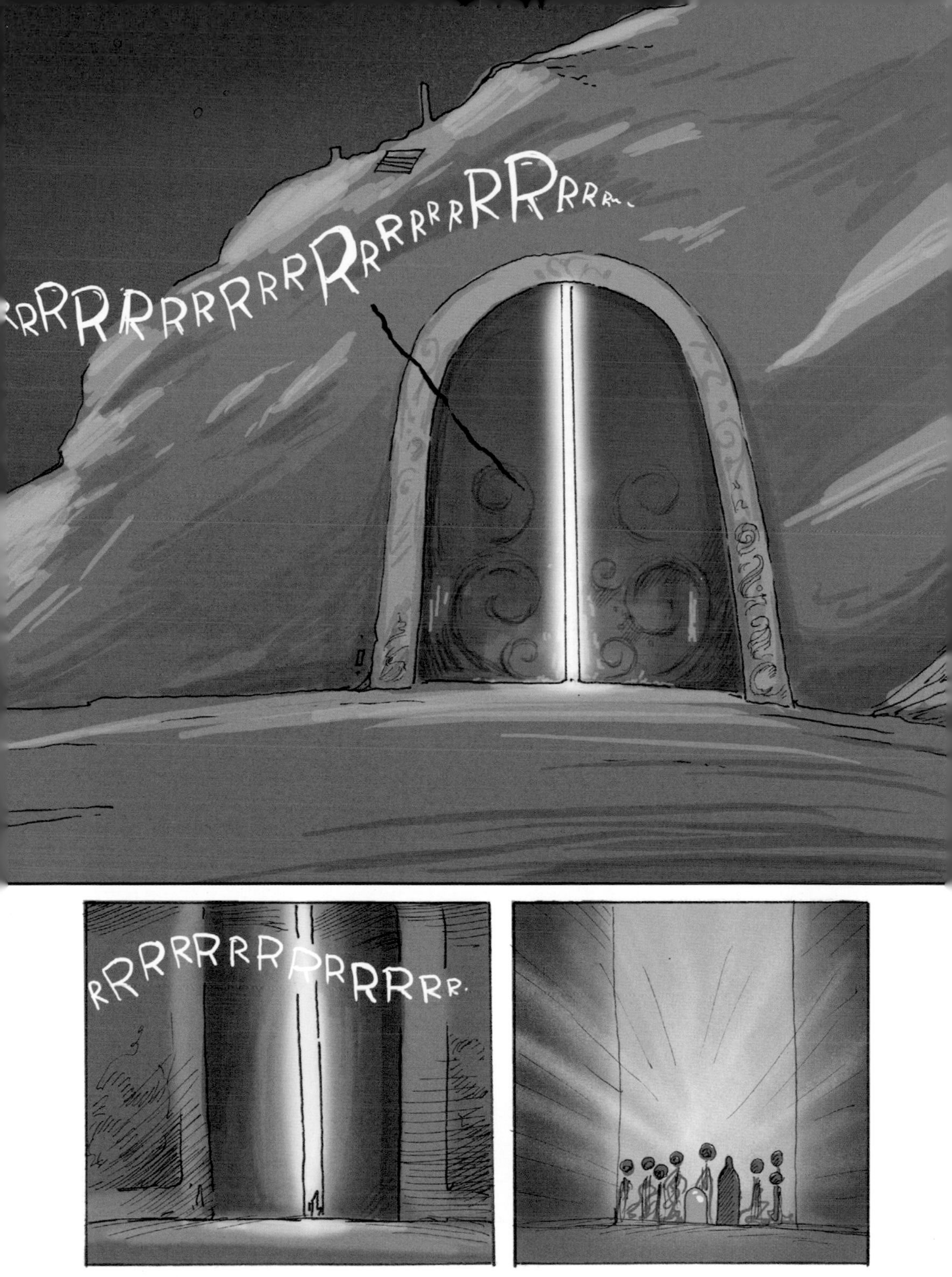
RRRRRRRRRRRRRRRRRRRRRRRRRRRRR
RRRRRRRRRRRRRRRRR

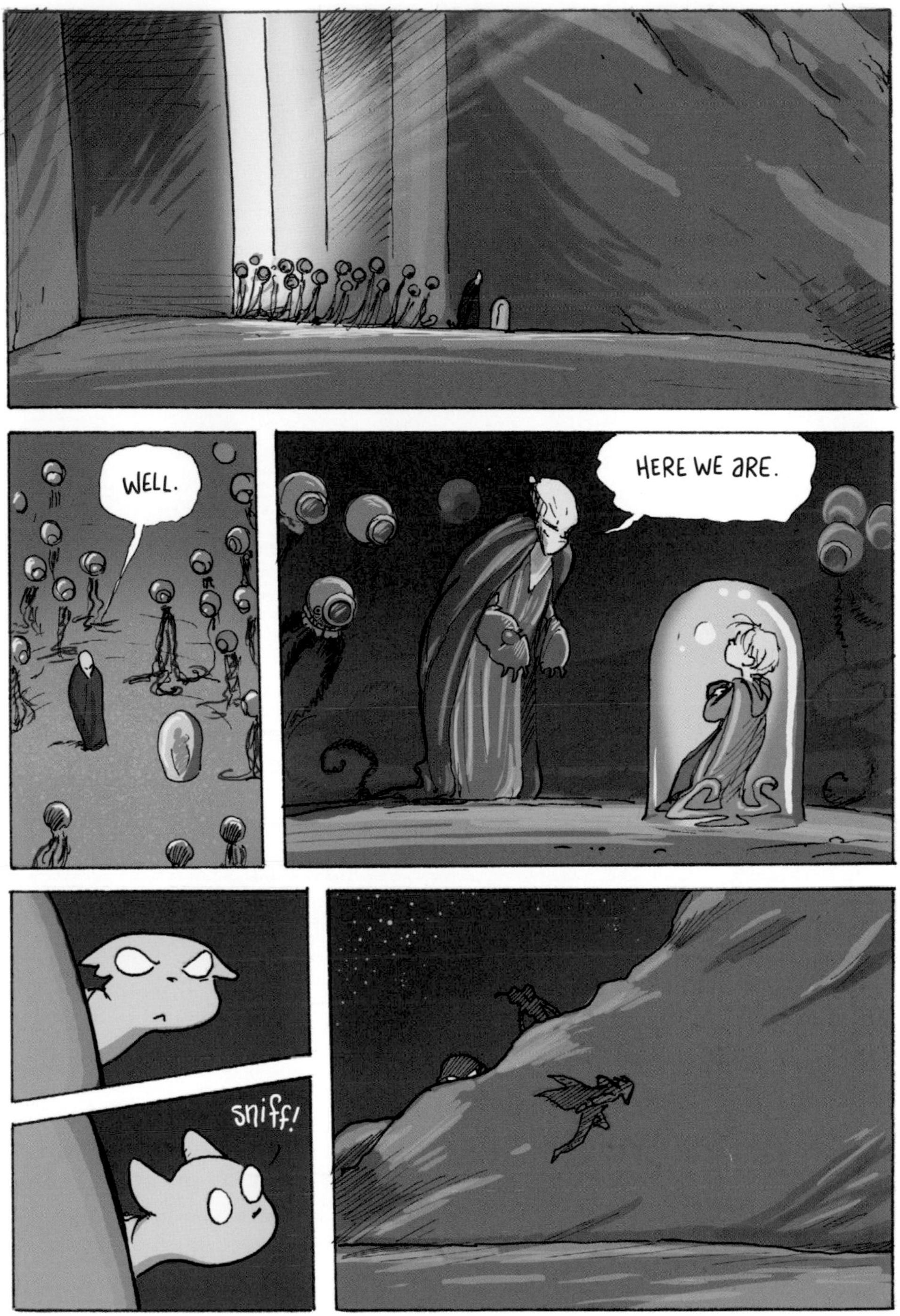
WELL.
HERE WE ARE.
sniff!

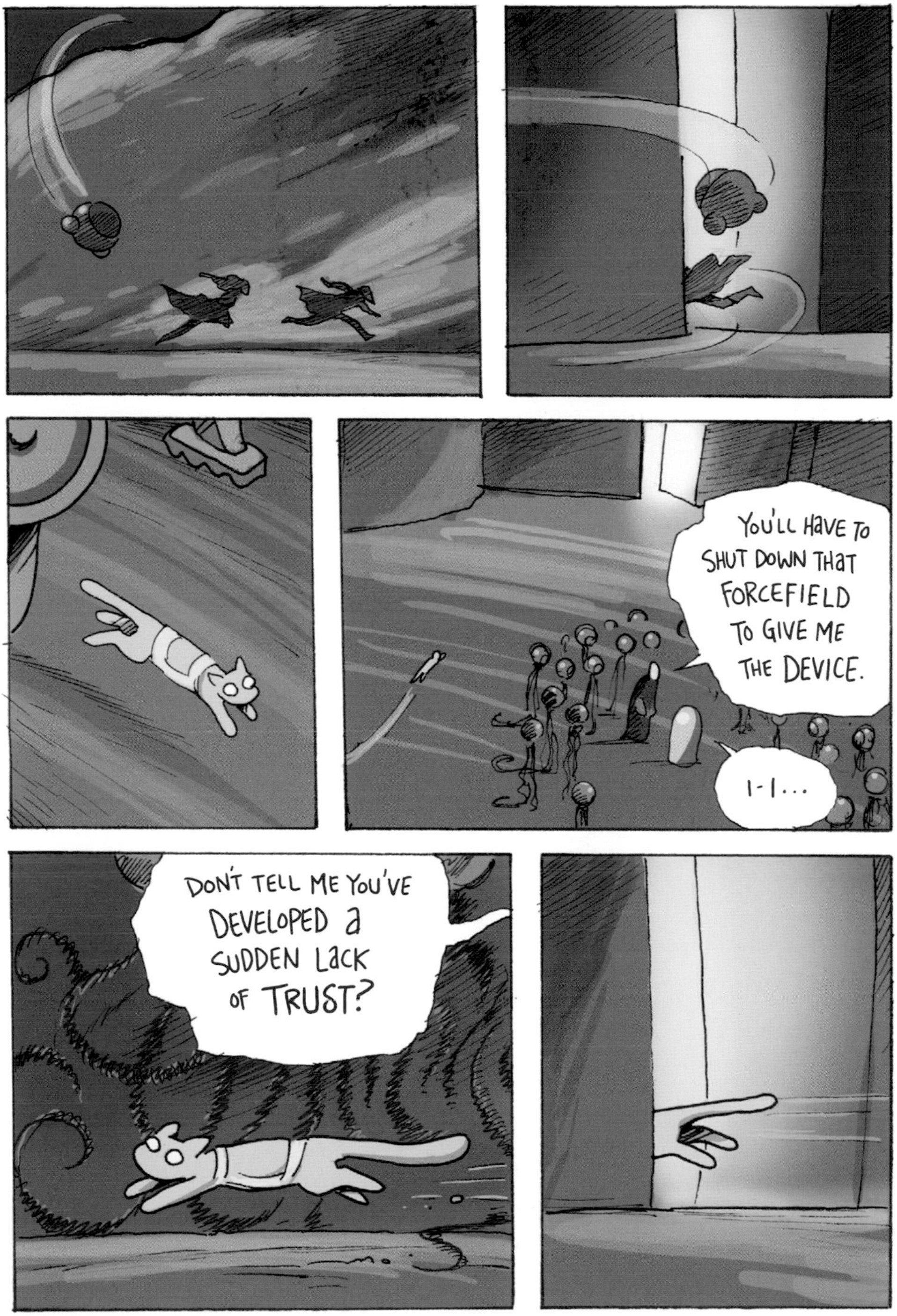
YOU'LL HAVE TO SHUT DOWN THAT FORCEFIELD TO GIVE ME THE DEVICE.
I-I...
DON'T TELL ME YOU'VE DEVELOPED a SUDDEN LACK OF TRUST?

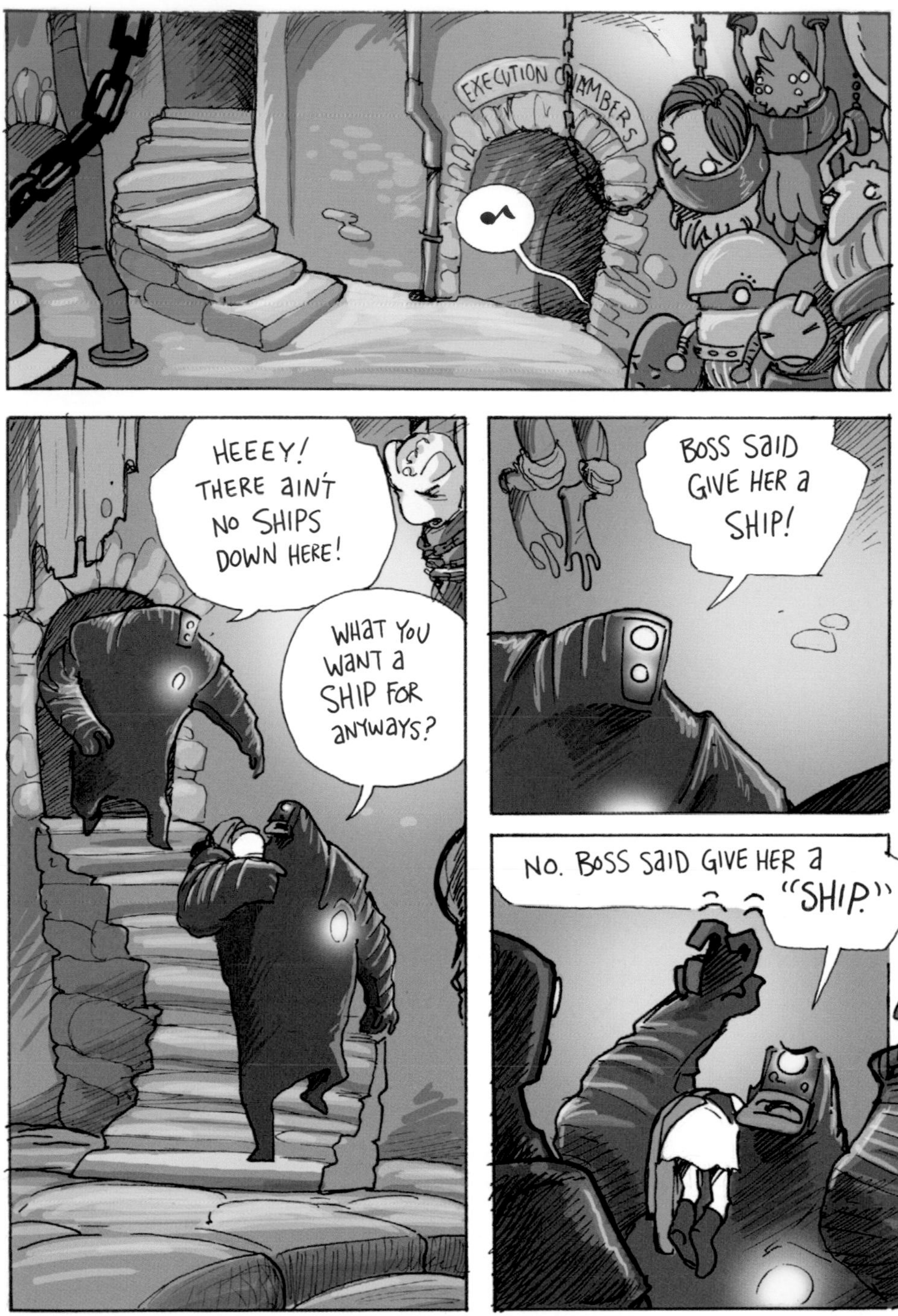
EXECUTION CHAMBERS
♪
HEEEY! THERE AIN'T NO SHIPS DOWN HERE!
WHAT YOU WANT A SHIP FOR ANYWAYS?
BOSS SAID GIVE HER A SHIP!
NO. BOSS SAID GIVE HER A "SHIP."

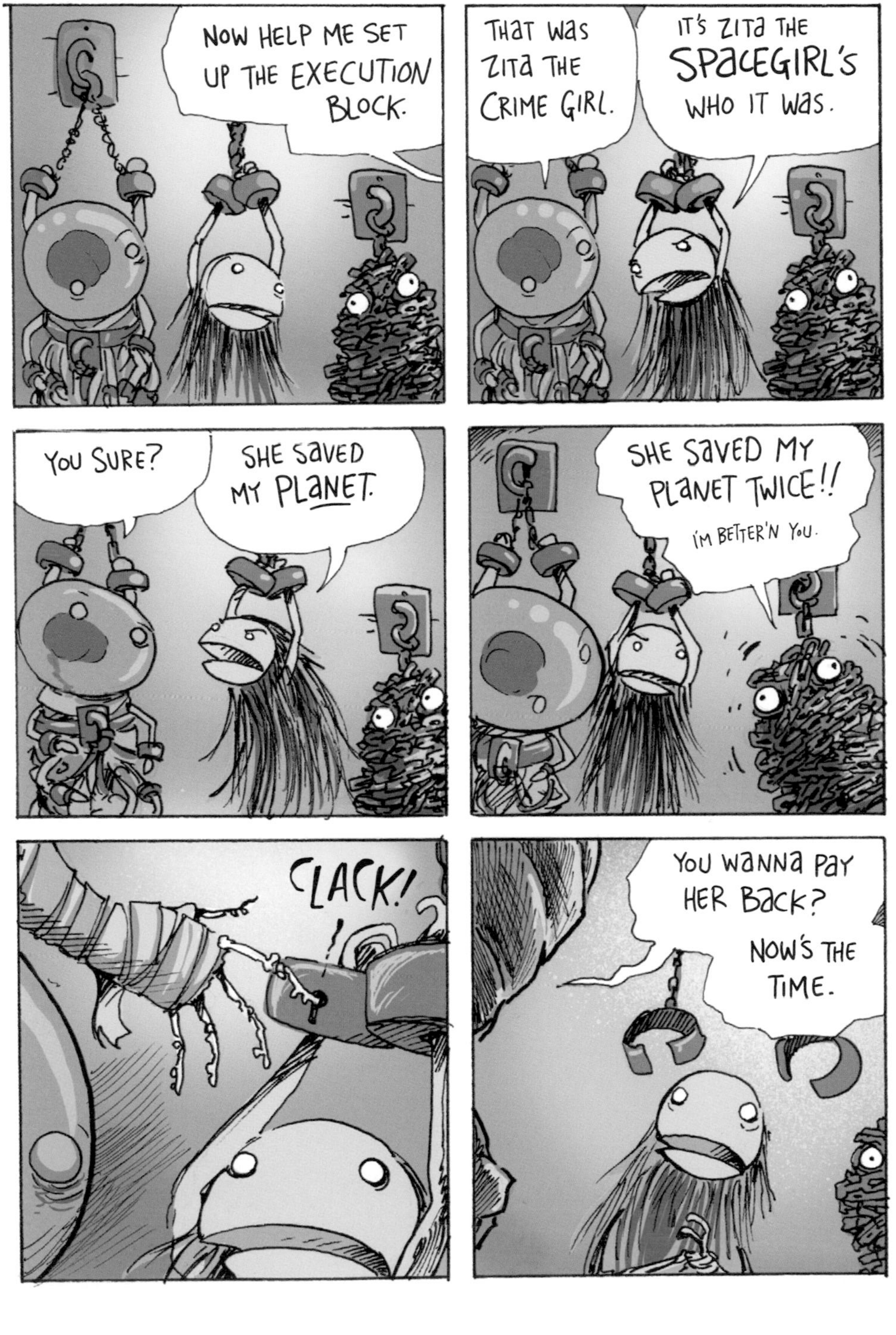
NOW HELP ME SET UP THE EXECUTION BLOCK.
THAT WAS ZITA THE CRIME GIRL.
IT'S ZITA THE SPACEGIRL'S WHO IT WAS.
YOU SURE?
SHE SAVED MY PLANET.
SHE SAVED MY PLANET TWICE!!
I'M BETTER'N YOU.
CLACK!
!
YOU WANNA PAY HER BACK?
NOW'S THE TIME.

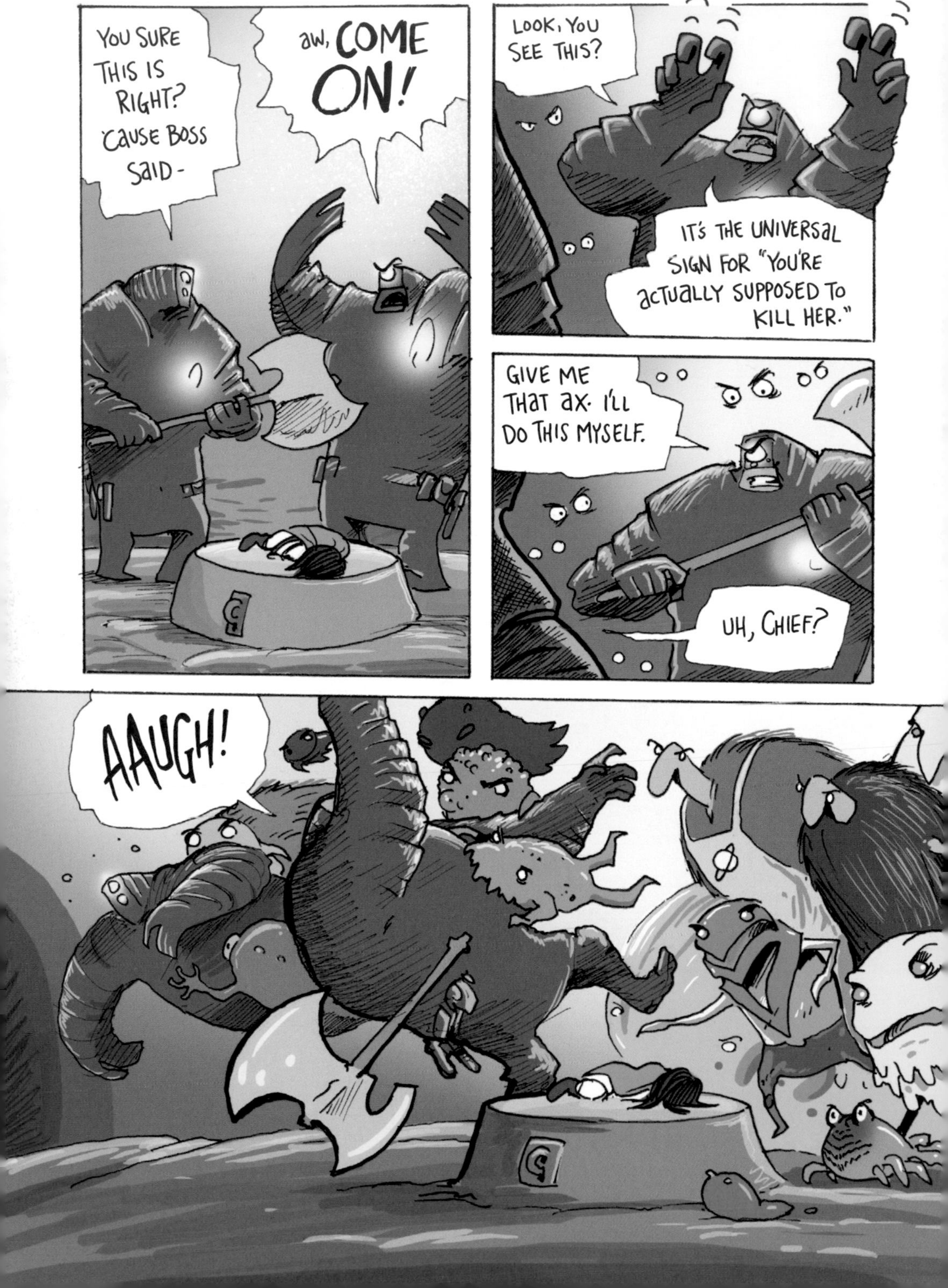
YOU SURE THIS IS RIGHT? 'CAUSE BOSS SAID -
aw, COME ON!
LOOK, YOU SEE THIS?
IT'S THE UNIVERSAL SIGN FOR "YOU'RE ACTUALLY SUPPOSED TO KILL HER."
GIVE ME THAT AX. I'LL DO THIS MYSELF.
UH, CHIEF?
AAUGH!

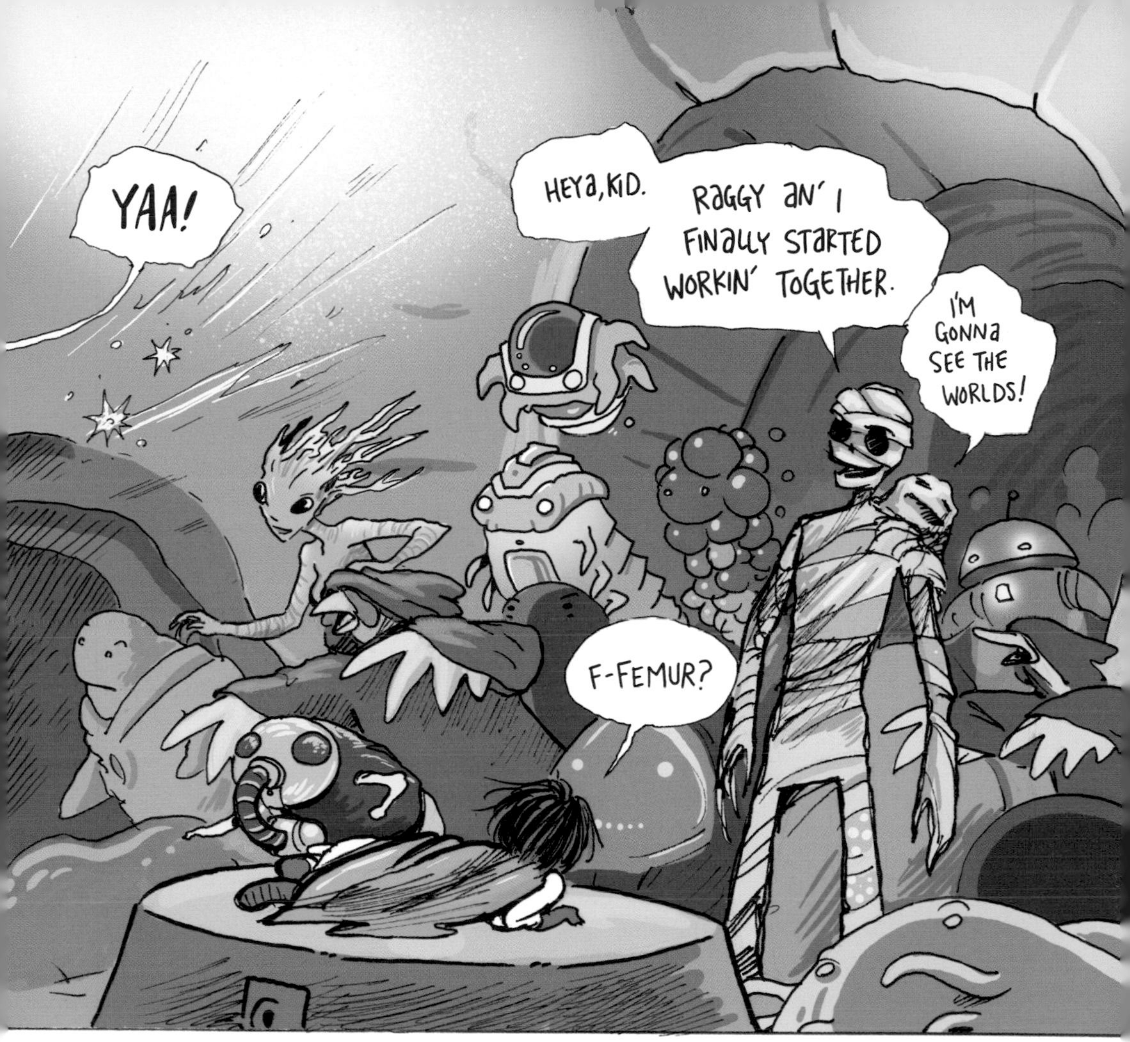
YAA!
HEYA, KID.
RAGGY AN' I FINALLY STARTED WORKIN' TOGETHER.
I'M GONNA SEE THE WORLDS!
F-FEMUR?

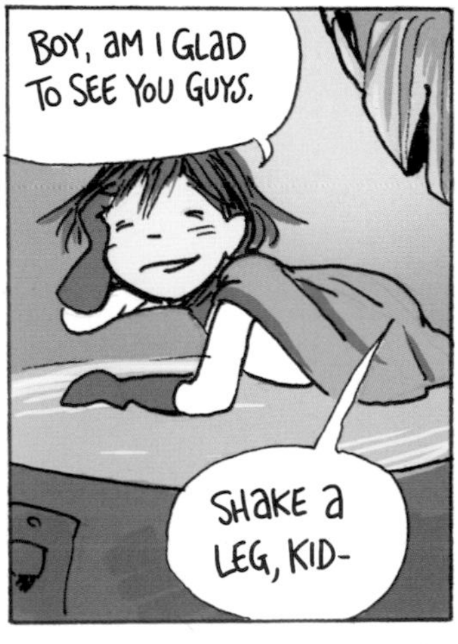
BOY, AM I GLAD TO SEE YOU GUYS.
SHAKE A LEG, KID-

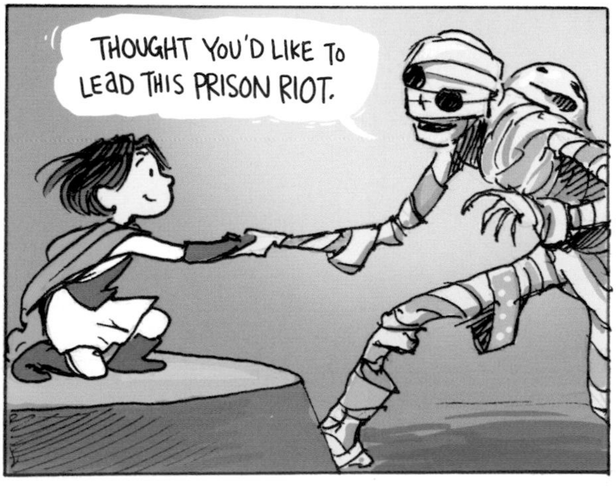
THOUGHT YOU'D LIKE TO LEAD THIS PRISON RIOT.

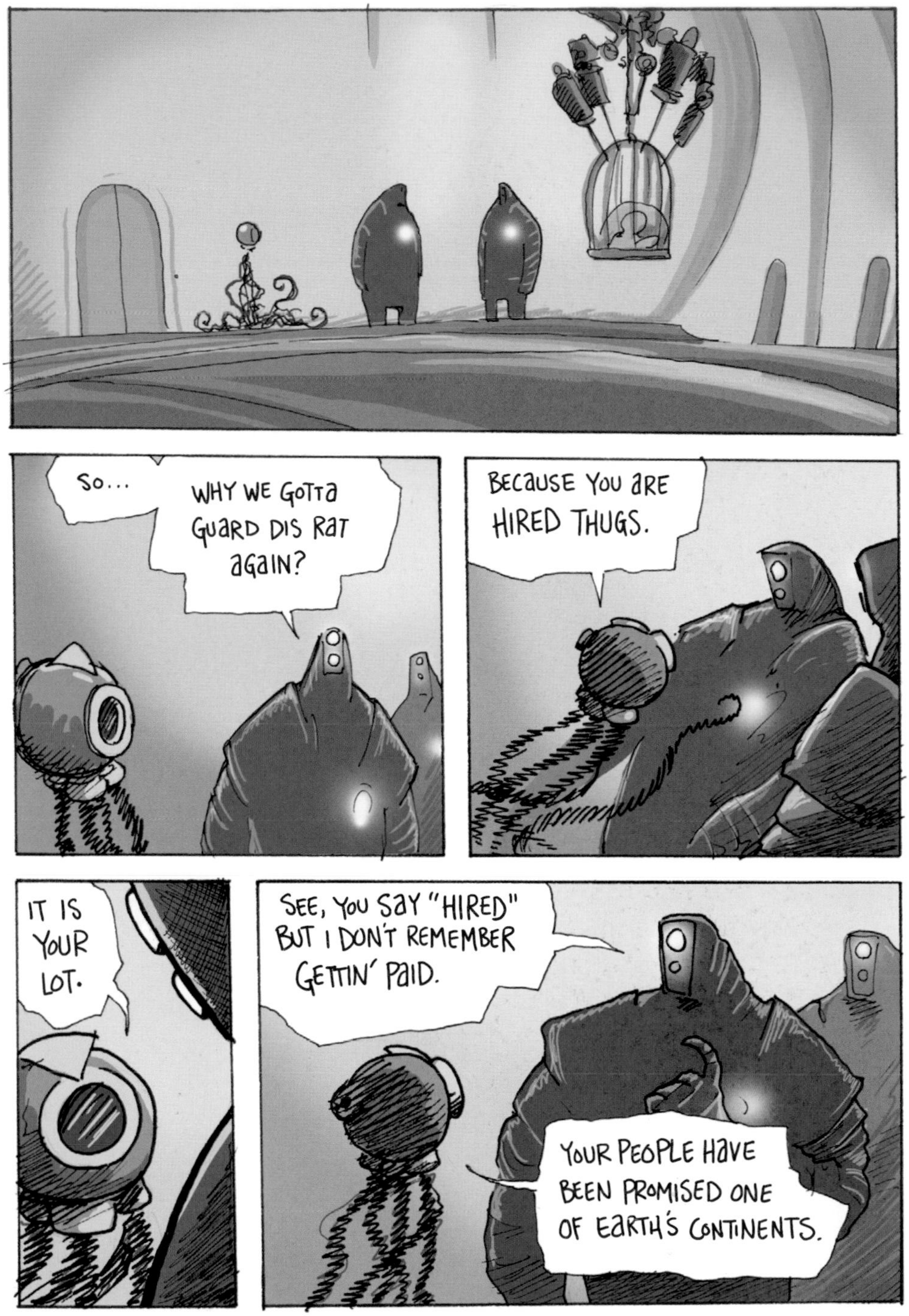
So...
WHY WE GOTTA GUARD DIS RAT AGAIN?
BECAUSE YOU ARE HIRED THUGS.
IT IS YOUR LOT.
SEE, YOU SAY "HIRED" BUT I DON'T REMEMBER GETTIN' PAID.
YOUR PEOPLE HAVE BEEN PROMISED ONE OF EARTH'S CONTINENTS.

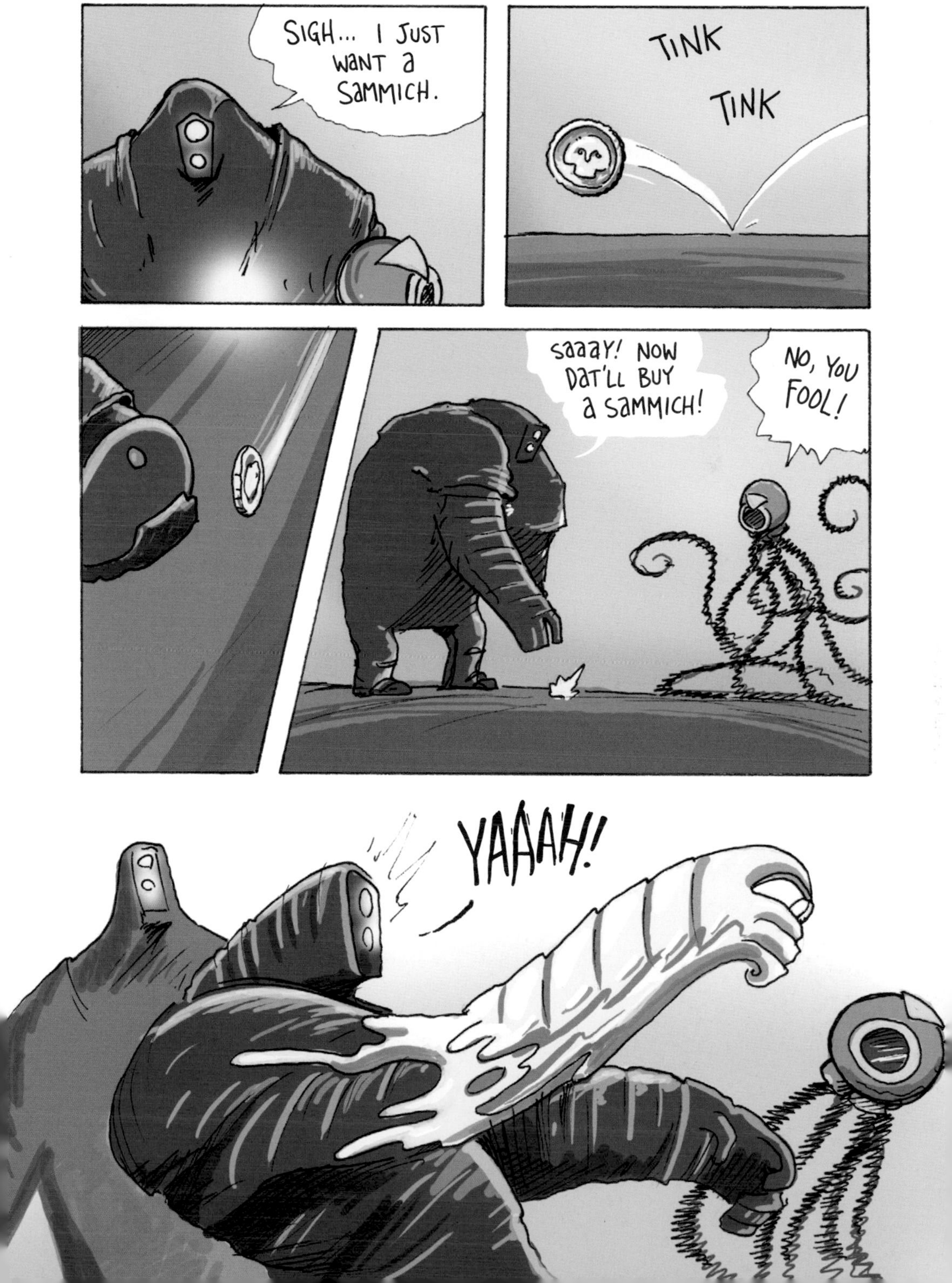
SIGH... I JUST WANT a SAMMICH.
TINK
TINK
saaaY! NOW DAT'LL BUY a SAMMICH!
NO, YOU FOOL!
YAAAH!

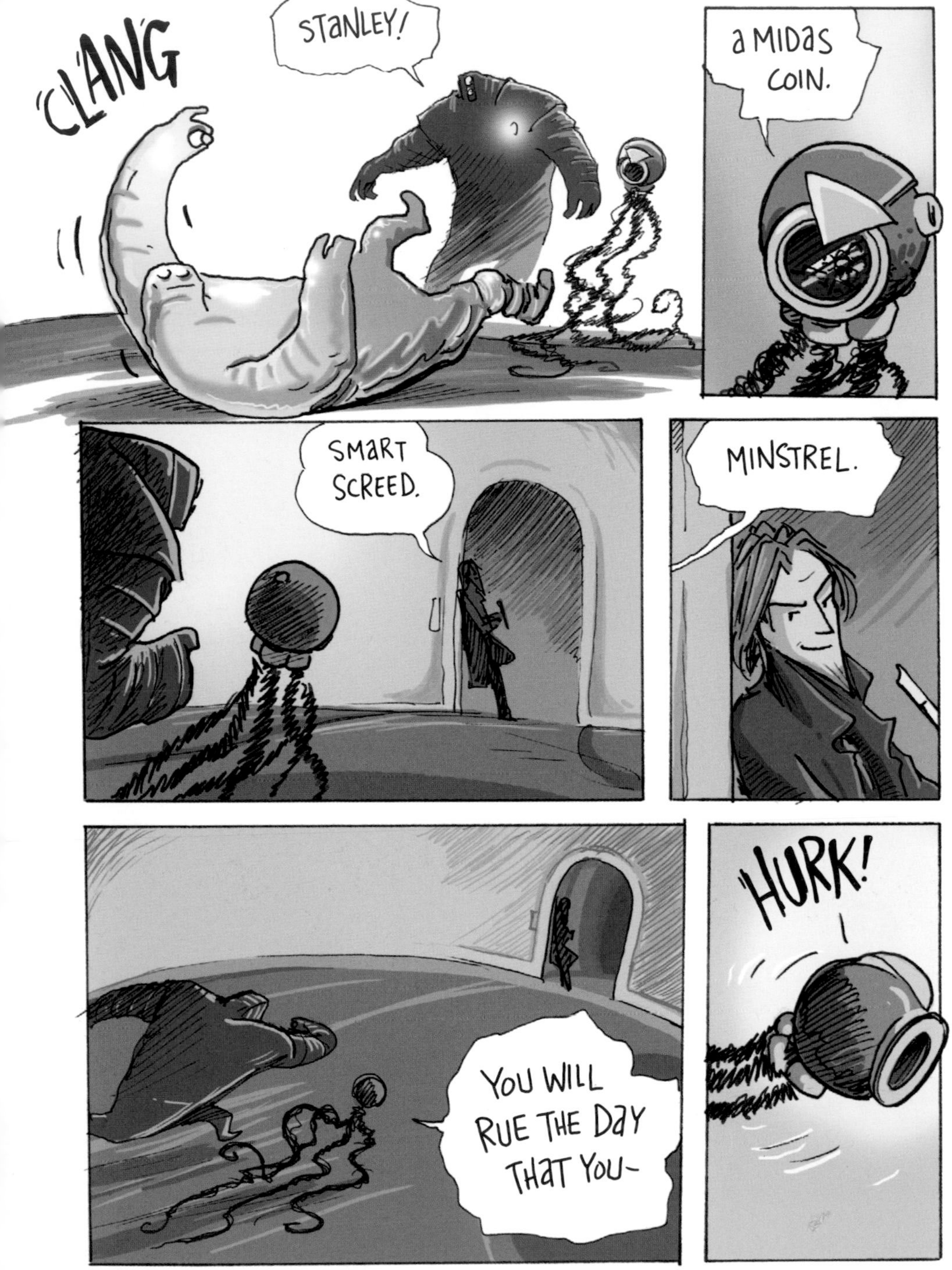
CLANG
STANLEY!
A MIDAS COIN.
SMART SCREED.
MINSTREL.
YOU WILL RUE THE DAY THAT YOU-
HURK!

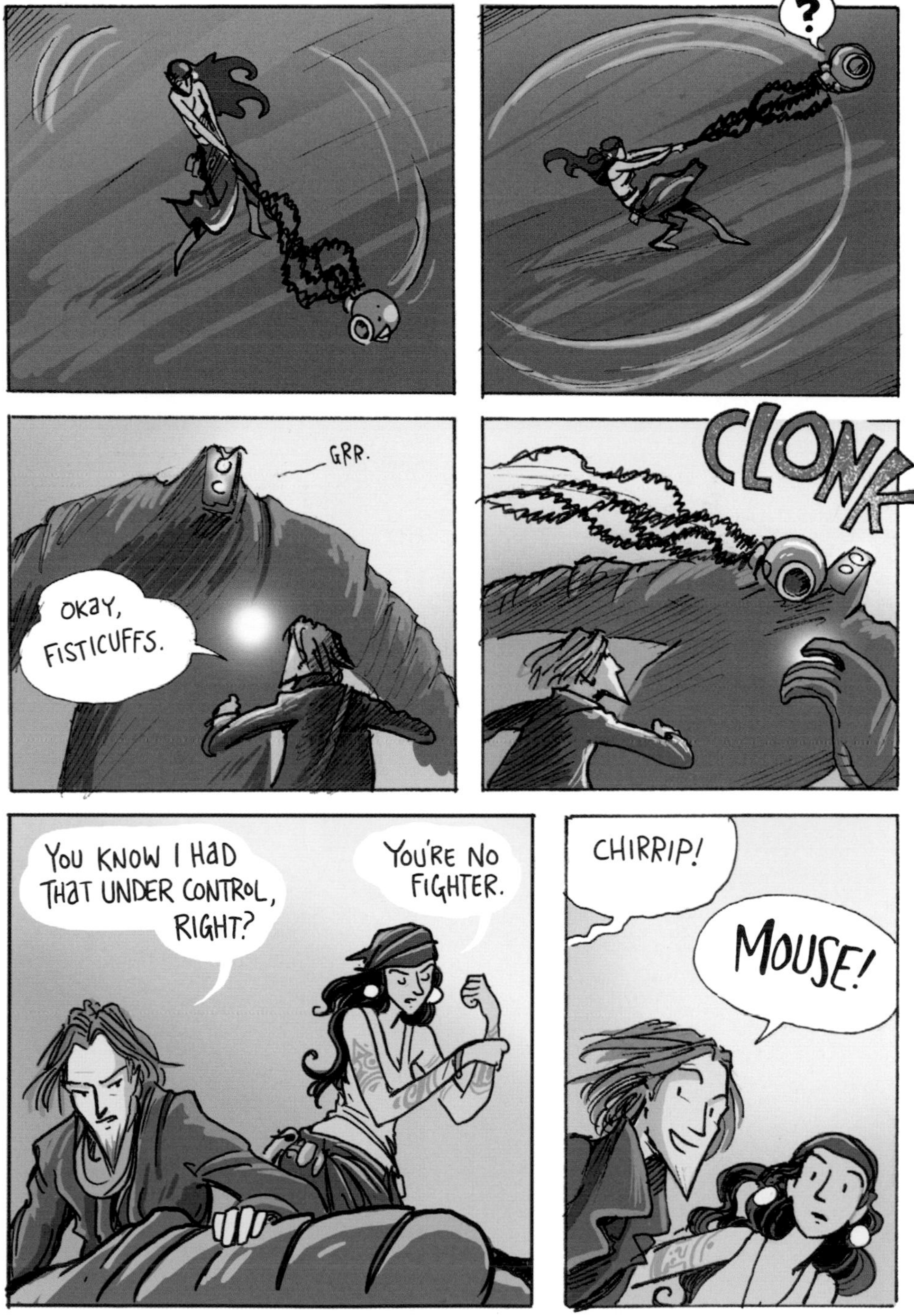
?
GRR.
OKAY, FISTICUFFS.
CLONK
YOU KNOW I HAD THAT UNDER CONTROL, RIGHT?
YOU'RE NO FIGHTER.
CHIRRIP!
MOUSE!

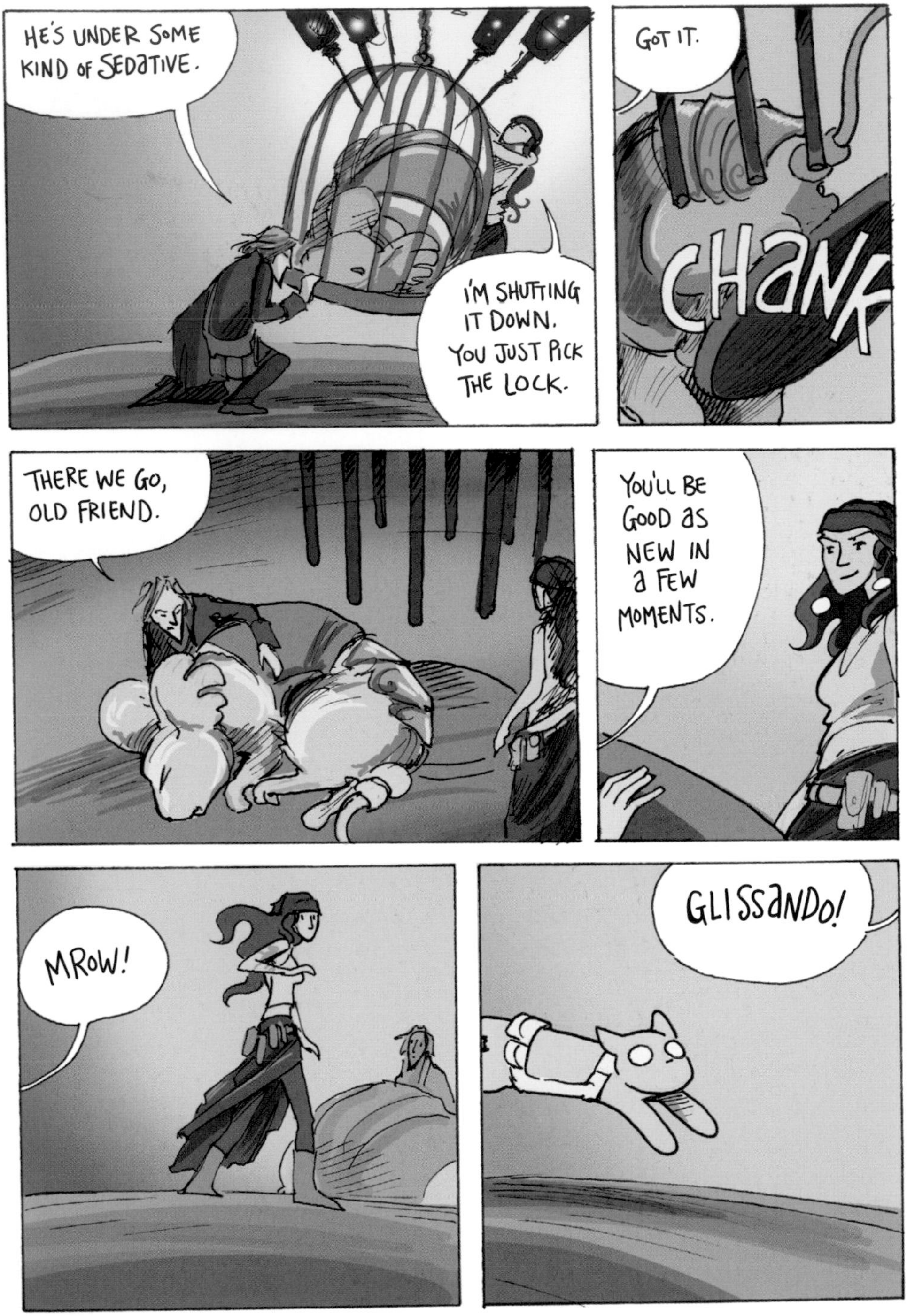
HE'S UNDER SOME KIND OF SEDATIVE.
I'M SHUTTING IT DOWN. YOU JUST PICK THE LOCK.
GOT IT.
CHANK
THERE WE GO, OLD FRIEND.
YOU'LL BE GOOD AS NEW IN A FEW MOMENTS.
MROW!
GLISSANDO!

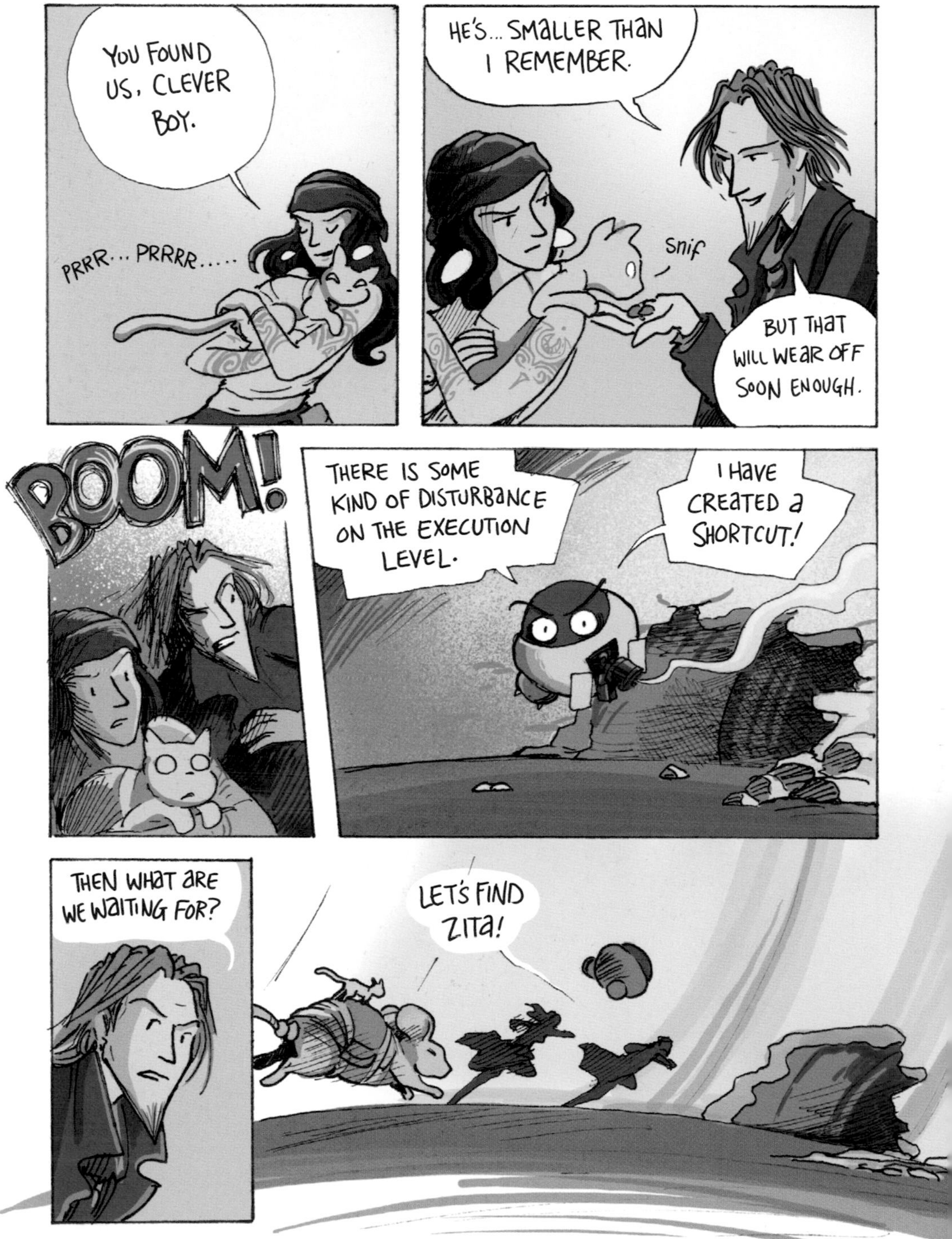

YOU FOUND US, CLEVER BOY.
PRRR... PRRRR.....
HE'S... SMALLER THAN I REMEMBER.
Snif
BUT THAT WILL WEAR OFF SOON ENOUGH.
BOOM!
THERE IS SOME KIND OF DISTURBANCE ON THE EXECUTION LEVEL.
I HAVE CREATED A SHORTCUT!
THEN WHAT ARE WE WAITING FOR?
LET'S FIND ZITA!

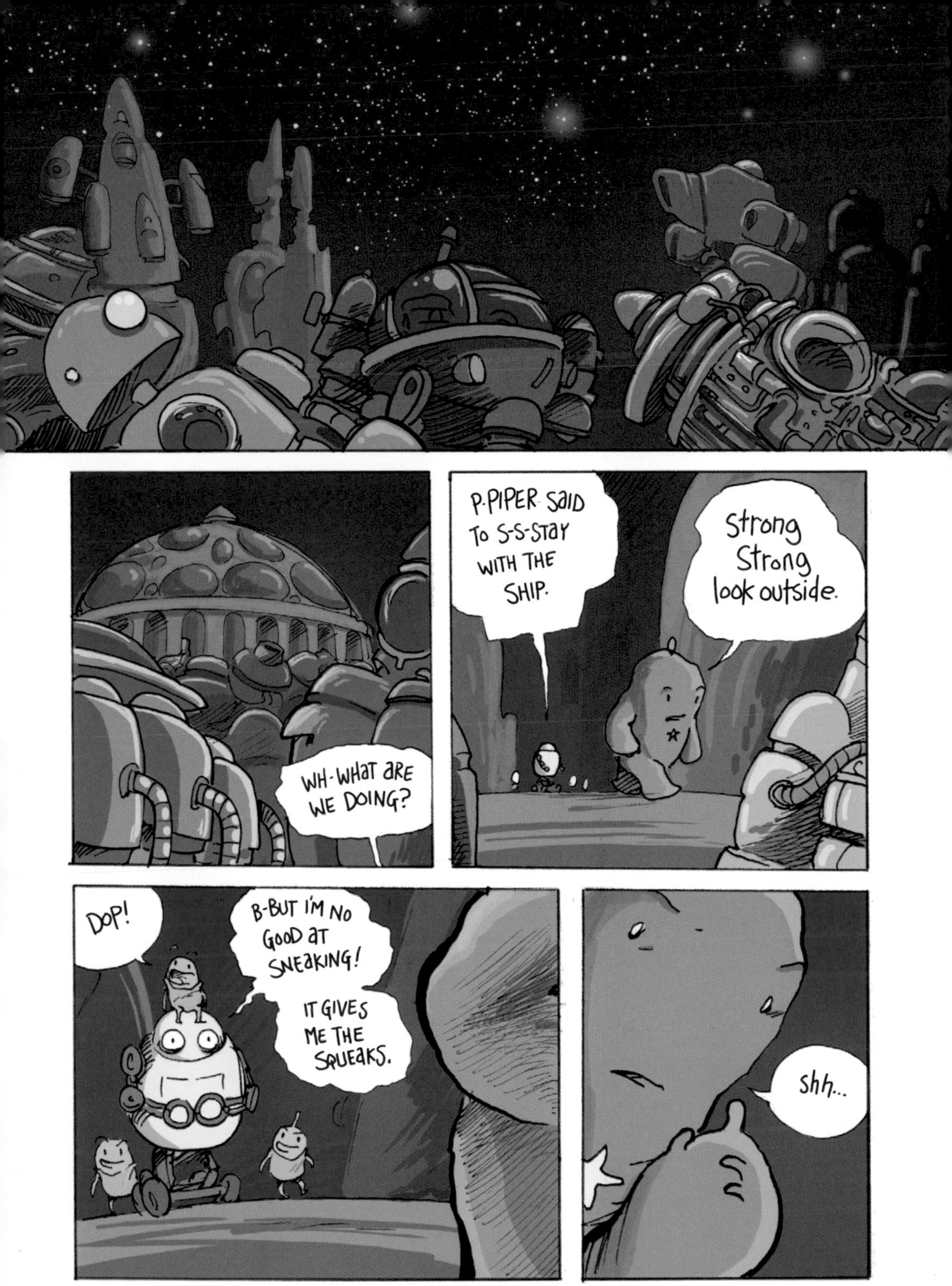
WH-WHAT ARE WE DOING?
P-PIPER SAID TO S-S-STAY WITH THE SHIP.
Strong Strong look outside.
DOP!
B-BUT I'M NO GOOD AT SNEAKING!
IT GIVES ME THE SQUEAKS.
Shh...

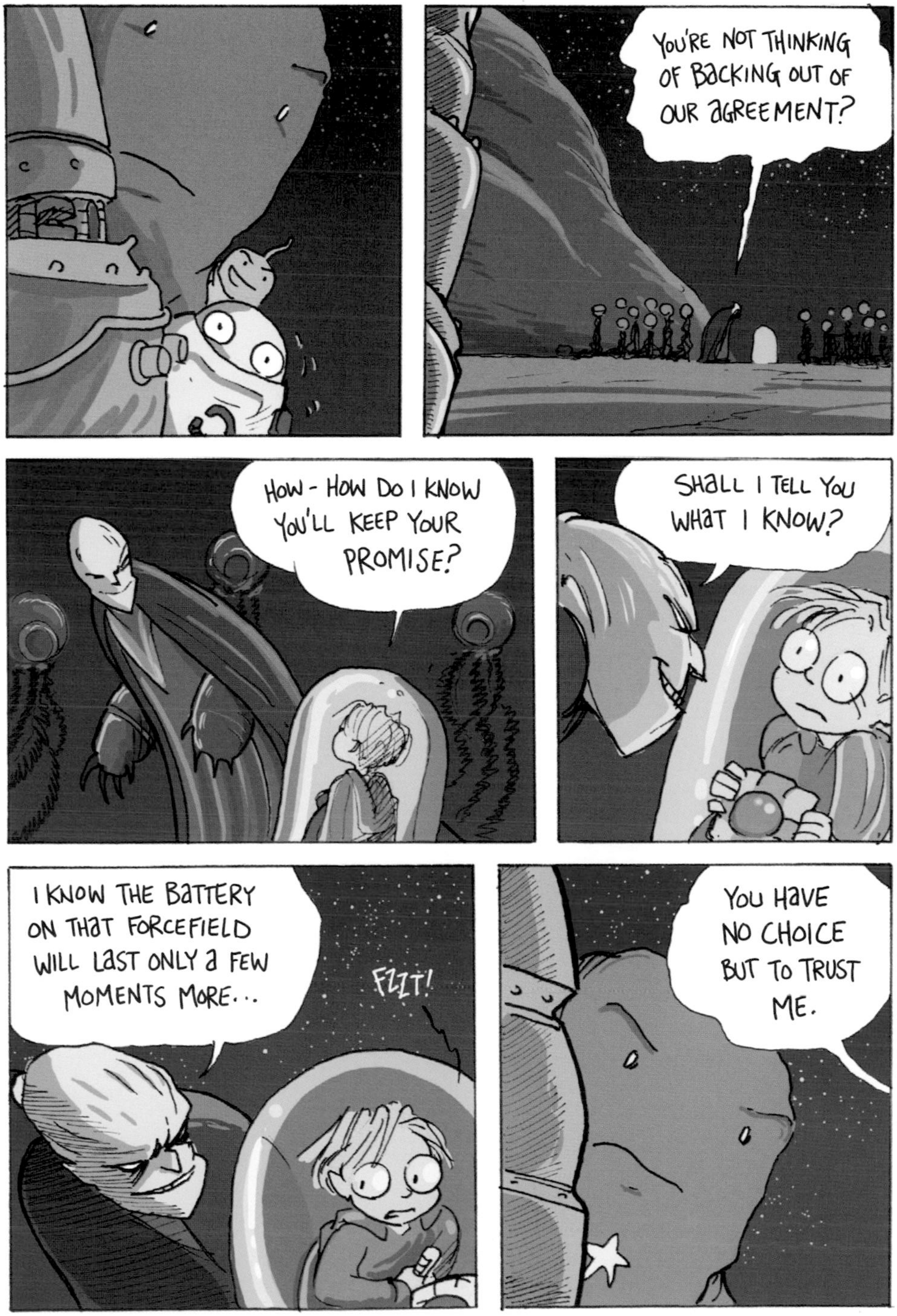
YOU'RE NOT THINKING OF BACKING OUT OF OUR AGREEMENT?
HOW - HOW DO I KNOW YOU'LL KEEP YOUR PROMISE?
SHALL I TELL YOU WHAT I KNOW?
I KNOW THE BATTERY ON THAT FORCEFIELD WILL LAST ONLY A FEW MOMENTS MORE...
FZZT!
YOU HAVE NO CHOICE BUT TO TRUST ME.

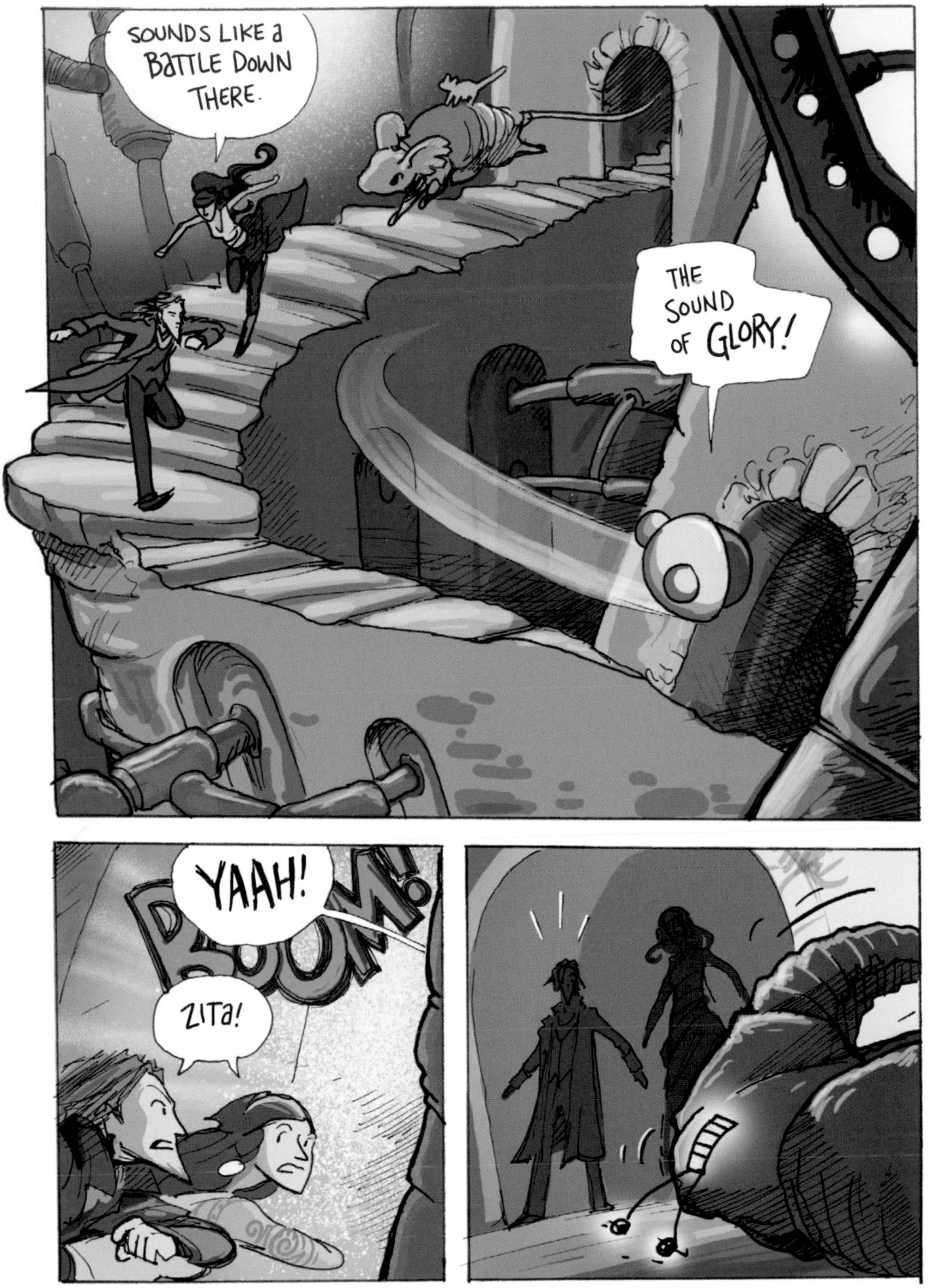
SOUNDS LIKE a BATTLE DOWN THERE.
THE SOUND OF GLORY!
BOOM!
YAAH!
ZITa!

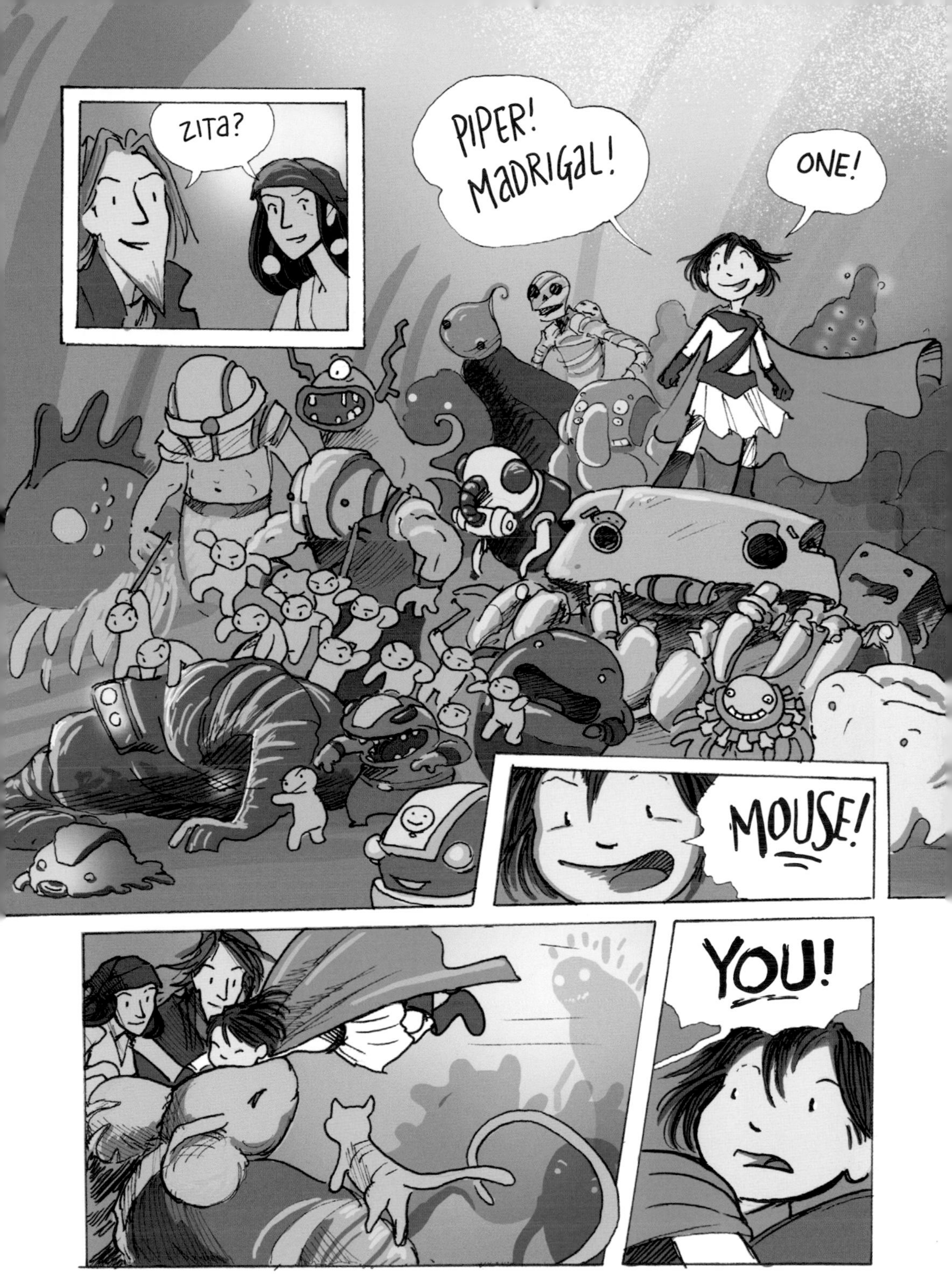
ZITA?
PIPER! MADRIGAL!
ONE!
MOUSE!
YOU!

RATTLE CLICK

RATTLE CLICK

HE SAYS HE WANTS TO FIND JOSEPH—

SAY THE WORD AND HE'LL "FIND" THE WRONG END OF MY CANNON.

NO!

NO FIGHTING.

BUT—!

IT'S WHAT WE WERE MADE FOR!

HE CAN HELP US IF HE WANTS.

WE'RE GOING TO FIND JOSEPH.

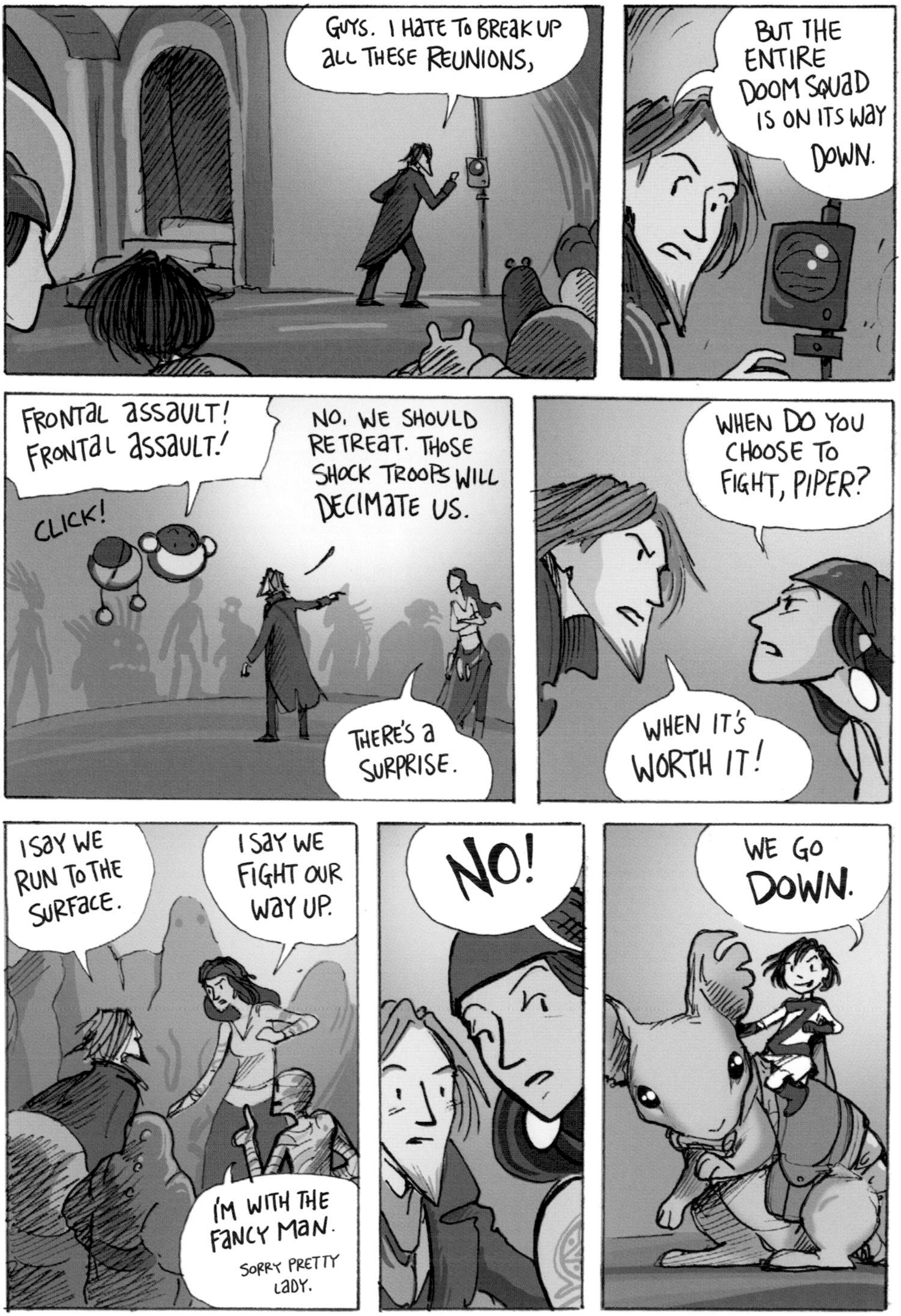
GUYS. I HATE TO BREAK UP ALL THESE REUNIONS,
BUT THE ENTIRE DOOM SQUAD IS ON ITS WAY DOWN.
FRONTAL ASSAULT! FRONTAL ASSAULT!
CLICK!
NO. WE SHOULD RETREAT. THOSE SHOCK TROOPS WILL DECIMATE US.
THERE'S A SURPRISE.
WHEN DO YOU CHOOSE TO FIGHT, PIPER?
WHEN IT'S WORTH IT!
I SAY WE RUN TO THE SURFACE.
I SAY WE FIGHT OUR WAY UP.
I'M WITH THE FANCY MAN.
SORRY PRETTY LADY.
NO!
WE GO DOWN.

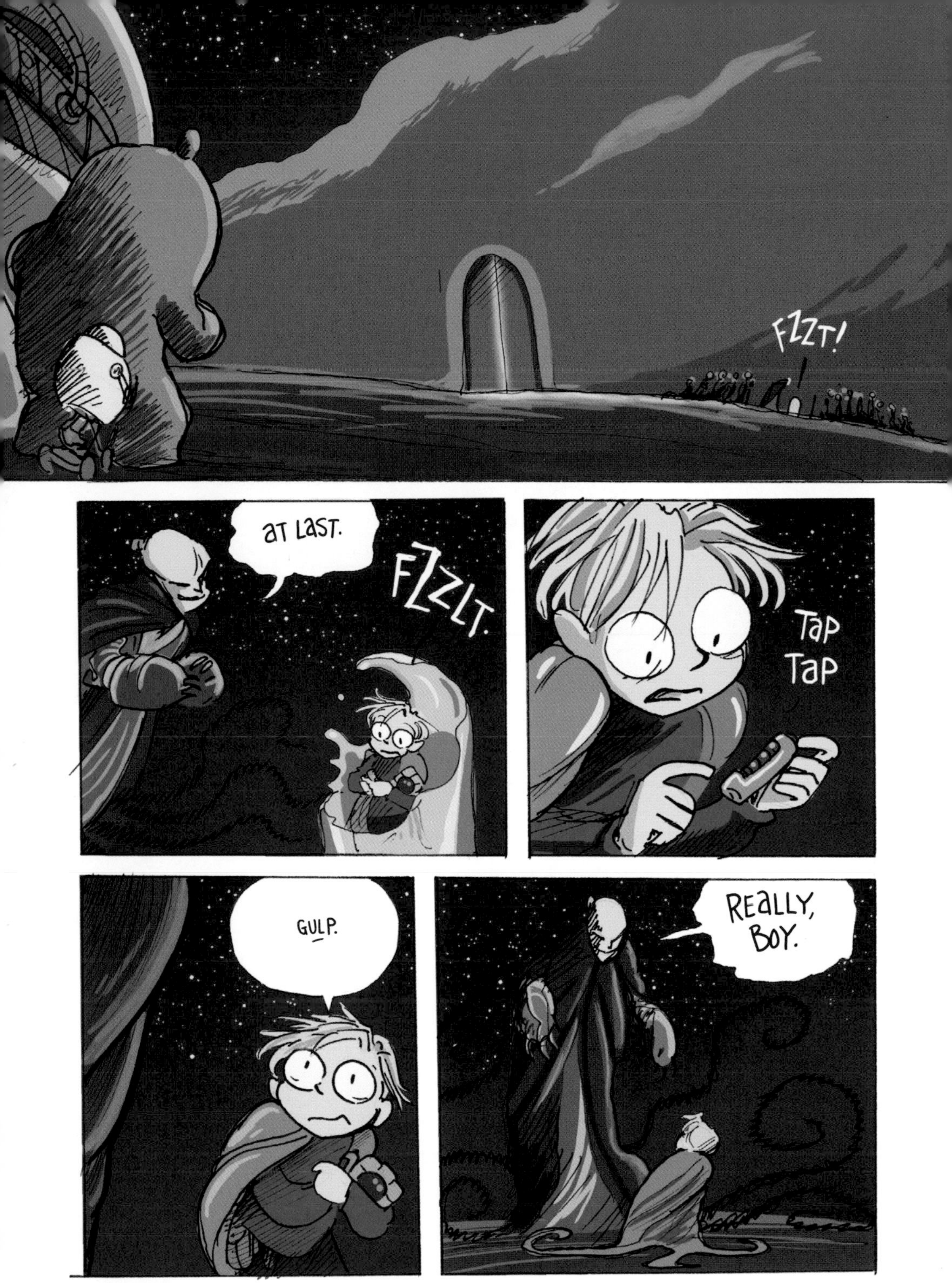
FZZT!
AT LAST.
FZZLT.
TAP
TAP
GULP.
REALLY, BOY.

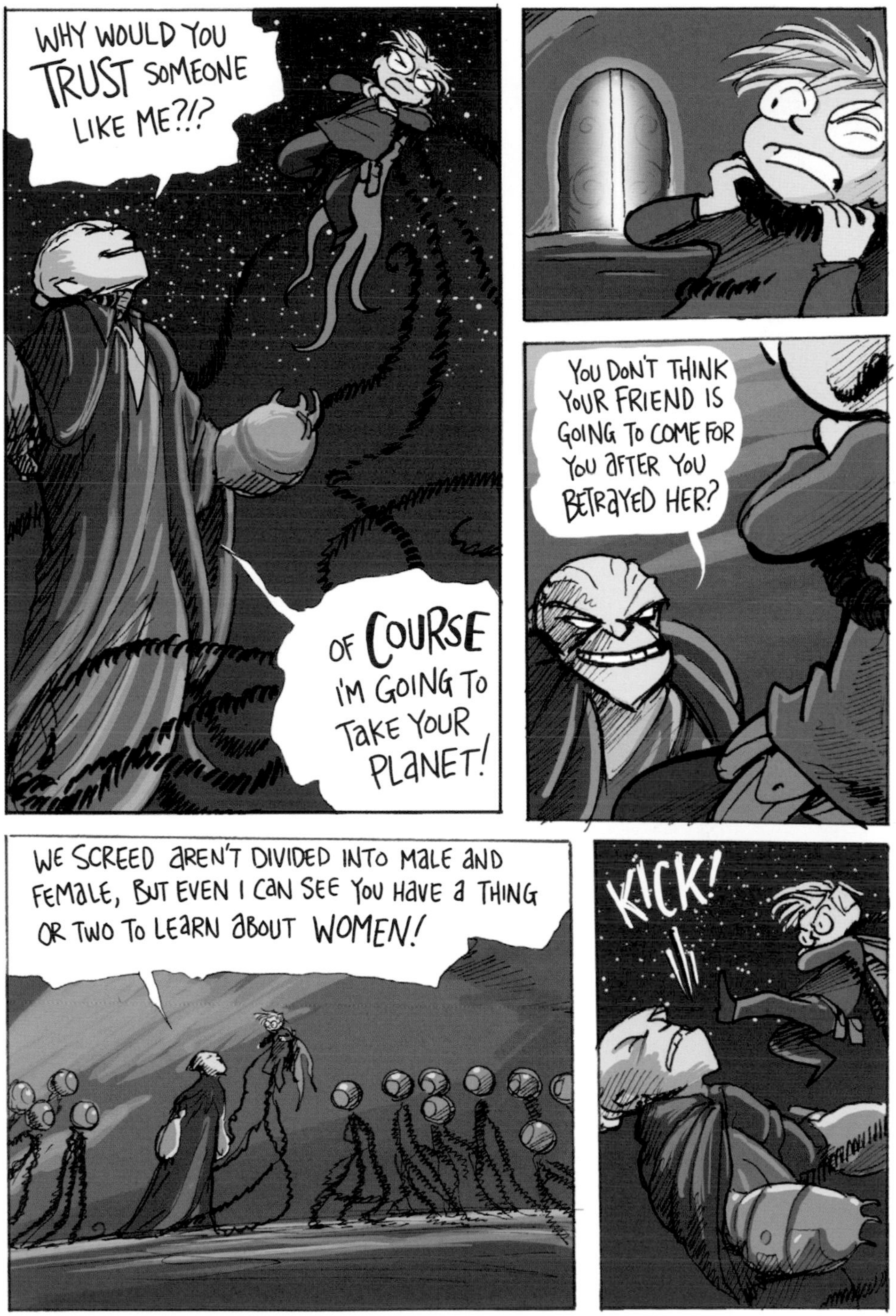
WHY WOULD YOU TRUST SOMEONE LIKE ME?!?
OF COURSE I'M GOING TO TAKE YOUR PLANET!
YOU DON'T THINK YOUR FRIEND IS GOING TO COME FOR YOU AFTER YOU BETRAYED HER?
WE SCREED AREN'T DIVIDED INTO MALE AND FEMALE, BUT EVEN I CAN SEE YOU HAVE A THING OR TWO TO LEARN ABOUT WOMEN!
KICK!

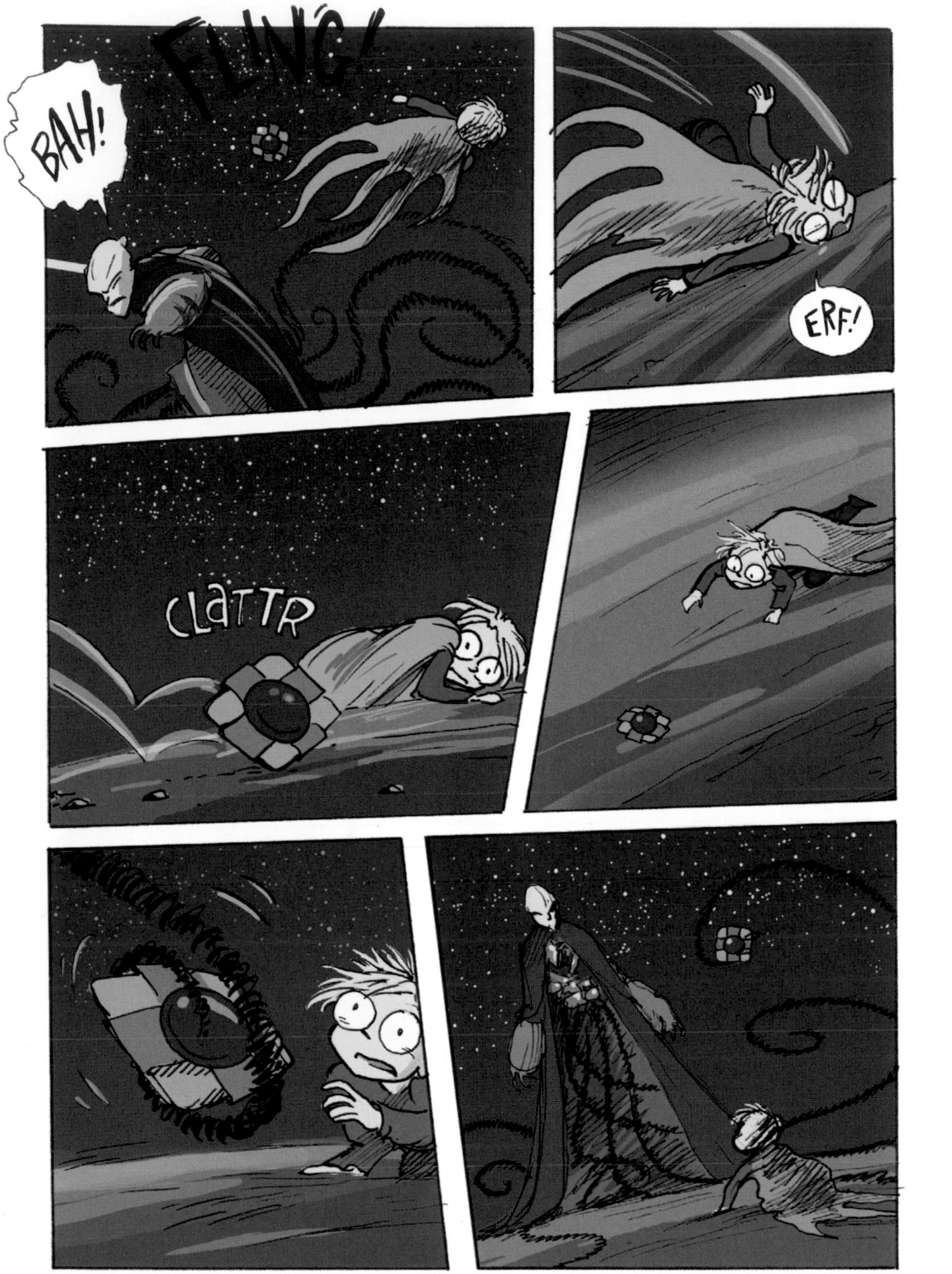
FLING!
BAH!
ERF!
CLATTR

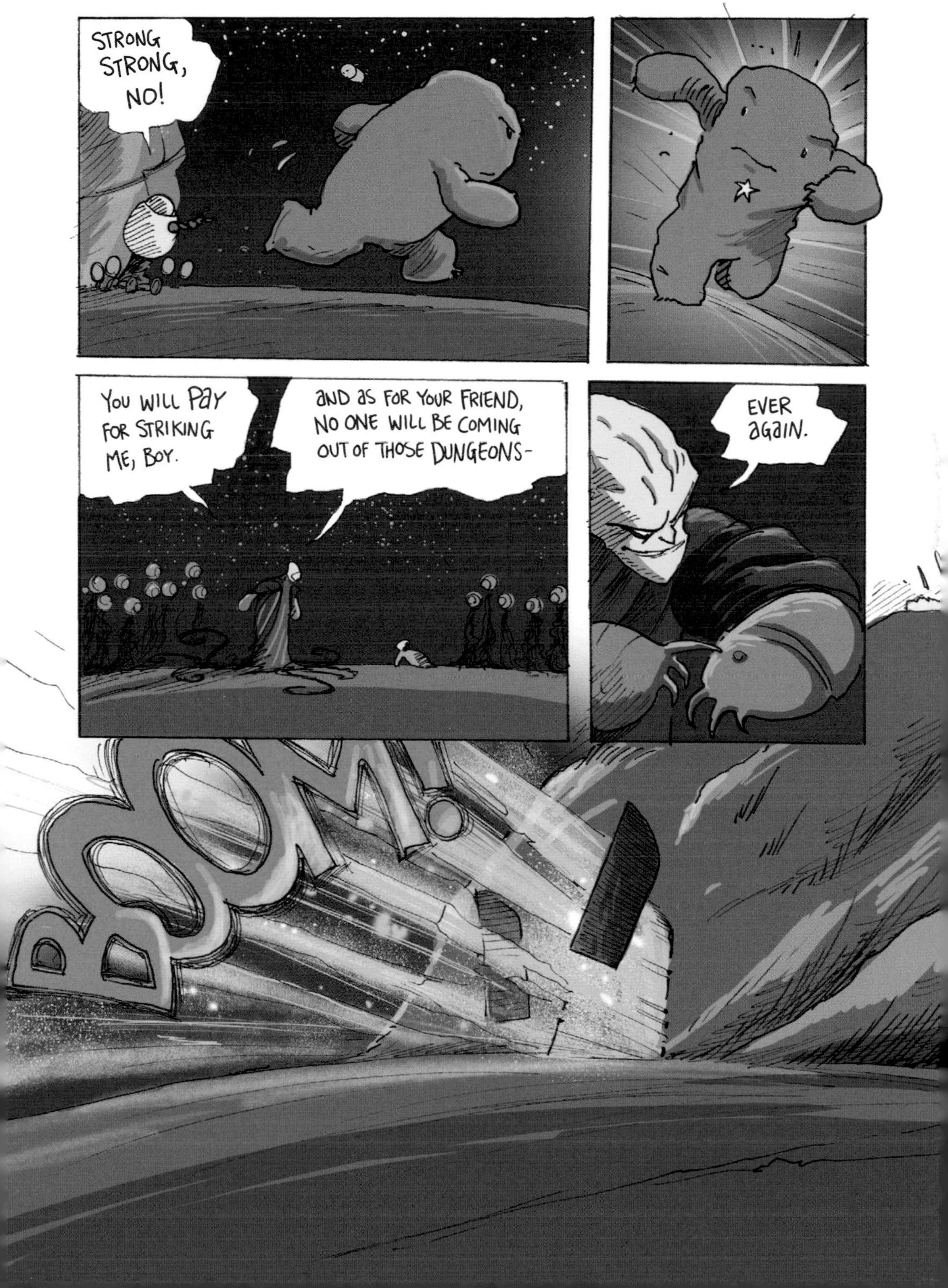
STRONG STRONG, NO!
YOU WILL PAY FOR STRIKING ME, BOY.
AND AS FOR YOUR FRIEND, NO ONE WILL BE COMING OUT OF THOSE DUNGEONS-
EVER AGAIN.
BOOM!

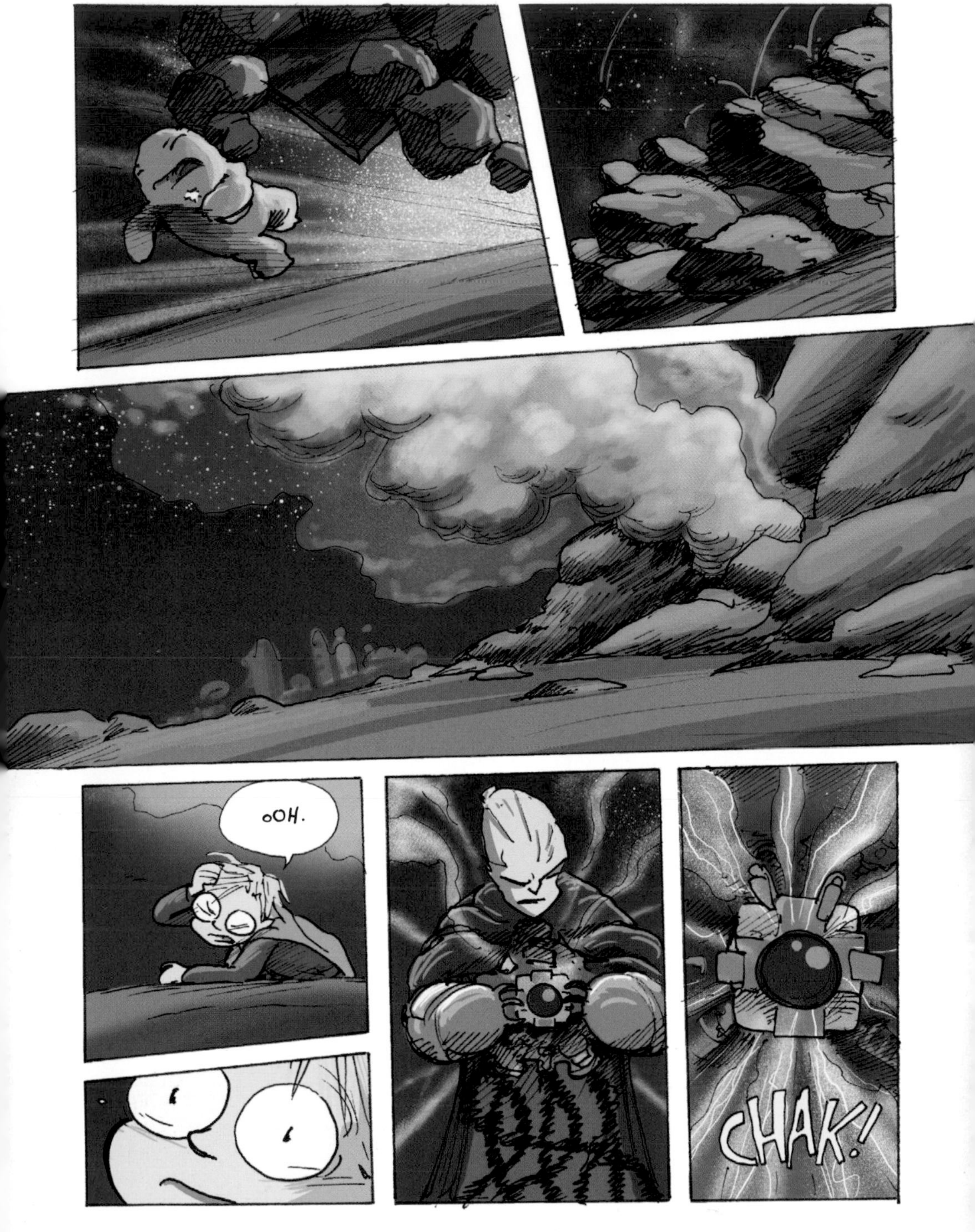
OOH.
CHAK!

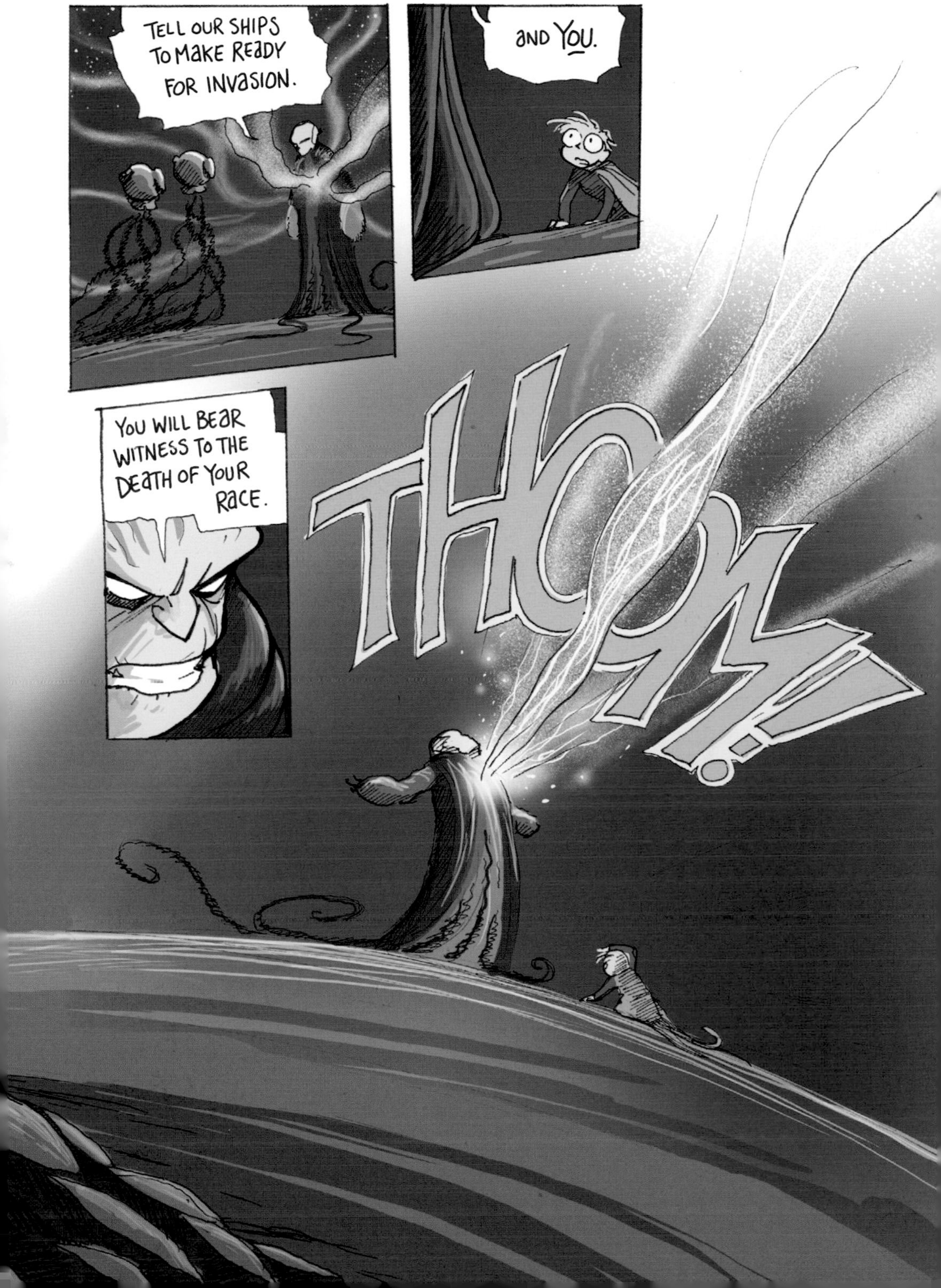
TELL OUR SHIPS TO MAKE READY FOR INVASION.
AND YOU.
YOU WILL BEAR WITNESS TO THE DEATH OF YOUR RACE.
THOOM!

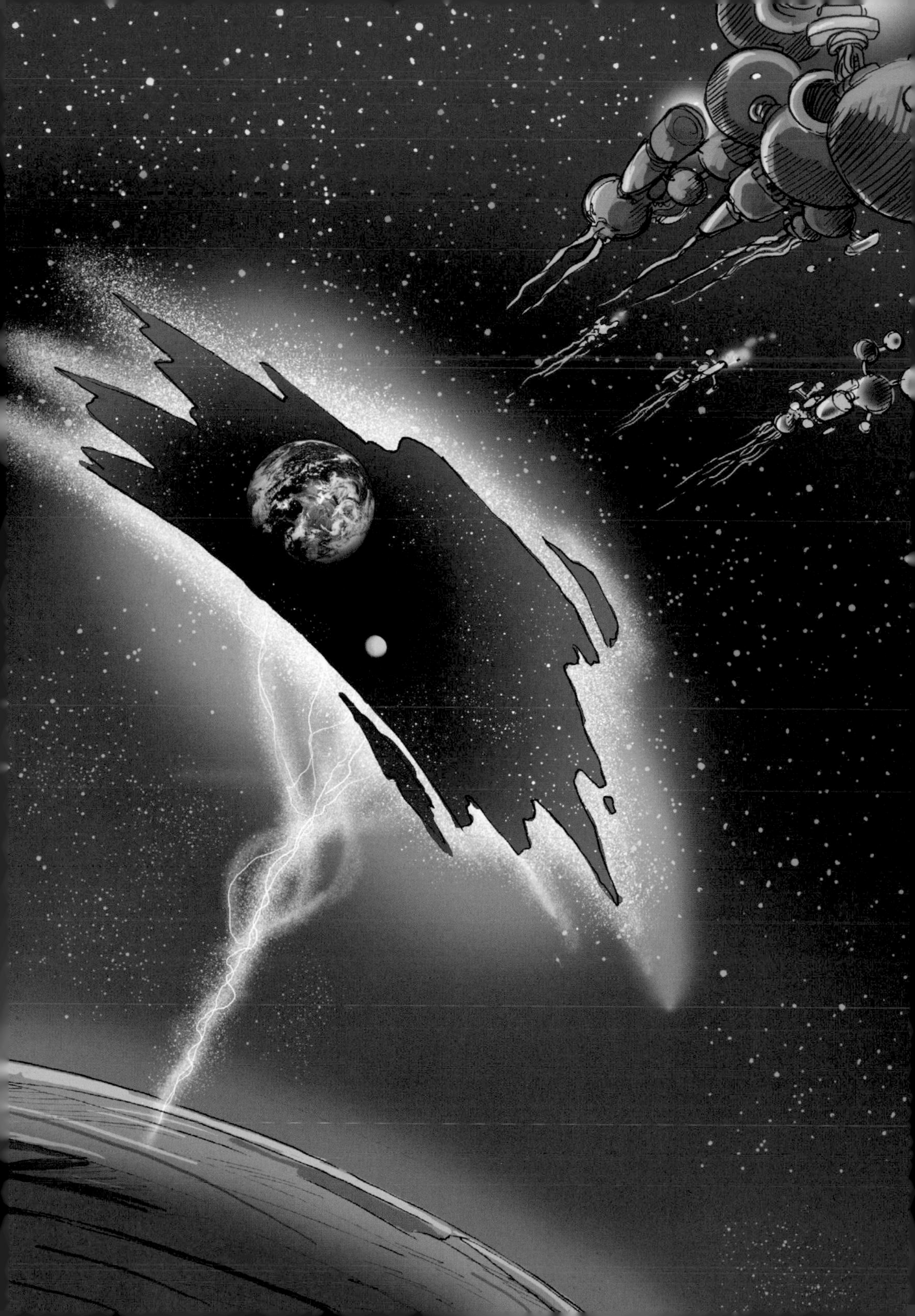

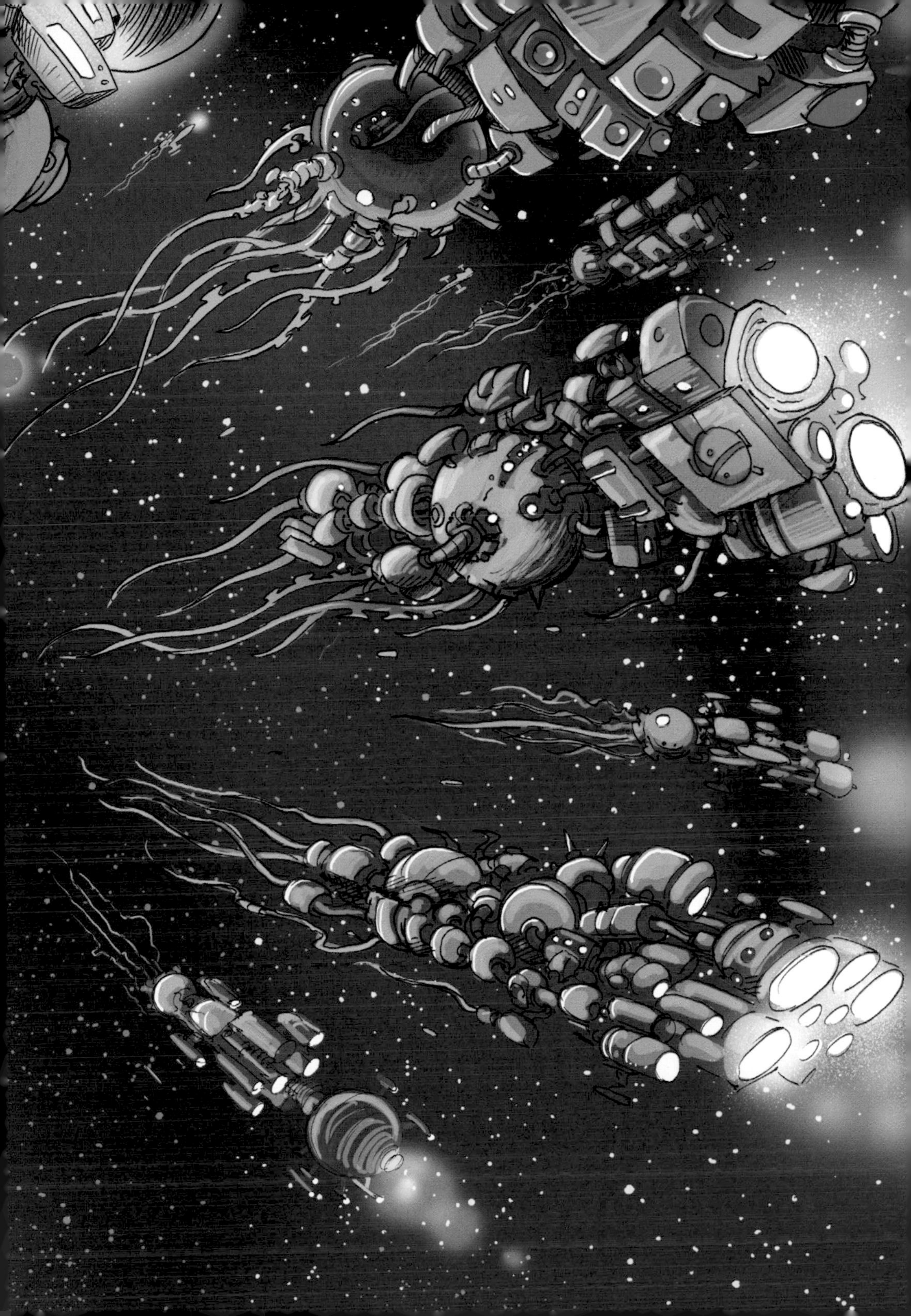

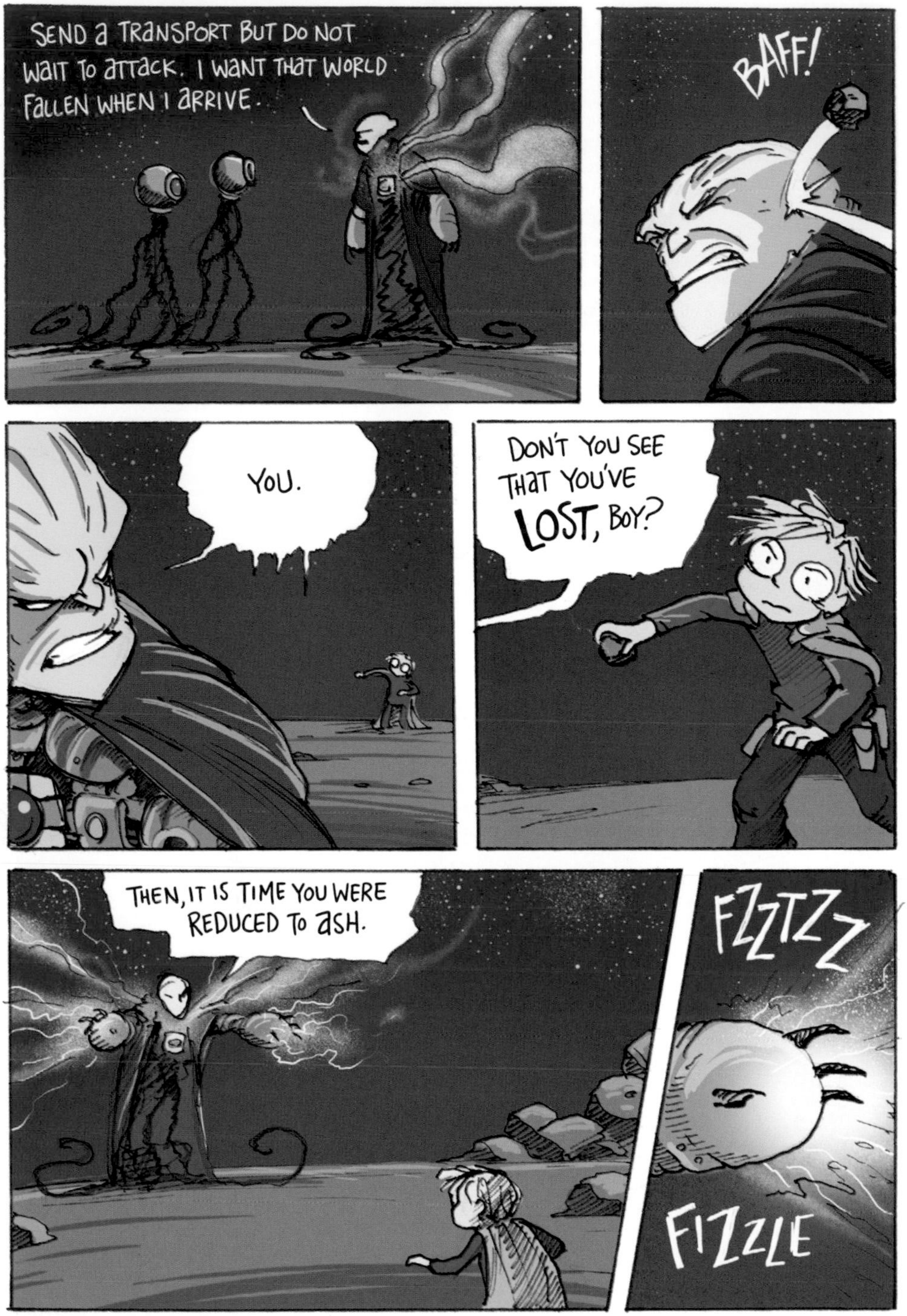
SEND A TRANSPORT BUT DO NOT WAIT TO ATTACK. I WANT THAT WORLD FALLEN WHEN I ARRIVE.
BAFF!
YOU.
DON'T YOU SEE THAT YOU'VE LOST, BOY?
THEN, IT IS TIME YOU WERE REDUCED TO ASH.
FZZTZZ
FIZZLE

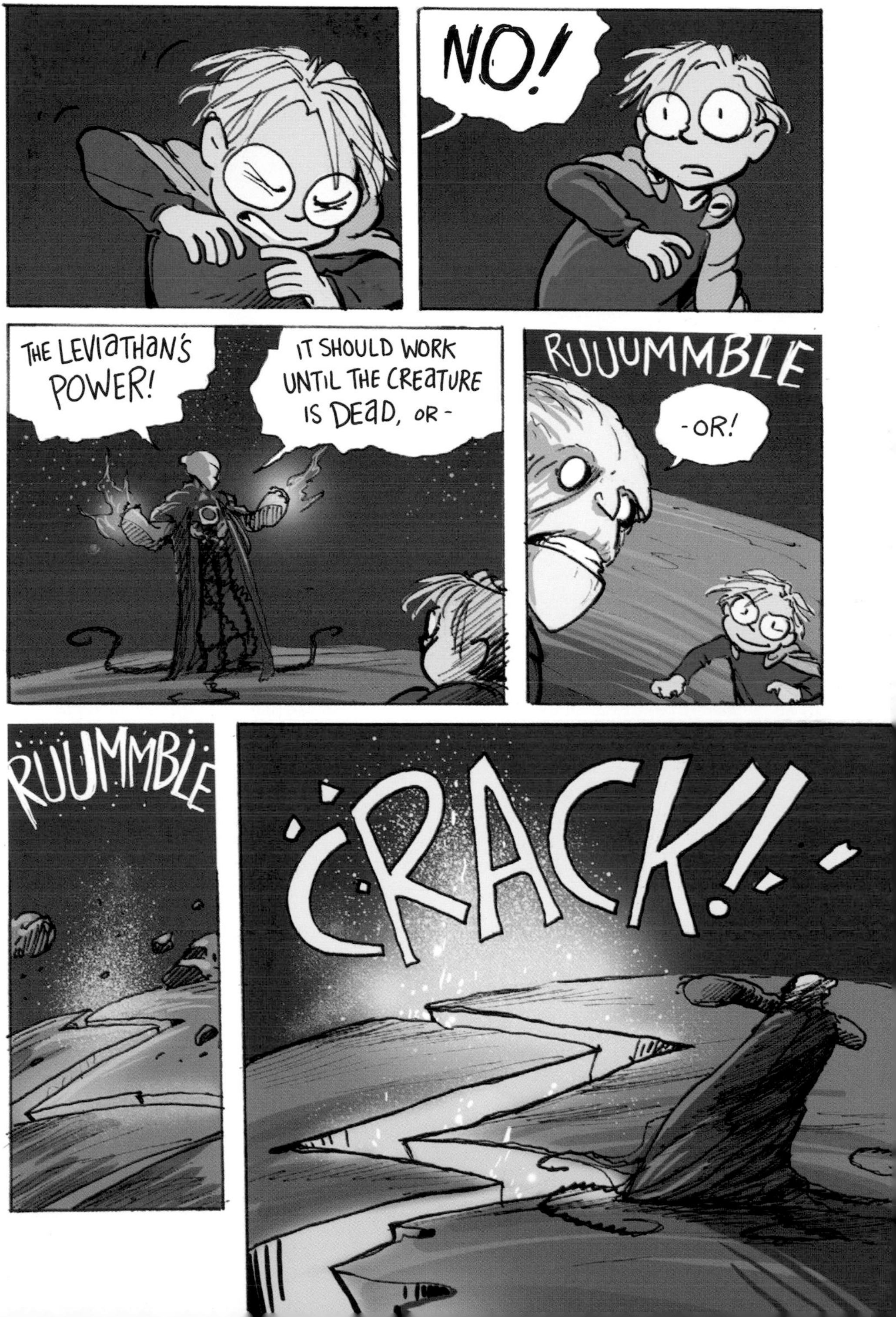
NO!
THE LEVIATHAN'S POWER!
IT SHOULD WORK UNTIL THE CREATURE IS DEAD, OR -
RUUUMMBLE
-OR!
RUUMMBLE
CRACK!!

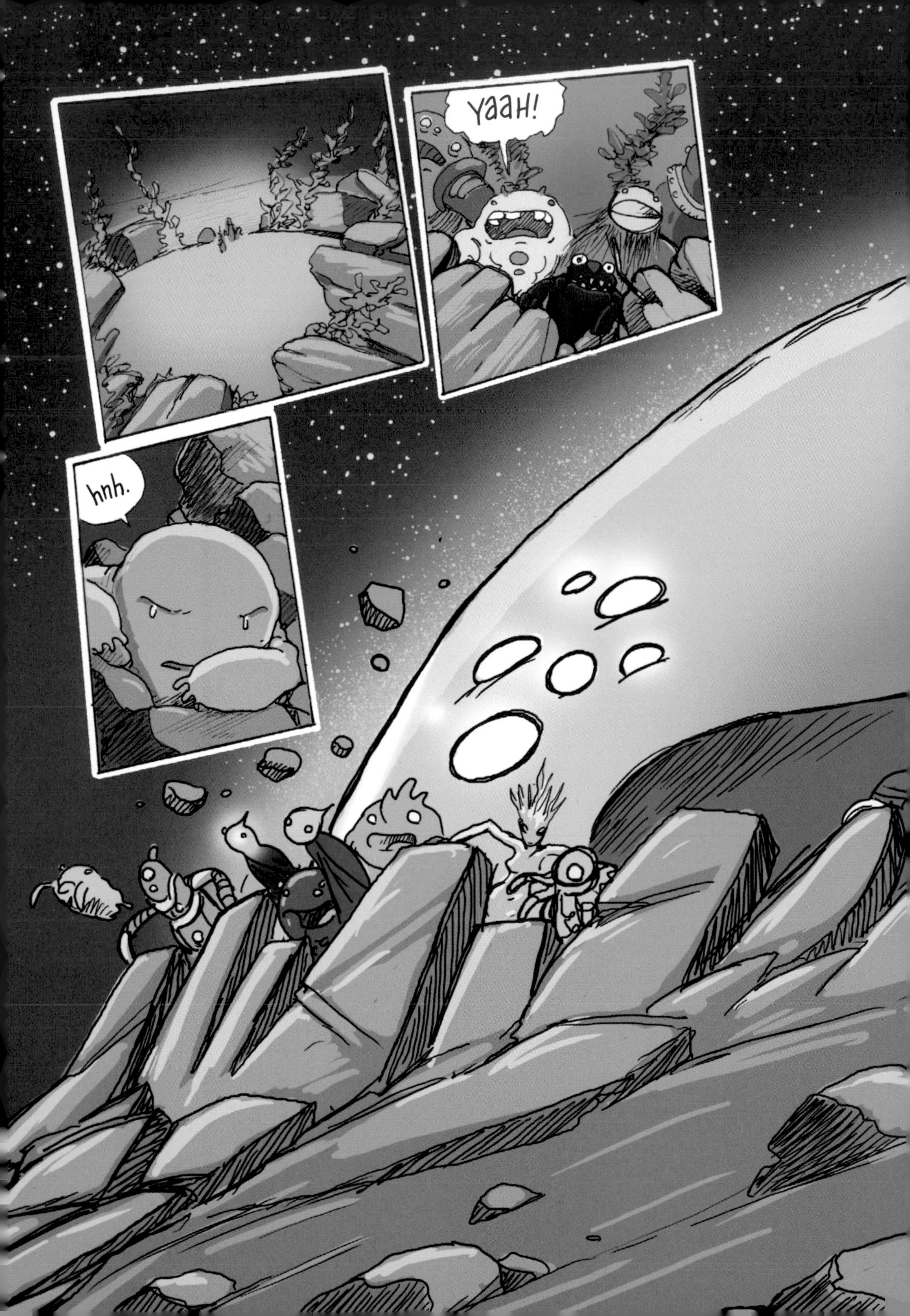
YAAH!
hnh.

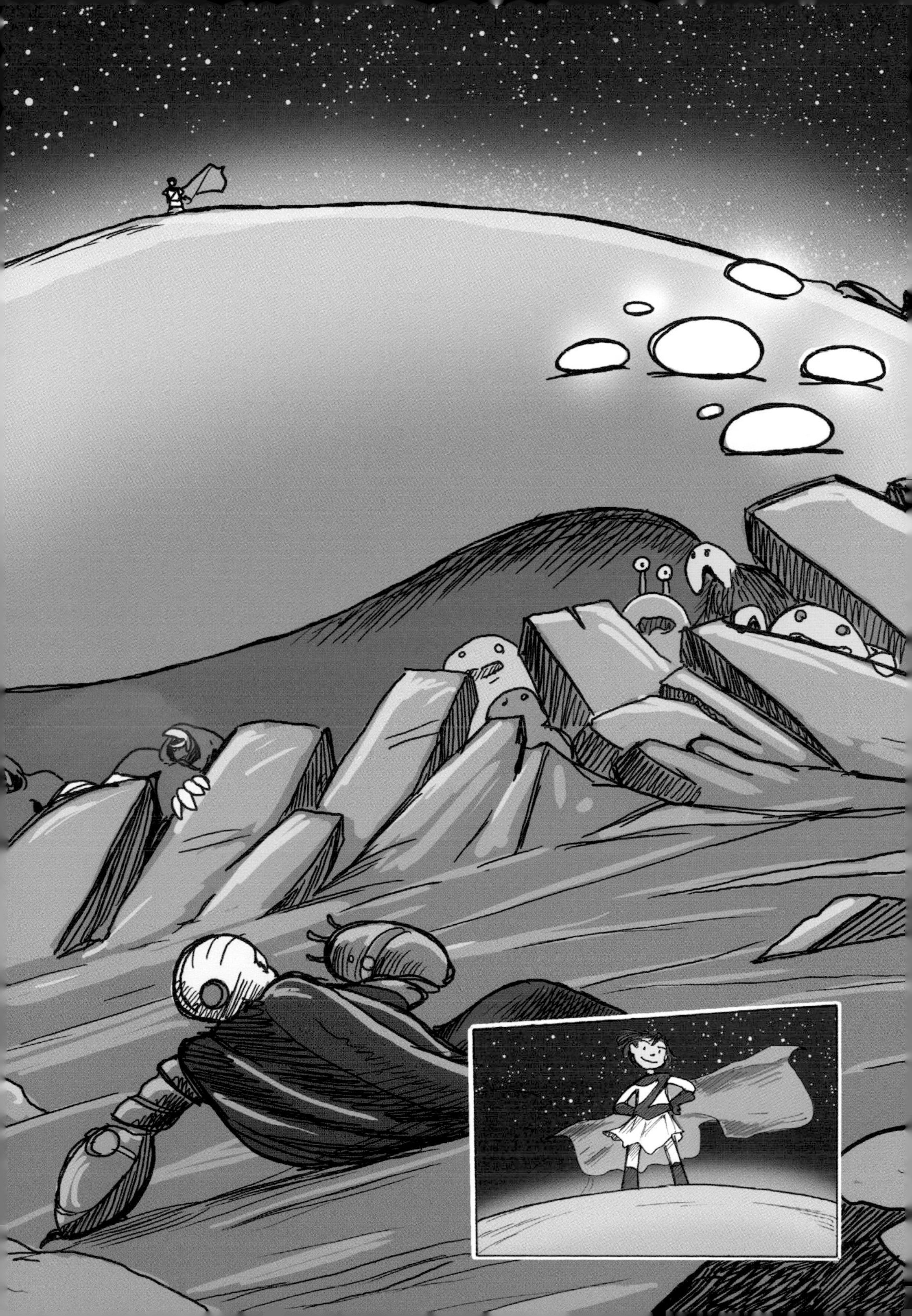

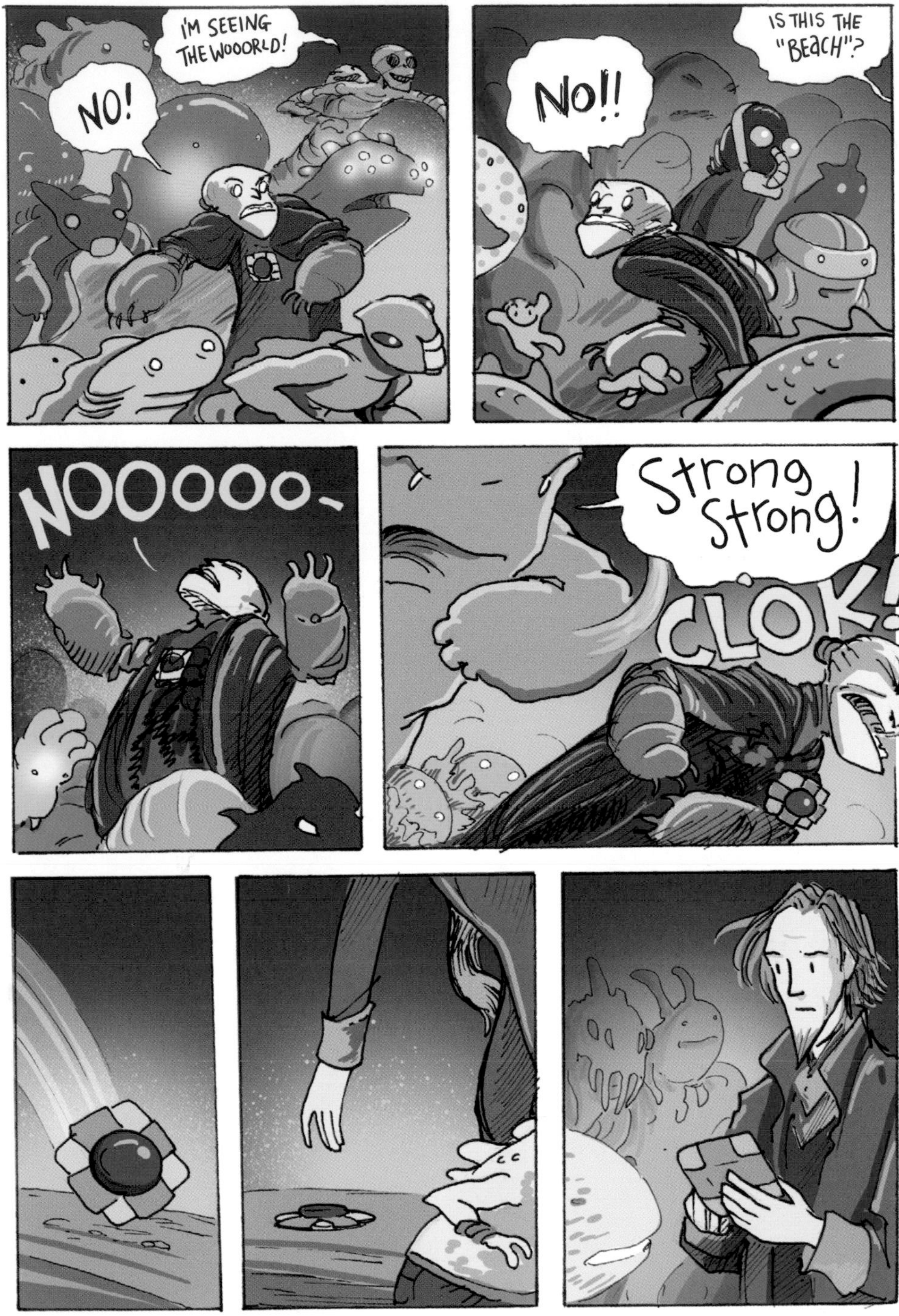

I'M SEEING THE WOOORLD!
NO!
IS THIS THE "BEACH"?
NO!!
NOOOOO-
Strong Strong!
CLOK!

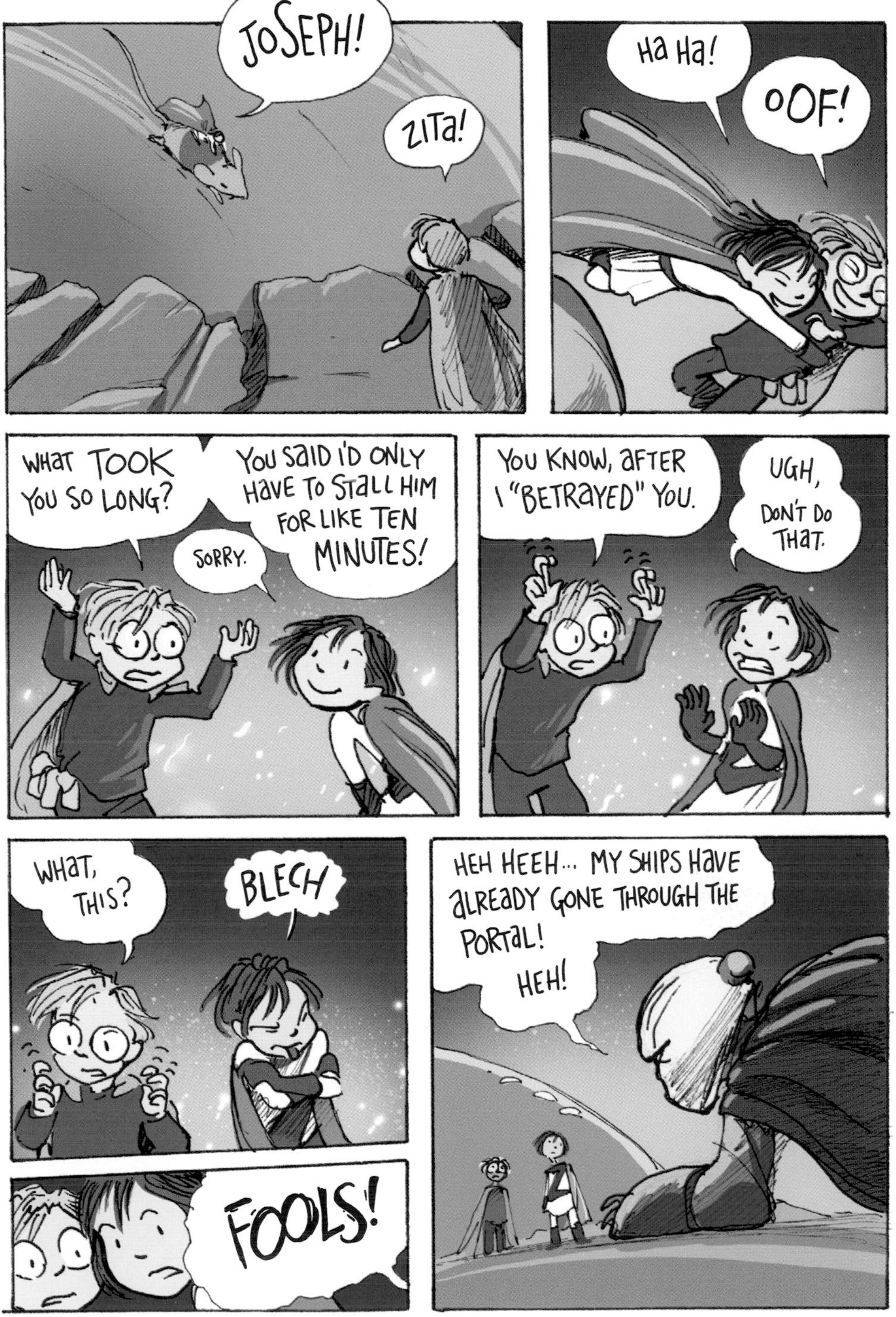
JOSEPH!
ZITA!
HA HA!
OOF!
WHAT TOOK YOU SO LONG?
SORRY.
YOU SAID I'D ONLY HAVE TO STALL HIM FOR LIKE TEN MINUTES!
YOU KNOW, AFTER I "BETRAYED" YOU.
UGH, DON'T DO THAT.
WHAT, THIS?
BLECH
FOOLS!
HEH HEEH... MY SHIPS HAVE ALREADY GONE THROUGH THE PORTAL!
HEH!

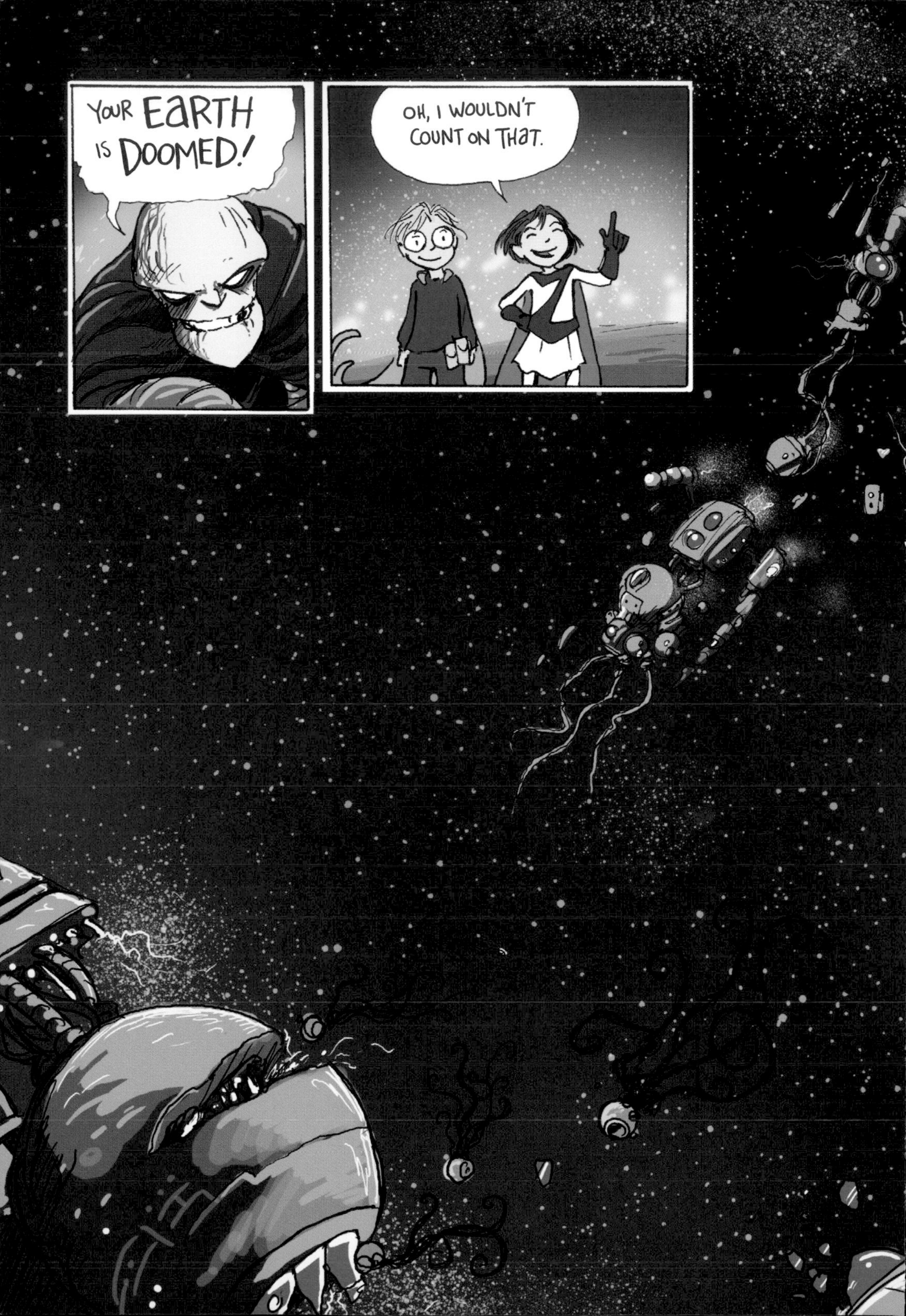
YOUR EARTH IS DOOMED!
OH, I WOULDN'T COUNT ON THAT.

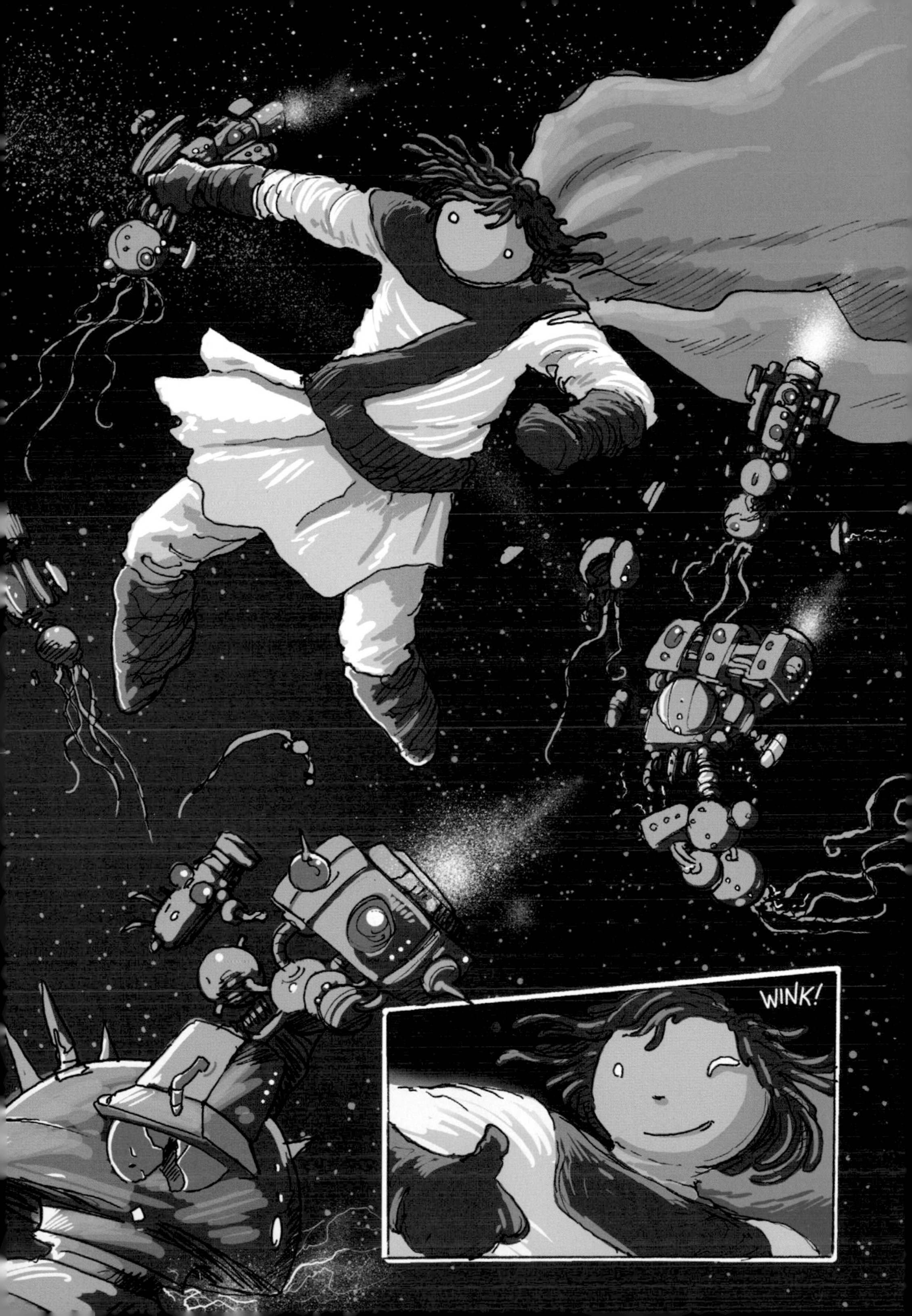
WINK!

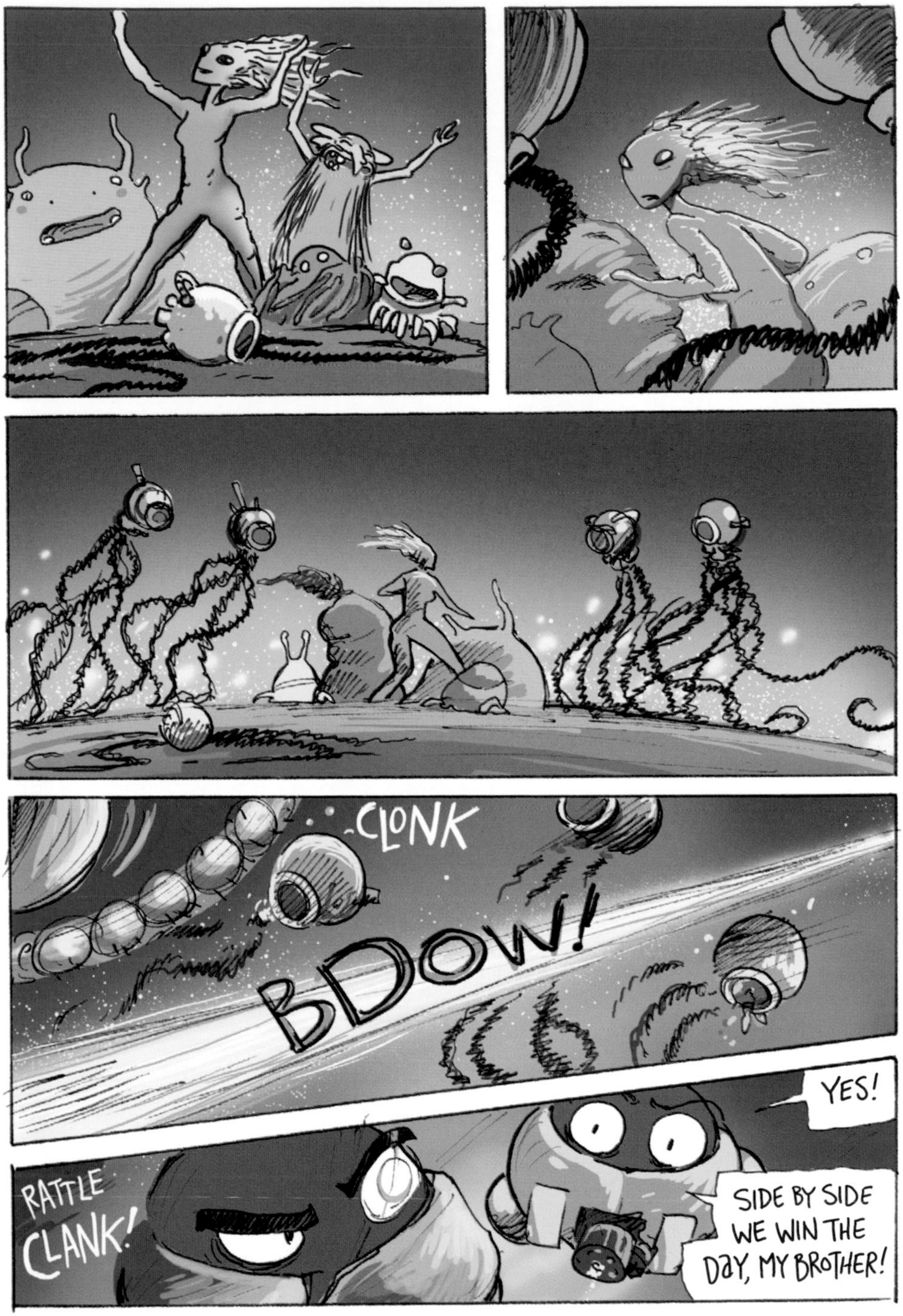
CLONK
BDOW!
YES!
RATTLE
CLANK!
SIDE BY SIDE WE WIN THE DAY, MY BROTHER!

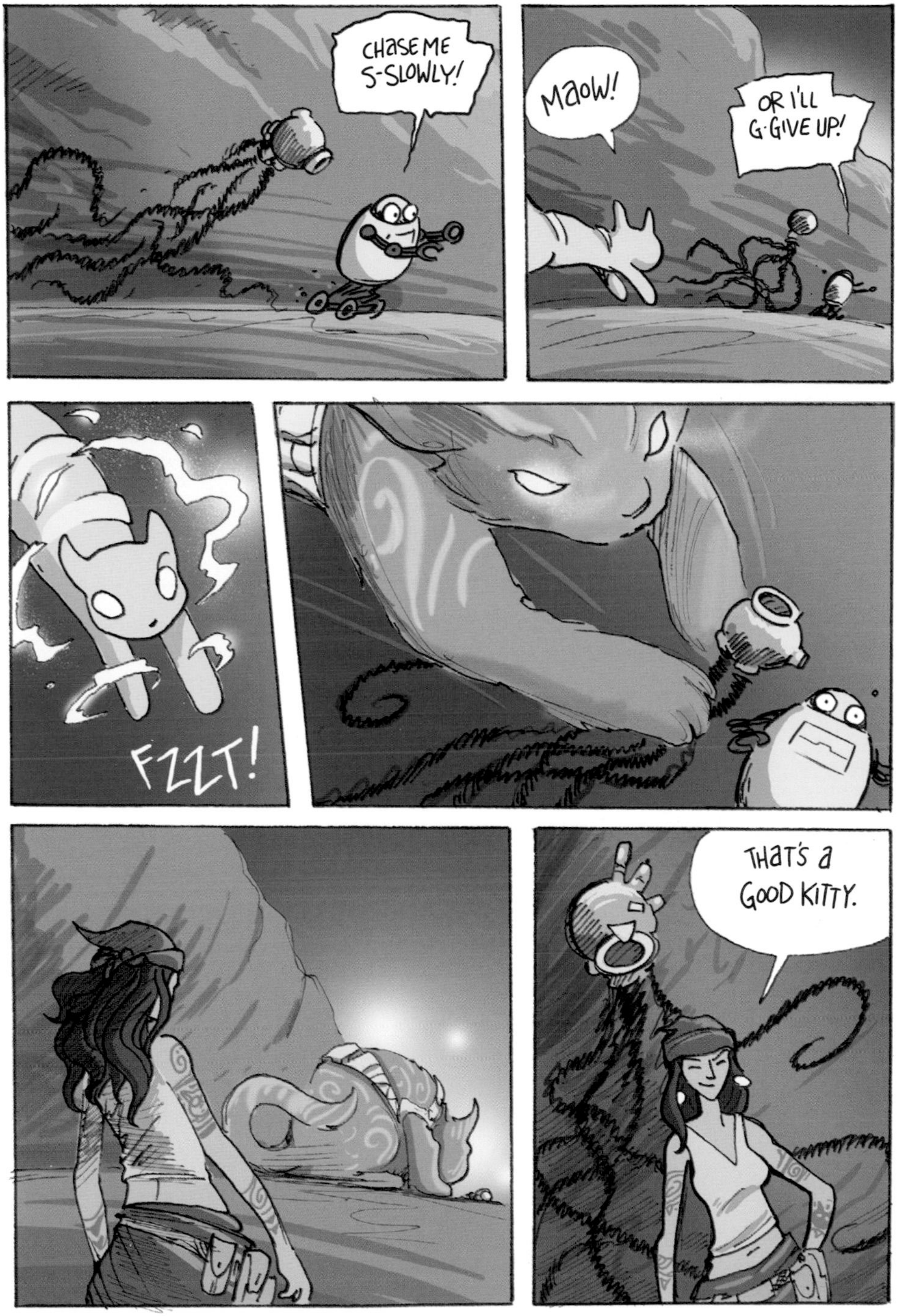
CHASE ME S-SLOWLY!
MAOW!
OR I'LL G-GIVE UP!
FZZT!
THAT'S A GOOD KITTY.

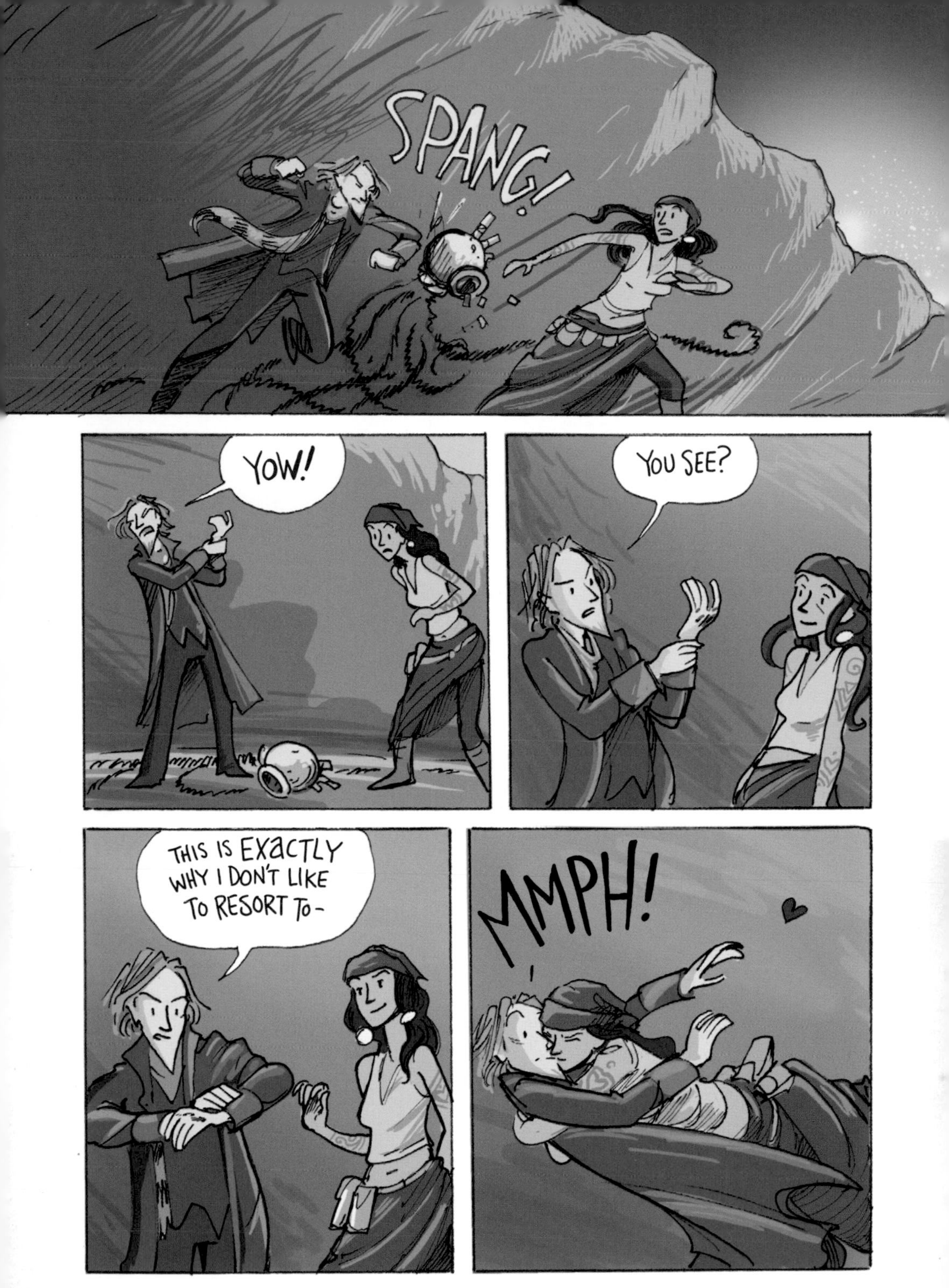
SPANG!
YOW!
YOU SEE?
THIS IS EXACTLY WHY I DON'T LIKE TO RESORT TO-
MMPH!

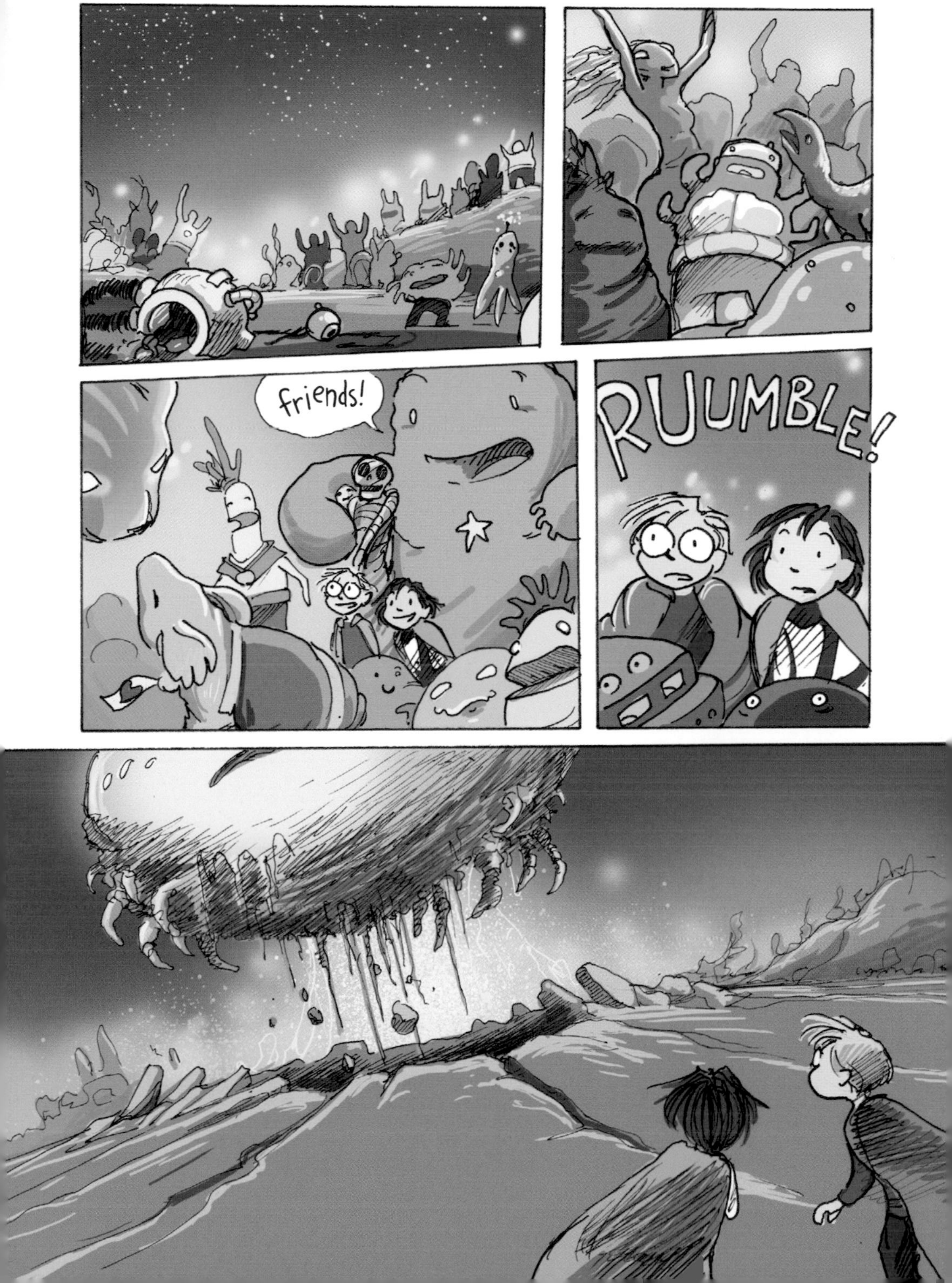
friends!
RUUMBLE!

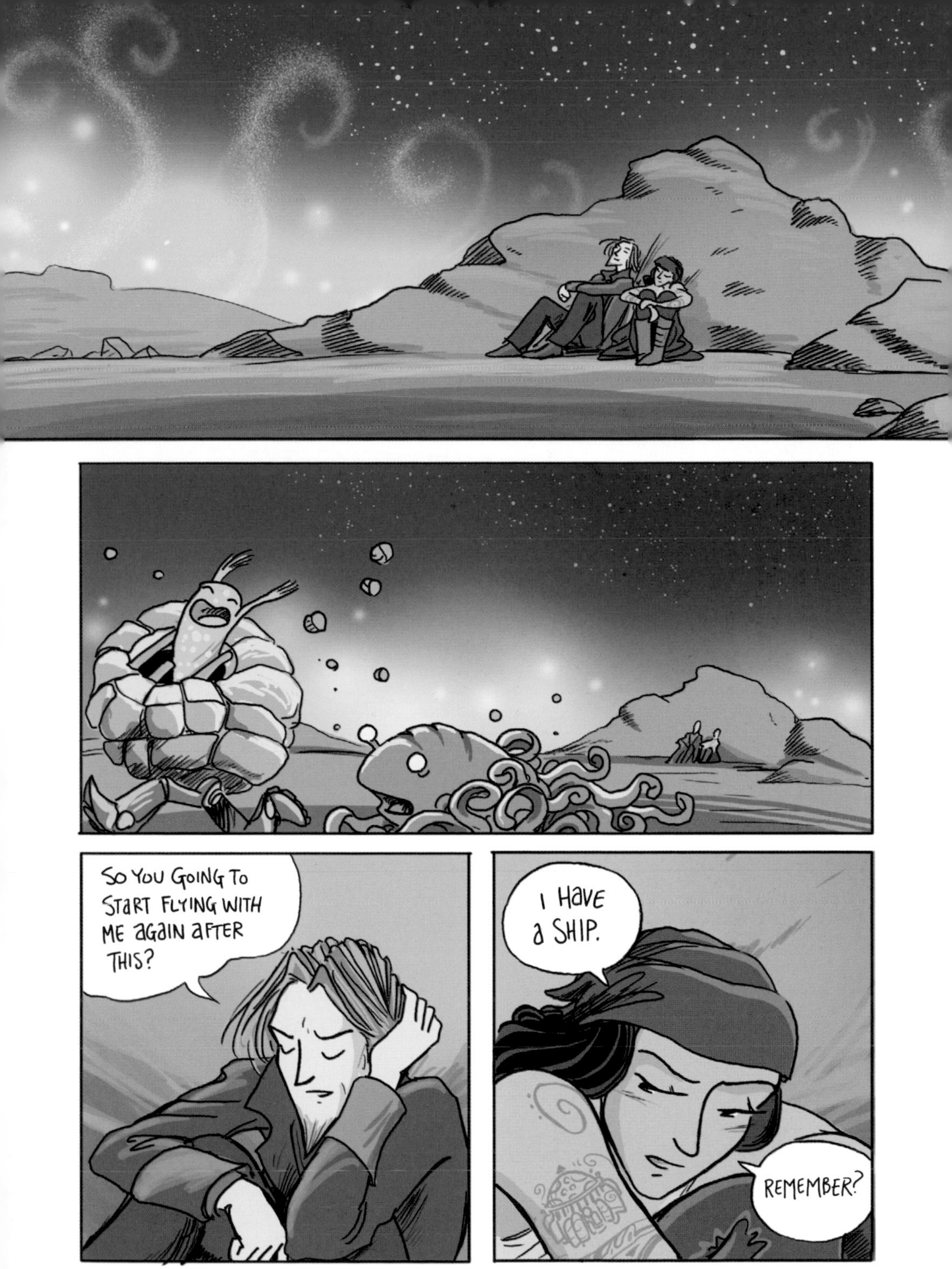
SO YOU GOING TO START FLYING WITH ME AGAIN AFTER THIS?
I HAVE A SHIP.
REMEMBER?

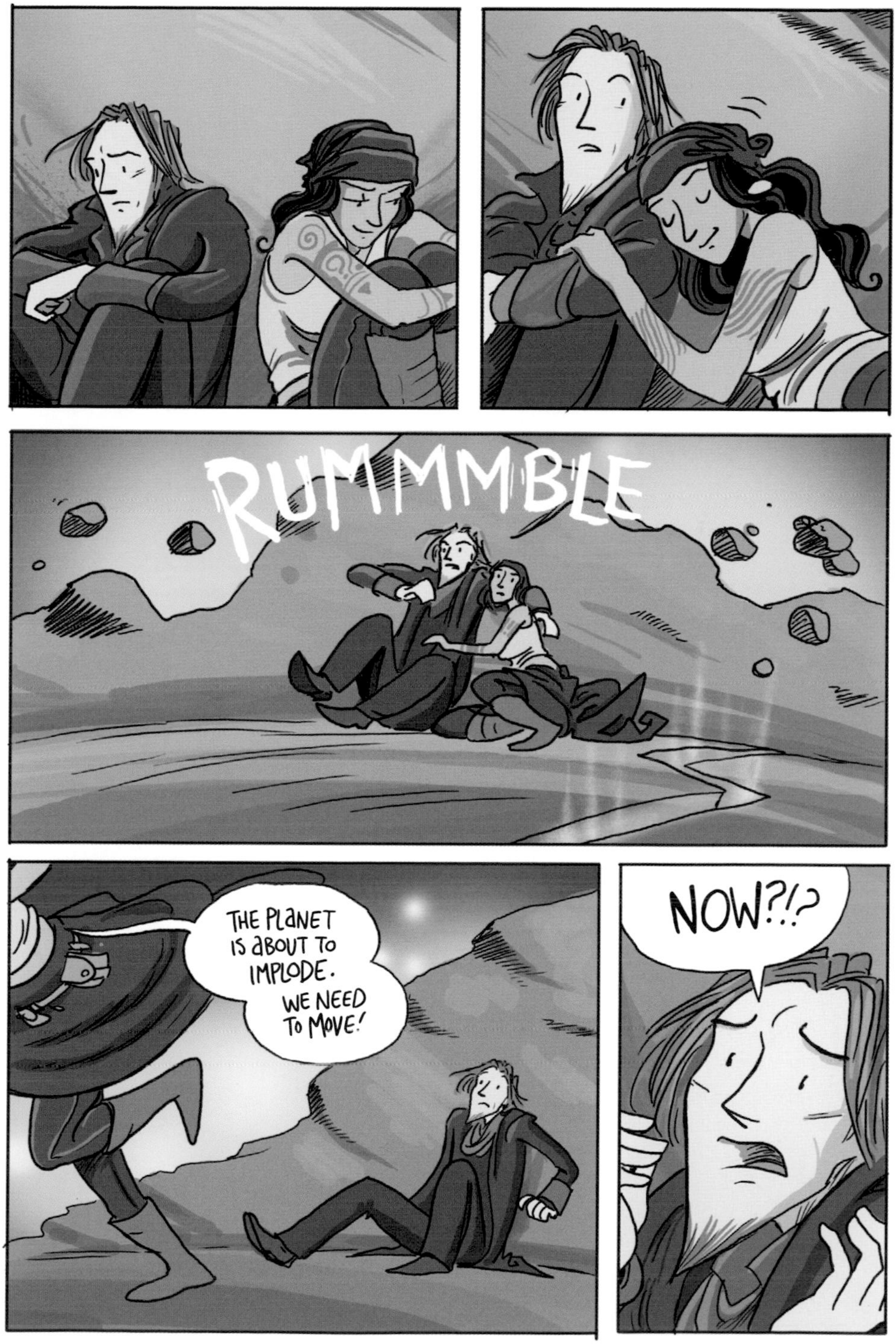
RUMMMBLE
THE PLANET IS ABOUT TO IMPLODE.
WE NEED TO MOVE!
NOW?!?

THAT'S RIGHT.

GO HOME.

RUUMBLE!

I TOLD YOU THIS PLACE CAN'T HOLD ITSELF TOGETHER WITHOUT THE LEVIATHAN!

IT'S GOING TO COLLAPSE!

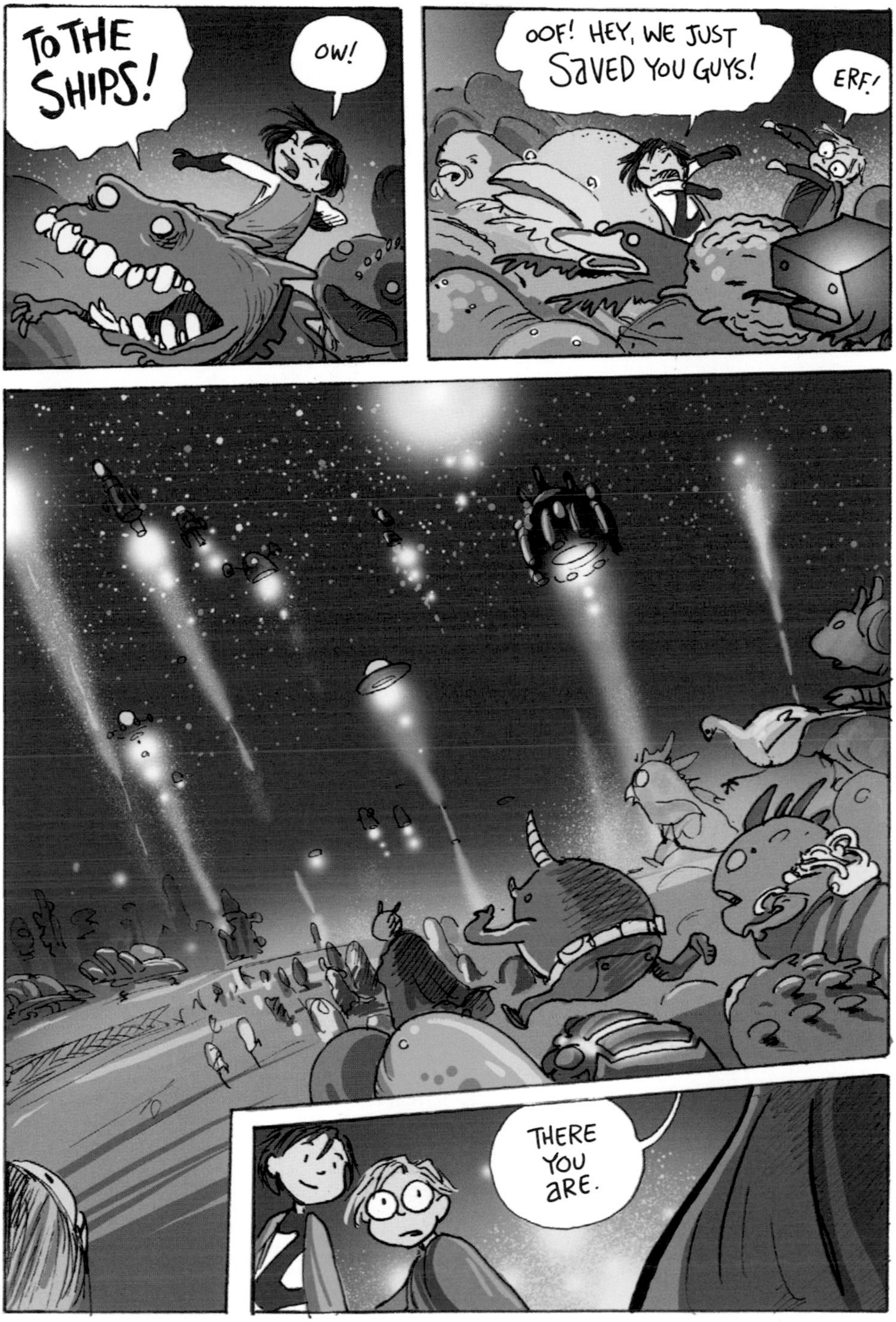
TO THE SHIPS!
OW!
OOF! HEY, WE JUST SAVED YOU GUYS!
ERF!
THERE YOU ARE.

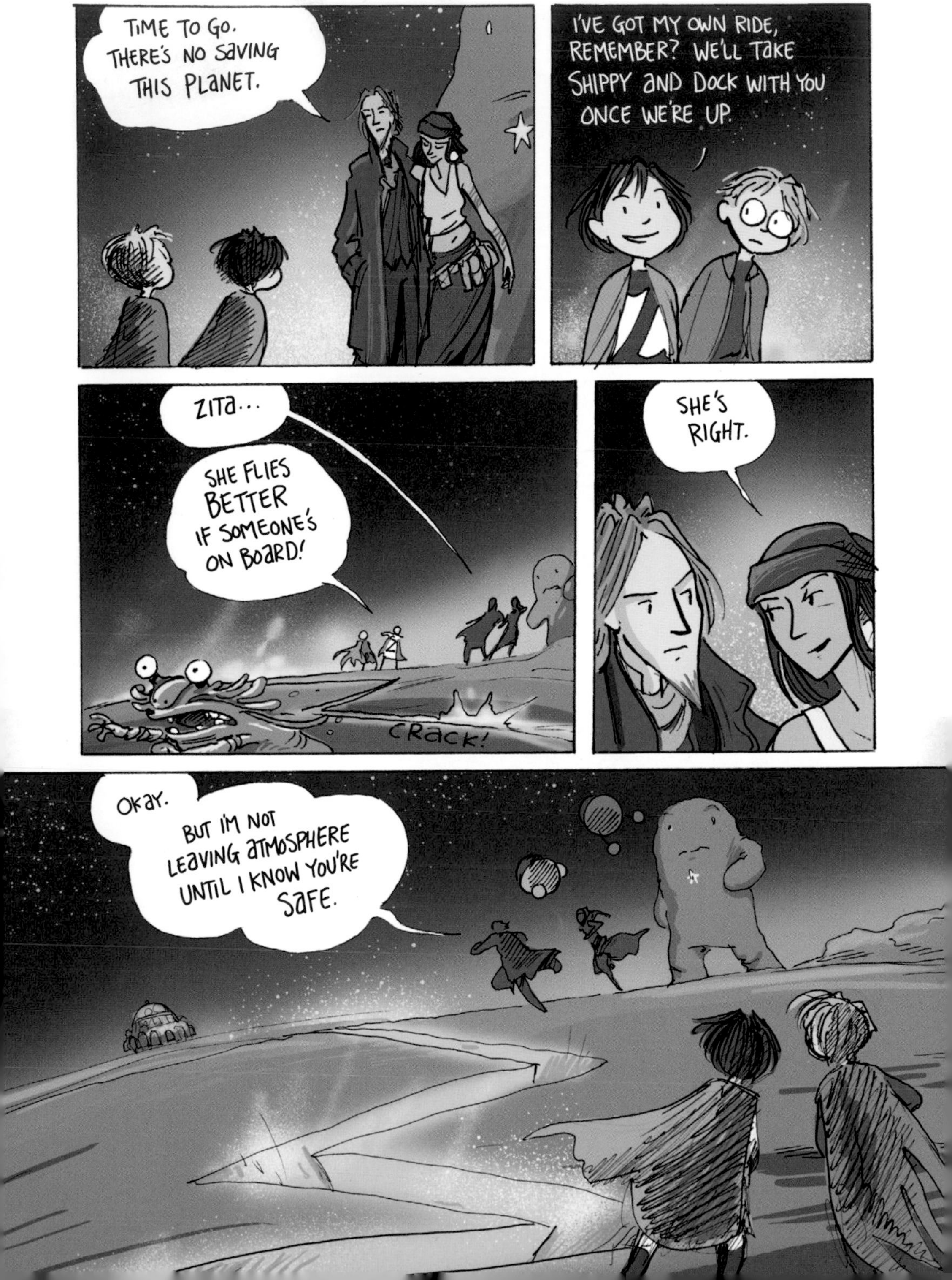
TIME TO GO. THERE'S NO SAVING THIS PLANET.
I'VE GOT MY OWN RIDE, REMEMBER? WE'LL TAKE SHIPPY AND DOCK WITH YOU ONCE WE'RE UP.
ZITA...
SHE FLIES BETTER IF SOMEONE'S ON BOARD!
CRACK!
SHE'S RIGHT.
OKAY.
BUT I'M NOT LEAVING ATMOSPHERE UNTIL I KNOW YOU'RE SAFE.

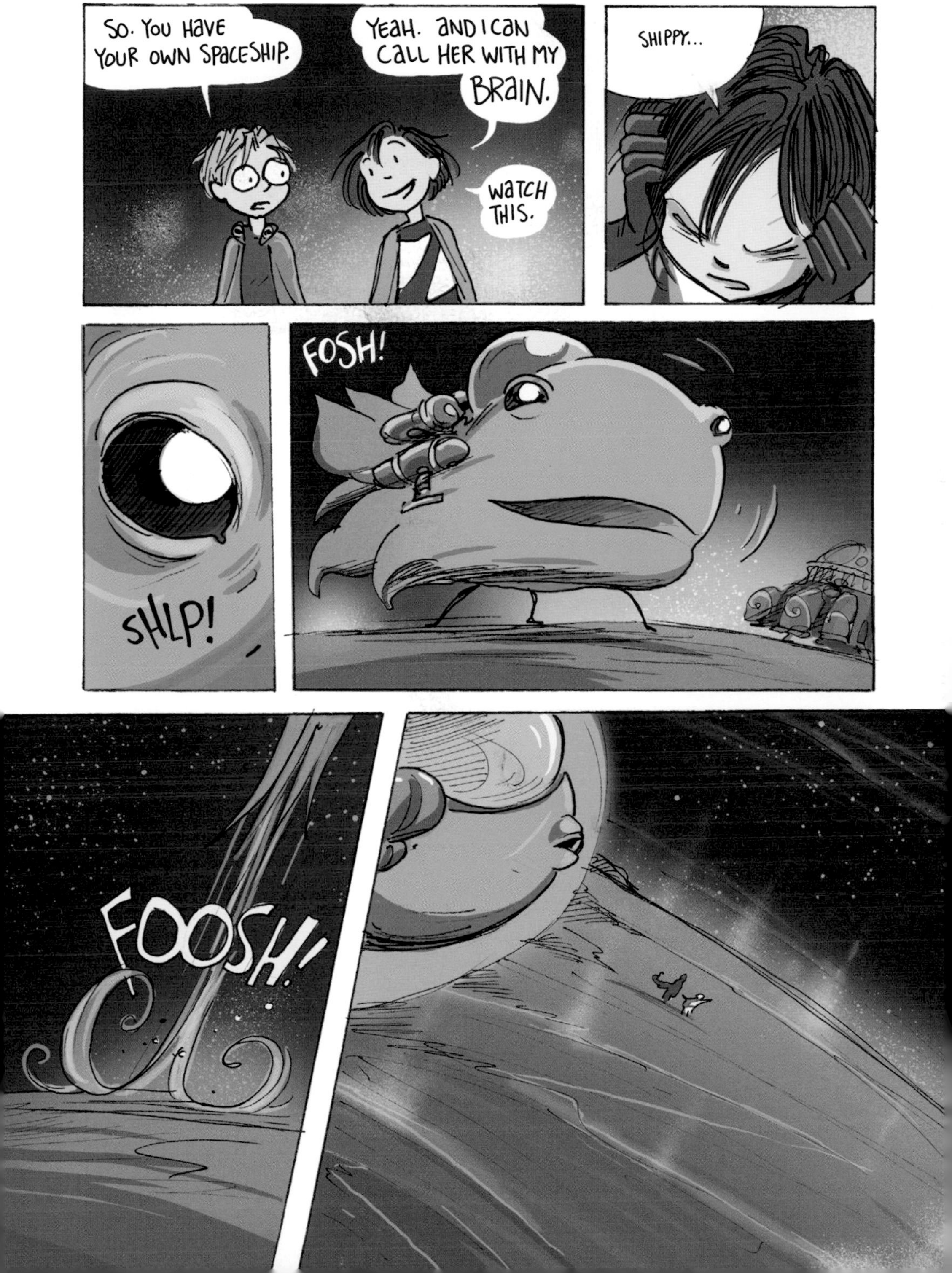
SO. YOU HAVE YOUR OWN SPACESHIP.
YEAH. AND I CAN CALL HER WITH MY BRAIN.
WATCH THIS.
SHIPPY...
SHLP!
FOSH!
FOOSH!

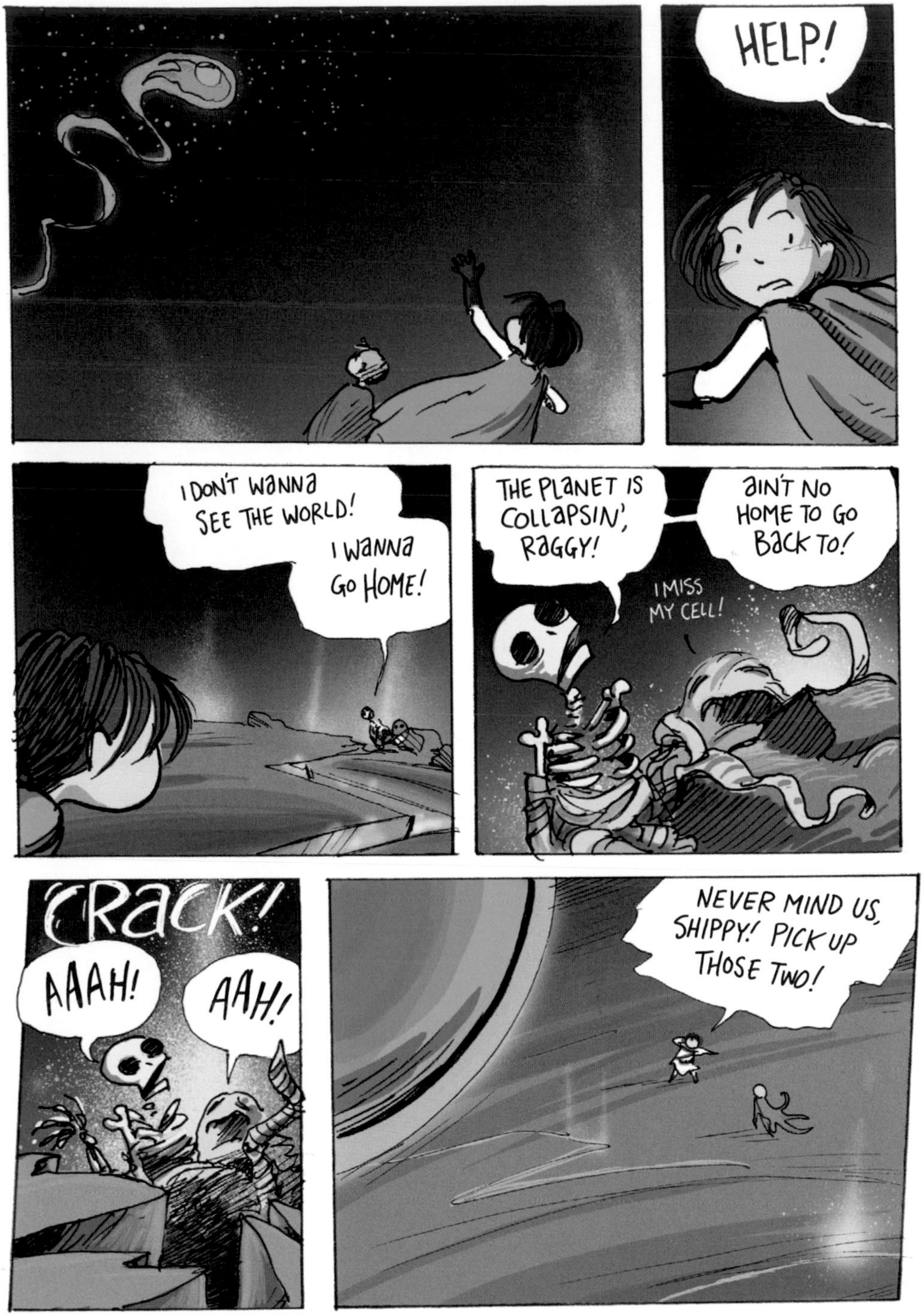
HELP!
I DON'T WANNA SEE THE WORLD!
I WANNA GO HOME!
THE PLANET IS COLLAPSIN', RAGGY!
AIN'T NO HOME TO GO BACK TO!
I MISS MY CELL!
CRACK!
AAAH!
AAH!
NEVER MIND US, SHIPPY! PICK UP THOSE TWO!

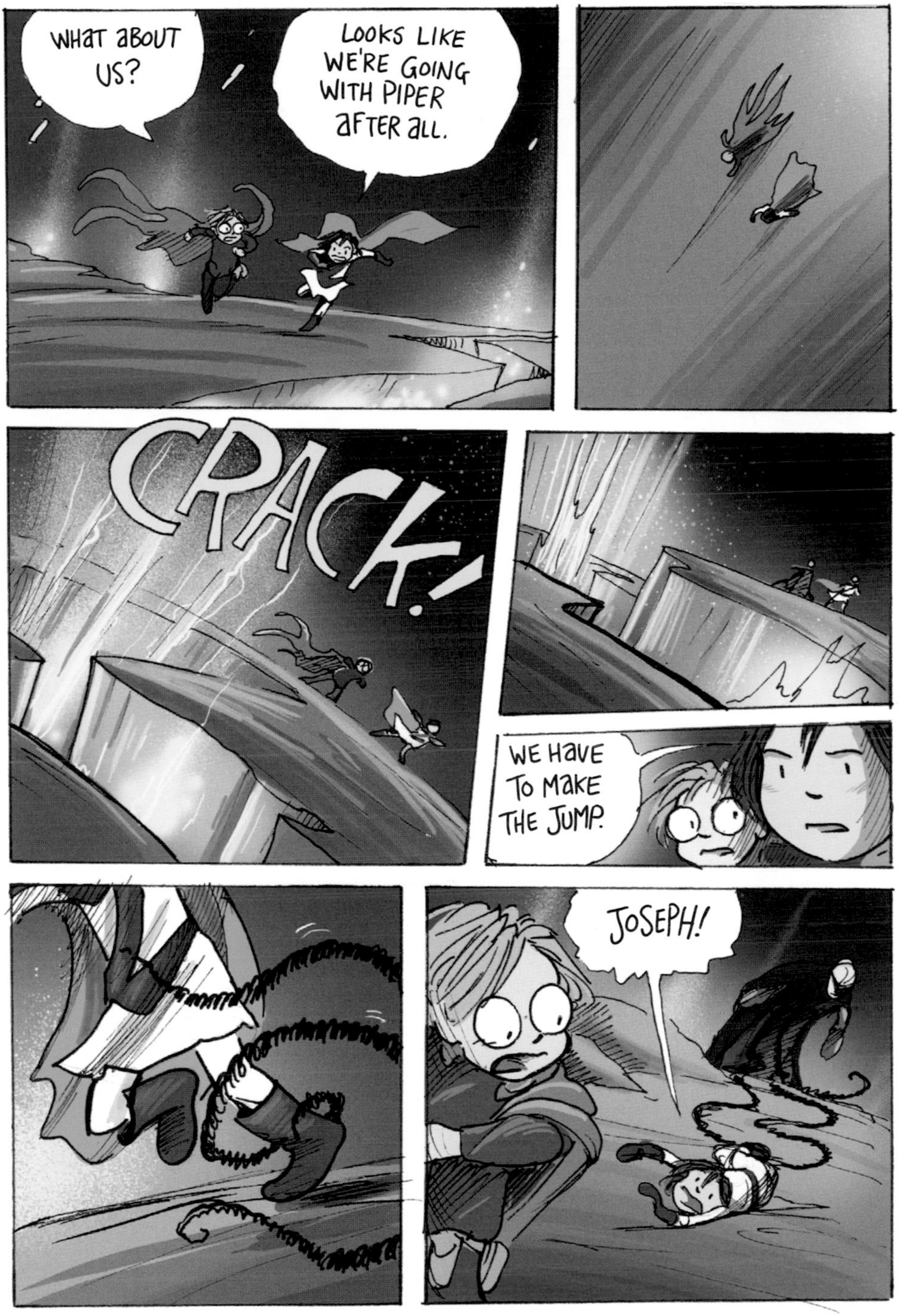
WHAT ABOUT US?
LOOKS LIKE WE'RE GOING WITH PIPER AFTER ALL.
CRACK!
WE HAVE TO MAKE THE JUMP.
JOSEPH!

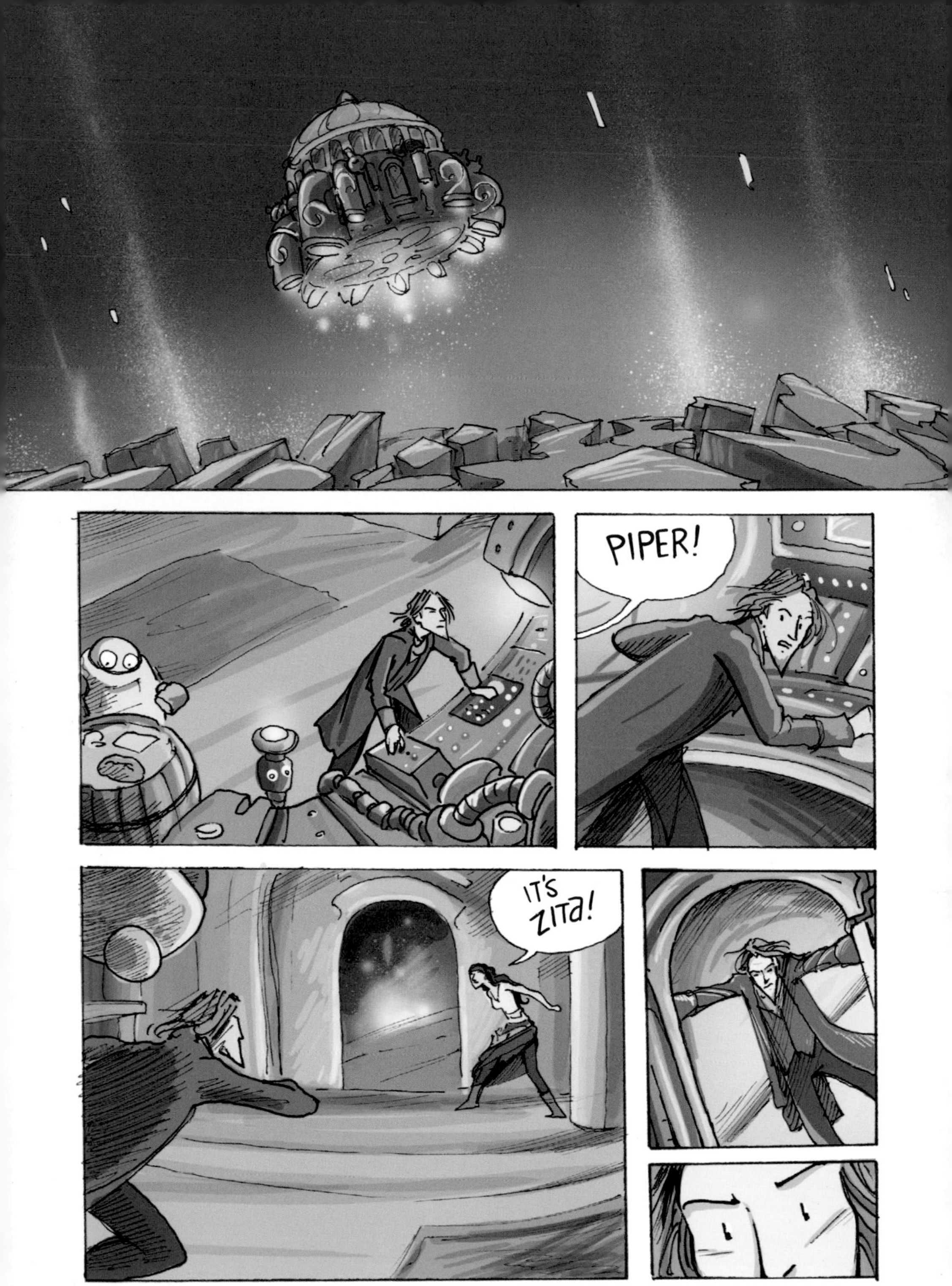
PIPER!
IT'S ZITA!

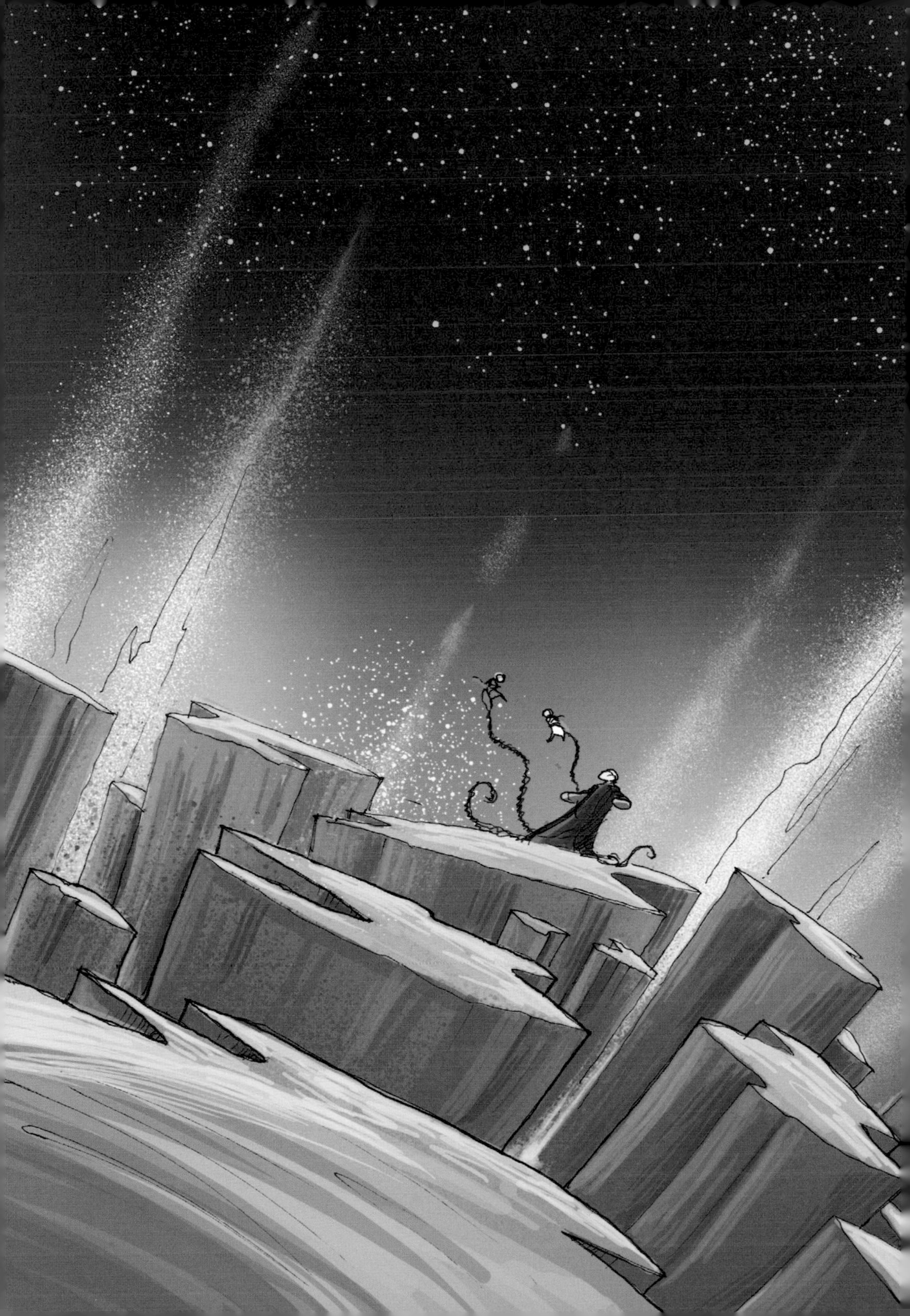

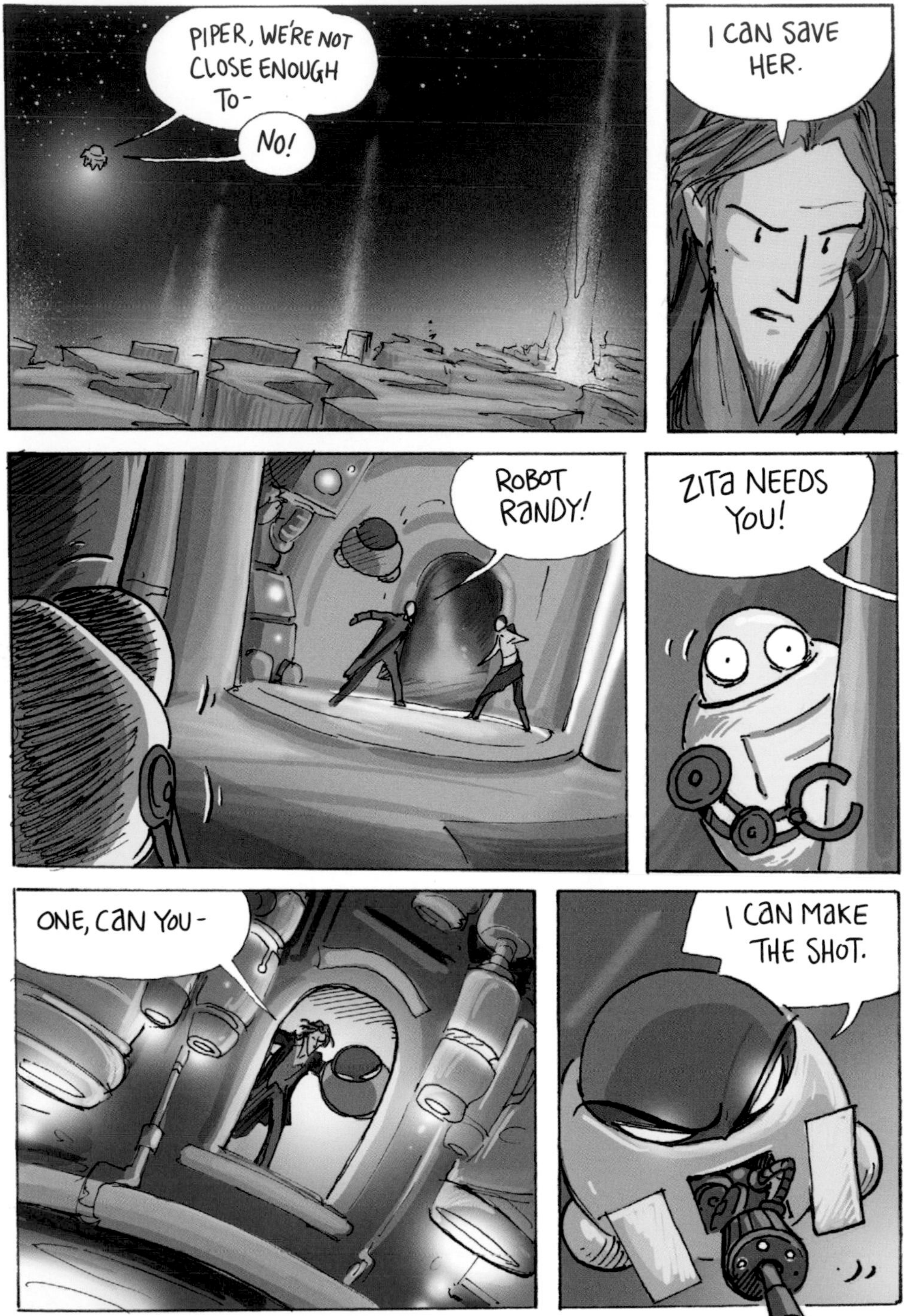
PIPER, WE'RE NOT CLOSE ENOUGH TO-
NO!
I CAN SAVE HER.
ROBOT RANDY!
ZITA NEEDS YOU!
ONE, CAN YOU-
I CAN MAKE THE SHOT.

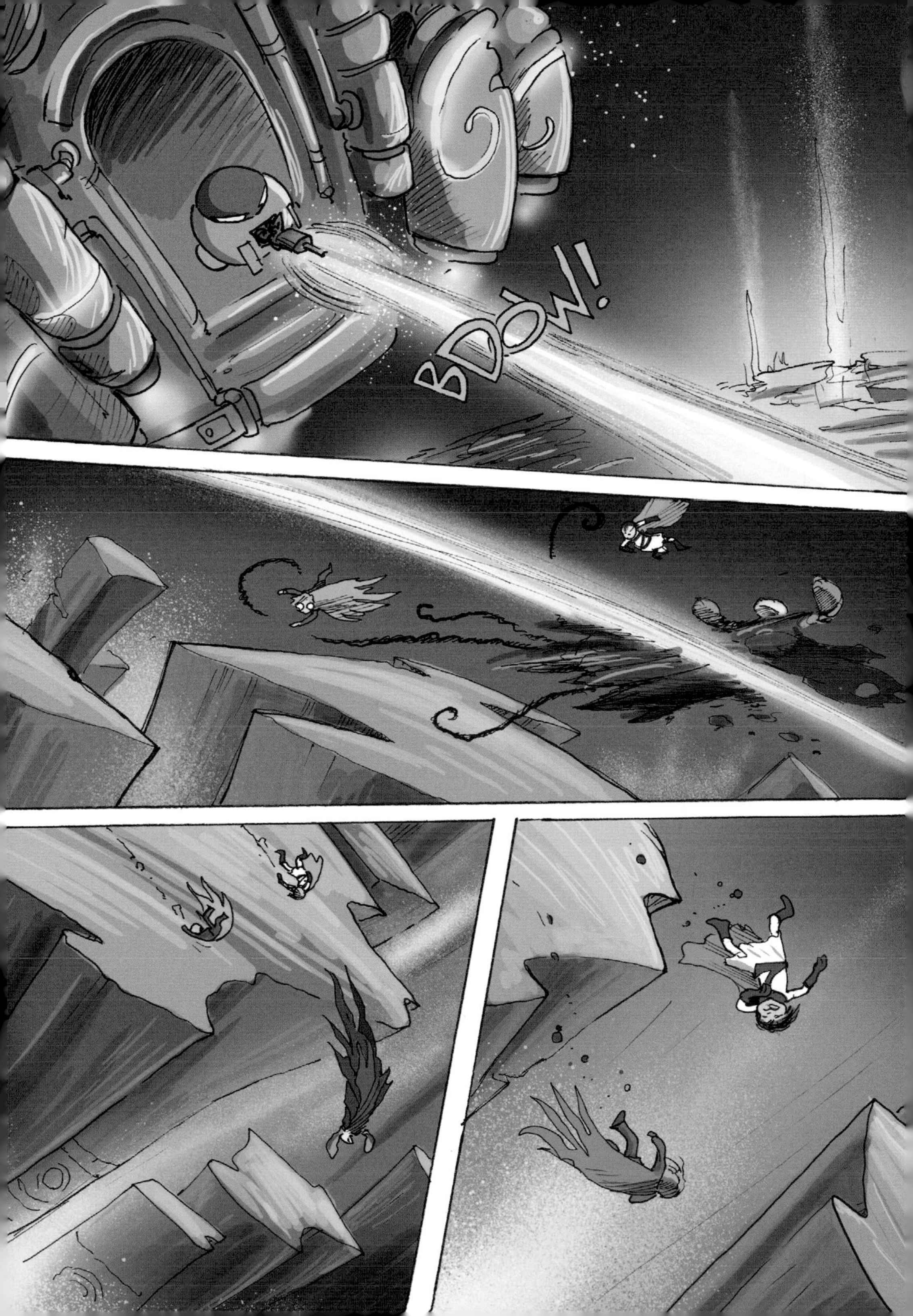
BDOW!

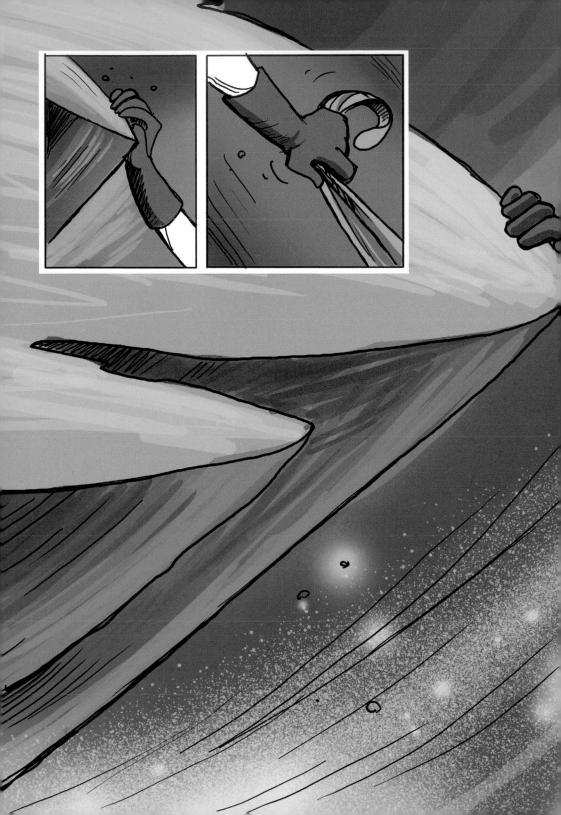

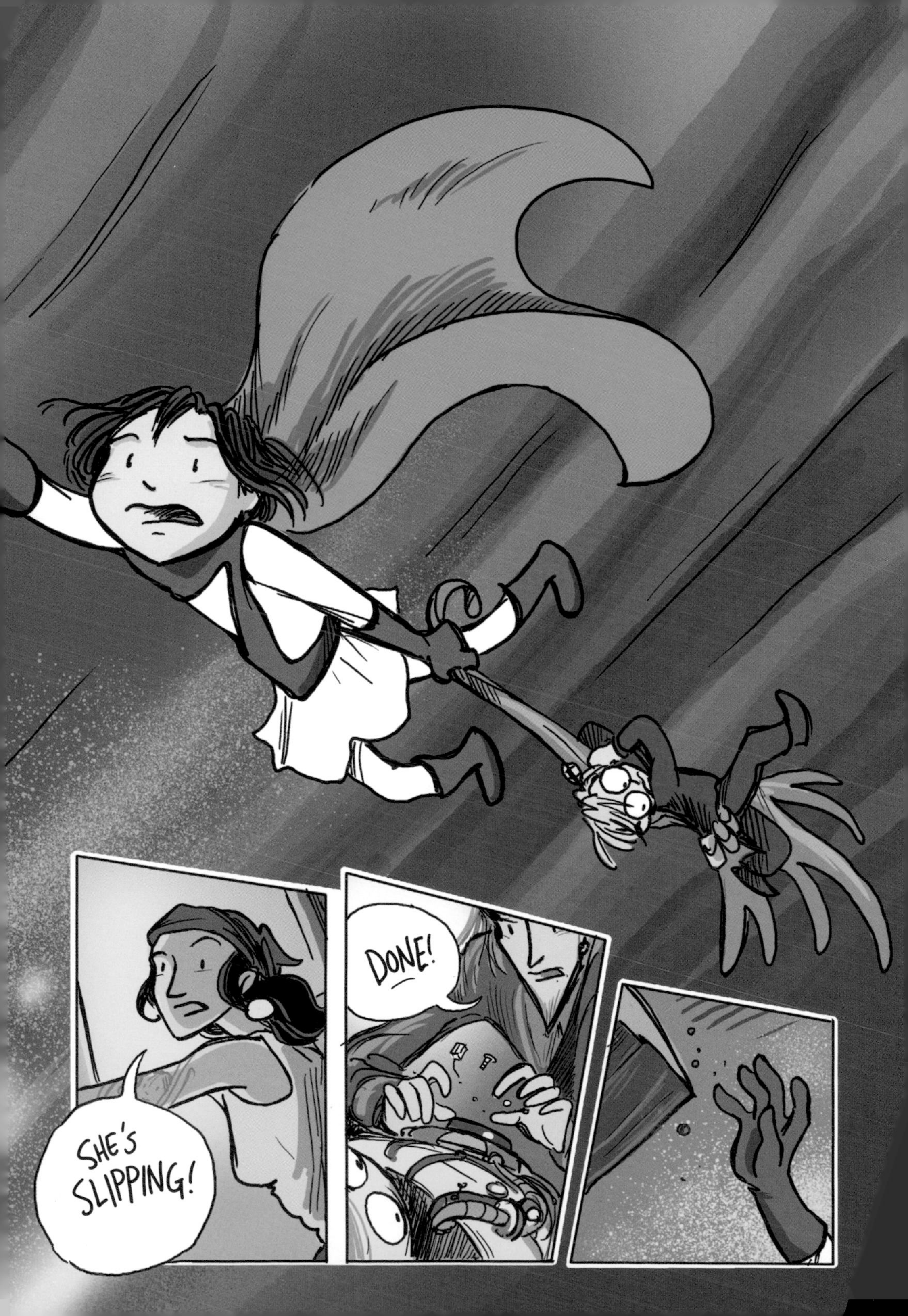

SHE'S SLIPPING!
DONE!

NOW, ROBOT RANDY!

THOOM!

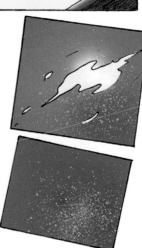

Chapter
Seven

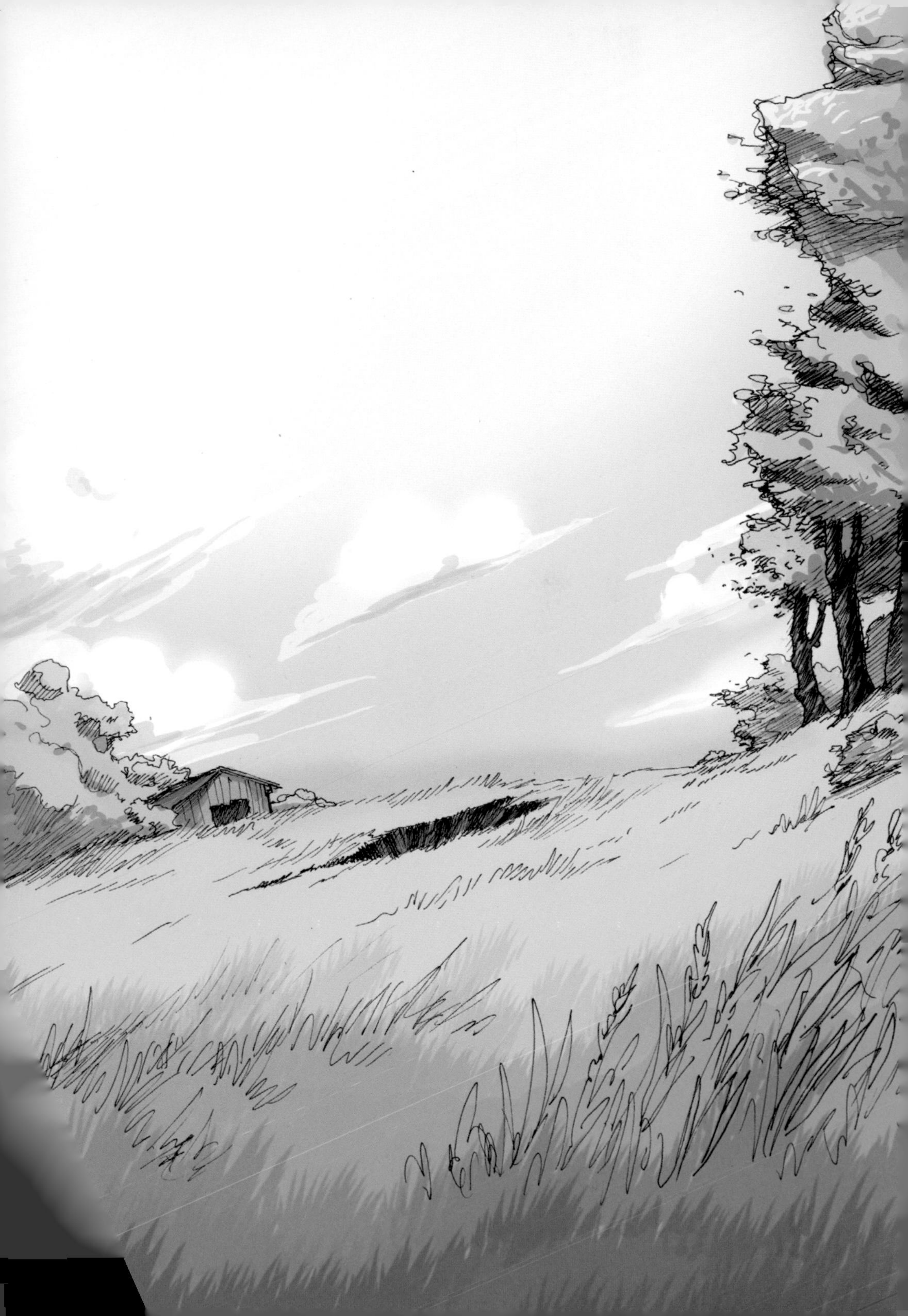

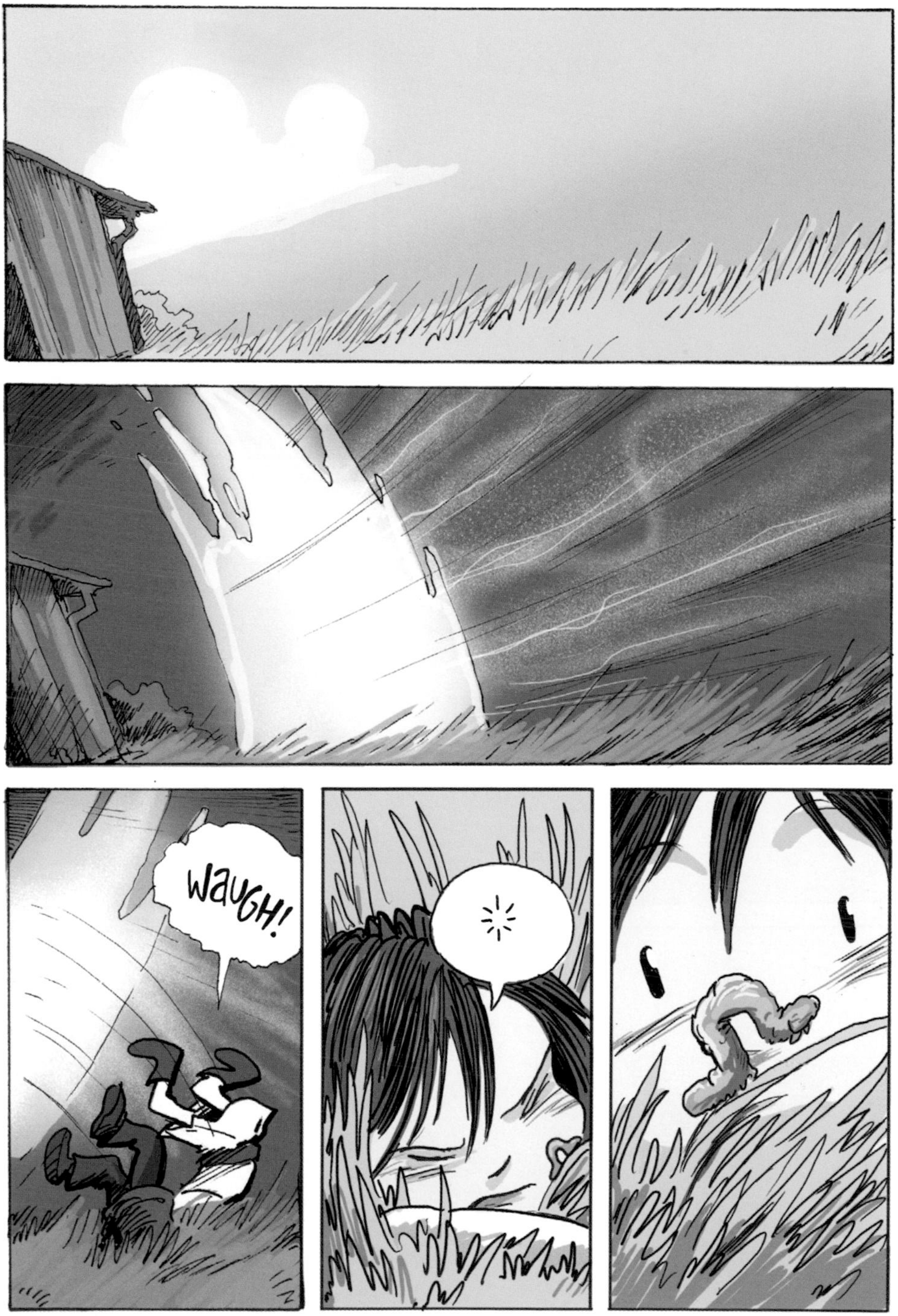
WAUGH!

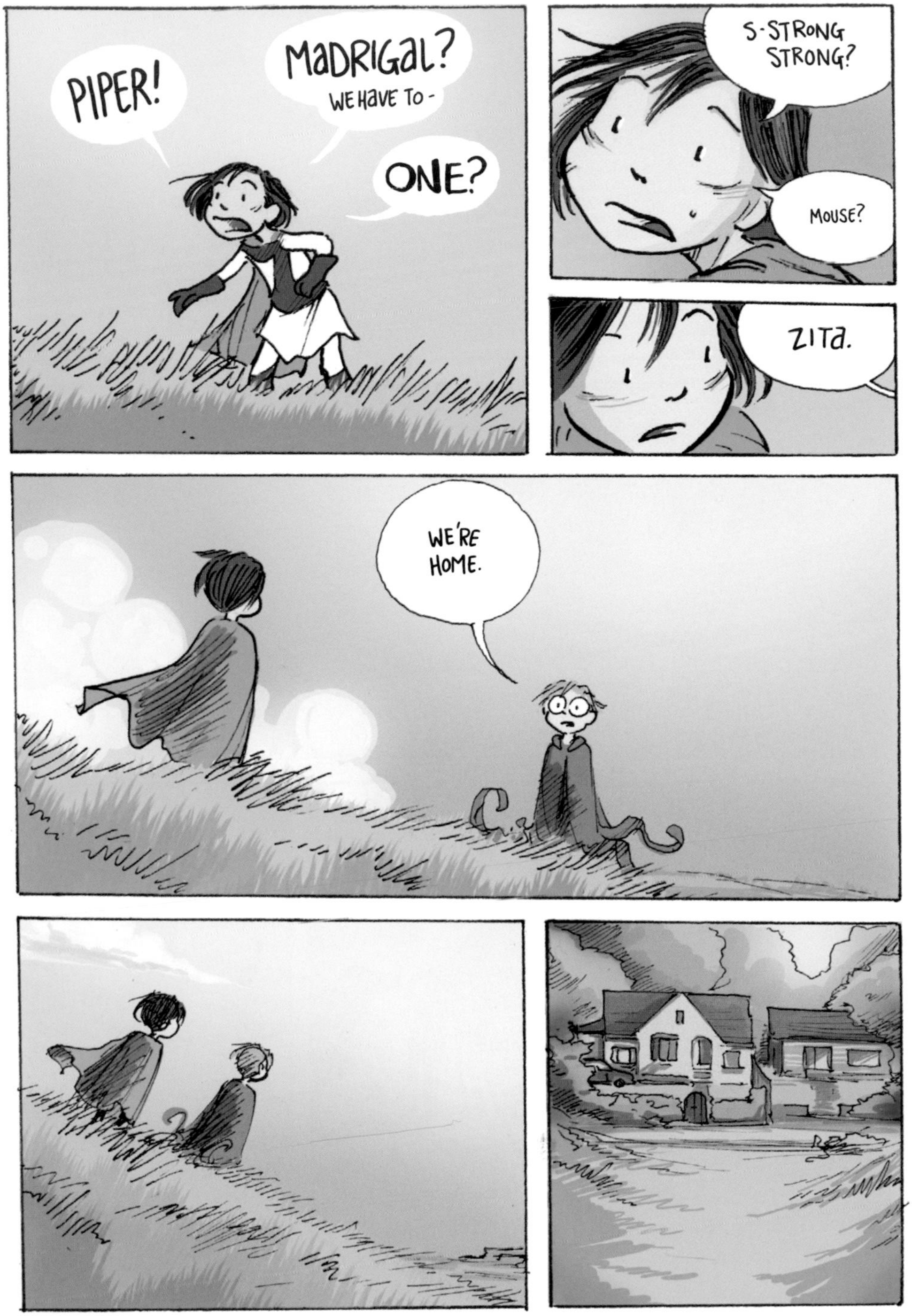
PIPER!
MADRIGAL?
WE HAVE TO -
ONE?
S-STRONG STRONG?
MOUSE?
ZITA.
WE'RE HOME.

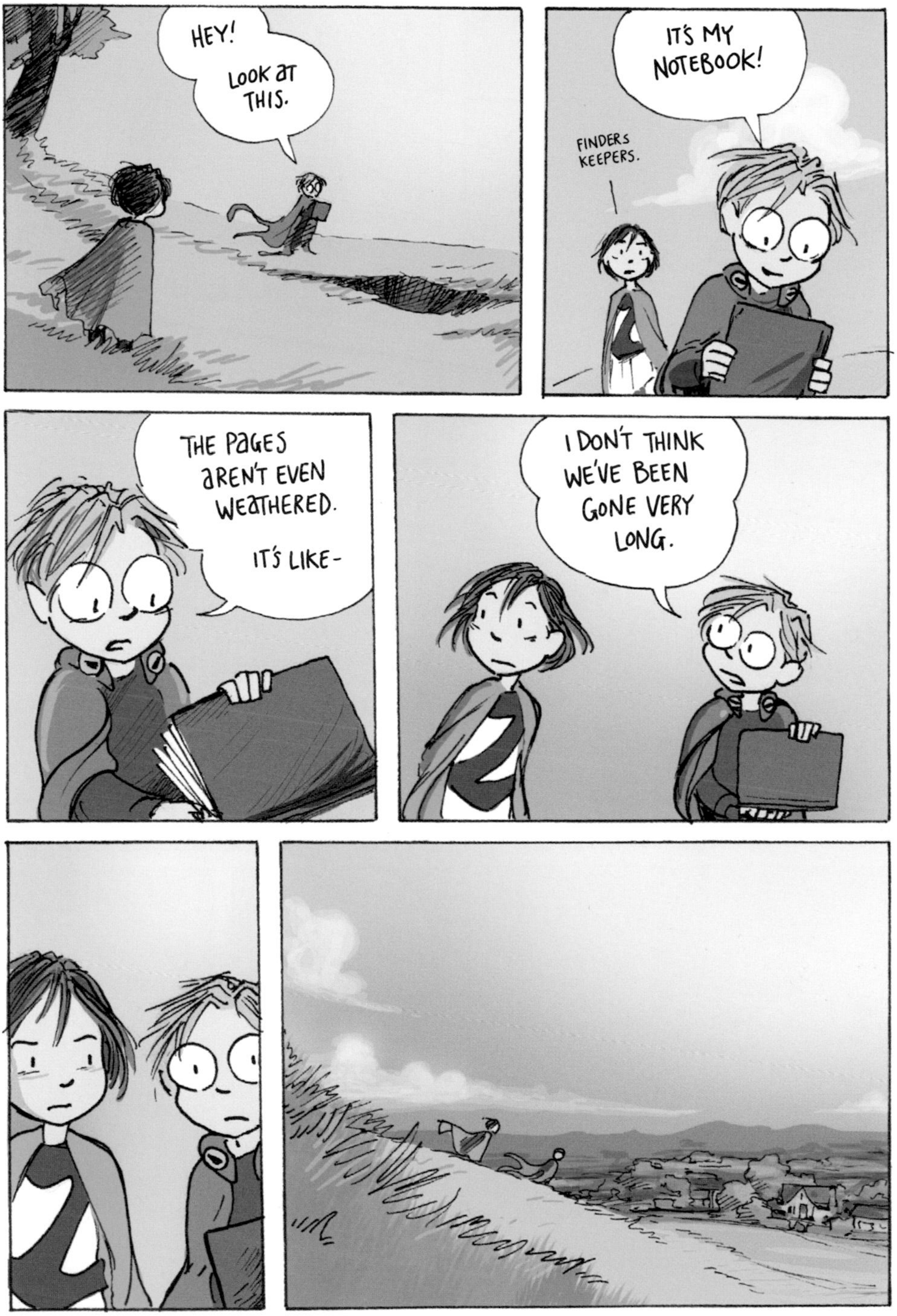
HEY!
LOOK AT THIS.
IT'S MY NOTEBOOK!
FINDERS KEEPERS.
THE PAGES AREN'T EVEN WEATHERED.
IT'S LIKE-
I DON'T THINK WE'VE BEEN GONE VERY LONG.

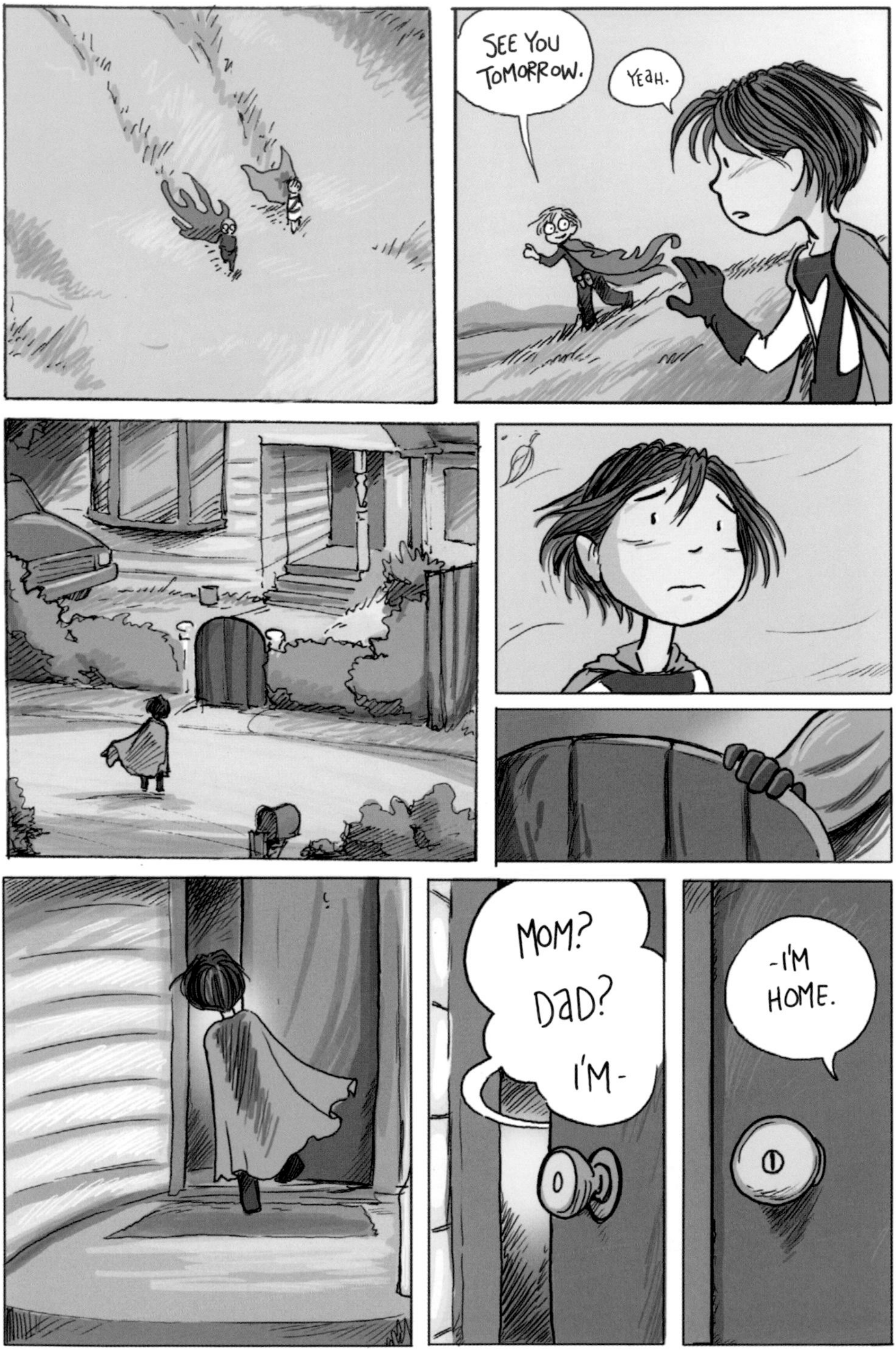
SEE YOU TOMORROW.
YEAH.
MOM? DAD? I'M-
-I'M HOME.

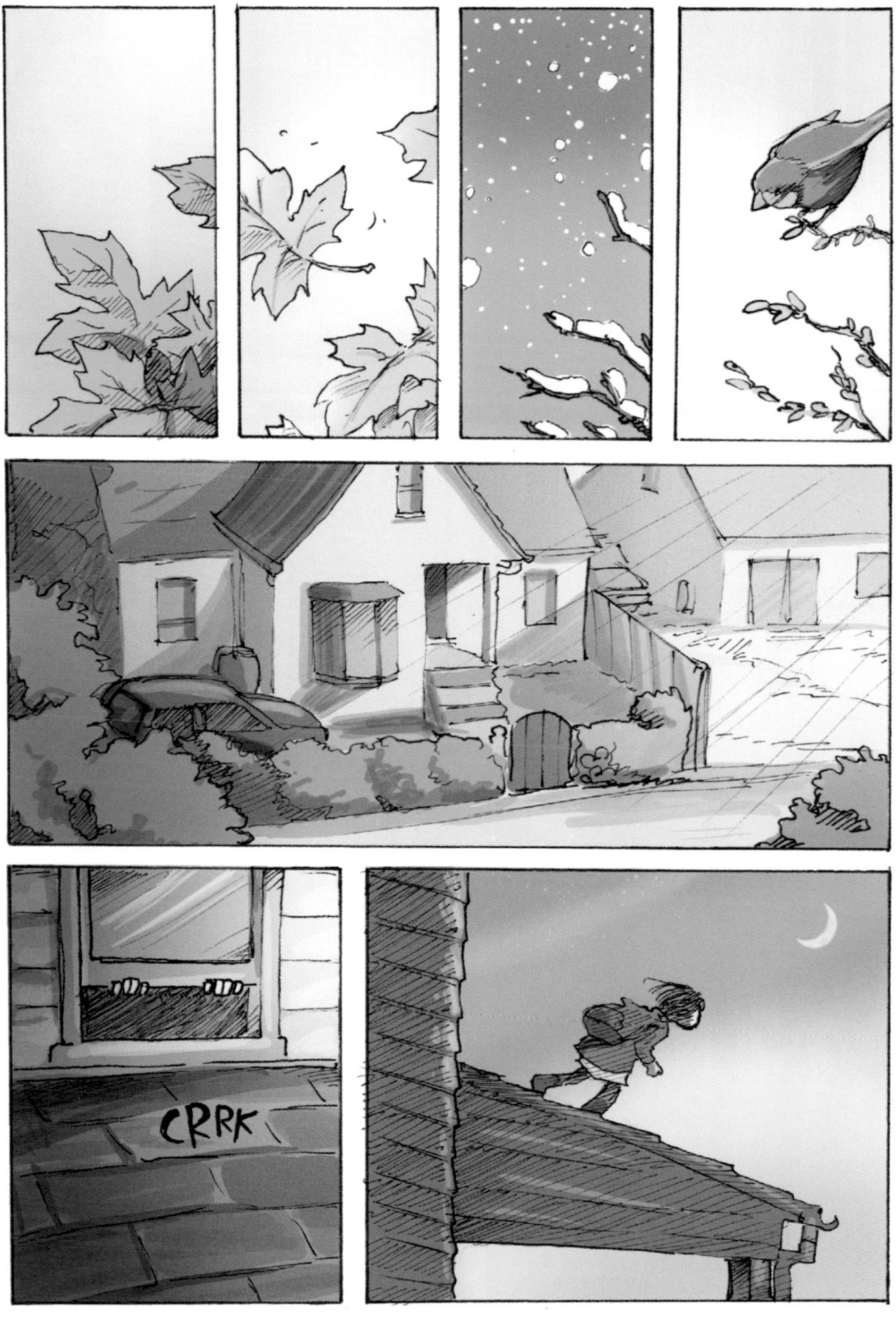
CRRK

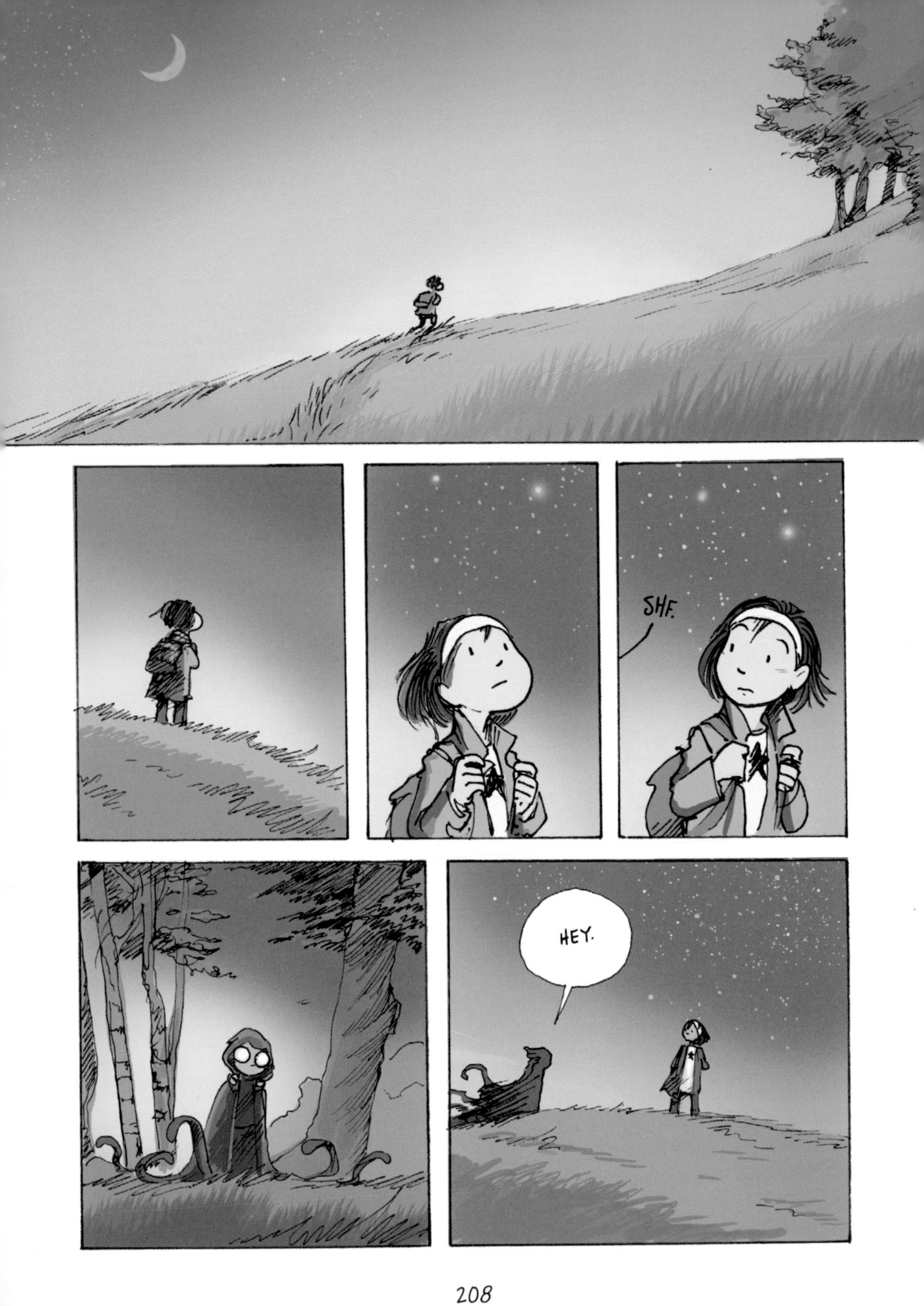
SHF.
HEY.

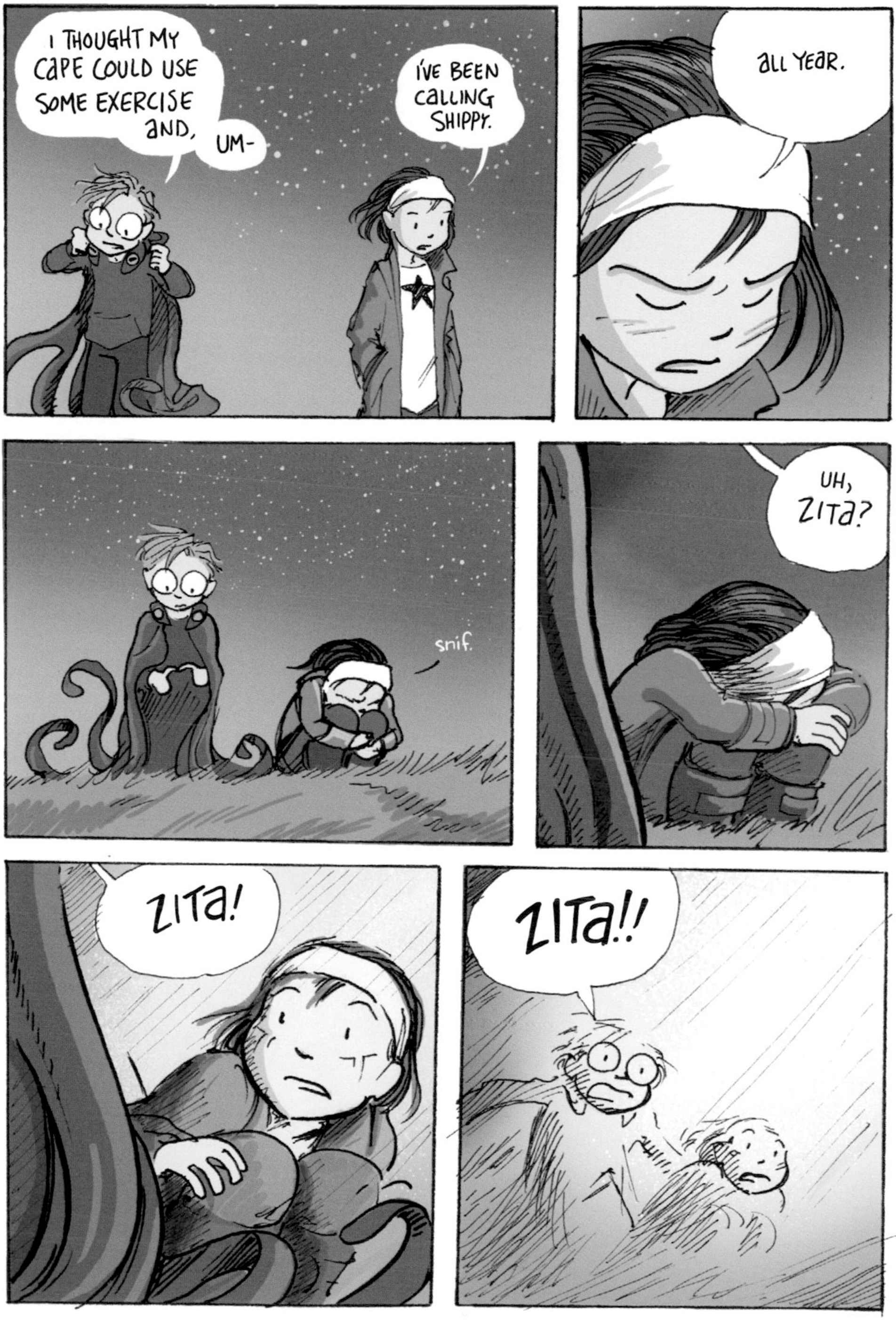
I THOUGHT MY CAPE COULD USE SOME EXERCISE AND,
UM-
I'VE BEEN CALLING SHIPPY.
ALL YEAR.
snif.
UH, ZITA?
ZITA!
ZITA!!

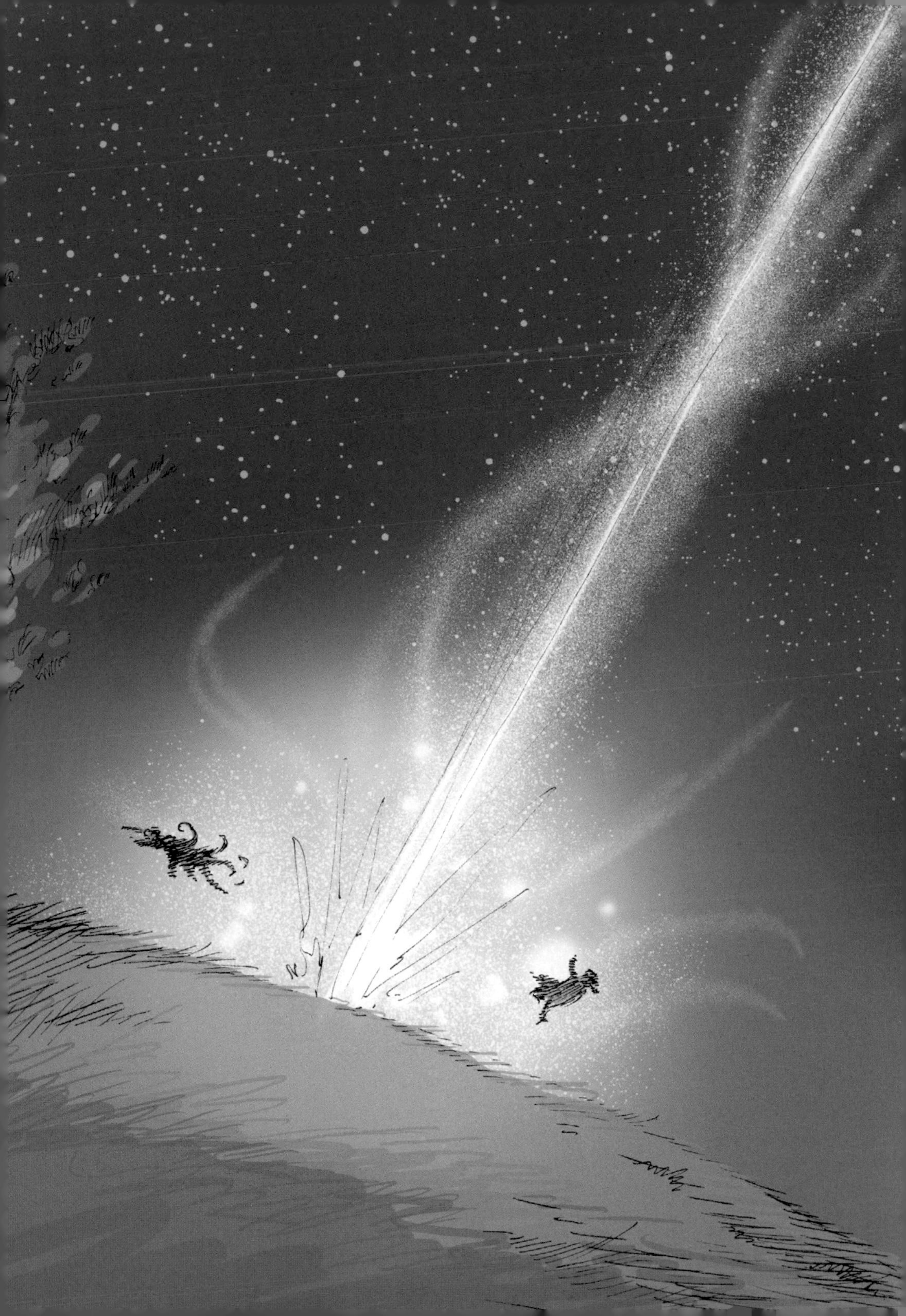

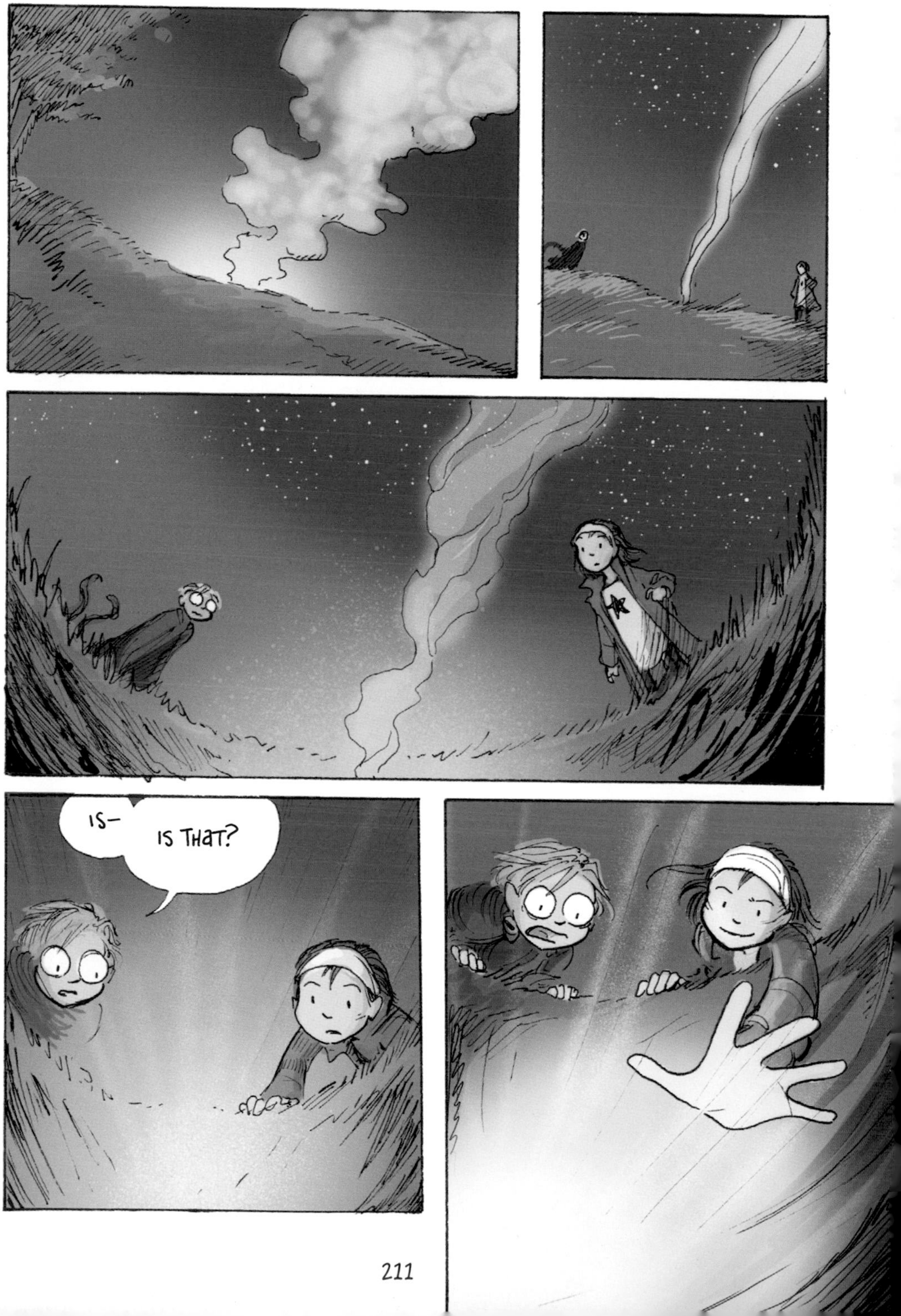
IS-
IS THAT?

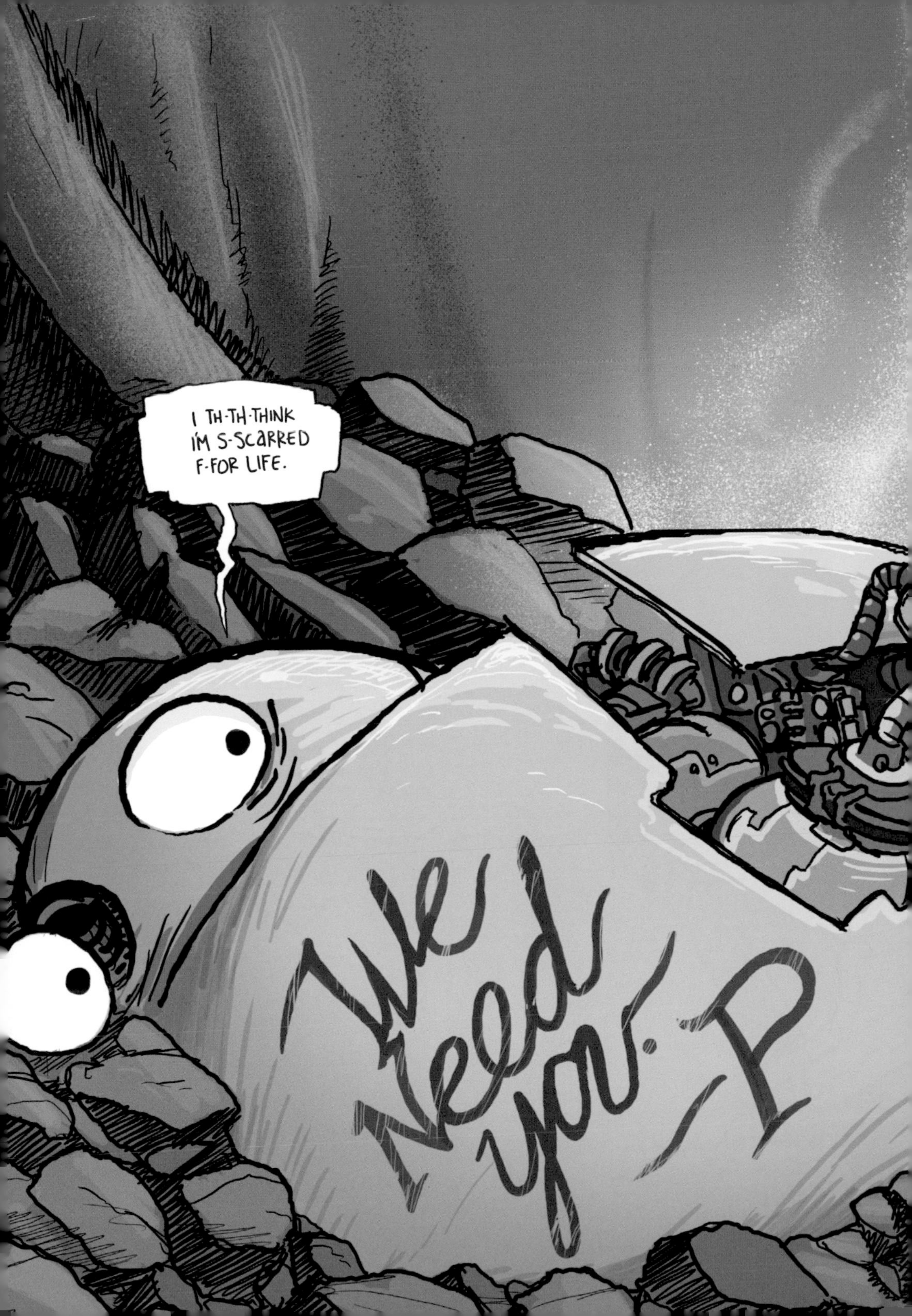
I TH-TH-THINK I'M S-SCARRED F-FOR LIFE.
We Need you. -P

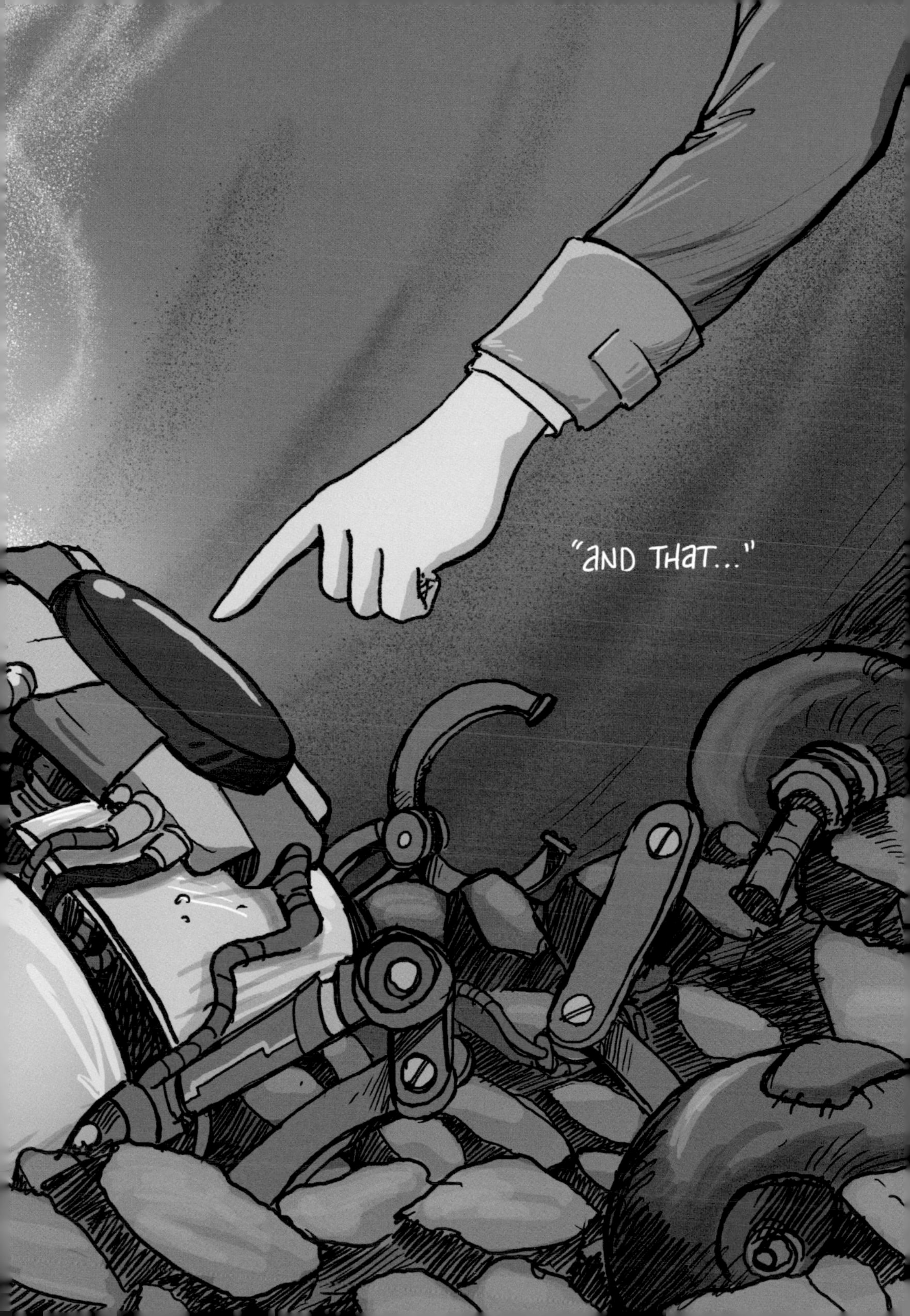
"AND THAT..."

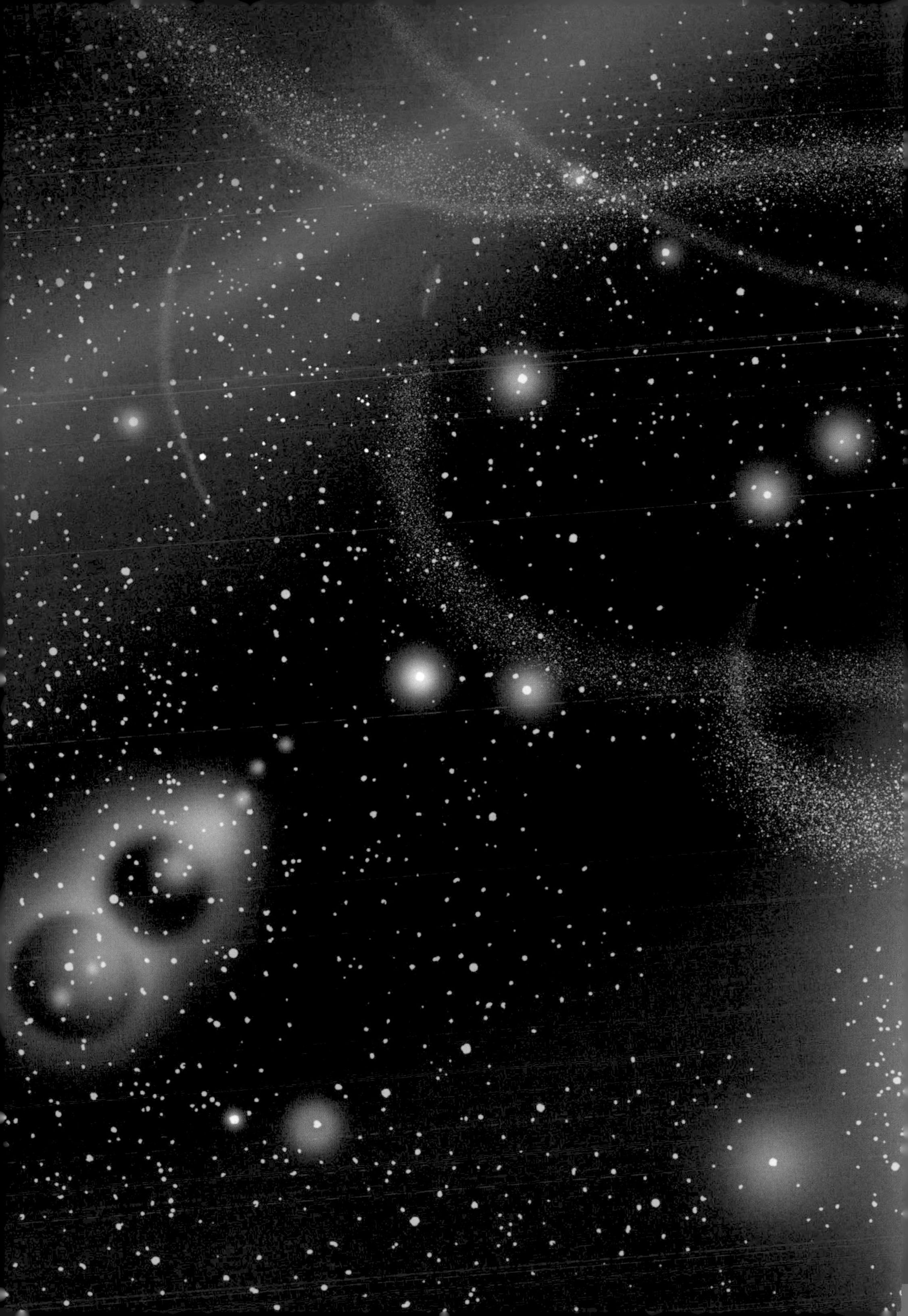

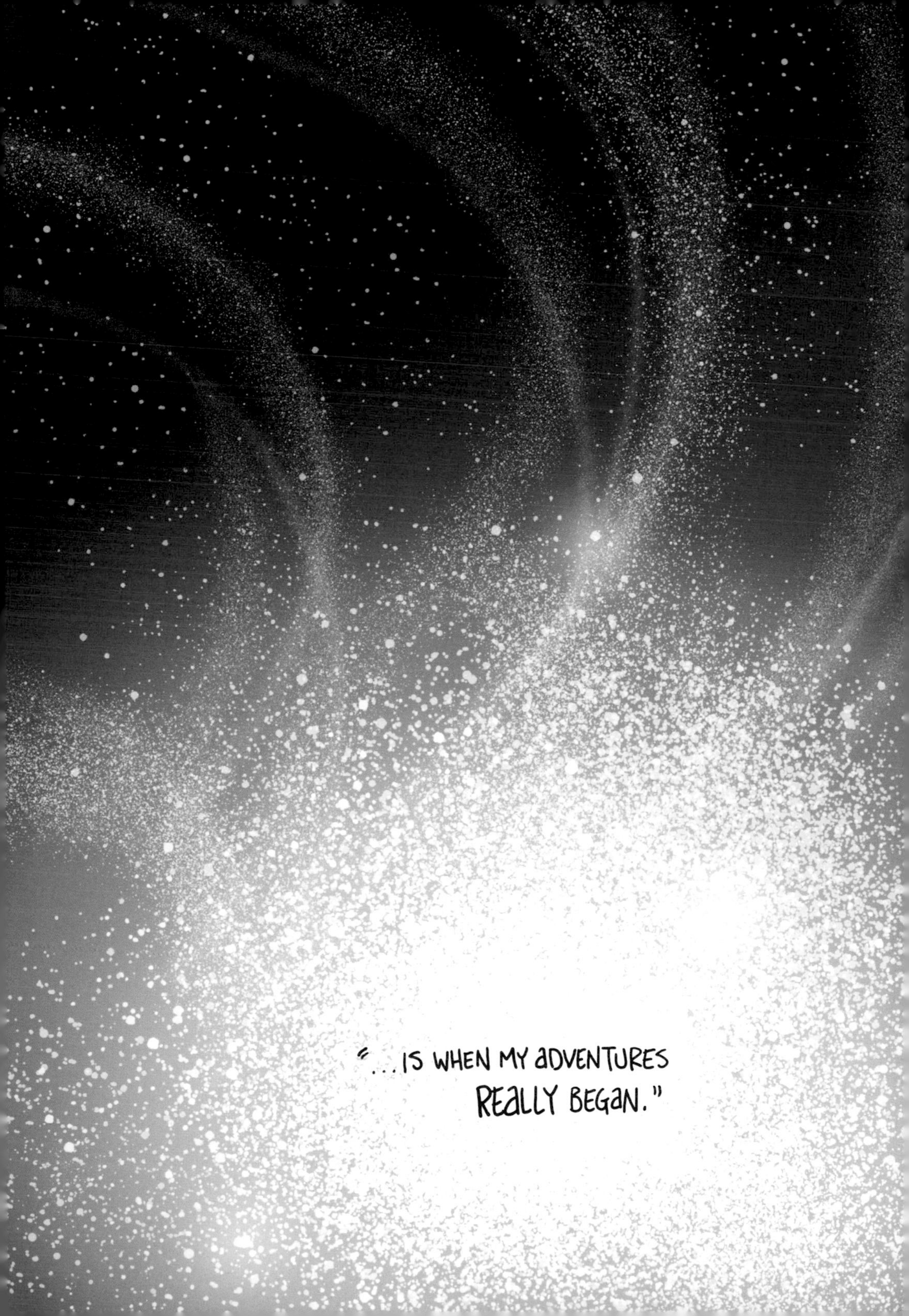
"...IS WHEN MY ADVENTURES
REALLY BEGAN."

THE ORIGIN AND EVOLUTION OF ZITA THE SPACEGIRL

Have you ever wondered where characters come from? Some characters seem to spring onto the page, fully formed and ready for adventure. Zita wasn't like that. As a character she took years to develop.

In college I met a REALLY cute girl named Anna. She shared with me some comics that she drew in high school about "Zeta the Spacegirl." They looked like this:

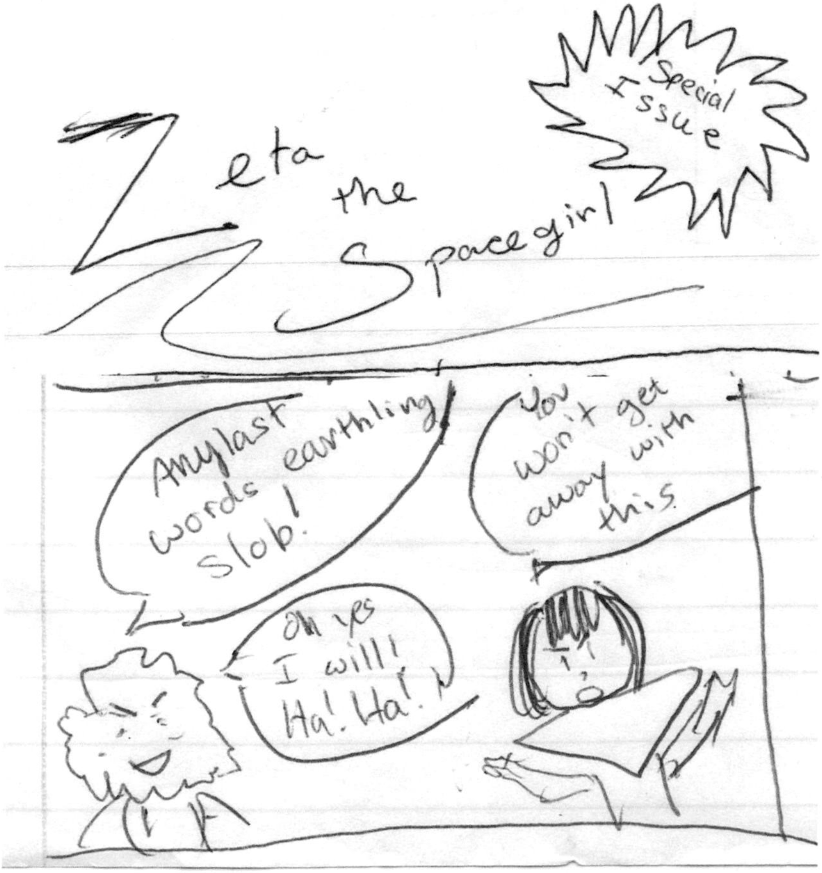
Zeta the Spacegirl
Special Issue
Any last words earthling slob!
You won't get away with this.
Oh yes I will! Ha! Ha!

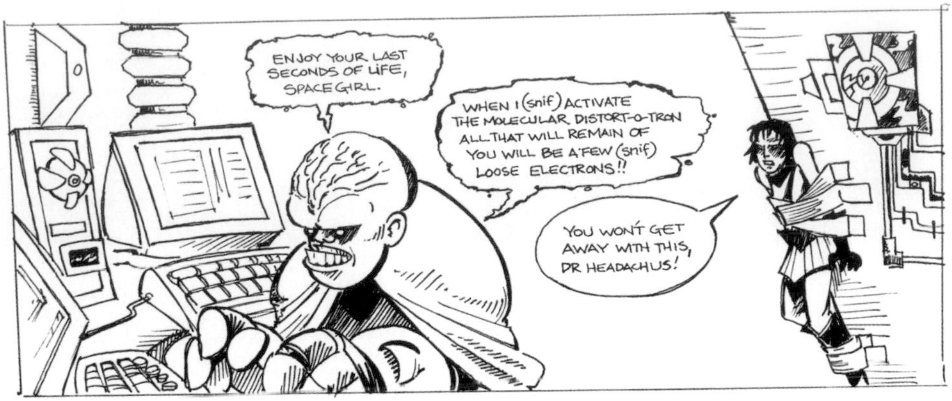
ENJOY YOUR LAST SECONDS OF LIFE, SPACEGIRL.
WHEN I (snif) ACTIVATE THE MOLECULAR DISTORT-O-TRON ALL THAT WILL REMAIN OF YOU WILL BE A FEW (snif) LOOSE ELECTRONS!!
YOU WON'T GET AWAY WITH THIS, DR HEADACHUS!

As a way to impress her I began developing the character and I drew comics for her featuring the new Zita the Spacegirl. In the early stories Zita was a time traveler from the future who teamed up with a couple of down-and-out superheroes.

We even had a Zita costume!

And my plan totally worked! That cute girl I made the comics for? She married me.

Later I took those early comics to conventions and showed them to editors, but no one was interested. And so for a time Zita the Spacegirl was forgotten...

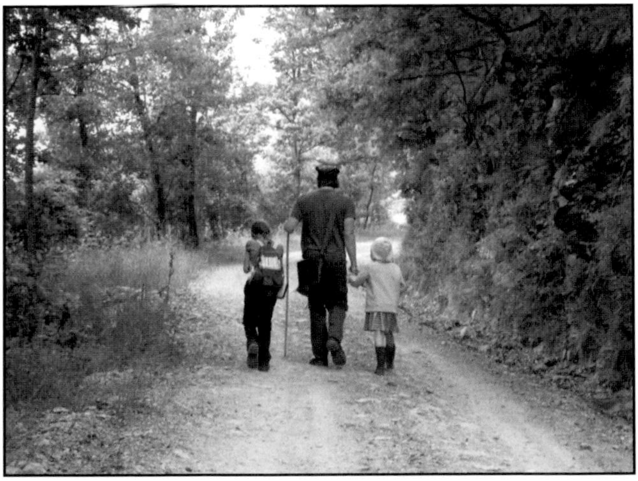

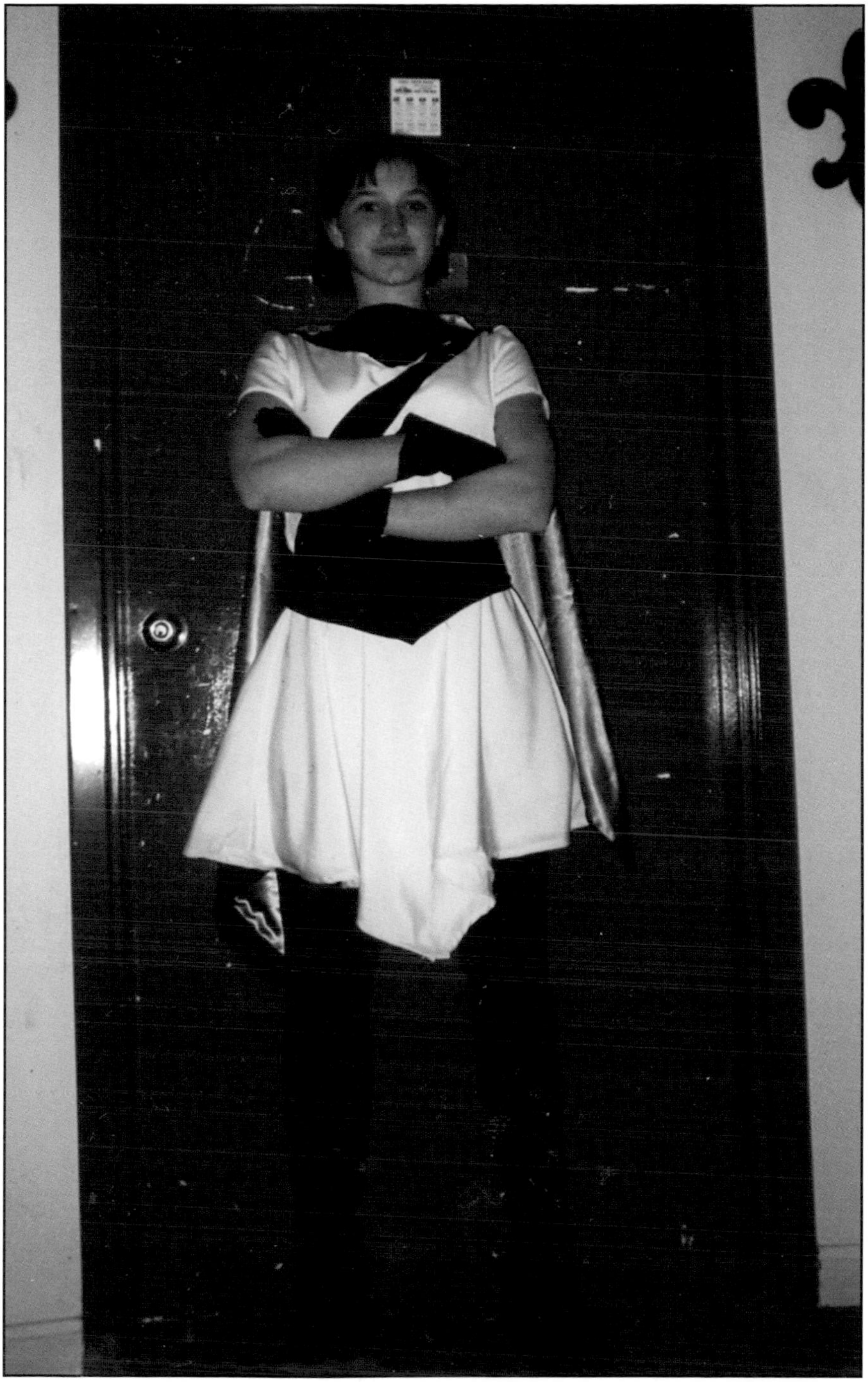

Anna in the original Zita the Spacegirl costume

...until I started making webcomics. That's when Zita's personality began taking shape, she started to look younger, and she found her friends Robot Randy and One.

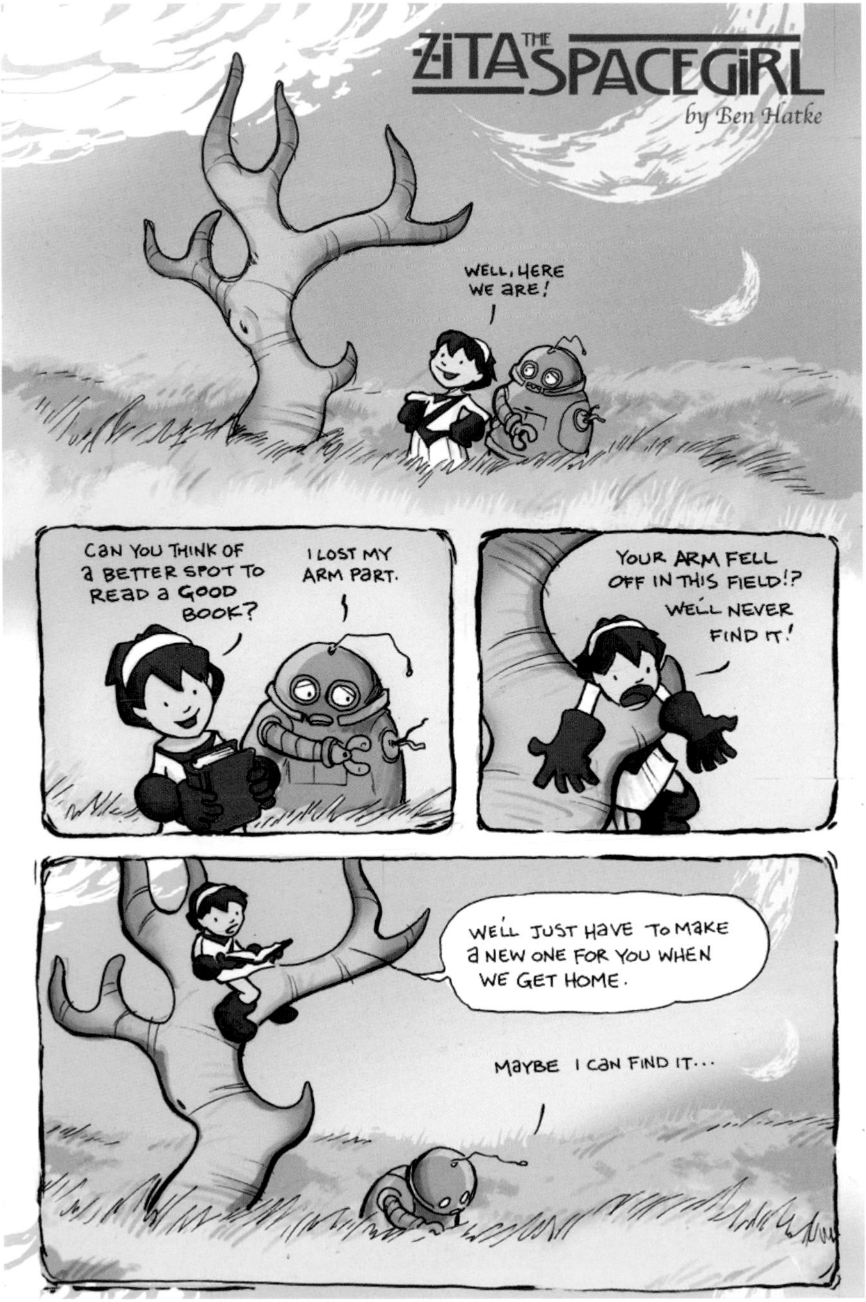
ZITA THE SPACEGIRL
by Ben Hatke
WELL, HERE WE ARE!
CAN YOU THINK OF A BETTER SPOT TO READ A GOOD BOOK?
I LOST MY ARM PART.
YOUR ARM FELL OFF IN THIS FIELD!? WE'LL NEVER FIND IT!
WE'LL JUST HAVE TO MAKE A NEW ONE FOR YOU WHEN WE GET HOME.
MAYBE I CAN FIND IT...

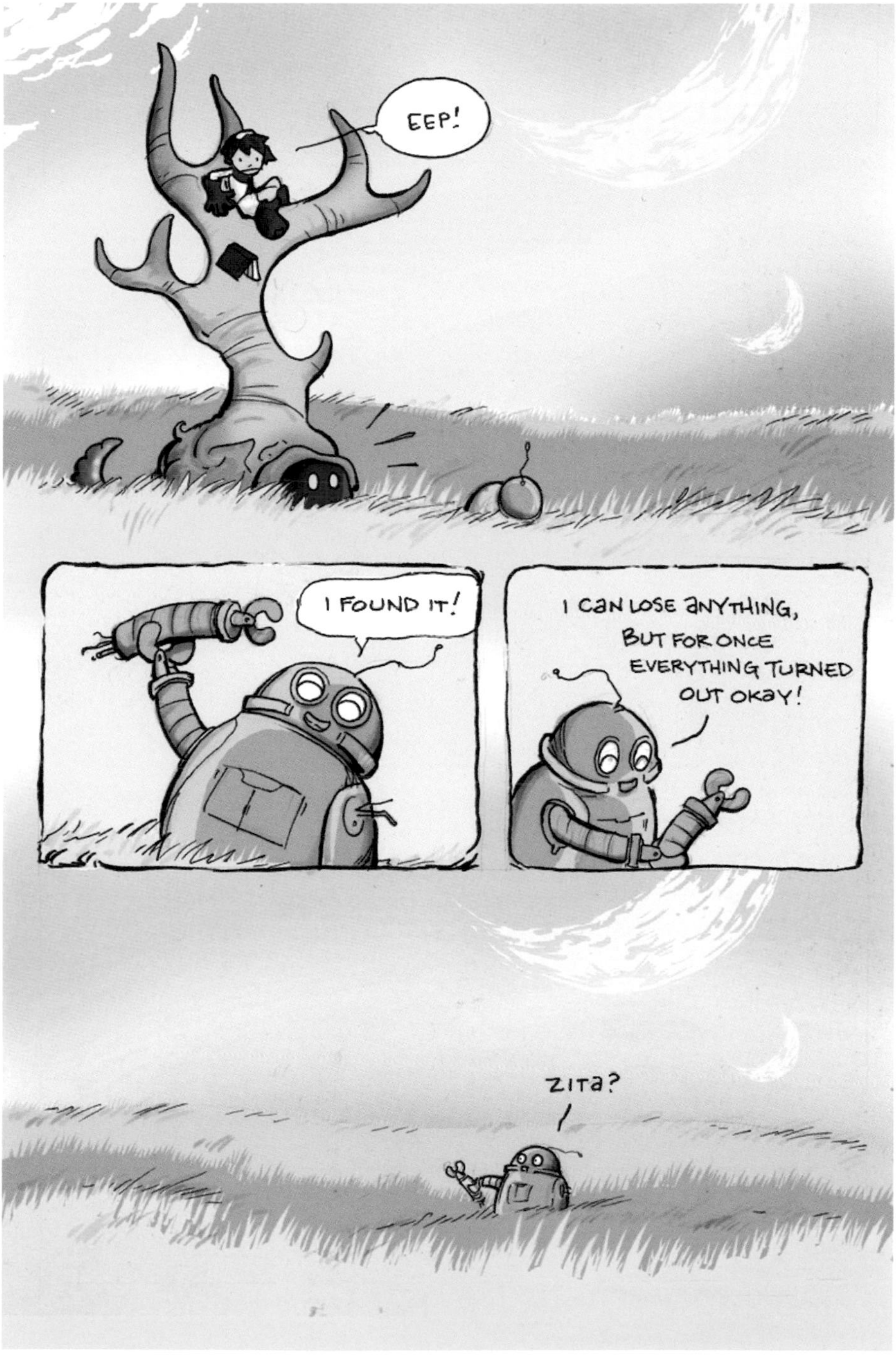
EEP!
I FOUND IT!
I CAN LOSE ANYTHING, BUT FOR ONCE EVERYTHING TURNED OUT OKAY!
ZITA?

A short Zita story called "If Wishes Were Socks" even appeared in a book called Flight: Explorer.

HE SAYS IT'S A MAGICAL WISHING SOCK. IT WILL GRANT ANYTHING YOU DESIRE.
WELL... THANK YOU!

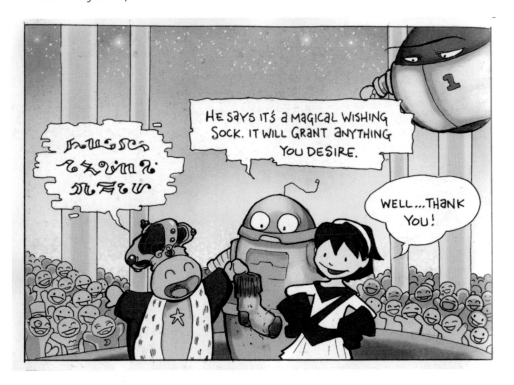

But one question remained: what was this girl doing traveling through space? What was she after? I realized that this was the story I wanted to tell. And that's the story you've just finished reading.

ANNA BERTOLINI DRAWS ZETA THE SPACEGIRL DURING CLASS
1994
BEN & ANNA MEET. BEN DRAWS ZITA COMICS
1999
BEN & ANNA MARRY
COMICS EDITORS NOT INTERESTED IN ZITA.
2001
BEN BEGINS MAKING ZITA WEB COMICS
2005
FLIGHT: EXPLORER STORY: IF WISHES WERE SOCKS
2007
WORK BEGINS ON ZITA THE SPACEGIRL TRILOGY.
2008
ZITA THE SPACEGIRL
2010
LEGENDS OF ZITA
2012
THE RETURN OF ZITA (THIS BOOK)
2014
?

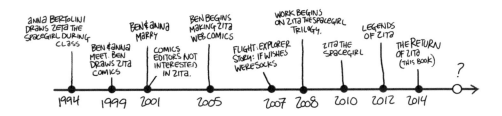

And what does the future hold for Zita? Only time will tell...

SKETCHES

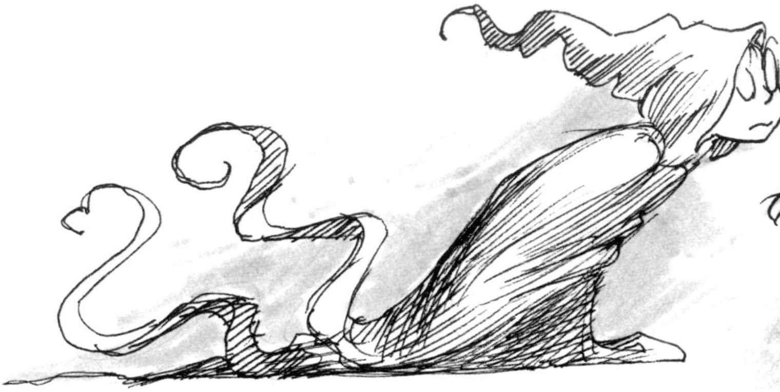

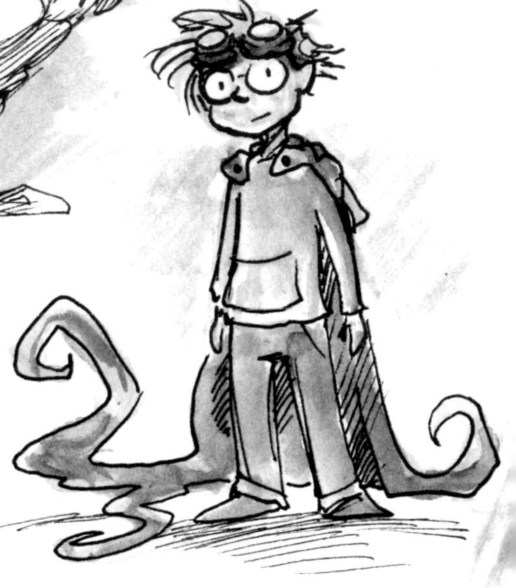

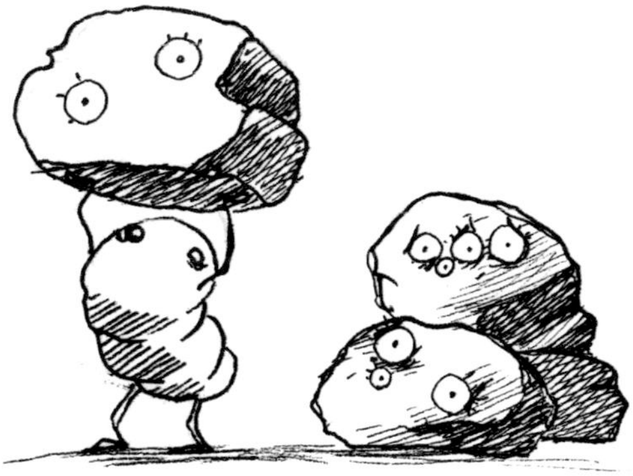

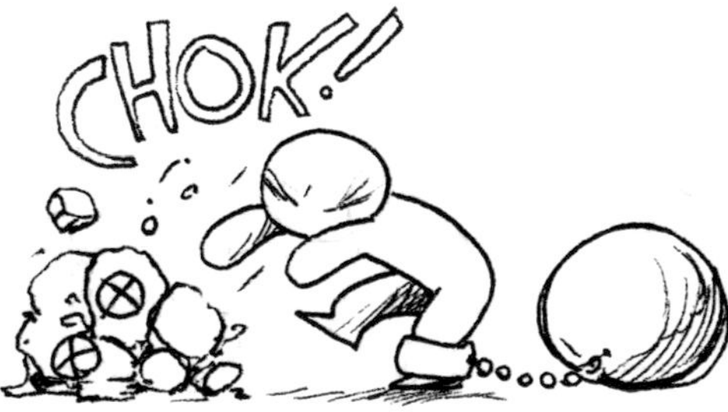
CHOK!

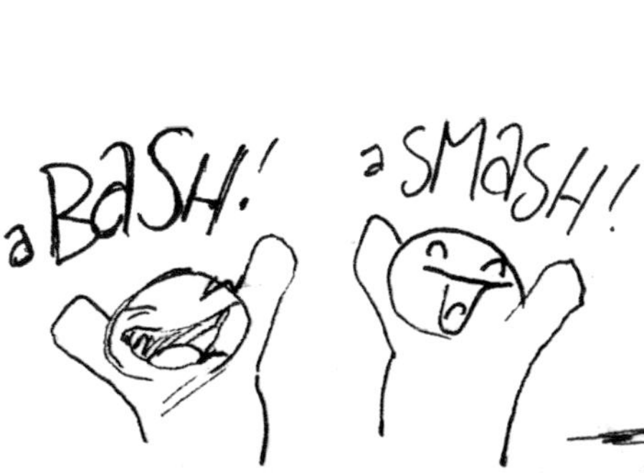
a BaSH!
a SMaSH!

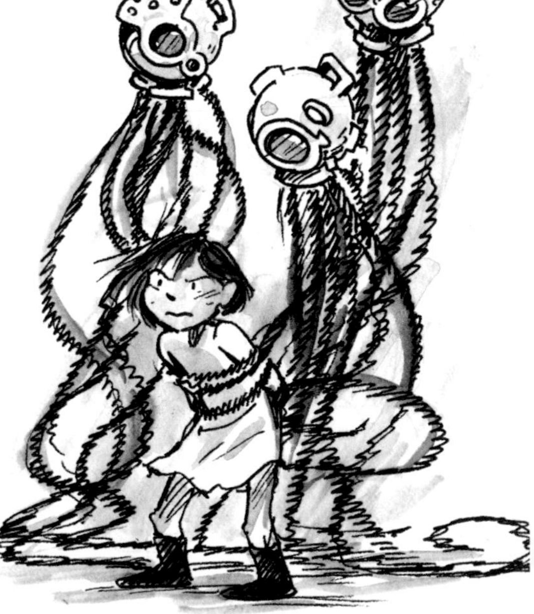

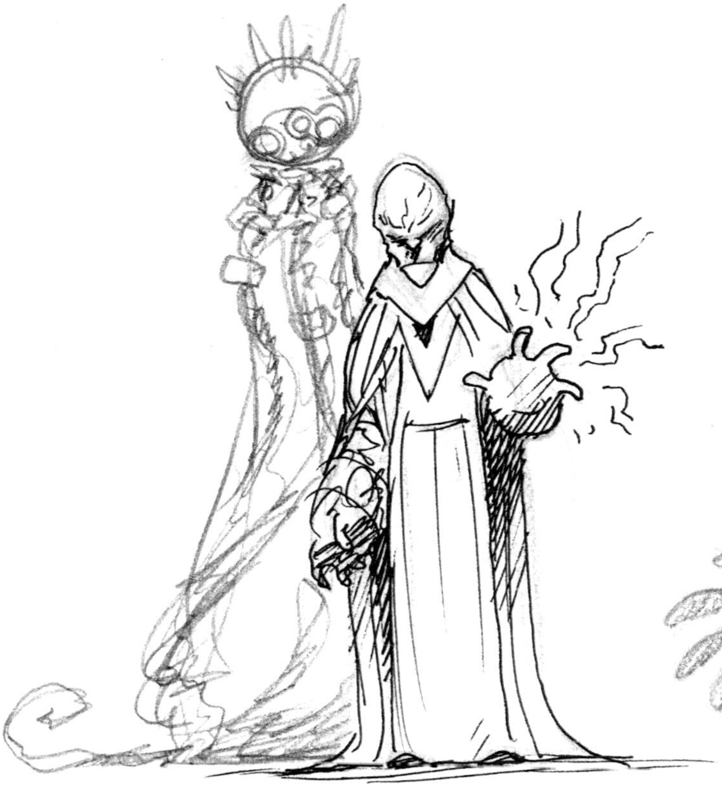

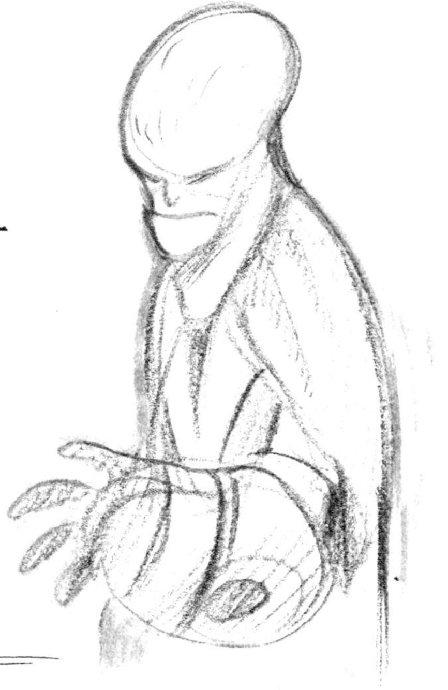

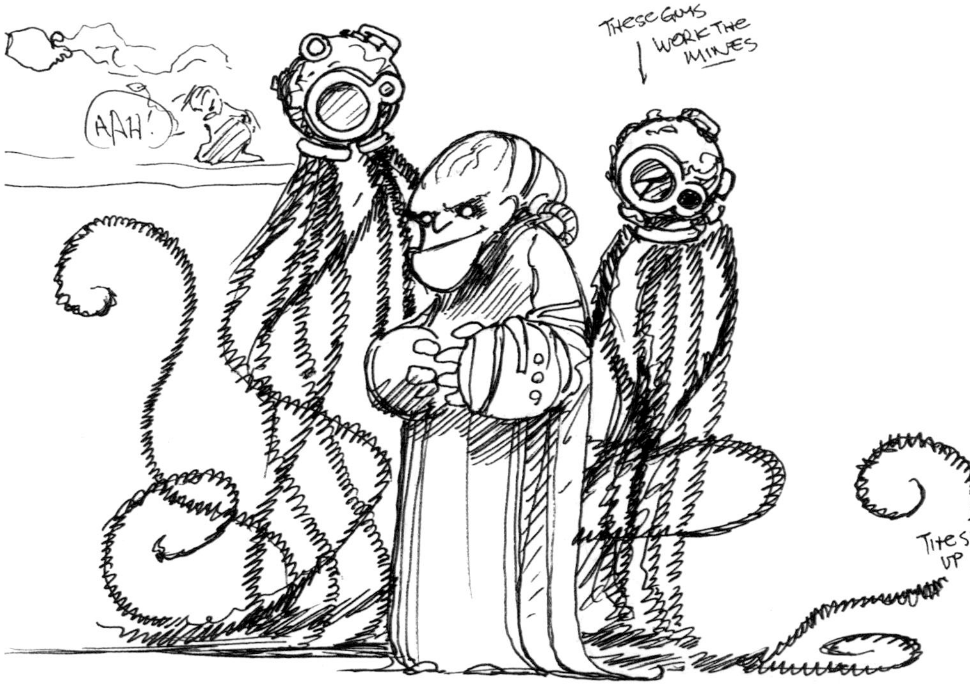
AAH!
THESE GUYS WORK THE MINES
THE SET UP

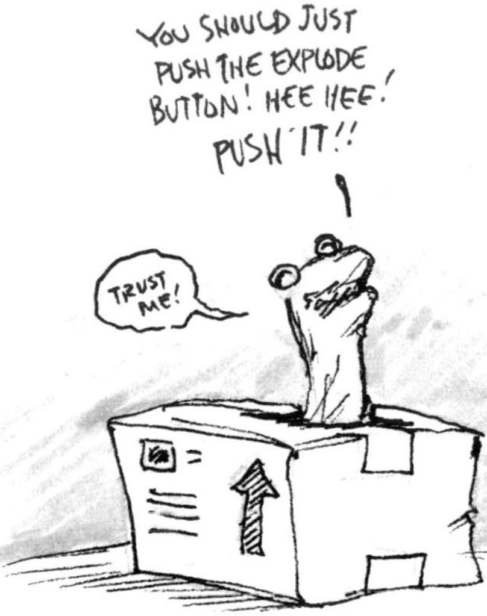
YOU SHOULD JUST PUSH THE EXPLODE BUTTON! HEE HEE! PUSH IT!!
TRUST ME!

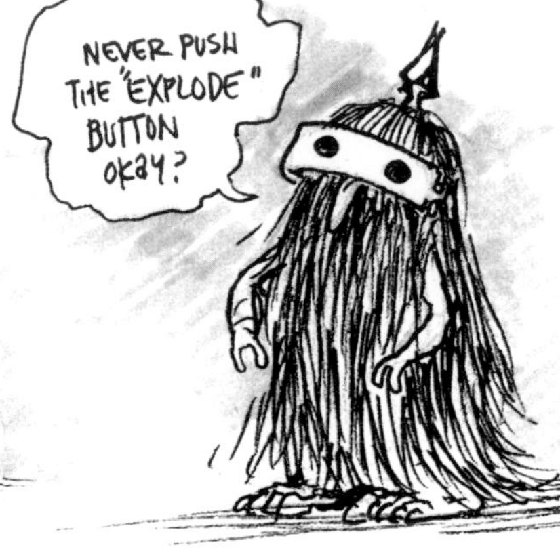
NEVER PUSH THE "EXPLODE" BUTTON okay?

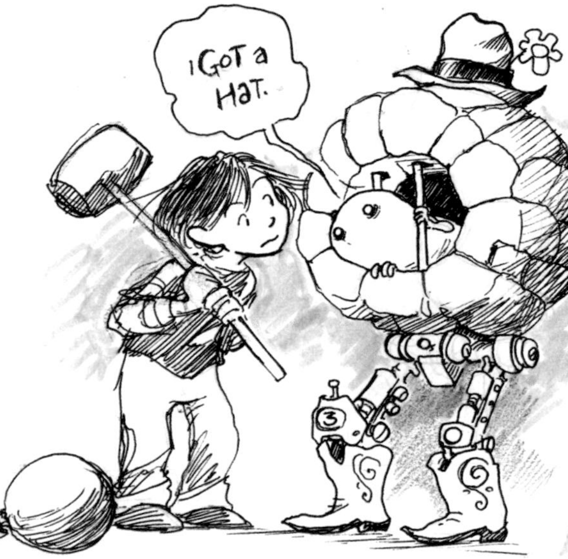
I Got a Hat.

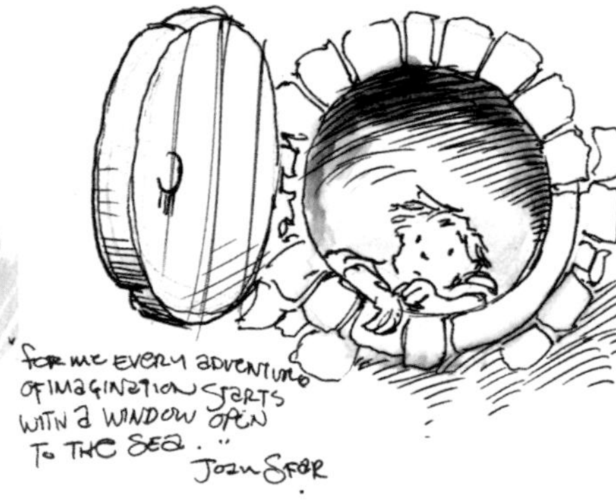
"for me every adventure of imagination starts with a window open to the sea..."
Joan Sfar

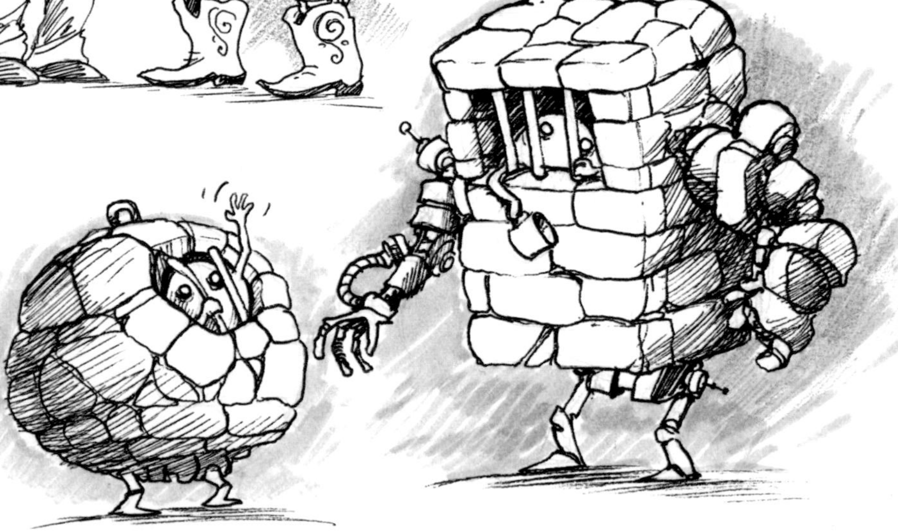

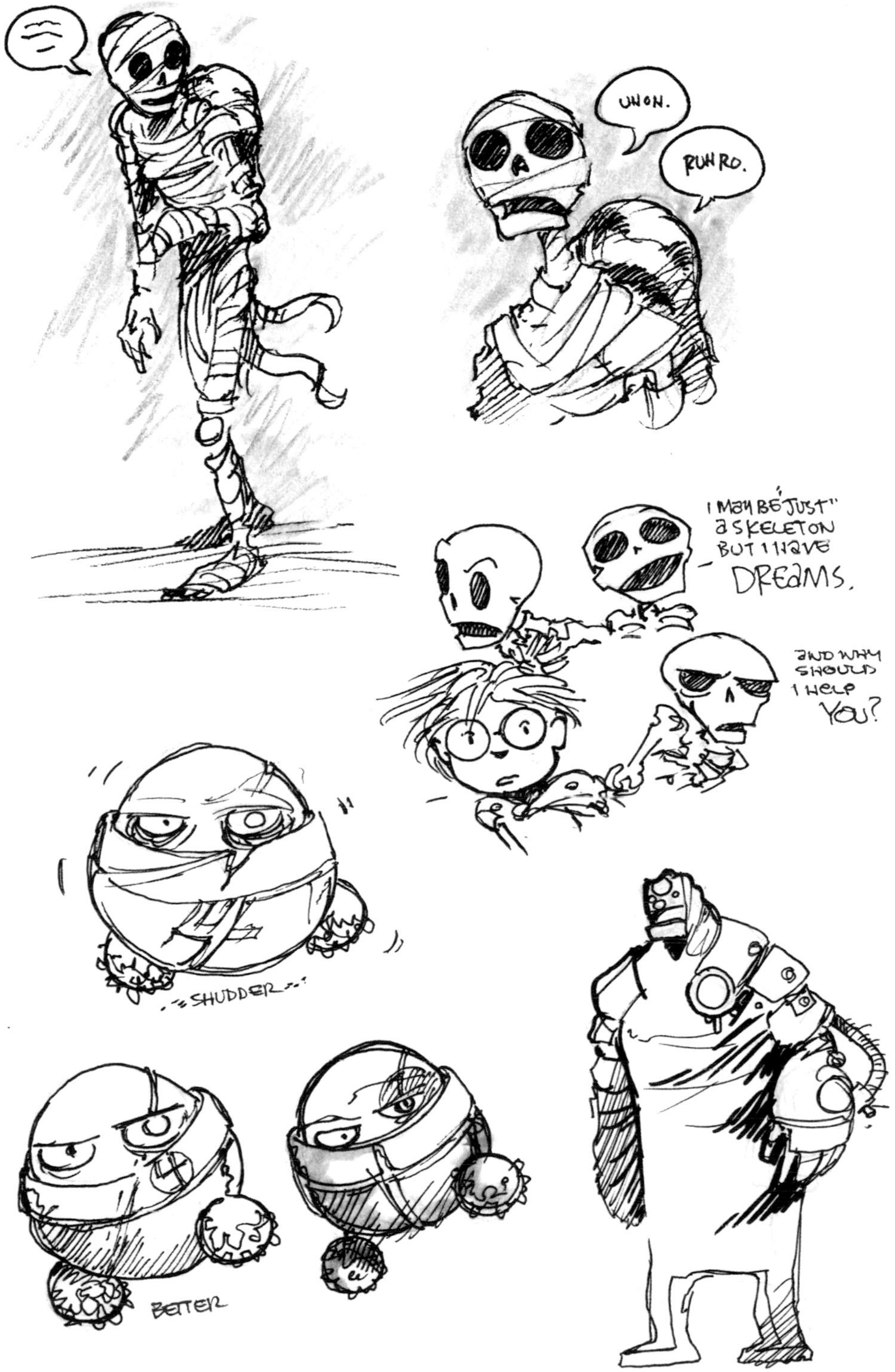
UHOH.
RUH RO.
I MAY BE "JUST" A SKELETON BUT I HAVE DREAMS.
AND WHY SHOULD I HELP YOU?
SHUDDER
BETTER

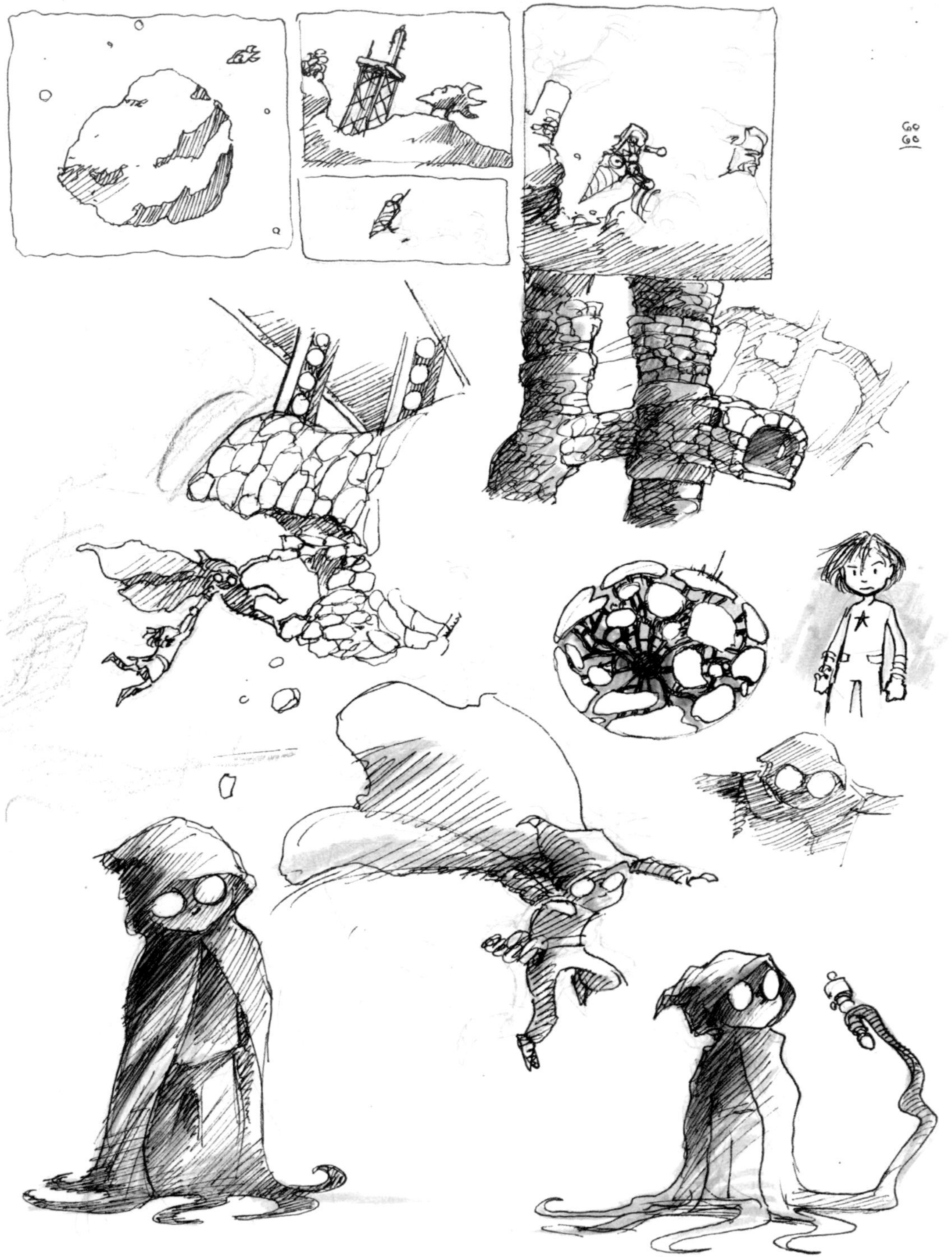
GO
GO

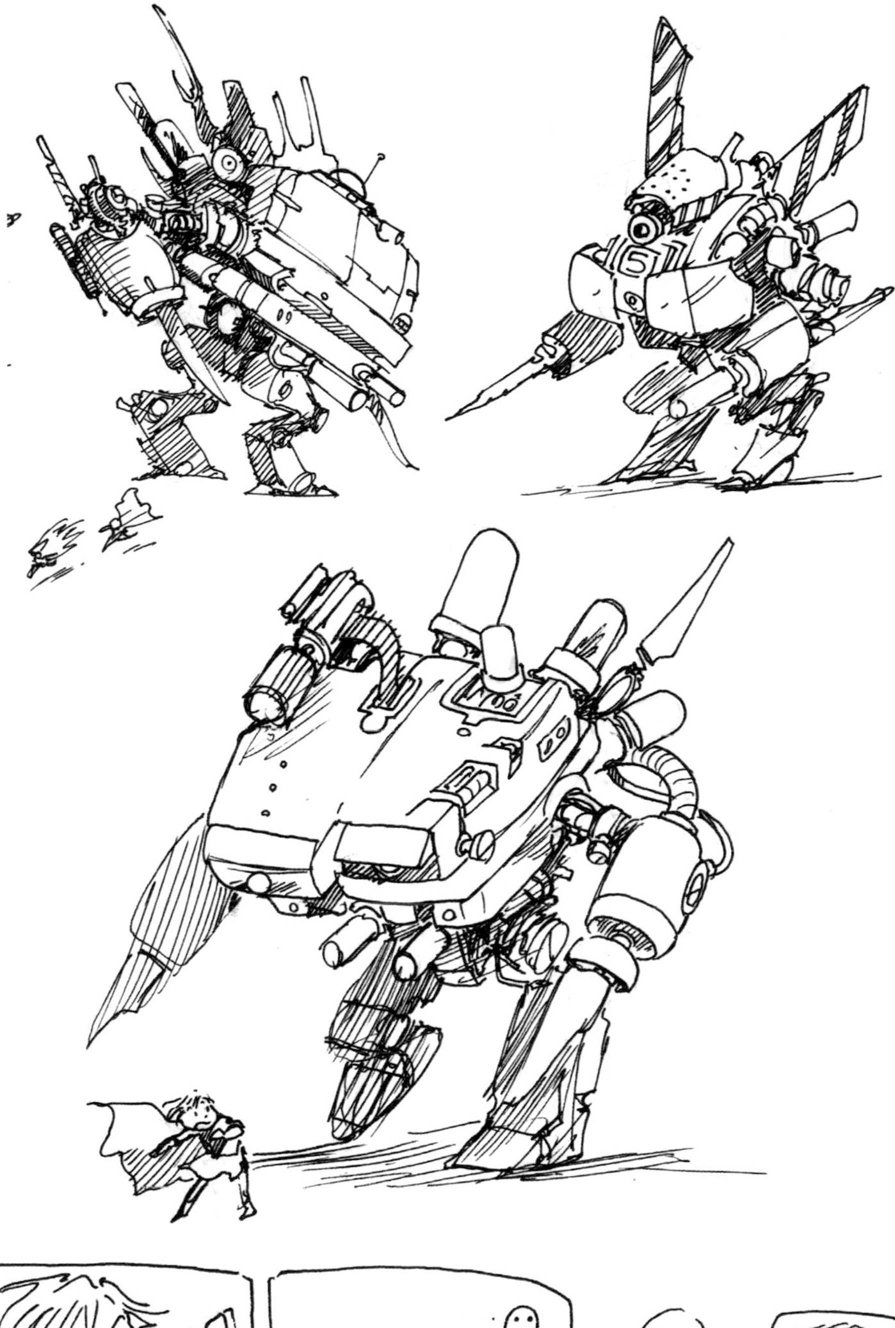

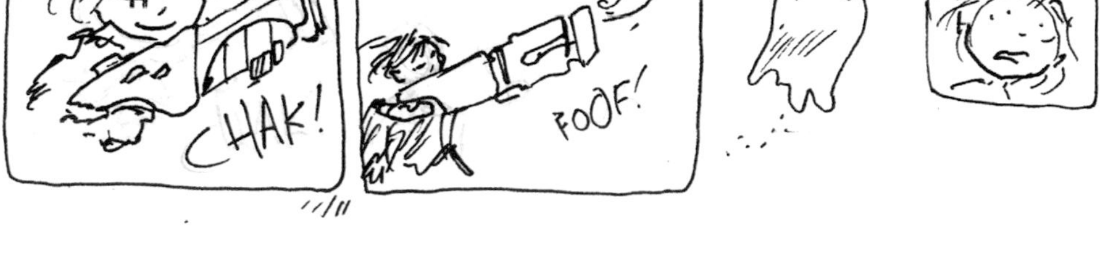
CHAK!
POOF!

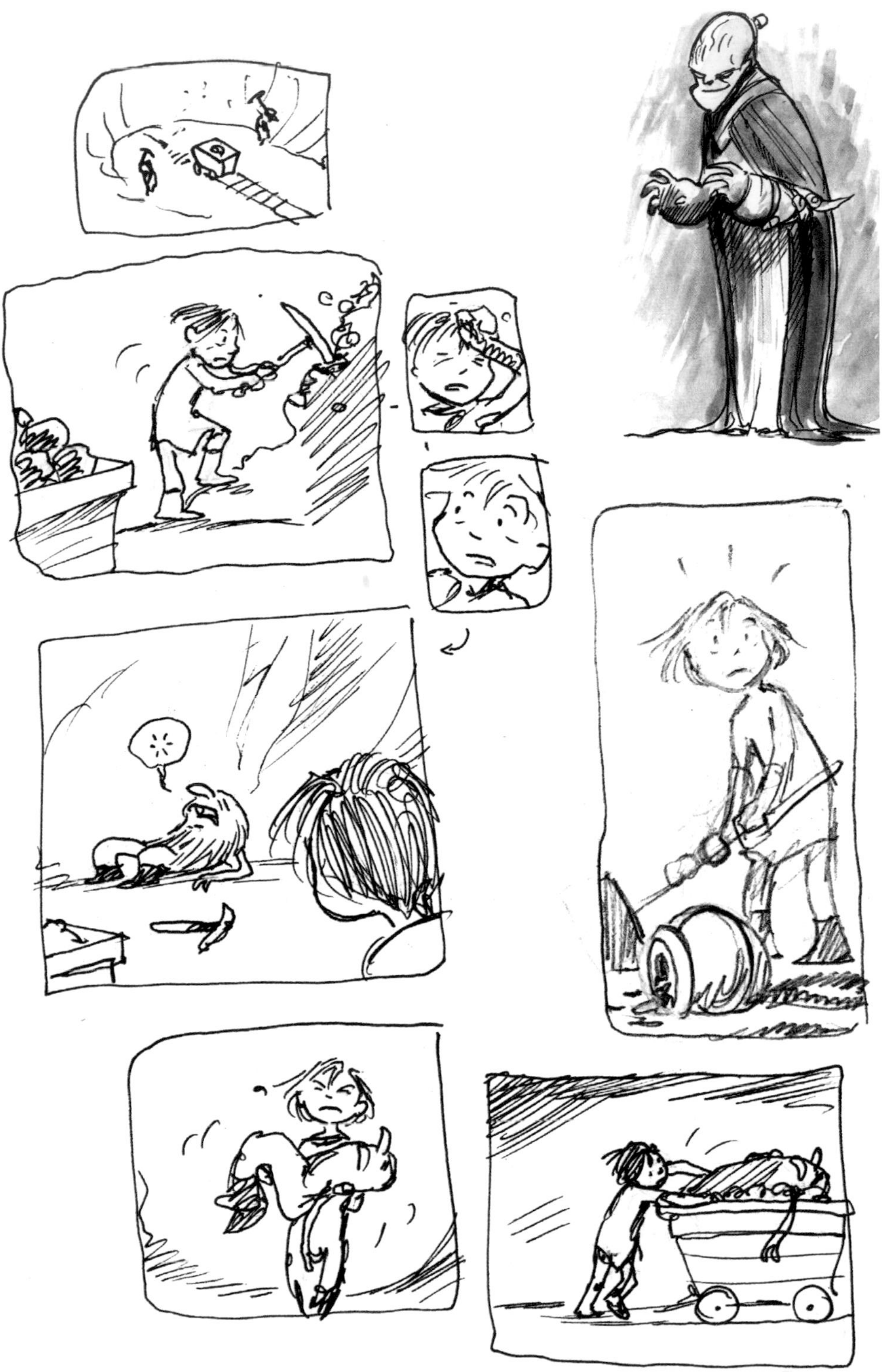

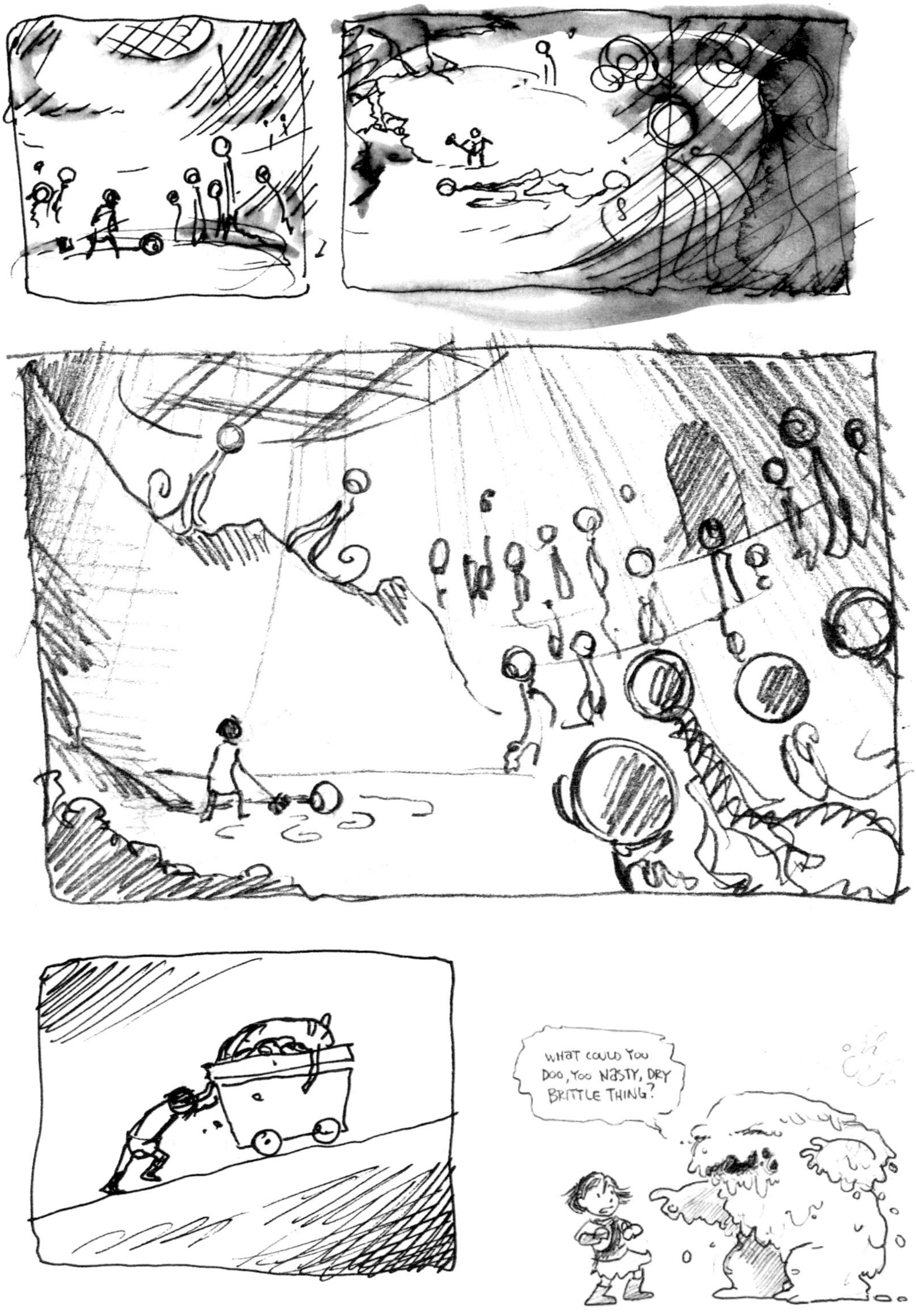
WHAT COULD YOU DOO, YOO NASTY, DRY BRITTLE THING?

ACKNOWLEDGMENTS

Special thanks to my mom, who sewed me a leather He-Man baldric and let me wear it to school under my clothes for two years. And to my dad, who helped me build a pair of gliding wings, but made sure I jumped off the retaining wall and not the garage roof. I won the cool parents lottery.

Thanks to my fourth grade teacher, Mrs. Berghoff, for letting me cut out and glue paper antennae to my head instead of paying attention during math class. You could have crushed a young artist there and you didn't.

Thanks to everybody in the little village of Gravagna, where I wrote and drew most of this book. I left my heart there, so please take care of it until I come back.

And thanks, of course, to the crew at First Second! Mark Siegel, Colleen AF Venable, Calista Brill, and Gina Gagliano! You're a pleasure to work with. Thanks also to my indomitable agent, Judy Hansen, for looking after me.

Most of all thanks to Anna and to my girls, Angelica, Zita, Julia, and Ronia. I'd be a smelly old hermit without you guys.

ABOUT THE AUTHOR

Ben Hatke is the father of four daughters and the author of three graphic novels.

He lives in the Shenandoah Valley next to a very old cemetery and he spends an awful lot of time thinking about turtles and robots.

Ben posts stories, art, and comics online at BenHatke.com.

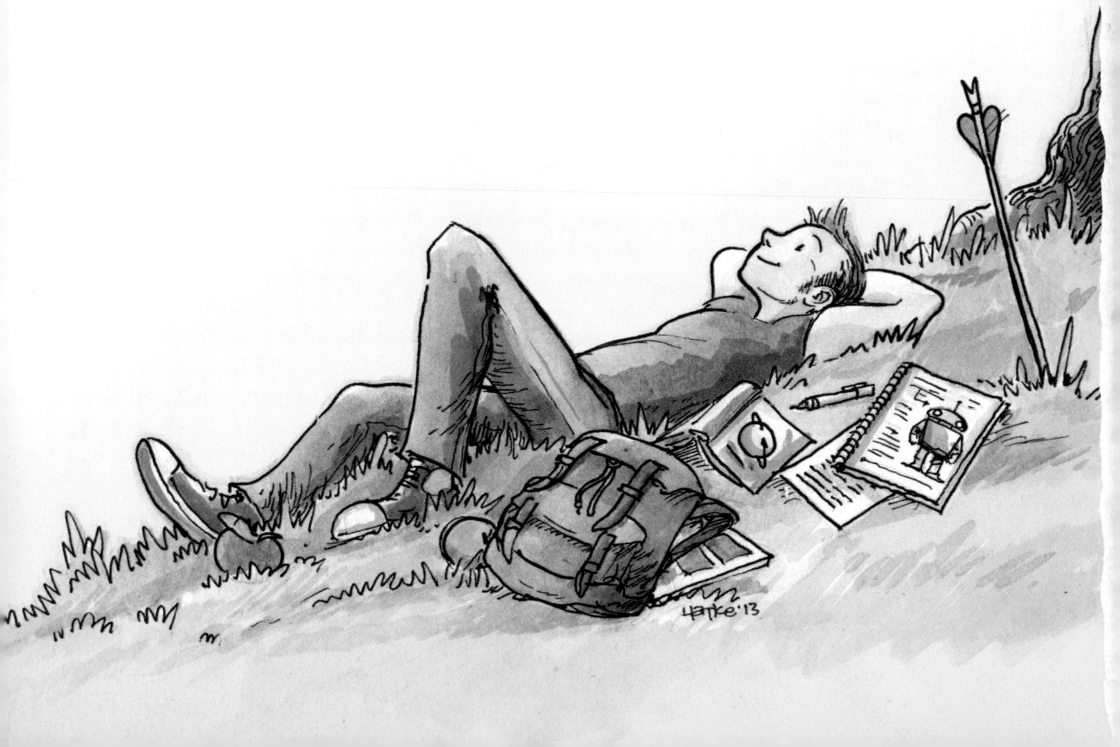
HATKE '13